OF MIST AND SHADOW

JENNA WOLFHART

Cover Design by The Book Brander

Character Art by Ruby Dian Arts & Beth Gilbert

Chapter & Scene Break Art by Etheric Designs

Editing by Practical Proofing & Contagious Edits

For those who dream of a better world.

AUTHOR'S NOTE

This series is intended for adult readers and will contain dark elements. To see a full list of potential triggers, visit www. jennawolfhart.com/books/content or scan the QR code below.

THE FAE OF AESIR

ELITE FAE

All the common fae powers, as well as additional magical abilities related to their bloodline.

COMMON FAE

Immortal life-span. Enhanced senses, strength, and speed.

LIGHT FAE

Power over fire.
Power over light.
Ability to create shields.

SHADOW FAE

Power over mist.
Animal communication.
Telekenesis.

STORM FAE

Power over wind.
Power over rain.
Power over lightning.

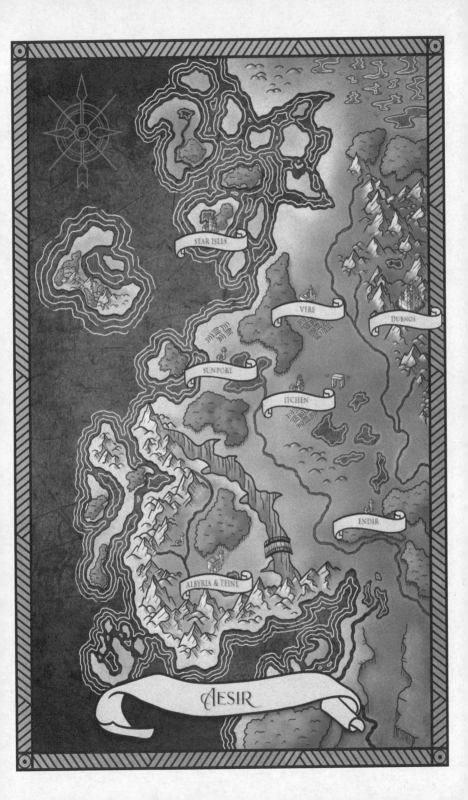

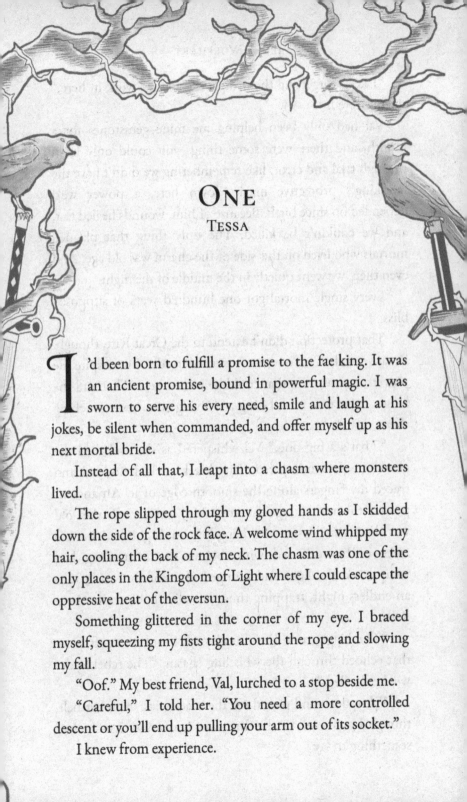

ONE

TESSA

I'd been born to fulfill a promise to the fae king. It was an ancient promise, bound in powerful magic. I was sworn to serve his every need, smile and laugh at his jokes, be silent when commanded, and offer myself up as his next mortal bride.

Instead of all that, I leapt into a chasm where monsters lived.

The rope slipped through my gloved hands as I skidded down the side of the rock face. A welcome wind whipped my hair, cooling the back of my neck. The chasm was one of the only places in the Kingdom of Light where I could escape the oppressive heat of the eversun.

Something glittered in the corner of my eye. I braced myself, squeezing my fists tight around the rope and slowing my fall.

"Oof." My best friend, Val, lurched to a stop beside me.

"Careful," I told her. "You need a more controlled descent or you'll end up pulling your arm out of its socket."

I knew from experience.

"I keep forgetting the protection doesn't work in here," she muttered.

Val had only been helping me mine gemstones for a month, and there were some things you could only learn through trial and error, like remembering we didn't have the fae king's protective magic down here, a power we'd depended on since birth. Because of him, wounds healed fast, and we couldn't be killed. The only thing that plagued mortals who lived on this side of the chasm was old age. And even then, we went quietly in the middle of the night.

Every single mortal got one hundred years of supposed bliss.

That protection didn't extend to the Great Rift, though. Because of that, no one ever ventured inside of it, despite the powerful gemstones that could be mined here. That and the king's strict rule prohibiting any living soul from touching them.

"That's a big one," Val whispered as she eyeballed the gemstone protruding from the black rock. I nodded and traced my fingers along the smooth edge of it. An ancient power thrummed against my skin, echoes of the old world. A time when the Kingdom of Light had been a force to be reckoned with, before the Mist King had vanquished the light and plunged most of the world into an endless night, trapping those left alive behind the Great Rift.

"The biggest one I've found yet," I said in a soft voice that echoed through the whistling chasm. "The rebel leader will be thrilled."

Val nodded and passed me the metal pick from her belt, though I could tell by the furrow of her brows that she had something to say.

The steel shrieked as I slammed it against the rock. "Go on then. Out with it."

She cleared her throat and waited to speak until after I'd knocked some of the rock free. "It's just...have you found out who he is yet? The fae asking you to do this?"

After brushing my thumb along the indentation I'd made around the flaming gemstone, I continued to use the pick to pry it free. Slam after slam after slam, sweat trickled down my neck, but I was used to this work. I'd once spent five hours on a single stone.

"No," I finally answered, handing the pick back to Val. "But it doesn't matter. He's trying to help us."

"How can you be sure of that?" She handed me a smaller instrument now, a little steel bar in the shape of an L.

I slipped the short end in behind the jewel and gave it a little jiggle. "He's the one who told us about these gemstones in the first place. They hold great power, Val. He said that if he gets enough of them, he can banish the mists. And then we'll be free from this place."

Val knew I was right, as cautious as she was. King Oberon had once been the most powerful fae alive, but the Mist King's curse had trapped him here. Mortals could cross the Great Rift, but no fae could—there was an invisible wall of power blocking them. Of course, none of us mortals even dared try. Out there, in the darkness and the mists, we no longer had the protection of our fae king. There were things on the other side, too. Monstrous beings, lurking in the shadows. Shadowfiends, joint eaters, and wraiths that drank blood. I'd even heard stories of the mists themselves turning men to ash when they spent too long out there.

And the Mist King was always in the shadows, watching and waiting.

"I'm just saying, maybe we should keep some of these gemstones for ourselves," Val said.

The gemstone popped free and landed in my open palm. It glowed red and orange, flickering like the depths of a blazing fire. The magic inside of it called to me. Temptation crept along the back of my neck. Maybe Val was right. I could keep it. Just this one.

Something sharp curled around my heart, like a thorny vine. I loosed a breath and slipped the jewel into the leather satchel slung around my neck.

"We can't, Val. What would we do with it? We're humans."

She pursed her lips, but then nodded. "Fine. But I'm coming with you to the drop-off this time. Me and Nellie. If something goes wrong, we don't want you to be by yourself."

"All right." I smiled and tipped back my head to gaze up at the lip of the cliff where my younger sister, Nellie, was waiting for us. She leaned forward with her hands gripping the edge, her chestnut hair tumbling around her face.

She and Val had insisted on getting involved when they'd discovered my weekly trips to the Great Rift. Even Nellie, who was afraid of heights. She wouldn't scale the cliff with us, but she wouldn't let me out of her sight, either. Until we were back on solid ground, she hunkered there at the top, ready to drag me up if she had to.

A shrill call echoed through the winding chasm, tickling the hairs on the back of my neck. A lump clogged my throat. Whipping my head toward Val, a dozen unspoken words passed between us all at once. She felt it, too—a shadowfiend was coming, and it was on the hunt.

Heart rattling in my chest, I shoved the tool between my teeth and hauled myself up the cliff, hand over hand, twisting the rope between my feet to help the climb. My back muscles groaned from the effort. When I'd first started mining these gemstones, I hadn't had the strength to go far down the cliff before my arms and back gave out. Over the months, I'd gotten stronger, even practicing at home when I thought no one was looking. I'd pulled myself up and onto the roof, over and over again, until I could do it without any trouble.

I just hoped it would be enough now.

Dust sprayed off the cliffside as Val kicked her boots against it. Her hands began to slip. Heart in my throat, I paused my climb and held out one hand toward her, grasping my rope with the other.

"You've got this," I whispered, not daring to speak any louder for fear my voice would carry to the monster hunting us. "Take my hand."

She stared up at me with defiant eyes and clung onto her own rope. "You're as strong as light now, Tessa, but you can't carry both of us back up that rope. You're not fae."

"You're right. I'm not. And thank the light for that," I replied. "But if you fall, I fall."

Her throat bobbed as she swallowed hard and cast a nervous glance at the yawning chasm beneath us. We couldn't see the end of it. It was one of the only things inside the Kingdom of Light to hold darkness inside it. Most of the time, the monsters never climbed up from the shadows.

I'd seen them only a handful of times. Every time they hunted me, I heard them long before I saw them. I could be fast up the rope. But Val had never done this until now.

Val's hands faltered, and she slid an inch down the rope. Her legs flailing beneath her, she bounced against the rock and spun around.

Gritting my teeth, I strained to grab her, but she'd fallen

too far out of my reach. Sudden tears burned my eyes, just as the entire chasm seemed to rumble.

"Val, come on," I hissed, my heart pattering. "Hold on."

She peered up at me with clear terror in the depths of her bottomless blue eyes. "I can't."

"Yes. You *can*."

Val was a year older than me. Twenty-six to my twenty-five. But it had never felt that way. Our souls were inexplicably entwined, as if we'd come into this world together. Seeing her struggle to hold on felt like my soul was starting to unravel.

She couldn't fall.

"You need to climb, Tessa. Save yourself. I'm not going to let you fall because of me."

We didn't say die. We never did. The word felt too alien in our mouths. The mortals of the Kingdom of Light did not know death, not until our hundredth year when old age finally took us away in our beds. To die here like this, barely over a quarter-century, was unthinkable.

Slowly, I inched down the rope and wound my hand around her wrist. My shoulder screamed from the extra weight, but I would never let her go.

"If you fall, I fall."

"Tessa! Val!" Nellie screamed from above. The rope jolted. "Find a cave! Let go of the rope! I'll get someone to—"

Her voice suddenly cut off.

I risked a glance up at the lip of the chasm. Nellie was nowhere to be seen. Dread sliced down my spine. That wasn't like her, especially at a time like this. She would never just leave us here dangling like bait above a monster.

A wail echoed through the chasm. Animalistic and full of

vicious anger. A tremor went through me. It was the first time I'd felt blinding terror in a very long time.

"We need to climb," I whispered to Val, clutching her hand tighter. "I know it's hard, but we're just going to have to do it, okay? Ignore the pain. Ignore your body telling you it's impossible. All we have to do is get up the cliff, and we'll be safe. They can't follow us there." Because for whatever reason, the shadowfiends weren't able to cross into the Kingdom of Light, either.

Her hand slipped on the rope. It was only a little, but it was enough to jolt me. I winced against the sudden flash of pain. My hand trembled to keep its grip. If she couldn't hold on, I'd have her entire weight in my hands, as well as mine.

Another dose of fear spiked my heart.

The rope suddenly shifted. We hurtled upward just an inch. A fistful of hope punched me square in the gut. Together, with our bodies trembling from effort, Val and I gazed up.

Had Nellie somehow managed to find someone that quickly?

The rope continued to inch higher as the growls beneath us grew louder. Up and up we went until we finally tumbled over the edge, onto solid ground. I was still gripping Val's arm. I couldn't seem to let go, even when we were lying on our backs in the lush grass.

"Nellie." The light of the eversun blinded me for a moment, filling my eyes with dancing stars. "How in the name of light did you manage to haul us back up?"

But it was not Nellie's sweet voice that answered. It was one deep and dark and full of raw power.

"Nellie isn't here," he said.

A tall horned fae with flowing crimson hair and eyes as

orange as flames stood over me. With a golden crown on his head and a glittering onyx necklace at his neck, he exuded gaudy wealth. His lips widened into a cruel smile, revealing a mouth full of sharp, elongated teeth. My heart flipped over, and my relief of being alive fled like a field mouse from a bird of prey.

It was the one person I'd hoped never to meet again, especially here with a pocket full of his precious stones. King Oberon had found us.

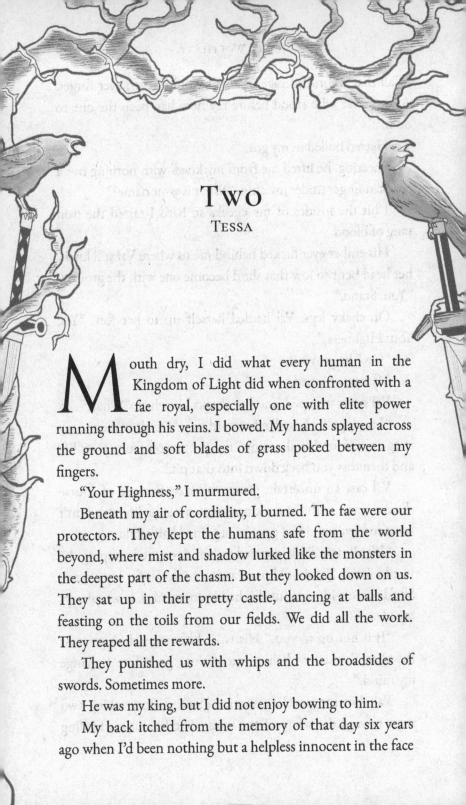

TWO

TESSA

Mouth dry, I did what every human in the Kingdom of Light did when confronted with a fae royal, especially one with elite power running through his veins. I bowed. My hands splayed across the ground and soft blades of grass poked between my fingers.

"Your Highness," I murmured.

Beneath my air of cordiality, I burned. The fae were our protectors. They kept the humans safe from the world beyond, where mist and shadow lurked like the monsters in the deepest part of the chasm. But they looked down on us. They sat up in their pretty castle, dancing at balls and feasting on the toils from our fields. We did all the work. They reaped all the rewards.

They punished us with whips and the broadsides of swords. Sometimes more.

He was my king, but I did not enjoy bowing to him.

My back itched from the memory of that day six years ago when I'd been nothing but a helpless innocent in the face of all that unbridled rage. A day I would never, ever forget. And the fae who stood before me now had been the one to do it.

Hatred boiled in my gut.

Sneering, he lifted me from my knees with nothing but a crooked finger under my chin. "What is your name?"

I bit the insides of my cheeks so hard I tasted the iron tang of blood.

His ember eyes flicked behind me to where Val still knelt, her head bent so low that she'd become one with the ground. "You. Stand."

On shaky legs, Val hauled herself up to her feet. "Yes, Your Highness."

"Go," he growled.

My heart flipped.

Val's eyes widened, and her cheeks blanched. "What?"

"I said, go!" He stalked toward her. "Don't make me say it again. Go or I will remove my protection from your life and then toss you back down into that pit."

Val cast an uncertain glance my way. Because of course she did. Even with the fae king threatening her life, she didn't want to leave my side. I gave her a pained half-smile.

"It's all right," I whispered to her, desperately hoping she would listen. Val should not have to go down for my crimes. She'd come with me, but this had been my idea. It was always my idea.

"It is not up to you." His voice boomed, echoing across the chasm's expanse behind me. "Now, go before I change my mind."

Val shot me one last worried glance before taking two steps toward the safety of the forest. She let out a whistling breath, her glassy eyes bubbling with unshed tears. Shaking her head, she twisted on her feet and ran.

As soon as she'd vanished into the trees, the king turned his full attention back to me. A strange smile curled his lips, the kind of smile I imagined lions might make when sizing up their prey. "Tell me your name."

I swallowed hard. I could refuse him, but I knew what would come next if I did. And as stubborn as I was, I didn't want to die this day. He wouldn't remember who I was, anyway. I wasn't the only human in Teine he'd punished. So, I forced it out. "Tessa."

"Tessa," he said slowly, as if he were rolling the word across his tongue. "Such a human name."

An insult, one of the fae's favorites. To them, being human was a fate worse than death. Even the common fae, the ones without extra magic like the elites, looked down on us. We were like ants beneath their boots. Mortal objects whose sole purpose was to do their bidding. And the king himself had just caught me blatantly disobeying him. This was not going to end well.

At least Nellie and Val had gotten away. I'd take the brunt of the king's anger if it meant they'd be safe.

His soft, smooth hands wrapped around my arms. He shook me so hard my teeth rattled. "Who are you to defy me? What's your surname?"

I winced and tried to pull away, but his grip was too strong.

"Answer me," he demanded, shaking me again. "And do not lie. I'll know if you do."

Raw terror burned through me. The rage in his eyes was unlike any I'd ever seen. Power hummed in his hands where his skin met mine. A power that seeped into my bones and scraped at my soul. I tried not to shudder, but I couldn't stop it. And what was worse, my trembling made him smile.

"Baran," I whispered.

"Baran?" His eyes went wide, and a cruel smile curved his lips. "Of course. It's *you*. Your father was a rebellious little insect, too."

I forced down the tears that threatened to fill my eyes. He knew who I was—the daughter of a traitor. King Oberon would never let me go now.

He released his grip on me and took a step back, sizing me up like cattle before the slaughter. What did he see? I couldn't help but wonder. A weak, little thing, shuddering before his gaze? Or did he see what I wanted to show the world? Strength, ferocity. Defiance.

Probably not. All he'd had to do was shake me, and I'd cowered like a mouse.

"Those gemstones are mine. You are forbidden from touching them." He snatched the bag tied around my shoulder, and the cord snapped like it'd been made of the mist itself. Glittering jewels scattered across the ground. Face screwed up, he knelt to gather them.

My lungs shuddered as I watched him. His gaze was focused on the ground. This was my chance to flee, not that it would do me any good. I couldn't hide from the fae king, not in Teine. Our little village flourished, but it was compact. Four hundred of us, all packed into the unremarkable buildings on the other side of the forest. He would know exactly where to look if he wanted to find me.

Still, I toed the ground behind me and cast my gaze toward the looming oak trees. Perhaps I could hide in there for a while. Val and Nellie would bring me food, and I could hunt. I'd learned how to—

"Do not be so foolish as to run from me after you've already tried to steal." His voice chilled me to the bone. "Tessa *Baran*."

Swallowing hard, I faced him once again. He stood before me now, the gemstones tucked into the stolen pouch once more. He pocketed them in his golden tunic and smiled that cruel smile. "You should know you have little hope of escaping me, not unless you wish to cross the Bridge to Death. And you know you'd never survive in the mists."

My heart pounded. I knew better than most. The image of my father's head on a spike haunted my dreams, even to this day. The mists had not killed him, but they had come close. And then Oberon had done the rest.

I fisted my hands. "You're right. It's useless to run. You'd stop me. Because you fae could never survive without your servants doing everything for you."

Anger flashed in his eyes. He strode forward with a predatory grace. I braced myself, expecting him to slam his fist into my jaw. "Every now and then, that village produces a little human just like you. One who thinks she's better than those who came before, than those who worship us. Spirited, some like to say. And do you know what I do with that spirit?"

I closed my eyes. I knew.

"I take it. I crush it. And then I smash it into a bloody pulp."

With a shaky voice, I asked, "So, what will it be then?"

"It?"

"My punishment."

The fae protected us mortals, but they did not hold back if provoked. Only a few idiots were brave, or stupid, enough to do what I'd done and rebel. Some were beaten. Some were put in stocks. Some were flayed, their twisted bodies strung up for the rest of the Kingdom of Light to see. The stench of death carried on the wind, drenching the village in it. It was an example. A warning. Stay in line or else.

"Ah." The fae king smiled. "I will set you free."

For a moment, all I could do was stare into the ember eyes of my captor. His words made little sense. Set me free? I'd stolen from him. I'd talked back. I'd defied him when no one else dared even narrow their eyes in his direction. He'd punished humans for far less than that.

And I was a Baran.

"This is some kind of trick, isn't it?" I couldn't help but ask. More defiance. We humans were not supposed to question the king, but I could not stop myself. This made little sense. "You're going to let me go and then hunt me down in the forest."

Another form of torture.

But he merely shook his head. "No, Tessa. You're free to go. Run home to your little human family."

I flicked my eyes to the pouch by his side. I would not be making my midnight rendezvous tonight, but at least I was still alive.

With a deep breath, I walked backward to the trees, keeping my toes pointed in the direction of the king, unable to tear my eyes away from him in case he planned to loose an arrow into my skull the second I glanced away.

When I made it to the forest safely, I twisted on my feet and dove into the carpet of bluebells. I didn't dare glance behind me to see if he followed. Heart in my throat, I ran. The sunlight slanted through the dense canopy, highlighting the beaten path ahead.

And so I raced home with the sting of fire on my heels.

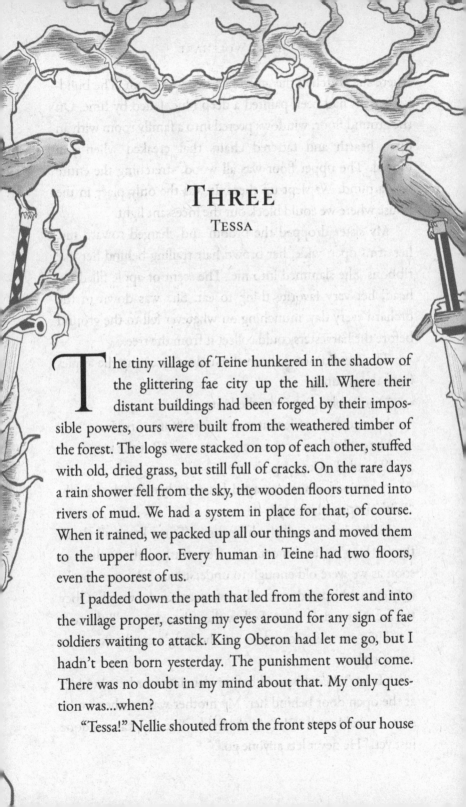

THREE
TESSA

The tiny village of Teine hunkered in the shadow of the glittering fae city up the hill. Where their distant buildings had been forged by their impossible powers, ours were built from the weathered timber of the forest. The logs were stacked on top of each other, stuffed with old, dried grass, but still full of cracks. On the rare days a rain shower fell from the sky, the wooden floors turned into rivers of mud. We had a system in place for that, of course. When it rained, we packed up all our things and moved them to the upper floor. Every human in Teine had two floors, even the poorest of us.

I padded down the path that led from the forest and into the village proper, casting my eyes around for any sign of fae soldiers waiting to attack. King Oberon had let me go, but I hadn't been born yesterday. The punishment would come. There was no doubt in my mind about that. My only question was...when?

"Tessa!" Nellie shouted from the front steps of our house

where she clutched the green handle of a broom. The building's walls had been painted a deep blue, faded by time. On the ground floor, windows peered into a family room with an open hearth and tattered chairs that creaked when you moved. The upper floor was all wood, stretching the entire way around. We slept up there. It was the only place in the house where we could block out the incessant light.

My sister dropped the broom and charged toward me, her arms open wide, her brown hair trailing behind her like ribbons. She slammed into me. The scent of apple filled my head, her very favorite thing to eat. She was down in the orchard every day, munching on whatever fell to the ground before the harvesters could collect it from the tree.

The fae did not demean themselves by eating the apples from the ground.

"You're okay," she breathed into my hair.

I pasted on a smile that wasn't true. "Of course I am."

She pulled back and searched my eyes. "But the king."

"Decided to let me go."

A strained whistle escaped between her clenched teeth. "Without punishment?"

Nellie, just like all the humans in Teine, knew all about the fae king's punishments. We were warned about them as soon as we were old enough to understand. Tales were probably even whispered to us when we were in the womb. Obey the fae. Never defy them. Follow the rules, and you'll thrive.

Then we were forced to see the king's cruelty in all its horrific glory.

"Tessa," she whispered before glancing over her shoulder at the open door behind her. My mother was nowhere to be seen. Probably still toiling in the fields. The day was not done just yet. "He never lets anyone go."

"I'm aware." Sighing, I slung an arm around her shoulder and steered her back to the house. She paused to collect the broom from where she'd dropped it, and then she leaned it against the house, green handle against the faded blue wall. Inside, Val was waiting for us, and by the mugs on the table next to her and the fuzziness in her eyes, I could tell she was already two drinks in.

She blinked up at me, winding her hand around the golden chain she wore. Another sign she was drunk. That necklace had belonged to her mother, and she couldn't let go of it when she'd had a few too many pints. Her parents, along with my father and uncle, had been victims of Oberon's wrath.

"Tessa?" she whispered.

"Val, you couldn't have gotten here even half an hour before me. How are you already drunk?" I grabbed a mug for myself and filled it from the keg tucked into the corner of the kitchen.

"I thought you were dead. I thought he'd killed someone else I love. I'm so sorry I ran," she whispered. She rubbed her eyes, sniffling. "Is this a dream? Am I dead, too?"

"For the love of light." I took a swig of my ale and raised my brows, looking to Nellie. "How much has she had?"

"Can't be sure." Nellie shrugged. "Several, at least, and she chugged them all within seconds. Might want to get her a bucket. Last time she did this, she got sick all over our floor. Mother's face when she saw..."

Mother had always been the perfect picture of a loyal, subservient human. Never once did she complain or gossip about the royal fae. Her dresses were pressed and crisp. Not a single hair on her golden head strayed from its perfect place. But when she'd seen Val's drunken state all over her polished floor...she'd let loose a horrified screech that had echoed through the entire village.

I took another swig and grabbed a bucket from the closet under the stairs. Then I plopped it before Val, who had begun to sway back and forth on her stool. "What did the king do to you, Tessa?"

"Nothing," Nellie answered for me, her voice thick with dread. "He did nothing, Val."

Val's brows pinched together. "That makes no fucking sense."

"You're right," I admitted, ignoring the chill in my veins. "It doesn't. But there's little I can do about it. I'm lucky he let me go, even if he might come for me later. Maybe I can be ready for him..."

My eyes trailed back to the closet where I'd hidden a stash of whittled wooden daggers. No one, not even Val and Nellie, knew about them. We humans weren't allowed to carry weapons. Not even to protect ourselves. *Fae protect*, the decree said. Humans had no need for such things. If we wanted to hunt, we had to find creative ways to spring traps.

But I'd always suspected there was more to it than that. They didn't want even a glimmer of an uprising. If humans joined together and attacked the fae...well, we could make things difficult for them, but they'd survive. They were stronger and faster than we were, even the common fae. Their wounds healed fast. It was *possible* for a human to kill a fae, but the chances of it happening were slim to none. Magic killed them much more easily than physical wounds did. There were only three things we could do—stab them in the heart, cut off their head, or burn them. Flames couldn't kill Oberon, though. As one of the strongest elite fae in the world, he drew power from fire and light.

The fae needed us, though, for more than just farming. After the Mist King trapped us all behind the Great Rift, the female light fae lost the ability to reproduce. So, King Oberon used his mortal wives to birth his offspring.

Maybe I could be prepared for when he came for me...or sent his soldiers to do the deed for him. If I fought back, I could flee. He said I couldn't survive in the mists, but I'd rather take my chances out there than in here, faced with certain death.

"I know what you're thinking," Nellie said quietly, twisting her hands into the shape of wings. "You want to fly away from here, like all the ravens did."

"Nellie, I—"

Her cheeks flamed. "You can't do that, Tessa. How could you forget what happened to Father?"

As I stared into my sister's eyes, the anger in my gut dissipated like smoke on the wind. The mists had not been kind to my father, but it was more than that. If I ran, the king would be forced to punish someone else in my stead. Nellie had been at the chasm. If he hadn't seen her, he'd heard her name. Val, too. They would both be in danger if I left.

"Don't worry. I won't run." Sighing, I grabbed the mug and drained the rest of it, relaxing at the fire in my belly. The sun beyond the windows was still high in the sky, but there was a slight orange hue to it now, signaling the end of our day.

Mother would be home at any moment, stumbling through the door on weary feet. It would be time for dinner, and then bed. First, we needed to sober Val up so Mother wouldn't ask questions about—

The door swung open, creaking on battered hinges. Mother filled the doorframe with the scent of wheat and dirt.

She wore gray trousers and a grass-stained tunic, as she did every day.

"Mother!" Nellie sprang to her feet, doing a terrible job of hiding the fact that something was going on. She twisted her hands, knuckles stained white. "You're home. I mean, of course you're home. It's the end of the day. We need to make some dinner."

Mother hobbled into the cottage on tired feet. Ula Baran's dark golden hair was pulled into a tight bun that sat high on top of her head. Her deep brown eyes bored into me. Even after a day working in the sun, she was flawless, though her hands were rough, calloused, and red. The opposite of King Oberon's.

"What are you three up to now?" she asked with narrowed eyes.

Val mumbled from where she hunched over the bucket.

"Having a drink." I lifted my mug. "Val had a tad too much."

My mother sniffed. "That seems to a regular occurrence these days. Why? Is there something else going on?"

My mother wasn't fae, but she had the instincts of a hawk. Nothing escaped her notice. We were oozing with guilt, and that delicate little nose of hers hadn't missed it. I was surprised I'd gotten away with my gem-stealing for so long. Somehow, she'd never puzzled it out. But after tonight, I doubted it would stay that way for long.

"The festival is coming up," Nellie said with a blush. "We're just trying to enjoy ourselves while we can. You know, before King Oberon makes his choice. As unlikely as it is, it could be one of us."

The Festival of Light only happened once every seventy-five years. Most mortal girls never got to experience the excitement of it, of being presented before the fae king. He would choose his next human bride. In return, the fae promised seventy-five more years of protection over Teine. Many of the girls in our village hoped to be picked. They'd spent weeks preparing their gowns, planning their hair.

I couldn't think of anything worse.

"You should be happy if you're chosen," my mother said. But then her eyes softened as she gazed down at poor Val. "I know this is hard for you. Just try not to make this drinking too much of a habit. All right? It's not good for you."

"Yes, ma'am," Val said.

"Good." Mother beamed as if she'd talked the king himself into doing her bidding. "Now, I'll make us some dinner. Val, you're welcome to stay here for the night if you'd like."

My heart ached for Val as she gave a silent nod. She didn't have a family to go home to, not like I did. As Mother bustled around the kitchen, preparing our nightly feast, I found Val some black tea to bring the life back into her cheeks. We ate well that night, just as we always did. As bad as the fae might be, they did make sure we had food in our bellies and warmth in our hearths. Never cold, never hungry, never alone.

Just so long as we fell in line.

After dinner, the dreams took me to another world, a place beyond the chasm, where shadows and danger lurked like thieves in the night. I never knew when a dream would come. Weeks would pass without one. Sometimes, they took me to the highest mountain peak, far beyond the borders of the Kingdom of Light. Other times, they showed me the rolling sea, or sweeping hillsides free of mist, or sand hot between my toes.

But in each one, there was always *him*. The leader of the light fae rebels, who lived in a forgotten city on the other side of the chasm.

Because he was masked and cloaked, I could tell little about him. He was tall, broad-shouldered, and gruff. His wavy dark hair fell to his shoulders, and his eyes were the color of ice. Not that I'd ever seen ice, other than in my dreams. The snowy hilltops were nothing more than a figment of my imagination as far as I was concerned. I'd never see any of that in person.

That night, my dreams took me to a shadowy forest where fireflies twinkled in the deepening dusk. No sunlight here. I always found it odd, like I was looking at something unreal. Which was just as well. These were only dreams, after all. A way for the captain to communicate with me.

"What happened?" he asked from his perch on the wide limb of an evergreen tree. The mossy needles drooped around him, transforming his figure into a gathering of shadows. Even though I couldn't see much of him, my heart still pounded, curiosity pulling me toward him like coiling string. "You didn't show up at the drop-off tonight."

We always met at the wooden wall at the base of the

mountains behind Teine. He stayed on one side while I was trapped on the other. I passed him the gemstones by shoving them through a hole in the wood. As a fae, he couldn't cross the bridge to mine the stones himself. That invisible wall of power kept him out.

"The king caught me." I hugged my arms to my chest, remembering the look of pure rage on King Oberon's face, and the warnings that had come after.

His head snapped toward me. Those glittering eyes raked across my body as if searching for answers. Heat brushed my cheeks. "*What?*"

"He caught me at the chasm and took the jewels," I said. "I had nothing to give you tonight, and I thought it best not to meet, just in case he has someone watching me. We can try again in a few weeks when he's forgotten about it. How many more gemstones do you need to banish the mists?"

Even though I could not see his face, not even his lips or his chin, I could have sworn he frowned by the way the corners of his eyes twitched down. "This makes little sense. The king would not let you go if he caught you stealing his gemstones."

The captain stood and strode toward me, his billowing cloak and elaborate mask hiding his face from view, except for those piercing blue eyes that bored holes into my skin. Anger churned in the depths of them. My blood chilled. I'd seen that anger from him before but never directed toward me.

"This isn't good, Tessa." His deep voice rolled over me. "Oberon does not allow rebellion in his kingdom."

"Trust me, I know," I whispered, a memory of Father's head flashing in my mind. I'd never told the captain about what had happened six years ago. We didn't talk about those kinds of thing. It was the gemstones and nothing else. Any time I asked him something personal, he turned the conversation around. "I'll be fine. You don't have to worry about me."

"You put yourself in danger every time you go into that chasm. I always worry," he murmured.

Tension crackled between us as he gazed down at me. A soft wind rustled my hair and blew a few strands into my eyes. The captain reached out toward me with a gloved hand. My breath caught in my throat. With fae-like grace, he brushed the hair behind my shoulder. Everything within me coiled tight.

For a moment, I forgot all about the king.

But then the captain shook his head and stepped back. "Oberon will never let this be. He'll be angry about what you did. If he hasn't done something yet, he will. You need to get out of—"

Suddenly, I was jolted out of my dream by hands wrapped around my shoulders, shaking me. I blinked away the image of the forest. My mother's concerned face hovered over me, her golden hair a mess of curls that fell into her eyes.

My insides churned, worry spiking through me.

"Mother?" I whispered up at her. "What's going on?"

Had the king come for me already?

"You were thrashing and mumbling in your sleep. Tessa, my love, you were having another nightmare."

I relaxed against the pillows. Thank the light. "Oh. I'm sorry if I woke you."

"Don't you be sorry." She pressed my damp hair away from my forehead. "You can't help these horrible nightmares of yours."

But what she did not know was that my dreamtime visit with the fae's rebel leader wasn't the true horror. If anything, it was my only escape. The nightmare was this. Being here, trapped in this place by the fae king who would one day, sooner or later, destroy me any way he could.

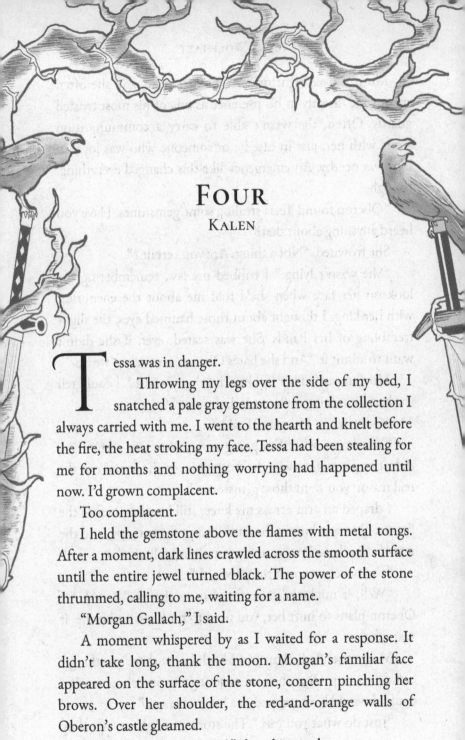

FOUR
KALEN

Tessa was in danger.

Throwing my legs over the side of my bed, I snatched a pale gray gemstone from the collection I always carried with me. I went to the hearth and knelt before the fire, the heat stroking my face. Tessa had been stealing for me for months and nothing worrying had happened until now. I'd grown complacent.

Too complacent.

I held the gemstone above the flames with metal tongs. After a moment, dark lines crawled across the smooth surface until the entire jewel turned black. The power of the stone thrummed, calling to me, waiting for a name.

"Morgan Gallach," I said.

A moment whispered by as I waited for a response. It didn't take long, thank the moon. Morgan's familiar face appeared on the surface of the stone, concern pinching her brows. Over her shoulder, the red-and-orange walls of Oberon's castle gleamed.

"What's wrong, Captain?" she whispered.

Morgan lived right under Oberon's nose, and she often spent time directly in his presence as one of his most trusted guards. Often, she wasn't able to carry a communication stone with her, just in case he or someone who was loyal to him was nearby. An emergency like this changed everything, though.

"Oberon found Tessa stealing some gemstones. Have you heard anything about that?"

She frowned. "Not a thing. Are you certain?"

"She wasn't lying." I rubbed my jaw, remembering the look on her face when she'd told me about the encounter with her king. I thought about those haunted eyes, the slight trembling of her hands. She was scared, even if she didn't want to admit it. "And she hates Oberon as much as we do."

Morgan pursed her lips but didn't say a word. I could tell she had something on her mind, though.

"Out with it, Morgan," I said.

"You know what I'm going to say. Are you certain she didn't find a way to twist the truth? Maybe she found out the real reason you want those gemstones."

I draped an arm across my knee, still kneeling before the flames. "No one knows the truth except for you, me, and the rest of the rebels. I'm assuming you didn't tell her."

"I've never even met the poor girl."

"Well, it might be time for that to change," I said. "If Oberon plans to hurt her, you need to find out. Intervene, if you can."

Morgan scoffed. "You and I both know there's nothing I can do to stop Oberon from enacting his punishments. If I could, I would have stepped in a long time ago."

"Just do what you can." The stone went glossy, signaling the impending end to the magic that powered the stone.

"Keep an eye on things and let me know if anything happens. In the meantime, I'm going to try to convince her to get out of there. I'm in Endir now. Close enough that if she flees, I can help her after she crosses the bridge."

"Are you certain you want to do that? She'll find out the truth."

"It might be the only way to keep her alive."

She nodded. "Listen, if you want me to get closer to Oberon, I will, but I won't be able to carry these stones with me when he's around. Otherwise, he'll find out we—"

The image of Morgan wavered and then vanished into smoke just as the gemstone cracked. The magic had run out, the conversation was done, and yet it felt like I'd gotten nowhere. With a frustrated sigh, I pulled the stone from the flames and dropped it into a basket with some others. The magic it had contained was gone now, so I could no longer use it for messages, but the seamstresses liked to sew the dead gems into gowns.

A knock sounded on my door. Leaving my thoughts beside the fire, I crossed the room to see who else was awake this time of night. Toryn leaned against the doorframe, a bottle of red in one hand and two chalices in the other. He was my oldest friend, a warrior with a buzz cut and an easy smile. He'd been by my side the past four hundred years, and he always knew when something was wrong.

"I knew you'd be awake." He held up the bottle. "Thought you might want a drink, seeing as we didn't get any new gemstones tonight."

I held the door wider and he sauntered inside. "Oberon caught Tessa."

Toryn stiffened and then took a swill of the wine straight from the bottle. "Well, fuck."

"Fuck is right." I gladly took the offered bottle and swigged. The sweet liquid coated my tongue, though it was strong enough to burn as it went down. "I don't know what he's going to do to her, Toryn. You know how he is. He'll chop her head off if it suits him."

Toryn held out a hand and I passed him the bottle. "What are you going to do?"

"I don't know." I shoved a hand into my hair and paced. There was little I could do. "Morgan is going to keep an eye on things, but Oberon keeps her on a tight leash."

"I hate that we can't cross that damn bridge and do something."

We'd tried many times, but it was as if a wall stood in our way, wrapping all the way around the Kingdom of Light. It was the power of those gemstones. They contained Oberon's magic, and he'd somehow used them to make certain that no fae could leave or enter his domain. There was only one way we could get to him. We planned to steal every gemstone in that chasm and then destroy them. It would break down that invisible wall protecting his realm.

The mists would swarm into the Kingdom of Light, and so would we.

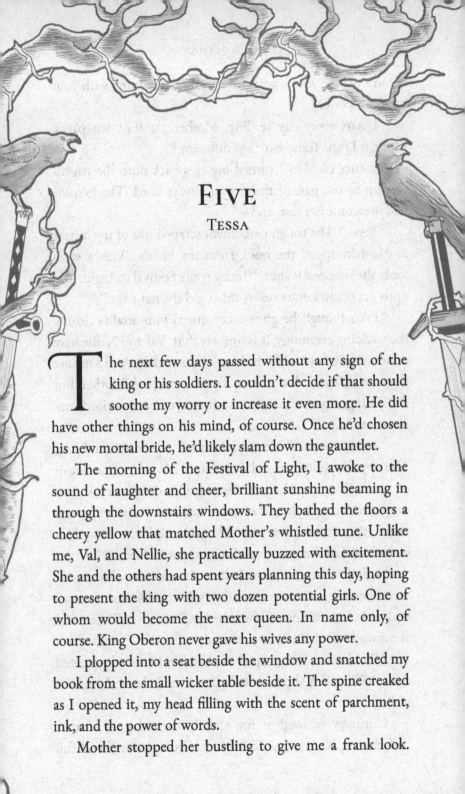

FIVE
TESSA

The next few days passed without any sign of the king or his soldiers. I couldn't decide if that should soothe my worry or increase it even more. He did have other things on his mind, of course. Once he'd chosen his new mortal bride, he'd likely slam down the gauntlet.

The morning of the Festival of Light, I awoke to the sound of laughter and cheer, brilliant sunshine beaming in through the downstairs windows. They bathed the floors a cheery yellow that matched Mother's whistled tune. Unlike me, Val, and Nellie, she practically buzzed with excitement. She and the others had spent years planning this day, hoping to present the king with two dozen potential girls. One of whom would become the next queen. In name only, of course. King Oberon never gave his wives any power.

I plopped into a seat beside the window and snatched my book from the small wicker table beside it. The spine creaked as I opened it, my head filling with the scent of parchment, ink, and the power of words.

Mother stopped her bustling to give me a frank look.

"Don't tell me you're going to spend *this* morning with your nose in a book?"

"I start every day reading, Mother. At least ten pages. More, if I can. Today isn't any different."

Mother tsked as I turned my eyes back onto the page. I was up to the part of the story I always liked. The heroine had overcome her fear, and—

"Tessa." The rough parchment scraped free of my fingers as Mother ripped the book from my hands. With a stern look, she snapped it shut. "Today is the Festival of Light. You must get ready, same as every other girl the right age."

"Even though he gives every queen immortality during the wedding ceremony, it is not worth it. Val and Nellie have no interest in becoming the king's bride either. And I'm sure there are others. I don't know if you've noticed, Mother, but the younger generation has realized our fae overlords are monsters."

"Tessa, my love." Her voice was full of concern and pity. The opposite of the anger I'd expected. It wasn't often one of us spoke ill of the king. It was considered distasteful. And dangerous. Even when they were nowhere near, we always feared they would hear us. "Do you think the rest of us haven't all had the very same thoughts you're having?"

"I find it impossible to believe the woman who eagerly meets her servant duties every day, with a smile and no word against it, has ever questioned the fae. Even after Father—" I cut myself off, choking on the words.

"Oh, Tessa." She grasped my hand in hers and squeezed tight. "What I'm about to tell you...it can't leave these four walls."

Curiosity gnawed at my already twisted gut. Mother had never spoken to me like this, her voice hushed and full of secrets. Surely she didn't have a story to tell. She and my father had agreed, twenty-five years ago, to produce two heirs to present to the fae king. They'd wanted to sacrifice their own children to keep our world ticking along the way it always had. And then when Father had changed his mind, when he'd rebelled...she'd stood aside and done nothing when Oberon put his head on a spike in the village square.

So what if she'd had *thoughts*? They'd pale in comparison to her deeds.

"All right, Mother. Tell me your thoughts, but don't think anything you have to say will convince me to get excited about this damn Festival of Light and the poor girl who will be forced to be the king's silent wife for seventy-five years."

One of the curious aspects of the *Oidhe*, the deal between mortals and fae, was this: The queen could never speak to anyone unless given permission, which she could not ask for. Even at court, during their raging balls full of drink, dancing, and lust, she never uttered a single word out loud. Or so the tales said—we weren't allowed in the fae city.

Oberon demanded silence and subservience. The queen was to produce offspring and shut up. Then, when a new bride came along, she was banished to the Tower of Crones, where all the old brides lived. That was the mortal queen's role.

No, thank you.

As my mother's hand tightened around mine, her fingers trembled. "I once considered crossing that bridge and joining the light fae rebels."

Shock slammed into me. I sat up straight and clutched her hand right back. "You can't mean that."

"I did," she said with a firm nod, her voice barely a whisper.

Taken aback, I searched her gaze. Those clear brown eyes I'd recognize anywhere looked the same as they had every day of my life, but it still felt as though I was staring at a stranger. My mother, the woman who had raised me *for* the Festival of Light, who had labored daily in the fields without a word of complaint, and who had sung the king's praises after my father's death...a rebel? Had the sun finally set in the sky? Because that was more likely than this.

"You better believe I did, Tessa." With a sigh, she released my hand and stood, her frame backlit by the blazing sun outside the window. "I grew up listening to my grandmother's stories about the previous Festival of Light. She was too old to be presented as an option for him, of course. The king never chooses a bride over the age of twenty-seven. But her sister, Marissa, was twenty. She'd hoped and dreamed and prayed for the king's attention. She wanted it. The promise of immortality is a powerful temptation. But she also had a friend, one just like you. Hannah, a girl who wanted to live the simple life here, surrounded by her friends and her family. Guess who got picked."

I swallowed hard.

"Marissa was devastated. Not because she didn't catch the eye of the king but because she knew she'd never see her friend again." My mother's breath rattled in her lungs. "She missed her horribly. So, Marissa sneaked into the castle to find her one night, to make sure she was happy. But when she did, Hannah acted as though she didn't know her. And then the king had Marissa beheaded in the square."

My back slammed into the chair as I slumped. I'd never met Marissa, my great-aunt, and no one had ever told me why, even though she would have been less than a hundred when I'd been born. The truth was worse than I'd thought.

"No one ever said. Gramma didn't tell me that story."

"You were a child," she said in a low voice.

I shook my head, a newfound fury burning through me. "Surely you know that's terrible, Mother? You must have, or else you wouldn't have wanted to join the rebels. What made you change your mind? Why didn't you do anything after Father died? What happened to turn you into...this?"

She folded her arms. "A mother who cares for her children, you mean?"

"You're as far from a rebel as anyone I've ever met."

"My grandmother explained something important to me. The rebels will never do a damn thing. They can't stop the mists, which is the only thing that traps us here. We can run, if we want, but where will we go? Out there, where the Mist King seeks to destroy us all? If I fall in line, Oberon will do nothing to hurt my daughters. I would do anything to protect you, do you understand? And as long as that's the reality of our world, we need to do what it takes to survive."

"That means obeying the king who murders anyone who dares question him," I said through clenched teeth.

A tense smile flashed across her face. "At least you understand, even if you can't bring yourself to agree with it. Maybe in time you'll see."

I pushed up from the chair. "If you believe all that, why would you ever want your daughters to marry him? I can understand falling in line and working in the fields and smiling when the fae give commands. But if you see him the same way I do, how could you have decided to have us *for* the king?"

"Oh, Tessa." She palmed my face, her eyelids fluttering shut. "I did not have a choice."

Blinking, I stepped back, my legs knocking into the chair.

"I'm sorry," she whispered. "I never wanted you to know, but I can see it's best if I no longer hide it from you. The king commanded every couple of the right age to produce two heirs for him in preparation for this Festival of Light. Twenty-six years ago. Some had sons, of course, but that's neither here nor there. We did what our king commanded, and we have to do it now. Or he'll murder us all."

Blood rushed through my ears, and my eyes instinctively searched for an exit path, a way out of this conversation. I didn't want to hear any more. I couldn't. My parents hadn't *chosen* to have me. Hearing the way my mother spoke, I could tell she wouldn't have, if the choice had been up to her.

A sob choking the back of my throat, I pushed past her and hurried toward the stairs, my book left behind. Words were often my escape, but they'd do me little good right now. I could only imagine how the ink would blur, my eyes dripping tears onto the precious parchment.

"Tessa," my mother called after me, her voice strained. "Please. Don't run before we've finished this conversation."

"I've heard enough," I managed to choke out.

My feet hit the stairs.

"I just wanted you to understand my heart."

Hands fisting, I paused. I couldn't bring myself to glance over my shoulder and see her crumpled face. I could hear the expression in the tone of her voice. "There's nothing more to say. Now, let me be. I have a festival to prepare for, because it seems I have no other choice. All hail the fucking king."

al perched on my bed, her boots laced up tight, the blue gemstone hanging from the gold chain around her neck. "Why in light's name are you wearing that ridiculous contraption?"

I glanced down at the puffy gown. It was a pearly white thing that edged past my toes, with gauzy sleeves that stopped just below my elbows. Lace wove together for the bodice, and a deep V dove between my breasts. Mother had been sewing it for months.

"I feel utterly ridiculous," I muttered.

"You look it, too."

"Lovely, thank you." I knelt, lifted the bottom hem, and slipped out my wooden dagger from where I'd strapped it to my ankle. With a smile, I pointed it right at her heart. "Fancy saying that again?"

Her jaw dropped, and she sprang from the bed. Hurrying over to the door, she slammed it shut and heaved as she slumped against it. Her words came out as a hiss between her teeth. "What the fuck do you think you're doing? Where did you get that? Do you want to get yourself killed?"

"Stop being so dramatic." Rolling my eyes, I tucked the dagger back into the sheath and dropped the gown. "No one will ever know it's there."

"The king will find out," she whispered. "He knows everything. And after what happened the other night at the chasm? You can't risk this, Tessa. What's it even for? Are you going to kill him when he chooses his bride?"

Not a bad idea, but...he'd be surrounded by soldiers and

other elite fae. Killing him during the Festival of Light would definitely make a statement, but even I understood how impossible that was.

"Protection," I replied. "I don't want to be unarmed in case he decides to make an example out of me in front of everyone."

Storm clouds rolled through her eyes. "You really think he would do that?"

I shrugged, trying to mask the icy blast of fear in my veins. The truth was, I hadn't been able to stop thinking about my encounter with the king. Why had he let me go? What did he have planned for me? When would be the perfect time for him to press a dagger against my throat? I'd wanted to ask the captain what he thought, but the nights had passed in a peaceful, dreamless sleep. The only person I could ask was myself.

And I'd come to an uncomfortable conclusion.

The Festival of Light.

"I think it's possible," I said quietly. "This is his chance to reinforce his rule over us. After he chooses a bride, he can stomp down any sign of rebellion. Those two things combined are a guarantee to keep the village in line for the next seventy-five years. Do it all in public. Make sure every mortal sees. When else are we all gathered like this?"

Val charged across the room, her eyes alight with anger. Roughly, she grabbed my arms. "Then you need to get out of here."

"There's nowhere I can go, Val," I said calmly. "And if I run, he'll take his anger out on someone else."

My family. Val.

She swore and spun away, stalking across the room, her boots thumping heavily with each dramatic step. A knock sounded on the door a moment later, and my sister poked her head inside the room, frowned. "What's going on in here? It sounds like you two are trying to knock the walls down."

"Val is a little anxious about the festival," I said dryly.

My dearest friend jerked to a stop in the center of the floor and shot me a growl.

I merely smiled. "See?"

"Geez, calm down, Val." Nellie inched into the room, her gown spilling around her feet, and edged the door shut behind her so silently it didn't even click. "You know he isn't partial to redheads."

"It's not me I'm worried about," she muttered.

Nellie's brows furrowed, scrunching up her cheeks. "You're worried about Tessa? I doubt he'll choose her."

They both pointedly looked at my very flat chest.

Not an insult, coming from them, but the king famously loved breasts, which had always made me worry for my sister. She had sweeping curves, tanned skin, and eyes big and wide and full of innocence.

I'd bury my dagger in his chest before I let him take her from me.

Just as I opened my mouth to calm them both down, my mother joined the party. Unlike us, she wore a simple frock. A brown linen thing that hung off her body like rags. Every mother and older woman in Teine would be wearing the same thing. King's orders. He liked to be able to pick out his prey from the crowd. Easier to spot them all when they were dressed up in feathers and bright silks.

"The three of you need to hurry up and finish getting ready. The festival is about to begin." She shot Val a very pointed look. My friend withered before her. My mother was the only person who could elicit that kind of reaction from Val. "You best get dressed, too, young lady. The king is unlikely to pick you, but you have to play your part."

Or else.

"I would rather be forced to sleep in a room made of windows for the rest of my life," Val said. "I don't even like men."

"I know, my love, but the king does not care about that. You must go to the festival, smile and nod, and then after he chooses his bride, you'll be free to live your life the way you want." Mother clutched her hands, and to my surprise, Val stood. "I set aside a gown for you, too. Come now. We can't leave the king waiting."

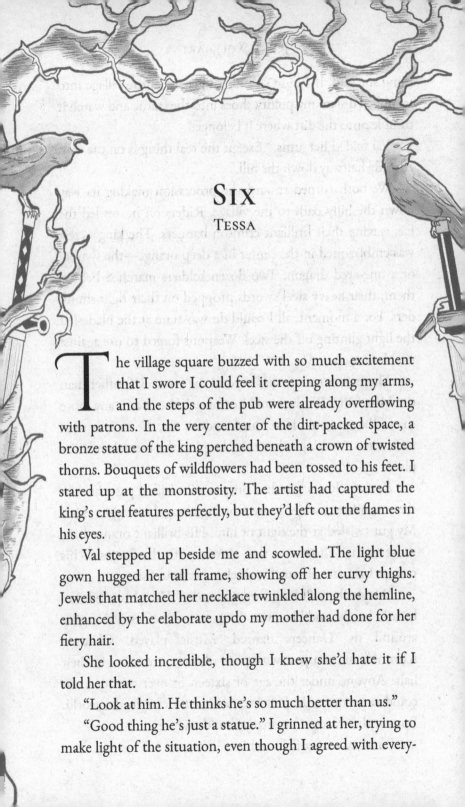

SIX
TESSA

The village square buzzed with so much excitement that I swore I could feel it creeping along my arms, and the steps of the pub were already overflowing with patrons. In the very center of the dirt-packed space, a bronze statue of the king perched beneath a crown of twisted thorns. Bouquets of wildflowers had been tossed to his feet. I stared up at the monstrosity. The artist had captured the king's cruel features perfectly, but they'd left out the flames in his eyes.

Val stepped up beside me and scowled. The light blue gown hugged her tall frame, showing off her curvy thighs. Jewels that matched her necklace twinkled along the hemline, enhanced by the elaborate updo my mother had done for her fiery hair.

She looked incredible, though I knew she'd hate it if I told her that.

"Look at him. He thinks he's so much better than us."

"Good thing he's just a statue." I grinned at her, trying to make light of the situation, even though I agreed with everything she said. If I didn't think I'd get the entire village into trouble, I'd slam my pointy shoes into the statue and watch it tumble onto the dirt where it belonged.

Val folded her arms. "Except the real thing is on the way. Already halfway down the hill."

We both turned toward the procession making its way down the hilly path to the village. Riders on horses led the fae, waving their brilliant crimson banners. The king's crest was emblazoned in the center in a deep orange—the symbol of a one-eyed dragon. Two dozen soldiers marched behind them, their heavy steel swords propped on their right shoulders. For a moment, all I could do was stare at the blades, at the light glinting off the steel. Weapons forged to use against us. No one else.

There were no enemies beyond the Great Rift other than the Mist King. But he could not breach the chasm any more than Oberon could leave this kingdom. So, the swords were useless for anything other than keeping the mortals in their place.

As the soldiers marched on, my eyes drifted past them to the magnificent white horse trotting along, bearing its rider. My gut twisted at the sight of him. His brilliant orange hair, those horns. Those eyes that glowed with the flames of his power. Instinctively, my hands clenched into fists.

"Maybe he will have forgotten you," Val whispered, her breath barely audible over the roar of the festival raging around us. Dancers danced. Music played. Children screamed and ran past with pink ribbons streaming in their hair. Anyone under the age of sixteen or over twenty-seven could carry on with their lives without a care in the world. Born at the wrong time, many would say.

But they were safe from him.

"You could be right." I said it for her sake more than mine. The king had surely not forgotten me.

One of the elders in the village, a gray-haired man named Caleb, hopped onto a stool and clapped his hands to gather everyone together in the square. Children shrieked and ran forward on bare feet, tumbling to a stop on the ground just in front of him, while the older generation hung back and exchanged expectant looks. It was time for the official start of the festival, when the elder passed down the Tale of War.

"Welcome to the fifth Festival of Light, where we will celebrate our three-hundred-and-seventy-five-year pact with the light fae." His voice boomed as we all fell silent. I exchanged a glance with Val, and she rolled her eyes. "The *Oidhe* began after the creation of the Great Rift, after King Oberon's war against the Mist King."

A rumble went through the crowd.

"The three fae kingdoms of Aesir, the Kingdom of Light, the Kingdom of Shadow, and the Kingdom of Storms, once lived in harmony. But that all changed when the Mist King decided to invade the Kingdom of Light after burning down human cities in the lands beyond the sea, mimicking the ancient myths of the five banished gods."

I shifted on my feet, ignoring the pinch of my shoes. The gods were nothing but stories, tales told around hearths, of a time when powerful beings used their horrific magic to feed upon the flesh of fae and mortals alike. The *burned* flesh. But while the gods weren't real, the Mist King had been inspired to follow in their fictional footsteps. He'd destroyed entire human kingdoms and feasted on the remains. Then he'd turned his deadly gaze here.

The elder continued. "But he did not account for the greatness of King Oberon, an elite fae with the power of the sun. Our Highness created the Great Rift, the barrier that keeps the Mist King from invading our village. He keeps us safe from the power of the mists and the monsters contained within it—the bloodthirsty shadowfiends and wraiths, and the shapeshifting joint eaters with vicious claws. To thank our great ruler for keeping us safe, we provide him with a new mortal bride every seventy-five years. Our sacrifice means that the fae can have more children, since the creation of the Great Rift had unexpected consequences and left the females barren. Whoever is chosen this day has been given a great honor. Long live the king."

Fuck the king.

I turned to Val. "If you ask me, I hope the joint eaters bite both kings' co—"

"Come now." Mother appeared behind me and ushered us toward the cluster of girls gathering at the eastern edge of the square. A table had been laid out with celebratory pies and cakes, the sweet scent of them wafting through the crowd. Once the king had chosen his bride, the mother of the lucky girl would cut the three-tiered vanilla cake and present it to the king himself. He'd take one bite, bless the village to eat the rest, and then he'd be gone with his new human companion. There would be no goodbyes. No gathering of belongings.

She'd just be...gone.

I could understand why Marissa had gone in search of her friend. I couldn't imagine watching Nellie or Val vanish down that path, only to be trapped up there behind the glittering walls of the fae city, never to be seen again. My stomach twisted at the thought. Losing either of them like that would burn.

Mother steered me to the back of the crowd, sandwiching me between Nellie and Val. Despite our earlier argument, I gave her a grateful smile as she bustled away to join the other mothers. For once, I understood what she was doing. We were less likely to catch the king's eye back here. Twenty-one other girls stood in the way.

I knew each of them by name and some were distant cousins. We'd grown up side by side, watching the endless sun slide from one corner of the sky to the next, plucking bluebells from the forest, daring each other to jump into the river where the fish liked to nibble on our toes.

Just in the front, there was Sanya, with long chestnut hair like Nellie's. Beautiful, timid, shy. She loved books and knitting and sweet chocolates. I could not imagine her at court with all those rowdy fae. Beside her was Lily, who stood tall with slim shoulders thrown back in defiance or determination. I wasn't sure which. In her younger days, she'd been part of my crew with Val. Always conspiring, always whispering dark words about our king.

But something had shifted in her during these past two years. Her eyes had begun to drift toward the city walls up on that hill. She fell silent when we whispered about the king. And when it had been time for our mothers to craft our gowns for the ceremony, she'd stopped speaking to me and Val entirely.

Worry whispered through me. Lily had blonde hair and a voluptuous figure. She had an aura about her that made her stand out from the crowd, but she wasn't too strong-willed. Unlike me, she knew when to be agreeable.

Out of all of us, she seemed like King Oberon's most obvious choice.

"Look what Ellen has done," Val whispered to me.

In the second row, Ellen shifted uneasily on her feet.

Beautiful, with midnight hair, wide eyes, and a perky nose, she smiled as she gazed at the approaching procession. Her mother had spent a fortune of time on her gown. Every single inch sparkled with crystal stones, catching the light so that Ellen herself seemed to shine.

A glittering jewel, destined to catch the eye of the king.

Only problem was, she'd stuffed her chest with rags.

"Ellen," I hissed at her, but she pointedly ignored me. Everyone knew you couldn't fool the king. Some redheads had once tried to dye their hair in order to tempt him to choose them. Like Marissa, they'd quickly been beheaded.

Shaking my head, I pushed the others aside and grabbed Ellen's arms. Shouts of irritation rose up around me, but I didn't care. I shoved my hands into her gown and ripped out the rags. Blood boiled on her face.

"How dare you?" she hissed at me. "Give those back." She snatched for the rags, but I held them out of reach.

I lowered my voice. "You can't. He *will* kill you."

"Girls, stop it," my mother exclaimed, grabbing the rags from my hands and shaking them right at Ellen's face. "You should know better than to try and trick the king into wedding you, my love. Now, everyone get back in line. He'll be here within moments, and we don't want him to catch you squabbling over fake breasts."

Ellen shot me one last look of rage before the mask of perfect civility slid back into place. Fake, bright smile. Empty eyes. She smoothed down her dress and tried to tighten it just so.

By the light, she really wanted to marry the king.

As I glanced around, I noticed a couple of the other girls were doing the same, though Milly and Pria hovered off to the side with folded arms and frightened eyes. I tried to catch their gazes to give them an encouraging smile, but they were too focused on the arriving procession.

The king's soldiers marched into Teine's buzzing square, their horses' hooves trampling down the grass and flowers along the edges. My jaw clenched as the roses were smashed into the dirt. With so little rainfall, we spent hours trekking to the river that wound down from the mountains and hauling water back for our plants. And now those roses were dead.

Power rippled through the square as the king swung off his horse and strode through the parting soldiers. Every single guard watched us closely, gazes narrowed, swords at the ready. The whispered conversations went quiet. The only sounds were the king's steady steps.

He stopped in front of the gathered girls, and those ember eyes scanned our faces. I held myself still, hoping he'd be so focused on someone else that he wouldn't notice me. Ellen straightened her gown once more.

The movement caught King Oberon's attention. He gave her an appraising glance, and his eyes dipped to her breasts. Lips thinned, he moved on to the next.

Ellen shot a scowl over her shoulder at me. I didn't meet her gaze. Any movement might draw his attention. Slowly walking down the front line of girls, he came to a stop just in front of Lily. She straightened and then gave a slight bow. His lips curved in an appreciative smile as he took in her hair, her dress, her figure.

It felt as though the entire village took a collective breath.

"Exquisite," he murmured.

My hands fisted. King Oberon had clearly made his choice. Lily was doomed. A vein throbbed in my forehead as I stared at the eager glint in his eye. The king promised his mortal brides luxury and unending youth and immortality, but I knew it was a trap. Someone needed to stop this. We couldn't let him take another girl from our village. But what could I do?

King Oberon suddenly lifted his gaze. He stared right at me. All the blood drained from my face as he pushed Lily aside. A few harsh whispers fluttered around me, shocked hands flying to mouths. The rest of the girls stumbled away, parting like the chasm. And then he lifted his finger, pointed it right at my face, and smiled.

My heart nearly stopped.

"You. Tessa *Baran*."

Chills swept across my bare arms as the world itself seemed to tilt. The taste of nausea roiled through me, thick and pungent, choking my throat. This couldn't be happening.

Gasps peppered the crowd. Even the music stopped. While no one in the village knew about my secret trips to the chasm or my rendezvous with the rebel leader, they all knew this was the last thing in the world I wanted. I'd never made it a secret. He'd killed my father.

Realization suddenly whipped through me, tossing me through another loop of vertigo. King Oberon was doing this for a reason. After he'd caught me defying him, he knew I didn't want this. And I didn't have a choice but to go with him. If I didn't, the humans would lose their protection.

The king had always been clear about the terms of the *Oidhe*. The mortals of Teine were required to sacrifice one mortal girl to him every seventy-five years. If we failed to follow through, that was the end of it all.

Rage burned through me. This was what he'd been planning all this time. This was why he'd let me go—to force me into a life he knew I didn't want. This was my punishment.

"Tessa," Nellie whispered, elbowing me. I'd been silent for far too long.

The king arched his brows, still smiling, still holding out his damn hand to see if I'd take it. What did he think I'd do? Refuse? He knew I couldn't. He'd made sure of that.

I ground my teeth. Truth be told, I couldn't think of a worse punishment than this. Try to behead me? I'd fight back. Worst-case scenario, I'd go out swinging. Force me into a dungeon? I'd find a way to escape. String me up as an example? Fine. But this...

I would have to spend the next seventy-five years by this monster's side. I'd have to bear his children...which meant I'd have to sleep with him at least a few times. Maybe more. He kept mistresses, but I'd heard tales that his appetite for sex was unquenchable.

The weight of my hidden dagger pressed against my ankle. If only I could move with preternatural speed so that I could stab him with it.

Every inch of my body rebelled as my breath hissed out between my teeth. Bracing myself, hating every single part of me that decided to cave, I lifted my hand and dropped it into his. His skin burned against mine, making me flinch.

His smile widened. "Good. It seems I have found my new bride."

My feet were as heavy as tree trunks as he pulled me from the crowd. Cheeks burning, I kept my gaze on the dirty hemline trailing along the ground by my feet. I couldn't bear to look at my mother, or Nellie, or Val, knowing what they must think.

He grabbed my arms and roughly placed me beside him.

I winced at his touch, wishing I could shove him away. But if I did, I'd pay for it. Nellie and Mother would, too. I knew better than anyone what happened to family when someone fought the king. The perpetrator wasn't the only one who bore the brunt of Oberon's anger.

"With this sacrifice," the king said, his booming voice echoing through the silent village, "the humans have held up their end of our ancient agreement, the *Oidhe*. One mortal bride in exchange for seventy-five years of bounty and protection."

A shiver went through me.

Seventy-five years. Bound to King Oberon's side. Sick burned the back of my throat.

He continued. "The fae of Albyria accept this gift from the mortals of Teine. And so our bargain remains. Enjoy your Festival of Light."

A small clap went through the crowd, timid and uncertain. As if oblivious to the halfhearted reaction to his speech, King Oberon turned to me and gripped my arms once more. My entire body seemed to hiss in answer.

"Time for you to return home, my bride," the king murmured to me as he steered me toward the waiting horses. Our transportation. I'd ride beside him, a prize on display.

"Albyria is not my home," I couldn't help but whisper with tears in my eyes. "This is."

"It is *not*. Say goodbye to Teine and everyone within it. You'll never see it or them again."

SEVEN
TESSA

The king ushered me through the crowd to where a horse sat waiting for me, a smaller version of his own. The ivory beast neighed, throwing his mane as if to communicate his displeasure. Wonderful. Even the horse realized I didn't belong with the fae.

"Climb on," the king commanded.

For a moment, I fought the urge to whip my hidden dagger out of its sheath and press the wooden tip against his neck. But it would do little good. The soldiers would stop me before I could kill King Oberon. And it might get my family killed.

My family.

Heart pulsing, I finally lifted my eyes to where my mother stood. Sandwiched between two other mothers, her hand pressed against her heart. The smile on her face was one I'd seen a thousand times, but I finally recognized it for what it was.

Fake.

The widening of her eyes. The paling of her cheeks. Those things told the truth. She was terrified for me.

As I gazed around at the gathered crowd, I spotted that same fear in every face I met, including several of the girls who had come to present themselves to the king. My stomach tumbled.

Did they all distrust the fae like me? Had it always been this way, and I'd just never seen it until now?

How could I have missed it?

Nellie caught my gaze. She raised her hands over her head and flared her fingers in the shape of wings. *Fly away from here, like the ravens.*

I wished I could.

"You know the rules," King Oberon said, roughly grabbing my arm and forcing me to turn back toward the horse. "No goodbyes. Get on."

My heart banged against my ribs, and I bit back every vicious word I wished to say. He'd soon realize he'd made a very terrible mistake. This was my punishment, but it would be his, too. As his bride, I'd make the next seventy-five years a living hell for him.

And maybe, just maybe, I could find a way to destroy the fae from within. It could be the answer to freeing my people.

So, I smiled sweetly and hoisted myself up onto the horse, keeping both legs on one side to demonstrate that I could play by the rules. Prim and proper and silent. Though it was more to keep my dagger hidden than anything else.

"Good." He flashed his sharp teeth at me. "Now, you're to remain silent until you reach your room inside the castle, which is the only place where you may talk freely. If someone says something to you when you're outside of that room, you're to nod and smile unless you're explicitly given permission to speak. Do you understand?"

I wrinkled my nose. "Why?"

"Because I said so," he sneered.

The rest of the mortals gathered around while the king left me behind to enjoy the slicing of the cake. I tried to meet the eyes of my mother, of Val, but they hung in the back of the crowd with my sister, all whispering fiercely amongst themselves.

Thankfully, their words did not drift on the wind. I couldn't bear the thought of the king hearing whatever they were saying about this.

My heart squeezed as I tried to commit every detail of them to memory. Val's gorgeous flaming hair, the wildness of her spirit and her eyes. My sister, the kindness of her smile, the dimple of her right cheek, the dancer-like gracefulness in the way she moved.

And my mother, the woman who was more like me than I'd ever dreamed. All this time she'd been pretending, just to keep us safe, but she held rebellion in her heart, too. I wished I'd known it sooner. I'd spent too many years angry at her for what had happened to Father, when none of it had been her fault.

As the king shot a sharp glance over his shoulder at me, I shuttered my emotions. I couldn't stand the thought of him seeing my sadness and knowing it was because of him. Or for him to think he'd won.

Steeling my spine, I turned my back on my home and gazed up at the gleaming city in the distance—the place I would make my stand against the fae.

Even if it was the thing that killed me.

Soon, the king was done with the cake, and he leapt on

top of his steed to the half-hearted cheers of the village. Could he hear the defeat in their voices? Did he see the fear? Did he even care? Likely not. Why care what was in the hearts of men as long as they fell in line?

The history books spoke of human kings in the lands beyond Aesir who had been just like Oberon, those who had used fear and terror to rule. The kind ones, those loved by their people, were few and far between. But mortal men withered away. They could be replaced. And with a new mortal reign came hope.

Fae did not die of old age. We might never be free of King Oberon. Not unless someone killed him.

Unfortunately, that was not a particularly easy thing to do.

The soldiers blew their horns, and the procession moved east, up the winding path toward the city. My gut twisted with every step. Albyria glittered before us in shades of orange and red, flaming chasm gemstones etched into the top of stone walls. In the very center, the castle rose up like two skinny fingers that scraped against low-hanging clouds. It was as horrifying as it was magnificent. So many riches, so much ravishing light. All for those inside the city walls, and no one else.

"Isn't it breathtaking?" the king asked with a smug smile from where he rode beside me.

I didn't answer. He'd told me not to, but I had a feeling he expected at least a nod. And I would do whatever it took to annoy him.

He glanced at me. "You may speak."

Pressing my lips together, I said nothing.

"*You may speak.* Isn't it beautiful?" he growled out, repeating himself. I got a little thrill out of that.

"No."

It was beautiful. But I also hated the sight of it.

"I will make you regret that." Power hummed in his voice, skittering across my skin like trails of fire.

I fought the urge to wince.

"You asked me a question. I answered truthfully."

"There was nothing truthful in your words," he bit back. "No one can gaze upon Albyria and not find her beautiful. I will not be lied to, least of all by someone like you."

"The only thing I see when I look at your castle is gaudy wealth. You're showing off. Probably to overcome an inferiority complex or something pathetic like that. You want everyone to think you have it all, that you're the best, that you are the great King Oberon. And because of that, your city just looks ugly to me."

Oberon did not reply. He stared ahead, a muscle in his jaw ticking, a dangerous glint in his eye. I'd probably pay for that, but I didn't care. Fuck him. Fuck all of them.

We passed through the city gates, the path between us morphing from dirt into gold. On either side of the street, lines of fae were waiting, craning their heads to get an eyeful of their future human queen. A few cheers burst up amongst them, but their celebration seemed muted.

King Oberon beamed as we passed beneath crimson banners whipping in the wind. He smiled easily at his subjects, a contrast to how he'd treated the humans down in Teine. I ground my teeth together to hold in my commentary.

"You see, my people love me," he said as we passed through the wide square and through another set of looming gates that led into the heart of the city where the castle stood.

"They understand that I have given them everything they need."

My lips remained firmly pressed together.

"Good. Silent. Just as I ordered."

My teeth bit the insides of my cheeks. Blood bloomed on my tongue.

I focused on the steady clatter of hooves on stone, the heavy breathing of the horse, the wisps of clouds scuttling across the sun-drenched sky. Anything but him. And his words. And his stupid smug smile.

We passed through another square before coming to a stop in front of a curving set of stone stairs that led to the arched castle door. Painted a hideous red, it clashed with all the orange and gold everywhere else. Two armed soldiers stood on either side of it, their spears pointed up at the sky. They both flicked curious gazes toward me, and then quickly resumed their blank stares.

King Oberon dismounted first as the rest of the party filed into the courtyard behind us. He motioned to a nearby soldier, a female fae with silver features and broad shoulders. Her steel armor clinked as she strode over to us.

"Morgan, take Tessa inside and get someone to show her to her room. Make sure she gets some food and drink and that she doesn't try to explore the castle on her own." He shot me a vicious look before parting. "We need to be careful with this one."

"Yes, Your Highness." The fae warrior bowed and then turned to me as the king bustled off. She gave me a quick once-over, nodding. "Well. Here we are. Welcome to Albyria. It's nice to meet you, Tessa."

I blinked, a little surprised she'd bothered with the niceties after the way her king had treated me. Of course, I *was* set to become her queen. Maybe she viewed me differently than he did.

"Come along," she said, nodding toward the castle door. "They'll have prepared a room for you, but it'll be only temporary, of course."

My brows arched in question.

She gave me a tight smile. "After the wedding ceremony, you'll join the king in his bedroom."

Horror whipped through me like a storm. My pointy shoe caught on the crack between two stones, throwing me forward. A shriek shot from my throat as I fell, my knees colliding with the hard ground. Pain flared like lightning. Teeth clamped together, I sucked sharp breaths in through my teeth, willing myself to stay strong, to block it all out. I couldn't show weakness here.

"Careful." Morgan knelt before me and held out a hand. "You mortals can be so clumsy. I forget how much you experience pain, even if you can't be permanently wounded because of the *Oidhe*."

I lifted my face to meet her tense gaze. Understanding flashed through her eyes, and she gave me a slight nod, as if to say she knew *exactly* why I'd lost my balance. Not because of mortal clumsiness but because of her words. I'd have to spend every night in bed with the king.

For seventy-five very long years.

Shudders shook my body.

She tsked and helped me stand. "Don't worry. Your mortal queens always fall in love with him after the wedding."

My neck popped as I whipped my head her way. "*What?*"

Her eyes widened, and she hurriedly shoved her fingers

against my lips. "Shush. Don't speak. Just do what he says, all right?"

Dread coiled in my gut as she led me up the stairs. My mind raced as she signaled for the guards to open the door. Mortals in my village often acted the way Morgan did now. They'd always repeated the same thing. Obey the fae, especially the king. Never complain. Don't say a word against him. But I'd assumed, maybe wrongly, that the fae of Albyria did not have the same fears we did back home.

The doors widened before us like the gaping jaws of a beast. My heart trembled in my chest as the cool air inside swallowed me whole. I stepped from one crimson monstrosity into another. A long hallway stretched out before me, the stone floor hidden beneath a pale orange rug. The wall to my right had been painted a deep red, and trails of orange stretched out in an elaborate, swirling design. The left wall was the opposite, red on gold. The sun streaming in from the enormous ceiling windows highlighted the glowing colors, almost blinding me.

It was even gaudier than the exterior, if that was possible.

A small figure stepped forward with her head bowed, her pale ginger hair pulled tight into a bun. I started when I saw the smooth curves of her ears and the short, stubby fingers. She was human.

But mortals weren't allowed to step foot inside the city walls. No humans other than Oberon's chosen future queen.

Confusion whipped through me. I turned to Morgan, my brows arched in question.

"You're wondering about the maidservant. She's human. They all are, including our cooks, our cupbearers, all of it. No fae inside this castle is forced to work."

I arched my brows even higher. We'd never been aware of

this, which made absolutely no sense at all. If humans were put to work inside the castle, surely we would know about it? Our village was not large enough for mortals to go missing without our notice.

"We have a stable of human families who have lived inside the castle for centuries. They are born here, and they die here. They never leave the city walls."

Revulsion twisted through me. I'd had no idea. All this time...

"But no matter," Morgan said briskly. "Maidservant, lead us to our future queen's room."

Maidservant. My stomach turned again. Morgan hadn't even used the poor girl's name. It was as though she wasn't even an individual to these fae. Just an object. A creature to serve...like me.

Queen was a meaningless title. It held no true power in the Kingdom of Light, though it hadn't always been that way. Before the Mist King had drenched most of the known world in darkness and shadow, the Kingdom of Light had been more than just Teine and Albyria. There'd been other cities, other castles, other lands. Women had sometimes ruled independently of their husbands. The responsibility went to whoever had the best claim—male or female, it hadn't mattered. Not like it did now.

Of course, in the lands of Aesir, the rulers had always been elite fae.

Morgan fell into step beside me as the hunched maidservant led the walk down the hall. We turned into an arched doorway that opened up to a curving stairwell. I tipped back my head as we began to climb, our footsteps echoing like thunder. The stairs vanished so far above that I couldn't see the end to them.

By the time we reached my floor, sweat dripped down my neck and my cheeks were flushed. As far as I could tell, my room was situated on the second highest floor, and I had a feeling whose room would be at the top. My gut churned. I might not have to live with him yet, but I was close enough that he could snatch me away any time he wanted.

"Here we are," Morgan said as the maidservant opened the door. I stepped into the room, started to take a look around, but was cut short by a *thunk* from behind me.

Tensing, I spun on my feet. Morgan and the maidservant had gone, leaving me alone in here. The lock clicked. My hands clenched. I was trapped inside.

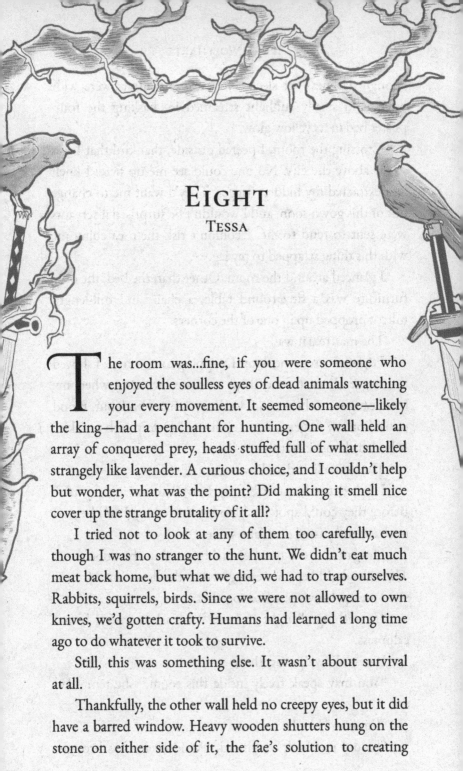

EIGHT

TESSA

The room was...fine, if you were someone who enjoyed the soulless eyes of dead animals watching your every movement. It seemed someone—likely the king—had a penchant for hunting. One wall held an array of conquered prey, heads stuffed full of what smelled strangely like lavender. A curious choice, and I couldn't help but wonder, what was the point? Did making it smell nice cover up the strange brutality of it all?

I tried not to look at any of them too carefully, even though I was no stranger to the hunt. We didn't eat much meat back home, but what we did, we had to trap ourselves. Rabbits, squirrels, birds. Since we were not allowed to own knives, we'd gotten crafty. Humans had learned a long time ago to do whatever it took to survive.

Still, this was something else. It wasn't about survival at all.

Thankfully, the other wall held no creepy eyes, but it did have a barred window. Heavy wooden shutters hung on the stone on either side of it, the fae's solution to creating enough darkness for sleep. Now, those shutters were wide open, and steady sunlight streamed in, basking the four-poster bed in its yellow glow.

Crossing the room, I peered outside, thankful that I was so far above the city. No one could see me up here. I knelt and extracted my hidden dagger. They'd want me to change out of this gown soon, and I wouldn't be surprised if servants were sent to tend to me. I couldn't risk them catching me with this thing strapped to my leg.

I glanced around the room. Other than the bed, the only furniture was a tiny round table, a chair, and full-length mirror propped up in one of the corners.

The mattress it was.

I tiptoed across the floor. Dropping to one knee, I shoved the dagger beneath the thick mattress, wincing when my hand caught on the wood. I yanked my hand back out. Blood pooled on my finger where a splinter dug deep into my skin. It healed almost instantly.

The door clicked and swung open.

I jerked up to my feet, my heart hammering my ribs. Before they could spot the blood, I shoved my hand behind my back and pasted on a false smile.

Morgan and the maidservant hovered in the doorframe. The mortal girl kept her eyes glued to the floor, but Morgan sized me up, brows pinched together.

"Everything all right in here?" she asked with a brutal calmness.

I pressed my lips together.

"You may speak freely inside this room," she reminded me.

"I'm fine," I lied.

She did not look convinced. "Maidservant has brought

you some food. We thought you might be hungry after such an exciting start to your day."

My stomach had the indecency to growl, betraying me. I hadn't eaten anything for breakfast. My gut had been too twisted up in knots ahead of the Festival of Light, and I'd been whisked away while the rest of the village feasted after the king's choice. It wasn't like me to skip a meal.

Still, as hungry as I was, I didn't think I could stomach food.

"I'm not hungry."

Morgan took the tray from the maidservant and inclined her head toward the door. The girl vanished into the corridor. My guard placed the tray on the table with an air of detached civility, but there was something about the way she moved that seemed lethal. The stillness before the pounce.

"This will go a lot easier for you if you just accept what's happening." She motioned at the room. "You only have to endure this for a month while we finish all the preparations for the wedding."

I arched a brow. "And then I have to endure *him* for seventy-five years."

Instead of acknowledging my comment, she continued. "I think you understand how the king behaves when someone defies him. Now that you're his intended, he won't lay a hand on you. You're far too valuable to him for that kind of punishment. But he can grind your spirit into the ground until there is nothing left of it, even in as little as a month. Just accept what is happening, Tessa. Do what you are told and keep your lips shut. I would hate to see him break you."

I scoffed, even as my heart faltered at her words. "Don't pretend you care."

She shook her head. "I should have known you wouldn't listen. Fine, speak your mind in front me all you like if that helps. But quiet yourself around everyone else. That includes your maidservant. She may be a mortal, like you, but she does not share your beliefs."

"Don't speak as though you know *anything* about my beliefs," I shot back.

"Eat this." She tapped the tray with her long, elegant finger. "Someone will come and force it down your throat if you don't do it yourself."

And with that, she was gone, leaving me alone to stew in my thoughts. Or so I thought. The maidservant hesitantly hovered in the doorframe, watching me with owlish eyes. I frowned as she just stood there, hands clenching and unclenching around her pale gray shift.

"What are you doing?" I asked.

"I'm to make sure you eat," she whispered. "If the food isn't gone within the hour, I have to inform the king."

I sat hard on the chair. "Morgan was serious about that?"

"Oh, yes. You're the king's bride-to-be. The bearer of his next generation of children. You must eat the correct amount of food to remain healthy."

"And if I don't?"

"He will send someone to make sure you do."

"That's..." I stopped myself, remembering Morgan's warning. While I didn't trust her, I did believe she'd been truthful, at least about that. It lined up with everything else I knew about the king. Fae females had been unable to bear children since the Battle of the Great Rift. The king needed a human to produce heirs, but it was difficult for us, even with the king's blessing of immortality. We struggled carrying a fae pregnancy, often requiring years to recover from it. The limit seemed to be three. After that, humans became sterile, too.

It was the one and only reason for the fae king's ritualistic Festival of Light. He wanted more children. So, by his twisted logic, I could see how he might be so obsessed with making sure I ate.

"That's fine," I said through gritted teeth. "I don't need any help. I can manage it myself."

Her shoulders relaxed. "That's for the best. I wasn't around for the previous *Oidhe* sacrifice, but I've heard tales. The girl who...well, the one you're replacing. She didn't eat the first day. Not willingly, at least. They say her screams echoed through the castle for hours."

A shiver raced down my spine. These people were monsters.

"I suppose she's glad she'll soon be freed from her duties, even if that means she has to go live in the Tower of Crones for eternity."

A strange expression flashed across the maidservant's face. "Oh yes. Certainly."

And then she coughed.

My eyes narrowed. There was more that she wasn't saying, but I could tell by the look on her face that she'd crossed some sort of imaginary line. There was nothing more I could get out of her. For now.

I sighed as I picked up the fork. "Can I at least have your name?"

"Maidservant."

Hand tightening around the fork, I forced the boiled potato into my mouth. It took all my effort to chew. When I was finished, I paused a moment before taking my next bite. "Surely you have a name other than that."

"If I did, I would not be able to tell you. It would be a secret, only spoken aloud when no fae is around to hear. Not that I would ever take another name," she said quickly. "It's just...some might. And if they did, you could never know it."

I chewed on a chunk of meat, half-wondering if it came from one of the animals that had been nailed to the wall. There was a strange spice to it, as if it had been dunked in a pot of overpowering herbs. A far cry from my mother's cooking.

I tried not to think about her or the rest of my family. Poor Nellie was probably sobbing into her pillow while Val paced the room, her scowl a permanent fixture on her face. They'd talk about breaking me out of here, but the words would be hollow. The only way out of here was by death. Mine or the king's.

I knew which one I preferred.

As I continued to eat, a strange sensation fluttered through me. My eyelids grew heavy. An incessant buzz filled my brain. The sunlight reached me through a haze. Everything felt far away, as distant as the stars I'd never seen.

I dropped my fork, and it clattered onto the plate. Dumbfounded, I stared down at the food I'd been forced to eat. The fork split into two, and then doubled itself to make four. Tongue heavy in my mouth, I understood at once what was happening.

The fae had poisoned me.

Heat caressed my cheek. A bell clanged, breaking through the heavy darkness. I sucked in a breath and shot up, eyes flying wide. I glanced around, trying to make sense of where I was, a certain dread punching down on my shoulders like two lead weights.

Light streamed in through a window beside my bed, which jolted my memory.

It wasn't *my* bed. This wasn't my home.

The fae had stolen me from my village, from my family, from my friends. They'd brought me here. And then they'd poisoned me.

But...I was still alive.

Throwing back the covers, I took stock of myself. They'd changed my clothes, removing the dress and replacing it with a soft pair of linens. Heart thumping, I swung over the side of the bed and felt beneath the mattress. Relief charged through me when my fingers brushed against the wooden hilt of my dagger.

I'd been smart to hide it. Thank the light.

A knock sounded on the door, and I jumped back up to my feet. No one gave me a chance to answer, Morgan and Maidservant bustling inside. I really ought to give the girl a name, even if she refused to use it.

"Good. You're awake." Morgan nodded as Maidservant deposited a tray of bread and eggs onto the table. "We don't have much time. Eat quickly, and then I'll escort you to the bathing chambers."

I eyed the eggs warily. "The poison didn't work well enough the first time?"

Morgan gave me a tense smile. "It was merely an herbal

remedy to ensure you got enough rest. The fae's special valerian concoction. It causes a deep, dreamless sleep."

Dreamless. That wasn't good. I needed to reach out to the captain and tell him what had happened. As long as I was stuck inside this castle, I couldn't steal gemstones. He'd need to find someone else who could smuggle him the goods. It was the only way he could destroy the mists and free the humans from this place.

"It was the middle of the day when I got here, and I'm guessing it's the next morning now." I folded my arms. "I've had plenty of rest. I don't need any more."

"Your food does not contain the valerian concoction this morning."

I blew out a frustrated breath. "How can I be sure of that?"

Morgan lifted her shoulders in a shrug. "I have no reason to hide it from you. You'll be eating that food either way, whether or not it contains valerian. Might as well be frank with you about it. Although, as you're well aware, it is not your place to question it."

She cut her gaze toward Maidservant. I fought the urge to roll my eyes. This place was ridiculous.

Still, I had no desire to have someone come and stuff food in my mouth, so I sat at the table and quickly finished breaking my fast. When I was done, Maidservant swept the tray aside and vanished into the hallway. Morgan motioned for me to join them.

I glanced down at my night clothes and frowned. "Shouldn't I get changed first?"

"No need," Morgan said. "Today, we began your pre-*Oidhe* ritual. The first step is a bath. You humans know what that is, yes? It's where we—"

"I know what a bath is."

She sniffed. "Could have fooled me."

"I could say the same right back at you," I countered. "When was the last time you washed that mound of hair?"

Her flowing silver strands were bound in a bun, but stray strands rioted against the string holding it together.

"Careful. You're mistaking my kindness for something more than it is. You are a means to an end and nothing more."

I frowned. What the hell was that supposed to mean?

"And don't forget, when we step out of these doors, you're to remain silent unless given permission. If you speak —and the king hears of it—there will be darkness to pay."

I snapped my mouth shut, hatred burning through me. But then I couldn't help but ask, "He refuses to harm me. Like you said, I'm to bear another generation of children for him. What's the worst he could do?"

Morgan pursed her lips, her eyes flashing. "You do not want to find out, Tessa."

Shuddering, I followed her out into the hallway where a line of soldiers was waiting to escort me, in my thin linen frock, to wherever this strange ritual process would begin. Their boots clomped on the floor, matching the dreadful beat of my heart. I kept my gaze forward.

We wound down several flights of stairs before entering a lower level of the castle where roses snaked in from flung-open windows and trailed across the inner floors and walls. I sidestepped a particularly nasty stretch of thorns while the soldiers marched on, their steel-encased boots protecting their feet.

Inside the bathing chamber, two more human servants waited for me beside a tub full to the brim with steaming water. They lowered their eyes when I entered, half-turning to a regal human woman whose twisting crown matched the crimson walls of the city.

I swallowed hard. That would be the current queen. The mortal I would soon replace.

Hannah.

"You may speak, Madam," Morgan said to the queen.

She pointed at the tub. "In."

Her voice shuddered across me like something from the depths of the chasms. Dark, dangerous, full of power. Even as a human, her seventy-five years spent in this court had changed her, transformed her into something else. My mother's words echoed in my mind. This was the girl who hadn't wanted to come here. The one who had changed.

She had bright blonde hair that fell to her waist and eyes the color of a fresh bruise—odd for a mortal, as most of us had brown irises. Her slender frame showed off her ample cleavage, and she wore her sweeping, violet gown, woven from the finest silks, as if it was a second skin.

Morgan explained. "During the pre-*Oidhe* ritual, the current queen gives you orders and dictates your preparations. She ensures that you are ready for your new role."

"And can I—"

"No," the queen said icily. "You cannot speak. You cannot argue. You cannot balk against any of my demands. What you can do is get into the tub."

Mashing my lips together, I stared the queen down. My mother had been right. There was nothing but hateful superiority in this woman's eyes. No sign of humanity, compassion, or love. If she'd once rebelled against the fae, she certainly didn't now.

She'd become one of them herself.

"Why are you like this? Don't you remember how he treats those of us in Teine? What he does to us?" I asked, balling my hands into fists.

She drew back her lips and hissed, whirling toward Morgan. "What is the meaning of this? You were under strict orders to make her understand that she cannot speak in front of me."

Morgan paled, her neck bobbing as she swallowed hard. "I apologize, Madam. I did warn her, but you know how they can be. It's a difficult adjustment. You remember how it was...last time."

I frowned.

"I don't care how *difficult* the *adjustment* is. She is my servant, to do as I say. Until the wedding, nothing she wants matters. The sooner she understands that, the better. Or I *will* tell the king."

Morgan turned back to me. "Get into the tub, Tessa."

The look in her eyes sent a chill down my spine. It was a look that communicated her feelings all too well. Fuck up and there was nothing she could do to stop the queen from enacting whatever justice she deemed necessary.

So, I climbed into the stupid, scalding bath. I didn't flinch when the queen insisted on chopping off an inch of my hair. I didn't scream when she brought a soldier in to tattoo Oberon's one-eyed dragon on my upper back—some kind of brand meant to mark me as his next bride. The ink-tipped needle felt like a knife scraping against my skin, but I stayed still. I wouldn't let her break me.

And I didn't say a word when she ordered Morgan to reduce my food rations.

"Too much muscle," the queen said with a sneer as she poked my shoulder. "We can't have her looking like that.

And what are these scars on her back? Why haven't they fully healed? Oberon's choice this time is...odd."

I didn't answer. She wouldn't like what I had to say. Oberon had given me those scars the day Ty, my father's friend, had carried my father's wounded body across the Bridge to Death after they'd both fought against the monsters in the mists. When the king's men had found them, they hadn't tended to their wounds. They'd taken Father's head and put Ty in the stocks for months.

For Oberon, that hadn't been enough. He'd punished me, too.

But I didn't break then, and I wouldn't break now. They'd have to kill me before I let them douse the fire in my heart.

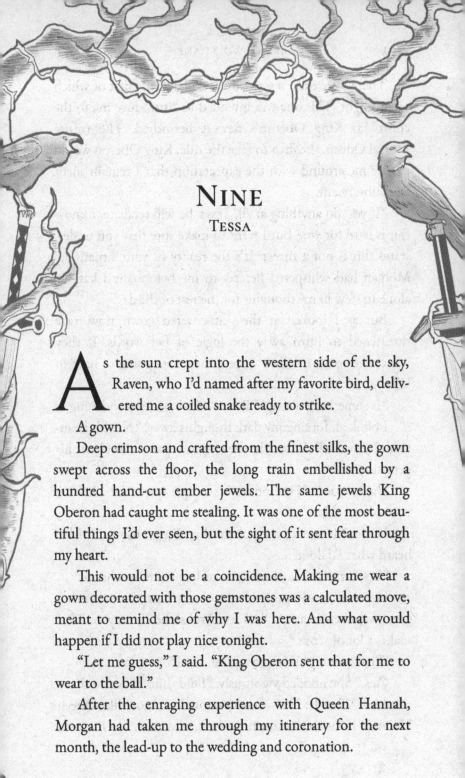

NINE
TESSA

A s the sun crept into the western side of the sky, Raven, who I'd named after my favorite bird, delivered me a coiled snake ready to strike.

A gown.

Deep crimson and crafted from the finest silks, the gown swept across the floor, the long train embellished by a hundred hand-cut ember jewels. The same jewels King Oberon had caught me stealing. It was one of the most beautiful things I'd ever seen, but the sight of it sent fear through my heart.

This would not be a coincidence. Making me wear a gown decorated with those gemstones was a calculated move, meant to remind me of why I was here. And what would happen if I did not play nice tonight.

"Let me guess," I said. "King Oberon sent that for me to wear to the ball."

After the enraging experience with Queen Hannah, Morgan had taken me through my itinerary for the next month, the lead-up to the wedding and coronation.

There were to be a series of lavish balls, the first of which was tonight. This one was intended to "introduce me to the court" as King Oberon's newest betrothed. The future Mortal Queen, the fifth to take the title. King Oberon would parade me around with the expectation that I remain silent and subservient.

"If you do anything at all, Tessa, he will retaliate. I know this is hard for you, but I want to make sure that you understand this is not a threat. It's the reality of your situation," Morgan had whispered fiercely to me before she'd left me alone to stew in my thoughts for the rest of the day.

But as I looked at the gem-covered gown now, rage threatened to burn away the logic of her words. If they wanted to make me their queen, they were going to have to kill me.

"Is something wrong?" Raven asked, her eyes widening.

I blinked, forcing my dark thoughts away. "No, it's beautiful. I just...well, I thought the king was particular about his gemstones."

She nodded. "He honors his future queen by allowing you to wear them."

Honor? It was a far cry from that. Raven must not have heard what I'd done.

"It's not that. He caught me stealing from the chasm."

Her eyes nearly popped out of her head, and then her gaze swept across me. "Oh. I see. And so he chose you. That makes a lot of sense."

What a strange thing to say. "It does?"

"Yes." She nodded vigorously. "I did think that you don't suit him. What he likes, I mean—someone more like Queen Hannah. I wasn't alive for the others, of course, but I've seen portraits. Well, I'm sure you have, too. Or do you not have books in Teine?"

"We have books, but I haven't seen the portraits. I just...I would think he'd want a bride who was more amenable than someone who stole from him. He has to spend the next seventy-five years with me."

Raven cast her eyes to the floor. "Well, it isn't as though your agreeableness will matter after the—"

"Maidservant," Morgan cut in from the open doorway. "The Eversun Ball has already begun, and King Oberon is waiting for his betrothed. He would not be happy to find out the reason why she is late."

I frowned out at Morgan, whose frosty eyes avoided meeting mine. "Don't threaten Raven. It was my fault. I was asking her questions."

Morgan arched a brow, her gaze finally meeting mine. "Raven?"

"Isn't it about time she had a name?"

Raven stood up a little straighter, but then she deflated again when she saw the look of pure venom on Morgan's face.

"Absolutely not. Maidservant, leave us now. Our future queen will dress herself."

Raven passed the dress to Morgan and rushed out of the door, her hands flying to her cheeks. I fisted my hands, watching as Morgan quietly closed the door behind her.

"You cannot do things like that," she hissed, shoving the gown into my hands. "And you cannot ask so many questions. Get dressed. And do it quickly. King Oberon is waiting, and he is not pleased."

"We spoke for a few moments at most," I argued back. "And what's the harm in calling her something other than

Maidservant, especially in the privacy of this room, where you told me I could speak freely?"

Morgan heaved out a sigh and rolled her eyes up at the ceiling. "She could tell someone. Then you'll bear the brunt of his wrath, and so will she."

Chills engulfed my entire body. "For just giving her a name?"

"He is an Albyrian light fae, Tessa. They are cruel and wicked and do not look upon humans as actual living beings with independent thought. You are the same as cattle."

"*You* are a light fae," I whispered back. "And even cattle are named."

She chuckled and shook her head. "You humans might name your cattle, but we certainly do not."

"You're all just monsters, aren't you?"

"Yes. And it's about time you truly understood that." She turned around, her armored back facing me. "Now, get dressed. We don't have time for this."

I clutched the gown to my chest and glared at her, my heart a hammer against my ribs. Everything within me itched to fight, to scream and rage against these people and this place.

I hated them all.

"At least give me some actual privacy," I said. "You already forced me to take a public bath today. If I'm to be paraded in front of a court full of monstrous fae tonight, at least let me dress in peace."

She heaved out a sigh. "Fine. I'll be right outside. Don't take too long."

She left me alone in the room. Quickly, I pulled off my clothes and donned the silky gown, topping off the look with my hidden dagger around my ankle. If I got the chance to stab the king in the heart, I would take it. They'd kill me for it, but at least I'd drag him down with me. Sometimes, you had to fight for others when no one else would.

Maybe it would be the start of a better world for everyone.

When I opened the door, Morgan gave me a nod. "Good. Your hair would look better up, but we don't have time for that." She motioned me into the hallway. "Brace yourself. It's going to be an...eye-opening evening for you."

Wonderful. My mouth went dry. That couldn't mean anything good. And going by what I'd experienced so far, it would probably be worse than what she was letting on.

Morgan led me to the ground floor where the scent of fire and smoke whispered toward me on a gentle wind, along with the sound of violins, harps, and flutes, all blending together in an upbeat, lilting tune.

It was a tune I'd heard all my life, one celebrating King Oberon's generosity. Usually, singers joined in back home.

King Oberon, the brave,
King Oberon, the kind,
To protect us from the mists beyond the gates.
King Oberon, the valiant,
King Oberon, the strong,
To save us from the Mist King's cruel fate.
Our enemy cannot feast upon our flesh,
He cannot munch on our burnt bones,
Long live King Oberon the great.

Thankfully, the fae weren't singing along. I found out why as soon as we turned the corner and came to the entrance to the Great Hall.

The Eversun Ball was in full swing. A set of looming wooden doors were flung wide, revealing the raucous party inside. At the far end of the Great Hall, King Oberon sat on a red-drenched throne, elbows on each knee, watching over the elaborately dressed court that was dancing, drinking, and...fucking.

Several naked couples and threesomes were scattered throughout the glittering hall, lit by black candles, humping and moaning and clawing each other's backs. On the floor by my feet, a male had his mouth latched on a female's breast while another straddled him, her fingernails digging into his muscular chest as she rode his cock.

My chest went hot, and I swallowed hard.

"Not what you expected, eh?" Morgan asked quietly from beside me.

I didn't give her the satisfaction of a nod. The parties back home were nothing like this.

"Don't worry. You aren't expected to participate. You're his." She inclined her head toward King Oberon, who had lifted his head to stare across the Great Hall, right at me. Darkness flickered in his flaming eyes. He wore crimson silks, his golden crown, and his black stone necklace, but there was no weapon in sight. "You'll stand beside him for the duration of the night. When the king decides the revel is over, I'll return you to your room."

The king narrowed his eyes as a furious rage crossed his face. I wanted to ask the cause, but I had a feeling it had something to do with me being late. And besides, I knew I wasn't to speak. So, I would keep my mouth shut. For now.

He lifted his hand and curled his fingers, beckoning me forward.

Morgan said, "Go on then. You have to do this part alone."

With a deep breath, I squared my shoulders and stepped

into the crowd. The reveling fae parted for me, edging aside, though several horned figures leaned in to sniff at my hair. I forced myself to keep my gaze forward.

Not a single one touched me. Thank the light for that. But they peered into my face. A nearby female with curling red hair wagged her tongue at my eye. Another cackled ominously. The trio from the floor got up and followed. The male tried to catch my eye, even with his cock still buried between the other fae's thighs.

Chest burning, I put one foot in front of the other, as the sudden realization struck me. Home was only a short walk away. Beyond the city walls, down the winding hill, and there it was. So close I could see it from my window.

But I was in a different world now. I was so achingly far from home.

The dais rose up before me. Two steps up, and I was there, in front of the king. He flicked his fingers at his side, and I moved to his left. Not a single word spoken. He went back to watching his court.

I picked a spot on the far wall to focus on. Between two crimson-and-orange banners, the servants had missed a little smudge of dirt. Lifting my chin, I stared at it. I knew what this party was. It was just as much about introducing me to the court as it was about intimidating me. If I didn't look at the faces of the fae, I wouldn't have to see their sneers, their sharp and twisted horns, their wagging tongues, their rage-filled eyes.

So, the wall it was. I could deal with that.

An hour passed before my feet began to ache. I wasn't unaccustomed to spending most of my day on the move, but these pinching shoes barely fit. My toes were smushed together, and the heels rubbed even when I didn't move.

"Ah, there she is," the king murmured, the first words he'd spoken to me so far.

I swallowed hard. He likely meant the current queen. Would she take up the empty spot on his other side? Thankfully, she wouldn't be allowed to speak, either. I had no desire to spend the rest of the night hearing her hateful voice.

The king chuckled. "I can see why you dubbed her Raven. Such a beautiful bird and a beautiful girl. A shame such beauty is wasted on a mortal."

Fear spiked through my heart. I sucked in a breath and shifted my eyes away from the wall. The fae below whirled through the hall, stomping their feet in time with the frantic music. They looped hands through arms, swinging round and round, wine staining their lips and their teeth.

Several naked fae were in the center of the dance floor, two males circling a female. She dropped to her knees as they crowded in around her.

And I understood at once what was about to happen.

Horror slammed into me, causing me to stumble back.

Her ginger hair cascaded around her bare shoulders, and her trembling hands palmed her thighs. Tears burned my eyes.

Another fae pulled off his clothes. "I have no heirs. She should be mine."

A fourth edged in. "No, the king said I could have her."

Raven sobbed.

King Oberon laughed.

The whole world seemed to slow in that moment. My dagger weighed against my ankle, as heavy as a stone. Breath hissing out between my teeth, I threw all caution aside. King Oberon had tossed Raven to the wolves, and I knew why.

It was because of me. Because I'd had the audacity to call her by a name.

I knelt, placing one hand against the cool stone floor and the other on my ankle, still hidden beneath my gown.

"What are you doing?" Oberon demanded. "Stand and watch what happens when you do not follow my rules."

"Fuck your rules," I hissed, shoving up from the floor as I whipped my dagger out of its sheath.

With a roar, I swung my arm, wooden blade pointed right at King Oberon's heart. I threw all my weight behind the blow, and the dagger sank into his chest. Not deep enough! Surprise flickered in his eyes as he grabbed my wrist.

The dagger had plunged only an inch into his chest. Blood drenched the wood. His fingers tightened painfully around my bones, nearly shattering them. I let out a strangled cry. He yanked out the dagger, shoving aside my trembling hand.

It clattered to the floor, the only sound in the sudden silence. The music had stopped. The fae were no longer dancing. Every single one of them stared right at me.

I breathed out.

King Oberon rose like a behemoth out of the sea. He jerked my arm behind my back, grabbed my other hand, and twisted it to meet the first.

Terror charged through me.

I'd misjudged his speed. His instincts were quicker than a snake's. Too fast for me to be able to catch him off guard. I'd even stabbed him, but it hadn't been enough. My heart pulsed. I'd had one chance. I would never get another.

I glanced at Raven. She gaped up at me, tears streaming down her face.

"Run," I whispered, but she stayed right where she was.

She knew just as well as I did that she'd never get away. We were both trapped.

"Apologies to my court." King Oberon spoke in a booming voice that shook with power. "You were provided with a just reward for your loyalty and service to me. Unfortunately, my betrothed thinks she can defy me."

The watching court responded with brutal silence.

It made my skin itch. After the past hour of constant, overwhelming sound, the lack of it now seemed to creep into my bones, scraping the very core of me.

The king leaned down, pulled me tighter against him, and hissed into my ear. "You don't seem to understand your place here, mortal. You and your kind are nothing more than vessels. If I say you do not have names, you do not have names. If I say that a member of my court may use one of you to procreate, then he may. I have warned you. I have given you a chance to obey. Everything that happens now is your doing."

He nodded toward the back corner of the wall where Morgan stood with an ashen face, her hand on the hilt of her sword. "Kill the mortal."

I sucked in a breath and tried to yank my wrists out of his impossible grip. Despite what Morgan had said about my safety, the king fully intended to kill me. I'd done the unthinkable—I'd tried to murder him. They'd discard me like an empty sack of grain, and then find someone more pliable. Someone they could dominate and subdue.

Morgan strode through the Great Hall, passing through the crowd of silent fae. She didn't meet my eyes. How could she? Her blade would take my life. Morgan had tried to pretend that she stood apart from the rest of them, but when it mattered, she was everything they were. And more.

She was the king's sword.

Morgan stopped beside Raven. The fae who had surrounded her pulled the poor girl from the floor, and that was when I realized the king hadn't meant me. Horror shook my bones.

"No," I whispered.

"Oh, yes," he hissed, his lavender-scented mouth against my ear. "You have forced my hand. You must see just how little you mortals matter to me."

I fought against him, my heart raging in my chest. Raven's terrified eyes met mine across the hall, and every single fiber of my being ached to do something, anything, to stop this.

Morgan pulled a dagger from her belt. She held it to Raven's neck and sliced.

Blood drenched the blade, and Raven's eyes went dark as the life left her body, faster than a breath. Morgan let go, and Raven hit the ground. I sucked in a choking gasp.

Tears blinded me. I closed my eyes and jerked my chin away.

As cheers filled the hall, revulsion roiled through me. Vomit bubbled up in the back of my throat. I couldn't stay here. I needed to escape. They would have to kill me, then, just as they'd done to my father. I'd die before I'd marry this monster. And the anger I'd felt before was nothing compared to the rage now boiling inside of me, its gnashing teeth desperate to rip through this entire kingdom.

"Silence," the king commanded as the cheers died down. "One more thing, just in case the mortal's death has failed to demonstrate to my betrothed what her place is in this court. Bring out the head."

My stomach twisted; my mind replayed the king's words.

The head, the head, the head. Terror clutched my heart. I could barely breathe.

The head. Whose head? Oh light, oh light, I didn't want to know. I couldn't look. I knew whoever it was would bring me to my knees.

But when the doors swung open, I couldn't turn away.

A guard strode in, his hand fisted around a tangle of chestnut hair. Her face was dirty, bloodied, and bruised, but I'd brushed that hair so many nights that I'd know the color of it anywhere.

He threw my sister's head right at my feet.

My legs buckled. All the fight went out of me.

The howl that ripped from my throat was the loudest human sound the court had heard in almost four hundred years.

And the king's victorious smile was the last thing I saw before I blacked out.

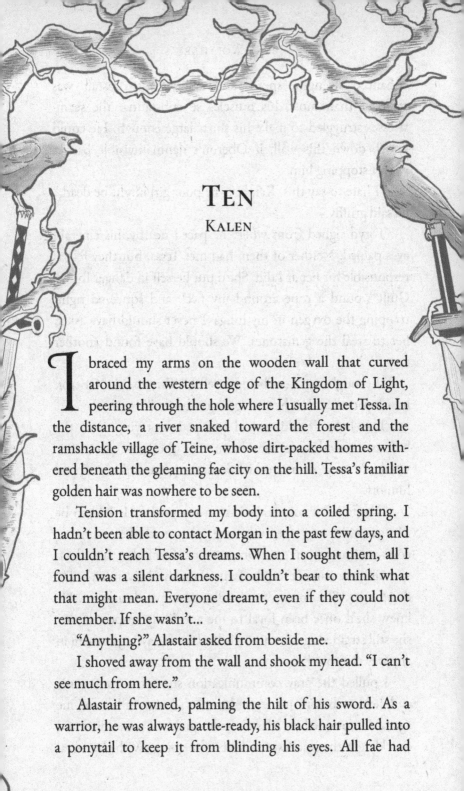

TEN

KALEN

I braced my arms on the wooden wall that curved around the western edge of the Kingdom of Light, peering through the hole where I usually met Tessa. In the distance, a river snaked toward the forest and the ramshackle village of Teine, whose dirt-packed homes withered beneath the gleaming fae city on the hill. Tessa's familiar golden hair was nowhere to be seen.

Tension transformed my body into a coiled spring. I hadn't been able to contact Morgan in the past few days, and I couldn't reach Tessa's dreams. When I sought them, all I found was a silent darkness. I couldn't bear to think what that might mean. Everyone dreamt, even if they could not remember. If she wasn't...

"Anything?" Alastair asked from beside me.

I shoved away from the wall and shook my head. "I can't see much from here."

Alastair frowned, palming the hilt of his sword. As a warrior, he was always battle-ready, his black hair pulled into a ponytail to keep it from blinding his eyes. All fae had enhanced strength, speed, and agility, but Alastair was stronger than most, his muscles so substantial the seamstresses struggled to make his shirts large enough. He could knock down this wall, if Oberon's damn invisible barrier wasn't stopping him.

"I hate to say this, Kal, but the poor girl might be dead," he said gruffly.

Toryn sighed from where he paced nearby, his emerald eyes pained. Neither of them had met Tessa, but they felt as responsible for her as I did. She'd put herself in danger for us. Guilt wound a rope around my neck and squeezed tight, trapping the oxygen in my lungs. I never should have asked her to steal the gemstones. We should have found another way.

"I thought we were being careful," Toryn said. "Oberon hasn't patrolled the chasm edge in centuries."

The light fae king had stopped worrying that the humans would scale the chasm. For the most part, they wouldn't even dream of it. Something must have tipped him off.

"Captain," a voice called from my pocket. It had to be Morgan. She was the only one who used that name to communicate with me. Oberon had forbidden her from speaking my name, even the twisted one he'd given me—*The Mist King*. She couldn't even discuss me with anyone. He knew she'd once been loyal to me and likely suspected that she still strained against his invisible bonds, sawing at them in any way she could.

I pulled the gray communication stone from my tunic and held it before my eyes. Morgan's voice called for me again. I motioned at Alastair, who grabbed some flint and quickly got the smallest spark of a fire going. With the metal tongs I'd carried with me, just in case, I held the stone over the flame.

Morgan's furrowed brows were the first thing I noticed, along with the hollow look in her silver eyes. My stomach dropped. Something terrible must have happened.

"What's happened to Tessa?" I asked through clenched teeth.

She pressed her lips together. "She's here at the castle. She's been chosen as the next queen."

I drew back as Alastair hissed. Toryn stopped pacing. His jaw dropped. Thank the moon she was alive, but to her, this might be a fate worse than death. Oberon would bind her to his side through fae magic. She would never be able to escape him. Even after he used her up and discarded her, she'd be forced to remain in the castle, hidden away in the Tower of Crones.

She would spend eternity stuck with him.

"We need to get her out of there," I practically growled.

Morgan blew out a breath. "It's going to be difficult. He has her under very close watch. Her new maidservant never leaves her quarters. And while I've managed to secure a position outside her door, Oberon has given me strict orders. You know that means my hands are tied."

Morgan was incapable of going against Oberon's direct orders unless she found a loophole. The only reason she was able to communicate through these stones was because he didn't know about it. The second he did, she'd be forced to stop.

"The wedding is in a month," she continued. "We have some time to plan, but I have to be careful. Guarding Tessa means being under close observation myself. I can't contact you often. Also, there's something else..."

I furrowed my brows. "What?"

"I'm forbidden to speak of it, to anyone. All I can say is something has happened, and Tessa is hurting because of it." She cast a quick look over her shoulder. "And I daresay she would be willing to do *anything* to destroy Oberon. Do you still have the Mortal Blade?"

Toryn popped in beside me with raised brows. "Not with us. It's safe and sound back in Dubnos."

Morgan dropped her voice into a hiss. "Let's get Tessa out of here. You can take her to Dubnos and give her the Mortal Blade. And then she can sneak back into the Kingdom of Light and kill Oberon."

"Morgan," I said, tensing. This was a terrible idea. We'd discussed doing something like this before, but we'd never followed through on the plan. It required smuggling a mortal out of the Kingdom of Light and then back in. Easy in theory. Hard as fuck in reality.

The stone wavered as the magic ran out.

"Think about it, Captain. You wouldn't need to steal his gemstones anymore. This would be a far easier way to destroy him."

A crackle followed her words, and the stone blinked out. With a frustrated sigh, I pulled it from the fire and tossed it away from me, wanting to rid my mind of Morgan's words. Oberon had chosen a cruel punishment for Tessa. And I had no idea how we were going to save her from it.

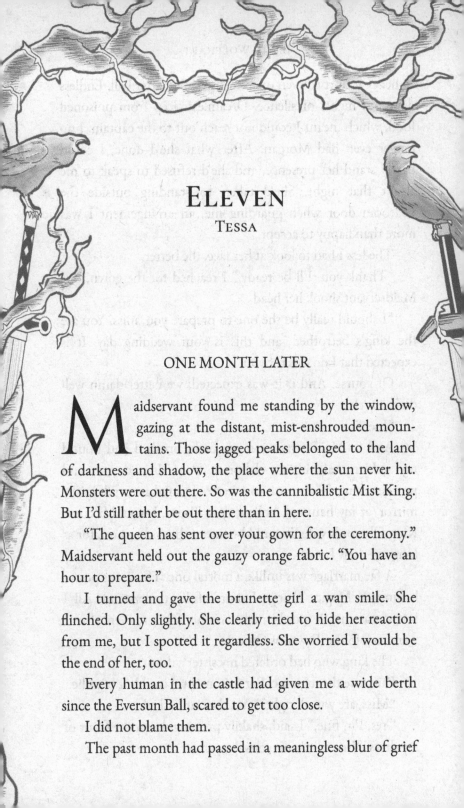

ELEVEN
TESSA

ONE MONTH LATER

Maidservant found me standing by the window, gazing at the distant, mist-enshrouded mountains. Those jagged peaks belonged to the land of darkness and shadow, the place where the sun never hit. Monsters were out there. So was the cannibalistic Mist King. But I'd still rather be out there than in here.

"The queen has sent over your gown for the ceremony." Maidservant held out the gauzy orange fabric. "You have an hour to prepare."

I turned and gave the brunette girl a wan smile. She flinched. Only slightly. She clearly tried to hide her reaction from me, but I spotted it regardless. She worried I would be the end of her, too.

Every human in the castle had given me a wide berth since the Eversun Ball, scared to get too close.

I did not blame them.

The past month had passed in a meaningless blur of grief

so heavy it hurt to even open my eyes. Ball after ball. Endless days and nights of silence. Dreamless sleep from poisoned food, which meant I could not reach out to the captain. I no longer even had Morgan. After what she'd done, I could barely stand her presence, and she'd refused to speak to me about that night. She'd taken to standing outside the bedroom door when guarding me, an arrangement I was more than happy to accept.

The less I had to look at her face, the better.

"Thank you. I'll be ready." I reached for the gown, but Maidservant shook her head.

"I should really be the one to prepare you, miss. You are the king's betrothed, and this is your wedding day. It is expected that I do this for you."

Of course. And if it was expected, we better damn well do it. Or else.

"I see."

And so Maidservant ran my bath, brushed and bound my golden hair in an elaborate bun, dressed me, and powdered my cheeks with rosy herbs. I stared at myself in the mirror, at my haunted, hollow eyes. Today, I would become King Oberon's wife. I would be forever bound to him, for as long as I drew breath.

A fae marriage was unlike a mortal one. There was power behind it. Magic. Things I didn't fully understand. All I knew was that it would make me his forever, even after I went to join the Tower of Crones.

The king who had ordered my sister's death.

Pain tore through me. For a moment, I couldn't breathe.

"Miss, are you all right?" Maidservant asked.

"Yes, I'm fine," I said, shakily pressing down the front of my dress. "Just a little nervous."

She nodded. "Of course."

I wanted to say more, to thank her for everything she'd done for me this past month. The days I'd struggled to get out of bed, she had pulled me from my stupor and washed the tears from my cheeks. But I knew she did not want to be thanked. She did not want me to feel anything toward her at all.

Because it could get her killed.

"I'm ready to go now, Maidservant. Tell Morgan."

With a nod, she opened the door into the hall. A moment later, Morgan stepped inside, bedecked in her steel armor, her gaze sweeping across me. I waited, silent while she inspected me.

"Beautiful, Tessa."

I did not speak.

"You're still angry with me."

I flicked my gaze toward her, narrowed my eyes, and then went back to silently staring at the wall.

"That's fine," she said tensely. "Let's go."

The wedding took place in the castle courtyard. The servants had been busy filling it with flowers in all shades of gold, orange, and red. A raised wooden platform squatted in the center of the gathering crowd where vines crept along an arched frame. I stood in the back behind a fluttering banner that hid me from view. The scent of fire filled the air, and the crowd buzzed with the promise of revelry and cheer.

I felt numb. Deep down, there was a part of me that yearned to fight back, to break through the melancholy that hung around my neck like a noose. But every single time a hint of it rose up within me, my sister's unrecognizable, bloodied face flashed through my mind.

They had killed her. And the king had promised to do

the same to my mother and Val if I even breathed the wrong way.

I could be reckless with my own life, but not with theirs.

He had done everything he'd said he would. Taken my spirit. Crushed it.

"Don't forget your bouquet," Maidservant said as she pressed a cluster of flowers into my hands. "Morgan had this made for you."

I hadn't realized Maidservant was there. I glanced down at the flowers. They looked like those tangled, messy bluebells from the forest beside my village, not the big, bright yellow ones in the square.

I frowned, wishing I could ask her if she was sure.

But my lips were sealed, and the music had begun.

Maidservant cast a nervous glance behind her, then leaned forward and whispered, "The king is about to give a speech. There is something for you in those flowers. Read it quickly, while they are all focused on him. Do what it says. Goodbye, Tessa."

She swept through the banner, leaving me alone with my thumping heart. I glanced around. Morgan stood at the far edge of the banner, her eyes focused on the square ahead, her hand on the hilt of her sword. She gave me the tiniest nod.

All the blood rushed into my cheeks.

My fingers dove into the bouquet, and they brushed paper. Lungs squeezing, I pulled out two pieces of parchment, each folded into a square. Quickly, I read the contents.

The first was written in a tense scrawl.

Be ready. A fight will break out. When Morgan approaches you, don't run away from her. Just do what she says. She's getting you out of this place.

Maidservant

I crumpled the note in my fist, sucked in a rattling breath, and stared at Morgan. She didn't meet my eyes, her gaze still locked forward, focused on the king.

Was this some kind of trick? How could this be real? Morgan was the king's right hand. His sword. The fae who killed for him. She'd done everything in her power to keep me in line. Why would she ever break me free?

But then my mind went over those early days at the castle. All her warnings. The silent looks. Her ashen face at the ball.

I needed to read the other note.

When I saw the handwriting for this one, I nearly toppled over. I'd seen that familiar looping scrawl a thousand times. My heart flipped over. Val.

> *I hope this reaches you, Tessa. I'm taking your mother, and I am getting her out of here. We're going across the bridge and into the mists. Morgan will bring you to us.*
>
> *I love you,*
> *Val*

My entire body shook, tears spilling from my eyes, as I read Val's note over and over and over until I could be sure I hadn't imagined every word. Val had somehow gotten me a note. To tell me she was taking my mother into the mists.

I reached out to grip something, but all I found was air. Val had escaped the Kingdom of Light...but she'd run straight into something far more dangerous. The mists.

Footsteps sounded nearby. Shaking, I crumpled the second note and shoved both of them back into my bouquet, tensing when a looming figure stepped through the banner. It was Cormac, a fae who had been part of the attack on Raven all those days ago. I gritted my teeth as he sneered down at me.

"I can't wait for the king to finally take you for his," he hissed, with eyes the color of blood. Spittle dripped down his chin, and the smell that drifted toward me was sharp and tangy, like a thousand barrels of ale. "Do you know how long I've waited to spread my seed? Two hundred *years*. And you took it away from me."

Heart hammering, I cut my eyes to the side, searching for Morgan. If that fight was going to break out as some kind of distraction, right about now would be a good time. But King Oberon's voice continued to drone on in the distance.

Cormac grabbed my chin and jerked my face toward him. "Look at me when I'm speaking to you, human. You stole that from me, do you understand me?"

My hands fisted by my sides. King Oberon no longer had any grip on my family. If I punched this fae, what could he do now? Kill me? Hardly.

I started to haul back my fist.

He laughed. "The king's little prize. I can't wait to see the look on your face when you realize what's *really* going to happen to you today."

My entire body froze.

What did he mean? Why did his eyes flicker with gleeful rage, as if he'd just trapped me in a web I couldn't escape?

A roar cut through the square. Clashing steel echoed soon after. Cormac's face screwed up, and he grunted, quickly glancing around the banner. I sucked in a breath, hauled back my fist and—

A strong hand grabbed my arm and dragged me backward.

"No," Morgan hissed into my ear as she spun me to face the opposite direction. "You have to go. Now."

A part of me wanted to throw my fist into *her* face. Trusting her seemed like a terrible idea. How could I be sure she wasn't plucking me out of the frying pan and throwing me into the fire?

But I also didn't have much of a choice.

I glanced behind me. Cormac had vanished behind the banner to join the fight. If I wanted to escape this nightmare, this was my only chance. I'd never get another.

"Fine," I said, hurrying my steps to keep up with her. "But I want you to know that I still don't trust you, and I definitely don't like you."

A ghost of a smile crossed her face. "I would expect nothing less, Tessa."

We raced through the silent streets of the fae city. It was the first time I'd seen anything other than the crimson castle walls for weeks. King Oberon had not let me outside, and even though my window had given me a view of the village and the wilderness beyond, those walls had felt like a coffin.

Close and suffocating.

As we rounded a corner away from the square, we passed through a wide cobblestone area with wooden huts lined up on each side. Barrels and baskets were piled next to each one, painted signs noting what each of them were. A shop for bread. Another for freshly picked fruit. There was one for meats and another for clothes. There was no one manning the market. They'd closed up shop for the day to celebrate the king's wedding.

But the sight of it made my soul ache. It reminded me so

much of home. A place I might never see again. If I got out
of here alive, the village would never be safe for me or the
other villagers. The king would look for me there. And if he
found anyone hiding me, he'd slaughter them as easily as he
had Nellie and Raven.

I'd be forever bound to the mists.

That thought haunted me.

"Have you ever been out there?" I asked, breath huffing.

"How could I have been? We're all trapped."

"Trapped because of the Mist King. Do you think he's
anywhere near the bridge?"

Her face paled. "I'm forbidden to speak of that person. I
cannot even say his name."

That was odd.

"Well, do you think it's as dangerous out there as they
say?"

She pressed her lips together. "I don't want to scare you,
Tessa, but there's no sense in lying. You'll find out soon
enough. Yes, the world beyond the bridge is dangerous.
There are things out there that can rip you to shreds before
you even know they're beside you."

My stomach twisted. "That isn't very reassuring."

"You need to know what you're heading into," she said
frankly. "Unfortunately, it's your only choice. You can't stay
here."

"I could hide somewhere. There must be a cellar or a cave
or something where the king wouldn't find me. We could
take Mother and Val there, too."

"Tessa, you know you can't do that." She stopped,
grabbed my hands, and squeezed. "You have no idea how
important you are to him. There is nowhere inside this
damned kingdom where Oberon cannot find you. It's too

small. No matter where you go, as long as you stay on this side of the chasm, he *will* track you down."

The passion in her voice startled me. All this time, she'd fallen in line, seeming like a good little soldier. But now I saw the truth. She'd been biding her time, just waiting for the right moment to make her move against the king.

"You're one of the rebels, aren't you?"

She pressed her lips together. "Yes. In my own way. One of the few on this side of the chasm. Now listen, you're going to have to do the rest of this on your own. I'm forbidden from taking you outside this city. There is a hidden gate in the wall just down this road. Go through it and make for the bridge. If the guards stop you, sneak back into the city and hide in the tunnels beneath the castle. There's a hidden entrance in one of the abandoned inns. No one ever goes down there. I'll find you, and we'll try again."

I nodded, my heart pounding.

"Run fast and head east. You'll cross a river, and then you'll reach the city of Endir. The rebels are hiding out there. I wanted to warn them of my plan, but I've been under close watch, too. I didn't want to risk Oberon finding out."

Then, she knelt and pulled out my little wooden dagger from where she'd hidden it beneath her trouser leg. The pointed end of it was still stained with the blood of the king.

"Keep this. Let it remind you of what you're fighting for."

"I should have known," a voice boomed from behind us. My heart lurched into my throat as we whirled toward the sound. Cormac stood in the center of the deserted street, his chest heaving as he clutched the golden hilt of his sword. He narrowed his eyes, sneering. "There's always been something about you, Morgan. Something I couldn't quite place. You never belonged."

Morgan smiled. Her steel sang as she pulled her sword from its scabbard. "I've been waiting a long time for this. Try your best, Cormac. Let's see what you can do."

Cormac raised his sword. "What I can do is slice your fucking throat."

Morgan matched his stance, shifting her body in front of mine. "Run, Tessa. Go. *Now.*"

My heart squeezed, my body frozen by uncertainty. How could I just leave her here to face Cormac on her own?

As if reading my mind, Morgan nudged my leg with the heel of her boot. "I'll be fine. *GO.*"

"Thank you." I yanked my wedding gown up from around my feet, and I ran.

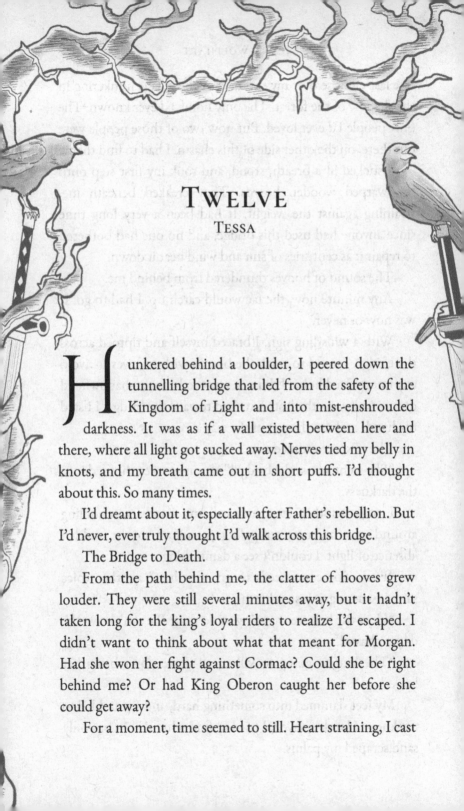

TWELVE
TESSA

Hunkered behind a boulder, I peered down the tunnelling bridge that led from the safety of the Kingdom of Light and into mist-enshrouded darkness. It was as if a wall existed between here and there, where all light got sucked away. Nerves tied my belly in knots, and my breath came out in short puffs. I'd thought about this. So many times.

I'd dreamt about it, especially after Father's rebellion. But I'd never, ever truly thought I'd walk across this bridge.

The Bridge to Death.

From the path behind me, the clatter of hooves grew louder. They were still several minutes away, but it hadn't taken long for the king's loyal riders to realize I'd escaped. I didn't want to think about what that meant for Morgan. Had she won her fight against Cormac? Could she be right behind me? Or had King Oberon caught her before she could get away?

For a moment, time seemed to still. Heart straining, I cast

one last glimpse over my shoulder at the village hunkering in the shadow of the forest. The only home I'd ever known. The only people I'd ever loved. But now two of those people were out there, on the other side of this chasm. I had to find them.

I sucked in a breath, stood, and took my first step onto the warped wooden boards. They creaked beneath me, straining against the weight. It had been a very long time since anyone had used this bridge, and no one had bothered to repair it as centuries of sun and wind beat it down.

The sound of hooves thundered from behind me.

Any minute now, the fae would catch up. I had to go. It was now or never.

With a whistling sigh, I braced myself and tiptoed across the bridge, careful to track the boards with my eyes to avoid any unexpected holes. I did not want to become shadowfiend dinner today. As the horses rushed toward the bridge, I fisted my hands and ran the rest of the way across.

The mists consumed me.

"She went across the bridge!" an angry voice shouted into the darkness.

I took another step forward, my hands windmilling around me, my eyes struggling to adjust to the sudden absence of light. I couldn't see a damn thing.

"Fuck. Someone needs to go after her," another voice said, just as angry, just as harsh.

"How the hell are we going to do that? We can't cross the damn chasm!"

"The king is going to kill us all if we don't bring her back."

My feet slammed into something hard, and I stumbled to my knees. Hands splayed, I tried to find what I'd hit, but only sand scraped my palms.

"Got you," a deep, melodic voice said. Strong hands wrapped around my arms and hauled me to my feet.

My heart nearly collapsed in on itself as terror ripped through me. The fae couldn't cross the bridge. So it couldn't be the soldiers. That only left one person. *The Mist King.* Tears of pure horror burned my eyes.

I screamed and shoved my dagger into his body. It hit, sinking into the skin, but I couldn't see in the darkness to know if I'd caught his heart. A grunt of surprise answered, and he loosened his grip on my arms.

Heart stuck in my throat, I ran. My legs wobbled beneath me, my wedding shoes pinching my toes and slowing me down. I breathed in the mists, desperately trying to see the ground before me. Everything was dark.

He grabbed my waist and dragged me back. "Stop running. It's—"

"Let go of me!" I screamed.

I writhed in his arms, bucking, kicking, twisting. I felt like a caged beast ready to drag my claws through his guts. But I was nothing more than a mouse.

All the stories of the Mist King filled my head, tumbling over and over. He burned humans alive. He feasted on their flesh. He wanted to destroy the world to become a god. And now he'd caught me.

I was going to die.

With desperation burning through me, I hauled up my foot and jammed the heel of my shoe into his boot. He barely flinched.

A soft cloth pressed against my nose and mouth, and the scent of valerian filled my head. As a heavy exhaustion dragged me under, the last remnants of light left me in brutal darkness.

A bright light dove into my mind and pulled me from a dreamless slumber. Head throbbing, I cracked open my eyes and found myself flat on my back, staring up at a torch flickering on the wall.

Groaning, I glanced around, trying to make sense of things. I was on a small bed with thick blankets draped over me. Across the room—

My heart stopped. A row of steel bars stood between me and...

I let out a rattling gasp.

Between me and the captain.

He leaned against the bars, arms crossed, a hooded cloak hiding his face from view as he stared down a dark tunnelling hallway. But I'd recognize that stance anywhere—relaxed but on edge at the same time, as if any moment something might lurch out of the night and swallow him whole.

It had been him. Out there, in the mists. But...why had he trapped me in a cell? And...my mind snapped on the memory. The cloth against my mouth. The valerian sweeping into my nose.

He'd drugged me. Just like Oberon had. Of course, I *had* been fighting him.

I threw back the covers, and pain bit my head. My vision blurred.

"Ah, you're finally awake," he said. That deep, lilting voice was so familiar. I should have recognized it the second I'd heard it, but the mists had disoriented me. "You might want to rest until the effects of the valerian wear off."

With my head braced in my hands, I hissed at him through clenched teeth. "What's going on? Why am I in a dungeon cell?"

"You seemed determined to flee from me. I didn't want you to run screaming again when you woke up."

Still trying to hold my head steady to dull the pain, I looked up to find him standing on the other side of those bars, staring at me with his deep sapphire eyes. Not an icy blue, like they'd been in the dreams. He'd dropped back his hood, the midnight color of his cloak matching the wavy hair curling around his pointed ears. The curve of his jaw was as sharp as a blade, and his entire body pulsed with power.

He was breathtakingly beautiful.

I swallowed hard as I stared up at him. I'd seen this face in a hundred portraits. It was one I'd *never* expected to see up close.

"You're the Mist King," I whispered, the blood draining from my face.

The enemy. The lethal fae who had murdered thousands in the human kingdoms beyond the sea. The one who'd trapped the people of Teine beneath King Oberon's cruel reign.

He flinched. "Don't call me that."

Despite my fear, confusion, and anger, a little smile tickled the corners of my lips. "Oh, you don't like that, *Mist King*?"

"I should have known you'd react this way."

"You have me trapped in a cell after poisoning me." I finally stood on trembling legs, fisting my hands by my sides. "You burned down entire cities and ate mortal flesh. You drenched the world in mist and darkness, and then you trapped those left alive beneath the rule of a cruel and wicked king. He probably isn't even as bad as you are, and that sure as light is saying something. Do you know what he does to us? Do you know what it's like to be a human trapped in that world?"

I laughed bitterly. "Why am I even asking that? You probably don't even care."

For a moment, the Mist King said nothing. A muscle in his jaw ticked. And then he turned on his feet and left me to stew in my thoughts.

A muscled fae with a buzz cut appeared outside of my cell sometime later. It was impossible for me to have any sense of time without the path of the sun to guide me. This male wore fighting leathers as black as the night and a gentle smile I wanted to punch. By now, the poison had fully worn off, and my head no longer felt as if it had been stuffed full of prickly thorns. I'd spent the past however long sitting on the cot with my back to the wall, eyes narrowed, body tense, trying to puzzle this whole thing out.

I hadn't gotten very far. None of it made much sense.

The warrior held up a plate of food. "Hungry?"

"Who are you?" I snapped back. "Wait, let me guess. You're one of the Mist King's loyal servants."

He laughed and shook his head. "I'm not a servant, and you really shouldn't call him the Mist King."

I arched a brow. "He doesn't like it. That's reason enough for me."

"Good one." He pointed at the plate. "You should really eat some food. It's been a few days."

Frowning, I stayed right where I was, though my belly ached. "How many days? Where has he taken me?"

"You're in Dubnos." He tried to keep a neutral face, but I could tell by the stiffening of his shoulders that he was worried how I'd react to that.

Dubnos, the ancient city up in the mountains, halfway across Aesir, where the Mist King ruled the Kingdom of Shadow. It was far, far away from home. Not that I was particularly surprised. I'd been stuck in this cell, alone with my own thoughts, for at least a few hours. I'd had a sneaking suspicion this was where he'd taken me. Had Morgan known? She must have. I never should have trusted her again. I couldn't trust anyone.

I folded my arms. "I'm not hungry."

"That's a lie," he countered with a smile. "You know we can sense them."

Narrowing my eyes, I scowled. No, I hadn't known that, though it made a lot of sense. Oberon and Morgan had always been able to tell when I lied. "I don't want to eat your food."

"Ah. There, that's true. You're angry, and I don't blame you. You've been ripped from your home and thrust into a strange world that you believe is ruled by a monster." He stepped a little closer to the bars, inching a brow upward. "But you need to eat. How can you fight back if you're weak?"

I tapped my finger against my thigh, hating that I still wore my stupid bridal gown. Dirtied along the bottom edges, it looked like I'd spent a year walking through mud. The loose gauzy sleeves exposed my skin to the air, and the chilliness of the castle had begun to dig into my bones, even with the blankets draped over me.

"Does he know you're down here talking to me?" I asked.

"Yes."

"And he knows you're encouraging me to fight back?"

The warrior sighed, and then leaned against the steel bars. "We're only trying to help you, Tessa. Can I call you that?"

I lifted my chin. "Only if you tell me your name. And don't make something up like he did."

"You mean when he called himself the captain?"

"Yeah. He's not actually a captain. Everyone knows he was called King Kalen Denare before the war."

"He's still called that," he said with a slight smile. "My name is Toryn. I'm one of the king's closest advisors, and I would give my last breath for him."

Well, that was...blunt. And more than I'd asked for.

"So, this nice act," I said, waving my hands around. "You're just trying to get me to lower my guard and trust you so that you can...do whatever it is you all plan to do with me?"

"No." He held up the plate again. "I'm just trying to get you to eat. You're skin and bones, and from the way Kal described you, you weren't that way a month ago. You need to get your strength back up."

Frowning, I stood. As much as I hated to admit it, he was right. Even though I'd recovered from the poison, my muscles felt drained. My head felt a little fluffy, and I could feel every rib through the dress.

"Fine." I strode toward the bars. "I'll eat. And I'll imagine stabbing him with every bite I take."

He chuckled, opened the door, and passed me the food. "All right. Enjoy."

After locking the door behind him, he started to walk away, but I had the urge to call out. "You aren't going to punish me for saying that?"

He stiffened and glanced back. "You're upset. It's understandable. Besides, they're just words. Why would I punish you?"

"For insulting your king. For not showing him respect." My hands shook a little, rattling the plate, despite my attempt to hold myself as strong as steel. It had only been a month since King Oberon had his guard toss my sister's head at my feet. Even now, it was in my thoughts every minute of every day. "For threatening his life."

Toryn loosed a breath. "Is that how Oberon treated you?"

Tears sprang into my eyes as the memories roared back to life in my head. I hadn't spoken a word out loud about my sister's death since it had happened. Oberon had broken me, but as long as I didn't talk about it, I could keep the fragments of my heart from shattering completely. My soul was in shards, but not splinters.

I hissed and turned away, clutching the plate. "Stop acting concerned. You and your Mist King are no better than he is."

"Hmm."

His footsteps echoed against the stone, fading into the distance. A moment later, a door creaked and then slammed shut. I sat hard on the bed, trying to still my racing heart, trying to block out all those horrible days and nights.

And they would likely pale in comparison to whatever happened to me here.

A fire within me lit, burning my memories away like ash. Toryn might have been messing with me, but he'd been right about one thing. I did need to eat. My strength could come back. And when it did, I would get out of this place, find Val and Mother, and then go where no fae kings could ever harm any of us again.

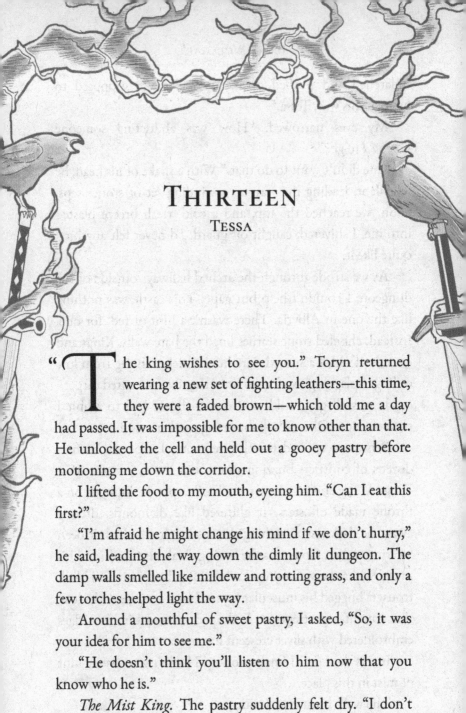

THIRTEEN
TESSA

"The king wishes to see you." Toryn returned wearing a new set of fighting leathers—this time, they were a faded brown—which told me a day had passed. It was impossible for me to know other than that. He unlocked the cell and held out a gooey pastry before motioning me down the corridor.

I lifted the food to my mouth, eyeing him. "Can I eat this first?"

"I'm afraid he might change his mind if we don't hurry," he said, leading the way down the dimly lit dungeon. The damp walls smelled like mildew and rotting grass, and only a few torches helped light the way.

Around a mouthful of sweet pastry, I asked, "So, it was your idea for him to see me."

"He doesn't think you'll listen to him now that you know who he is."

The Mist King. The pastry suddenly felt dry. "I don't want to go."

"Yes, you do." We reached a wooden door that he

unlatched and pushed open. "It was never supposed to happen this way, Tessa."

My eyes narrowed. "How was abducting someone *supposed* to go?"

"He didn't want to do that." With a shake of his head, he fell silent, leading the way up a winding set of stone steps. Soon, we reached the top, and a cold, fresh breeze blasted into me. I shivered, caught off guard. I'd never felt anything quite like it.

As we strode through the arched hallways outside of the dungeon, I couldn't help but gape. This castle was nothing like the one in Albyria. There wasn't a hint of red, for one. Instead, chiseled stone statues lined the bare walls. Kings and queens of old, I assumed. Fire-lit chandeliers hung from low ceilings, splashing a soft glow onto the silver-accented carpet.

It was all gray, cold, and dreary. But I had to admit I preferred it to Oberon's flashy orange and crimson.

When we entered the throne room, I expected to find dozens of courtiers buzzing about, but it was just the Mist King. At the end of a long stretch of carpet, he lounged on a throne made of...stars. It glittered like diamonds, driving away the darkness, matching the crown that he hadn't been wearing earlier. Gone was the boring cloak, the mask, and his pretense that he was a simple rebel. His silver tunic and black trousers hugged his muscular frame, but it was the dark cloak that caught my attention. It draped around him, its edges embroidered with silver crescent moons.

It was then that I finally noticed I hadn't seen even a hint of mist in this place.

The walls must keep it out.

"Come forward," he commanded, beckoning us with a wave of his hand. A single silver ring glinted on his forefinger.

Even with the carpet to muffle my steps, they still echoed through the vast, empty space. My eyes were drawn to the distant ceiling, curving up and away, a hundred feet above. It was magnificent, of course, but it just all felt so *empty*.

"Stop," he said when my feet hit the edge of the carpet. He leaned forward, his sapphire eyes flashing with something I couldn't quite place. "Toryn suggested we try this again. Will you listen or will you try to run?"

Irritation flashed through me. "I'd lie, but you'd be able to tell."

The Mist King turned to Toryn, who hovered just behind me. "I told you this was a bad idea. She thinks I'm the bloodthirsty Mist King."

"Don't try to tell me you aren't. I've seen portraits of you."

The Mist King—or *Kal* as Toryn liked to call him—furrowed his brows. "I am who you think I am, but I don't feast on human flesh or burn down cities. I brought you here to help you, Tessa. You would have been bound to Oberon forever if you'd stayed in Albyria. I know you think I'm this wicked, monstrous creature, but—"

"Why did you want me to steal those gemstones?" I demanded. "You told me it was so you could banish the mists and free the mortals from Oberon's kingdom. So that we could go across the bridge without risking our lives to the monsters that live in the shadows. That's not true, though. It can't be. Because *you're* the Mist King. The mists are yours."

His eyes went dark. "You're right. I lied to you about that. The gemstones are somehow holding the barrier in place. I wanted to break them all, so that I could invade the Kingdom of Light. I didn't tell you the truth because I didn't think you'd help me bring the mists into your village."

"I knew it," I whispered, anger ripping through me. "Why did you bring me here? What are you going to do to me? Burn my body?"

He lifted his eyes to Toryn. "I told you. She's not going to listen. Take her back to her cell."

"Kal..." Toryn said.

"See, you're just like him." I flinched when Toryn touched my elbow. "You act like he's a monster. And you're right. He is. But so are you."

The Mist King stilled. "You say it with such conviction. What did he do to you, Tessa?"

I folded my arms. "Looking for some pointers, Mist King?"

His lips curled. Anger whipped through his eyes like a storm, one that would drench me in unyielding darkness. "That is not my name."

"Yes, just like *that*," I said, my voice hushing. "Anytime you say something he doesn't like, just see what happens."

"What happens?" Toryn asked from behind me.

My heart throbbed, painful memories ripping through me. The silence in the room was heavy as my hands fisted, as my lungs struggled to gain enough breath. The Mist King's eyes dropped down, tracking my every move. I wished I could wash all the tension away, act like it didn't matter. The last thing I needed was for him to have another hold over me.

"What did he do to you?" the Mist King repeated in a soft, dangerous voice that curled across me like the mists.

"No worse than whatever it is you'll do."

"I am not like him." His voice boomed through the empty hall. Power washed over me, cold and dark, the opposite of the fiery heat of King Oberon. Anger curled his lips. Tension pulsed the muscles beneath his fitted shirt. I braced myself. I'd pushed him too far. And now I was going to pay for it.

At least he did not know where my mother and Val were. He could not get his hands on them.

With a shuddering sigh, he jammed his fingers into his hair and turned away. "Make sure she has a bath and a fresh change of clothes. And for the moon's sake, make sure she eats some fucking bread."

I stood frozen on the spot until he stormed out of the throne room. A door slammed behind him, the sound reverberating through my bones. My blood rushed through my ears as I stared after him. He'd brought me here, and for what? I still didn't know anything more than I had before.

Toryn sighed. "That didn't go as well as I'd hoped."

"How exactly did you expect a conversation to go between a girl and her captor?" I asked, my voice more full of bite than I'd intended. Even though Toryn was the Mist King's loyal guard, I could recognize that he hadn't been cruel to me. That didn't mean I liked him. I just didn't hate him. The kings were the problem.

"Well, for starters, I thought you'd tell him what happened in that castle." He began to lead me out of the throne room. "Don't tell me nothing did. It's as clear as day."

"That's an odd thing to say, coming from you," I said. "Your days are as far from clear as a day can be."

"Our world wasn't always permanently drenched in mist and shadow, Tessa."

"I'm well aware."

We strode out of the throne room and drifted into the hallway. He led me in the opposite direction from which we'd come, through another set of barren archways. I noted we didn't pass a single soul. Where were all the Mist King's subjects?

"He isn't the monster you think he is. There will be no burning and flesh-eating. Whatever stories you heard, they aren't true."

Clearly, that was what they wanted me to think, but how could I believe any of them?

"So, he'll let me go?" I asked, brows arched.

"Well." A pause. "No. The mists are dangerous. You wouldn't survive out there alone."

A bitter laugh popped from my throat. "That is exactly what Oberon said to keep us in line."

Toryn fell silent. Clearly, he couldn't come up with a good argument. Because there wasn't one.

A few moments and corridor turns later, we came upon a fae lounging against a wall. He was the most muscular person I'd ever seen in my life. All of these fae were. Unlike the tall, lithe Albyrian fae, he looked as though he had been hardened by battle. His black hair was pulled up into a ponytail, showing off the rows of silver rings lining each ear, glittering against his deep bronze skin.

"This is Alastair," Toryn said.

He flashed me a grin as we approached. "Look who it is. The famous Tessa."

I shot Toryn a look. "The famous Tessa?"

He smiled. "It's a small castle and not much happens around here. Word gets around fast." To the fellow warrior, he said, "Where's Niamh?"

"Polishing her boots and her sword." He rolled his eyes. "Like always. Why?"

"Tessa here needs some clothes." Toryn pointedly did not

glance down at the horrid gown, but the new fae had no such hesitation.

He gave me a once-over and let out a low whistle. "Straight from the wedding, I see. What kind of material is that shit? Doesn't look very warm."

"Gauze and linen."

"Need something warmer," he said with a grunt before leaning to the side. His fist pounded the nearest door. "Niamh, open up!"

I shifted on my feet as something boomed from beyond the door. Another thump followed soon after, and then the door swung wide. A fae sidled out with woolly violet hair, black skin, and a wicked smile, her steps full of confident swagger. Tall and powerful, she wore leather armor topped with steel, and boots that looked like weapons themselves. A jagged scar ran down one cheek. I tried not to look too closely. Fae never had scars.

"What the hell is this?" she asked, pointing at me.

"It's King Oberon's betrothed, our famous gem thief," Alastair said with a laugh. "How did you not know she was here?"

"Oh, right." Leaning against the doorframe, she folded her arms and cocked her head. "Not what I expected. She's not Oberon's usual type."

"I take that as a compliment," I said.

She grinned. "And bold, too. Where is she staying?"

"In the dungeon." Toryn cleared his throat. "Kal's orders. She isn't here willingly."

"Oh, for the love of the moon," she groaned with a roll of her eyes. "Gem thief, would you try to escape if we let you sleep in a normal room?"

"No."

All three of them nodded in unison.

"Dungeons it is, then," she replied. "Guess Kal needs to do a better job of convincing her to join our side."

"Bit of an understatement," Toryn muttered back.

This was strange. They bantered like siblings, but I supposed that was to be expected. Clearly, all three were warriors who fought for their king, and they'd likely spent centuries side by side. It was just...

Well, it all seemed so *normal*.

They seemed normal.

Monsters of myth, they were not. In fact, they reminded me more of the humans back home than of the Albyrian fae I'd met inside Oberon's castle. Except Morgan, of course, who was clearly part of this crew. But as nice as they seemed, I needed to be on guard. The only thing I knew with certainty was that I could never trust anyone again.

"You look confused, gem thief," Niamh said, reaching out to flick the ragged ends of my hair. "And you look like you've had a rough few days. How would you like a hot bath and a fresh change of clothes?"

"I wouldn't like that at all."

She grinned. "Stop lying to us. A bath it is. Come on inside. And don't look so worried. I promise I won't let any kings into the room until you're done."

FOURTEEN

KALEN

The mists whipped through the exposed battlement of the North Tower, bringing with it the scent of snow and ice. I grasped the stone crenel and leaned out into the darkness, pulling the air into my lungs to steady my racing heart. Tessa was frustrating me to no end, and I'd only spoken to her twice. If only she would stop for *one* moment, she might realize all that wrath needed to be directed somewhere else.

"She's taking a bath," Toryn said from behind me as he strode out onto the battlement. "Shockingly, she seems to listen to Niamh."

I grunted and shook my head. "Of course she does. Niamh is just as much a pain in the ass."

"You shouldn't have stormed out like that," Toryn said quietly. "It did nothing to gain her trust."

"She's never going to trust me. I'm the monstrous Mist King who lied to her about the gemstones. What's the point in even trying to change her mind?"

"Yes, that's an issue."

"Has she told you what Oberon did to her?"

Toryn pressed his lips together. "No."

I sighed and pushed away from the crenel, striding down the winding staircase to the war room below. Torchlight flashed across the etched oak table in the center of the damp room. A carved map of the fae region of the world, Aesir. The Kingdom of Light, The Kingdom of Shadow, and the Kingdom of Storms. Little figurines were scattered across it. Ships and swords and crowns and tiny carved men.

Toryn joined me at the table, frowning down at the cluster of swords gathered just beyond our border. "The scouts say those storm fae are still there?"

"They haven't moved for weeks. That could be a good thing. Maybe they're just camping there because they have nowhere else to go." I left the rest unsaid. Toryn knew how I felt about a group of hostile fae from the Kingdom of Storms camping near our borders. It had been centuries since we'd been locked in battle, and we still traded food and wool, but I'd long suspected their queen was biding her time.

She knew the power of King Oberon's chasm gemstones. They could do far more than create barriers that kept fae from crossing a bridge. And I was standing right in her path.

"They don't dare set foot in the mists," Toryn said as he braced his hands on the smooth edge of the war table. He pointed at the pile of swords. "They might be testing us, trying to draw us out. For now, they have no idea what our numbers are."

A situation I hoped would never change.

Queen Tatiana of the Kingdom of Storms hadn't been at the Battle of the Great Rift. She hadn't seen just how many warriors we'd lost. When the mists had thickened, she'd tried sending scouts ahead to learn our secrets, but many don't survive the mists. Even shadow fae could struggle against the things found in the darkness.

"Well, let's keep it that way," I finally replied. "For now, we'll do nothing. Just keep one scout's eyes on them."

Toryn nodded.

The door creaked open, and Niamh entered the war room with Alastair hot on her heels, like always. The look in her eyes was pure defiance, and I fought the urge to scowl. She'd been prickly the past few months, itching for a fight. Niamh didn't like to go long without stabbing an enemy in the gut.

"We need to talk." She strode over to the table and punched a finger beside the Kingdom of Light's figurine crown. "When the *fuck* are we finally going to take care of this asshole?"

I folded my arms and gave her a level stare. "I'm working on it."

"Well, you're not working fast enough. Stealing the gemstones is taking too long, and our thief is no longer on the right side of the chasm. We need to kill him."

"That's a fantastic idea." I shot her a smile full of teeth. "Except for the bloody fact that none of us can cross the Great Rift to get to him."

"We've stolen his mortal bride. He'll hate that," Toryn said. "There's not much more we can do. At least not right now."

Niamh stilled. "Alastair told me that Morgan had an idea. I think we should do it."

My boots clicked against the stone floor as I paced

around the table, moving from the Kingdom of Storms to King Oberon's small pocket of light-drenched land. "I thought it was a terrible idea before but even more so now. She'd never ever agree to it. She hates me."

"You're right. She does hate you." Rage flickered in her eyes. "But she hates Oberon so much more."

Toryn cocked his head. "Did you do the impossible? She actually told you something?"

"No," she hissed. "She has scars. It looks like someone dragged a knife down her back."

For a moment, a blind rage rose up within me like a venomous snake. With a low growl rumbling in the back of my throat, I turned my gaze onto the stupid golden crown figurine. It was such a gleaming, bright thing, but it hid the true darkness beneath. "That's what Morgan was alluding to. He tortured her."

"Him or one of his soldiers. When I asked her about it, she tensed, shut up, and wouldn't look at me anymore." Niamh's voice held the same fire as my heart. I'd known things were bad for the humans of Teine. They were forced to forever remain in the shadow of their king, but it seemed I didn't know the full extent of it. "She also has that dragon tattoo we heard about. The one the brides get. It feels of magic."

"Does she have any idea what it does?" Toryn asked. "Morgan still hasn't been able to figure it out. The queens stop talking to her after the weddings."

"I didn't ask her," Niamh said tightly. "She's clearly traumatized."

"Where is she now?"

"Back in her cell." She paused. "Are you sure we need to keep her locked up in there?"

"For now," I said with my eyes locked on Oberon's crown. "She'll try to escape if we don't, and it's not safe for her outside. The mists would eat her alive."

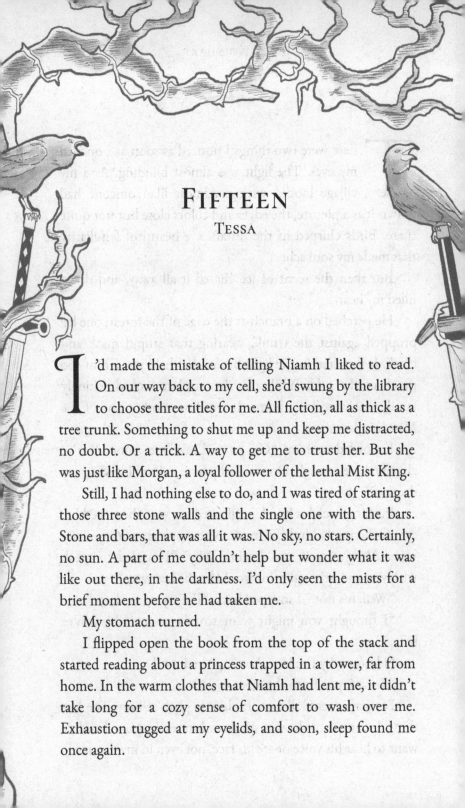

FIFTEEN
TESSA

I'd made the mistake of telling Niamh I liked to read. On our way back to my cell, she'd swung by the library to choose three titles for me. All fiction, all as thick as a tree trunk. Something to shut me up and keep me distracted, no doubt. Or a trick. A way to get me to trust her. But she was just like Morgan, a loyal follower of the lethal Mist King.

Still, I had nothing else to do, and I was tired of staring at those three stone walls and the single one with the bars. Stone and bars, that was all it was. No sky, no stars. Certainly, no sun. A part of me couldn't help but wonder what it was like out there, in the darkness. I'd only seen the mists for a brief moment before he had taken me.

My stomach turned.

I flipped open the book from the top of the stack and started reading about a princess trapped in a tower, far from home. In the warm clothes that Niamh had lent me, it didn't take long for a cozy sense of comfort to wash over me. Exhaustion tugged at my eyelids, and soon, sleep found me once again.

There were two things I noticed as soon as I opened my eyes. The light was almost blinding. And my village looked wrong. Almost like someone had drawn it as a picture, the edges and colors close but not quite there. Birds chirped in the distance, a beautiful familiarity that made my soul ache.

But then the scent of ice chased it all away, and dread filled my heart.

He perched on a branch at the edge of the forest, one leg propped against the trunk, wearing that stupid mask and cloak. It fluttered in the light breeze that held just a hint too much of the cold. While this dream place looked achingly familiar, it wasn't my home. It was just another one of the Mist King's games.

I scowled at him. "Go away. Leave me alone. You've already done enough. Do you really have to keep invading my dreams?"

Pushing back his hood, he glanced my way, those ice-blue eyes flickering behind the mask. Not sapphire, as they really were. Always icy in the dreams. Why? "I needed to speak with you and I thought this would be the best way."

"Well, it's not," I snapped back. "I'm trying to sleep."

"I thought you might want to talk about why you're here."

"I know why I'm here. You captured me."

"To save you from the mists."

For a moment, all I could do was glare at him. The last thing I wanted to do was speak to him ever again. I didn't want to hear his voice or see his face, not even in my dreams.

At least he was masked.

"Fine." I folded my arms and lifted my chin. "Let's say that's the truth, though I'm not convinced. You still lied to me about the gemstones. You still pretended to be a rebel."

He nodded, and then pulled off his mask. The muscles in his strong, angular jaw clenched. Those icy eyes were even more piercing than they'd been a moment before. "I didn't pretend to be a rebel, Tessa. I am one. We all are. That's who the shadow fae are to your king."

My eyes narrowed. "The rebels are light fae who live near Teine. In Endir, just on the other side of the chasm. A few of our villagers even left to join them once, after my father's death."

I thought back to Rock and Jon, their youthful faces and determined eyes. They'd done everything I'd wanted to do. Leave and fight back. Little did they know the group they'd hoped to join was led by the very fae who had destroyed the world.

"If you're the rebels, what happened to *them*?" I whispered. "Where did they go? Did you burn them?"

"I don't burn people, Tessa, and I don't know what happened to them. Fae and humans do live in Endir. Perhaps they made it that far. Perhaps not. The mists are dangerous."

"*You* caused the mists," I argued.

His face tensed. "I did, but while I can *use* the mists, I cannot make them go away. And I cannot stop them from pushing forward into new lands. Not anymore."

Shaking my head, I turned away, unable to look at him even a second longer. "I don't know why I'm having this conversation with you. How can I believe anything you say?"

"Because you know how cruel your king can be. And I'm trying to stop him."

I whirled back toward him. He stood there watching me with hawkish eyes, like I might kick him and run at any moment. And I damn well might if it could actually do me any good. But if I ran, I wouldn't be going anywhere. I'd still be stuck in my dream with him. "You poisoned me, just like he did, and then you threw me into a dungeon cell."

"How much do you know about the magic of the wedding ceremony?"

I frowned. "All I know is that the vows are binding."

"Exactly," he said. "You would have been bound to him for the rest of your life. For the mortal queens, that is eternity."

"Oh, I see what you're doing now." I shook my head and took a step back. "You want me to...to thank you for saving me from him? You do realize how ridiculous that sounds, right? You lied to me. You've trapped me."

"I just hit Oberon with a very powerful blow," he said, his voicing dropping into a low growl. "He no longer has a queen. His old bride will soon be off to the Tower of Crones, and his new one has escaped. This will hurt him."

I scoffed and rolled my eyes. "Please. He doesn't care about her, and he definitely doesn't care about me."

"He needs a mortal to produce more heirs."

"Unfortunately, there are still plenty of human women in my village. He'll just take someone else. He'll force another to become his queen." My voice hushed. It was something I hadn't thought about until now. Yes, I'd escaped, but at what cost? Mother and Val were out of reach, but the rest of the villagers were still there. He needed a bride. It was essential to his reign. Who would he take? Would he treat them the way he'd treated me?

Of course he would. Fear shuddered through me.

The Mist King lifted one thick brow. "That remains to be seen, but...wouldn't you like to stop him, just in case he does? Wouldn't you like to save your people from his reign? Because you could do that, Tessa."

My heart twisted in on itself. Holding my body perfectly still, I asked, "What do you mean?"

Saving Teine from King Oberon was one of the main reasons I'd gotten involved with the "rebels" in the first place. It had been a little slice of defiance in a world where independent thought rarely existed, at least when it came to the important things. And then, when I'd had the chance, I'd slammed my dagger into Oberon's chest.

A much bigger defiance. One I wished I could take back.

Pain flared in my heart at the thought of my sister.

The Mist King's eyes zeroed in on my face, as if he'd spotted my shifting mood. Toryn kept asking what had happened to me, and he wanted me to tell his king, too. Even Niamh had seemed interested. I understood why. They knew of Oberon's cruelty. But the wound was too fresh, too close to me. I couldn't talk about it or I'd lose the will to fight. Besides, I couldn't share it with any of them. Even if they were working against King Oberon, they were still my enemies.

"Oberon needs to die." He pulled a dagger out of thin air and angled it toward me. Instinctively, I flinched. The Mist King frowned. "Don't look at me like that. I'm not going to stab you with it. This is a dream, remember."

"I don't know the extent of your powers." I folded my arms and nodded at the dagger. "But I'm guessing that's intended for King Oberon?"

Hatred churned in his eyes. "Oh yes. And you will be the one who makes the killing blow."

"Ah." The memory punched me in the soul once more. I fought to hold back my tears. I couldn't cry in front of him. "Your plan won't work. I already tried to kill him once, and I failed, and I can't do it again because...because..."

No. I couldn't say it. Not out loud.

"You tried to kill Oberon?" He sounded surprised.

My eyes searched the forest for something to focus on. Something that could ground me. I swept my gaze beyond the tree where the Mist King had been sitting and found a rabbit bouncing along the mossy ground beside some fallen apples, its whiskers twitching. But all that did was remind me even more of Nellie.

"I know you fae think of us mortals as weak and spineless, but...it doesn't even matter. It didn't work." Turning away from the rabbit, I got caught in the Mist King's stare. He'd stepped closer when I hadn't been looking, so close that I could smell the frosty scent of him. Those piercing eyes bored through me, searching for answers I would never give. He could sense my pain, like the predator he was. And he wanted to use it. So that he could get what he wanted.

Never mind that it was what I wanted, too.

I just couldn't do what he asked. Driving another blade into King Oberon's heart would only end in more innocents' deaths. It wouldn't work.

"What kind of blade did you use?" he asked quietly. "Was it the little wooden thing you stabbed me with when I found you?"

"When you captured me, you mean."

Irritation flashed in his eyes. "Could you just stop arguing with me for one moment?"

"What are you going to do?" I snapped. "Burn me to death if I don't, *Mist King*?"

"For the love of the moon!" He threw up his hands and stalked away from me, vanishing into the forest. Heart hammering, I sat hard on the tree he'd vacated, hands splayed across the rough wood. My sister's tangled hair flashed in the back of my mind. Her bruised cheeks. The blood that had dripped onto the floor.

Shuddering, I squeezed my eyes shut, but that did nothing to block out of the vision of her head rolling toward me...the echo of her laughter...the softness of her once-brilliant smile.

Shaking, I balanced on the branch and pulled my knees to my chest. I couldn't do this. Any of it. I'd shut down when King Oberon killed my sister. It was the only way I could survive, by making myself numb to the pain. Morgan's determination to break me free had brought me back to life, momentarily, but I'd had enough.

The numbness called to me.

"Mother," I whispered, pressing my tear-streaked face against my legs. "Val."

No matter how much I wanted to give up, I couldn't. They still needed me. As long as they did, I couldn't break again.

The scent of mist washed over me. "What did he do to you?"

I didn't look up. "It doesn't matter. Why do you think that blade will work when mine wouldn't? I got him in the heart. A little bit, anyway. He was too fast for it to go in very far."

"I'm sure you'll take this the wrong way." The branch swayed as he leaned his weight against it. "But the truth is, mortals aren't strong enough to kill powerful elite fae. Like kings, for example. You would have had to chop off his head with a massive axe."

After pressing my face against my trousers to dry my tears, I finally looked up at where he leaned, arms crossed, only inches away. His eyes drank me in, but he said nothing about the streaked stains on my cheeks I'd failed to hide.

"Why do you think your dagger will make any difference?"

"This?" He held it up, his lips curving. "It's called the Mortal Blade, forged in the Iron Mountains. Use it against a fae, even a king, and he will die. All you'd have to do is scrape him. And, more importantly, only mortals can wield it. If a fae tried to use it, the power of the blade would turn against him and destroy him."

Lips parting, I gazed at the weapon. It was fairly nondescript for such a powerful dagger. It had an ordinary steel hilt without any ornamentation, and the blade itself was flat and plain. The single orange gemstone in the center was the only thing that stood out.

"That's one of King Oberon's gemstones," I said.

"That's right," he said. "The blade sucks out the magic of the gemstone to power it. The gemstone is powerless once it's used. Of course, you can replace it, but you'd need extra gemstones for that. Not ideal for a warrior on the battlefield but perfect for an assassin."

Assassin.

Was that how he saw me? A tool to wield this blade? It was then that I realized the Mist King actually *needed* me. He couldn't cross the chasm, and neither could any of his fellow shadow fae. If he wanted to use that blade to ensure the death of his enemy, he needed a mortal hand. He could not wield it.

I could do both of these things.

I hated that I was considering it. He was the Mist King, and he'd lied to me. How could I be sure he wasn't lying about this, too? Still, my hatred for Oberon ran deep.

Dropping my legs on either side of the branch, I leaned toward him with arching brows. "What do I get if I do this for you?"

His lips curled. "Revenge for whatever he did to you. King Oberon would be dead. Your people would be free of him."

"But he's the only one keeping the mists at bay. His power is what stops it from entering Teine, right? If I kill him, my people lose that protection. Don't they?"

His eyes searched mine. "Yes, I assume that's what would happen, but there are places in this world where your people can go that are safe from the mists."

Frowning, I shifted on the branch. "There are?"

"Outside of Aesir, in the human kingdoms across the sea. It would require a journey, but yes."

I blinked at him. "I thought you burned down all those cities."

"I keep trying to tell you. None of that happened."

I wasn't sure I believed him. For a moment, I chewed on my bottom lip, thinking. He'd finally given me some explanations I sorely needed, and he'd stopped stomping around angrily, but I still didn't like him, and I certainly didn't trust him.

He was right about one thing, though. I wanted King Oberon dead and my people to be free.

What was worse? I could refuse to work with the monster who had destroyed the world, while Val and Mother got lost to the mists. I could do nothing while my people back home suffered beneath King Oberon's rule.

Or I could accept his offer. Get my revenge. And help mortals take a step toward a better future, hopefully.

I'd need some assurances, though.

"How do I know this isn't some sort of trick?" I folded my arms. "You've lied to me once. I don't trust you."

"I'll make a vow," he said. "Fae magic will bind me to my words. The only way to undo it would be through death or if we both agreed to release each other from it."

"A magic vow?"

"Yes. Neither of us will be physically capable of doing anything that jeopardizes that vow without permission from the other."

"That sounds...like a lot." I cocked my head. "What's the catch?"

"No catch. If you do what I ask, I'll personally ensure your people find a safe place to live, where there are no mists and monsters."

"I'm going to need you to do one better than that," I said, my heart thumping. "Before Morgan convinced me to run, I found out my mother and my closest friend crossed the bridge to escape King Oberon. They're out there. Somewhere. I need you to help me find them. And I want to go with you."

He arched a brow. "That's a lot of demands."

Swinging one leg over the side of the branch, I hopped down and brushed off my trousers. And then remembered it was only imaginary dirt. "Two demands. One, help me find my family. Two, make sure my people find somewhere safe away from *your* mists. That's the only way I'll agree to a magical binding vow."

"You said it was your friend who escaped."

"Val is as much my family as my own fucking blood," I whispered harshly.

He ran a hand along his jaw, and then nodded. "All right. But I must warn you, the lands outside this castle are—"

"Dangerous? I know. Is it true the mists themselves can kill mortals?"

"Some humans, and even fae, are allergic to the mists, but you'd already be showing signs of it. The monsters, though, are very real."

"I don't care." I balled my hands. "Just help me find Mother and Val."

"You'll have to vow you won't run from me out there. I can't help you find your family if you're dead."

I pressed my lips together. "Fine."

One corner of his lip curved. "I vow to help you find your family and find a safe haven for your people to live far away from the mists, as long as you swear not to run from me. And then you'll use the Mortal Blade to kill King Oberon."

My chest felt tight, but I spoke the words. "I vow it."

Magic rushed along my arms, prickling the hair on the back of my neck. I sucked in a breath as the Mist King shuddered. Power pulsed between us, a darkness so great that I felt suffocated by it. I stared at him, stomach twisting. His will was now linked to mine, and I had no way of escaping him. A single thread wove between us, wrapping around our souls, and tying tight. Maybe this had been a terrible idea.

I'd made a deal with the Mist King.

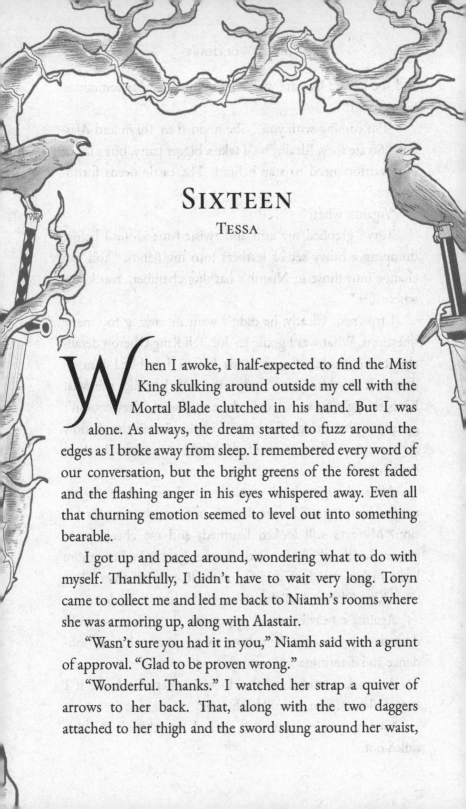

SIXTEEN

TESSA

When I awoke, I half-expected to find the Mist King skulking around outside my cell with the Mortal Blade clutched in his hand. But I was alone. As always, the dream started to fuzz around the edges as I broke away from sleep. I remembered every word of our conversation, but the bright greens of the forest faded and the flashing anger in his eyes whispered away. Even all that churning emotion seemed to level out into something bearable.

I got up and paced around, wondering what to do with myself. Thankfully, I didn't have to wait very long. Toryn came to collect me and led me back to Niamh's rooms where she was armoring up, along with Alastair.

"Wasn't sure you had it in you," Niamh said with a grunt of approval. "Glad to be proven wrong."

"Wonderful. Thanks." I watched her strap a quiver of arrows to her back. That, along with the two daggers attached to her thigh and the sword slung around her waist, and she looked like she was striding into war. "Is something happening?"

"I'm coming with you." She nodded to Toryn and Alastair. "So are they. Ideally, we'd take a bigger party, but a lot of our warriors need to stay behind. The castle needs fortifications."

"Against what?"

Toryn grabbed my arm and twisted me around before dumping a heavy set of leathers into my hands. "You can change into those in Niamh's bathing chamber. You know where it is."

I frowned. Clearly, he didn't want me asking too many questions. What was I going to do? Tell King Oberon details about this castle's fortifications before I stabbed him to death? It wouldn't even matter if I did. Just like the Mist King, the light fae were stuck where they were. They couldn't get across that bridge. So, even if I told him all the shadow fae's secrets, Oberon could do nothing to breach these castle's walls.

After changing and running my hands through my tangled hair, I stood before the mirror to see the transformation. My eyes still looked haunted, and my cheeks were gaunt. But the thickness of the leather gave me a little more bulk, making me look and feel more like myself than I had since King Oberon had chosen me to become his bride.

Against a heavily armed opponent, these clothes would do little to protect me. Somehow, they gave me a hit of confidence and determination anyway.

A knock sounded on the door. I stiffened. Maybe if I stayed silent, no one would bother me.

"Surely you're not still naked in there," Niamh called out.

I sighed and crossed the room. When I opened the door, she strode inside and gave me a once-over. With an approving nod, she said, "Fits you well, though the sleeves and legs are a bit long."

"Well, you're taller than me." Most fae were.

"True." She knelt and fiddled with the trouser cuffs. A flicker of shock went through me. Fae never, ever knelt in front of mortals. They certainly didn't lower themselves to the ground to fix their clothing. It was just not done.

"What's the matter?" She rolled up one of the legs, tucking the material in place to make it stay there.

"This is not how the light fae act around humans."

"The light fae are bastards," she muttered, moving on to the other cuff. "The ones in Albyria, anyway. The ones who didn't follow Oberon aren't quite so cruel. Unfortunately, there aren't many of them left."

She stood and brushed some dust from my shoulders. "This one has been in my closet too long. Sorry it's not in great shape."

"I like it," I said, unable to stop a slight smile from creeping up my lips. "It's the only time I've ever worn armor."

"Can't say I ever wear anything *but* armor, even when I'm here at court." She glanced at her reflection in the mirror and ran a finger down the jagged scar on her cheek. "Always be ready for anything."

"Is it rude if I ask what happened there? I thought fae power could heal anything."

She chuckled. "Not at all. In fact, it's been a long time since I met someone who didn't know. This scar here? It came from Oberon."

My eyes widened.

"That's right," she said bitterly. "He got me, too."

I pressed my lips together. Despite her many questions, I hadn't told her where my scars came from, though I supposed it wasn't difficult to piece together.

She continued. "Before the Battle of the Great Rift, we fought Oberon and his army in the fields just beyond our mountains here, on the border between our kingdoms. It was the first of many battles in our war with him. I was an archer, so I wasn't in the thick of it myself. All I could focus on was Oberon out there laughing while he slaughtered shadow fae on the front lines." Her voice went rough. "I got to the point where I couldn't take it anymore. So, I went down there to kill him myself."

Toryn drifted into the room from the open door. "Don't tell me she roped you into listening to this story."

I cast a glance between them as Niamh pursed her lips. "She asked me about it."

Toryn turned to me. "You'd think it was the only battle she was ever a part of, the way she goes on about it. Do you know how many times we've had to hear her rant about the Battle on the Borders? An unspeakable number. That's how many. Come on, Alastair and I can tell you much more interesting stories."

"I want to hear what happened," I said, lifting a brow. "Have *you* ever tried to rush Oberon in the middle of a battle?"

From the other room, Alastair let out a guffaw.

"I see." Toryn rolled his eyes and gestured at Niamh before backing out the door. "By all means, carry on."

"As I was saying," Niamh said, raising her voice to be heard in the other room, "I left my post and fought my way to Oberon's side."

"Kal still doesn't like that you defied his orders, Niamh," Toryn called out from the other room.

She ignored him. "I got as close as I could, and then I aimed an arrow at his head."

I felt myself leaning forward, even though I knew she hadn't won. If she had, he'd be dead. "What happened?"

"The bastard sensed me coming and shot some of his light magic at my face." She pressed her fingers against her cheek. "It knocked me out. I'd have been trampled if Kal hadn't seen. He got me out of there before Oberon could do any more damage, and my healing magic did all it could. This never went away, though. It's my reminder of everything he's done, everyone he's killed."

I swallowed hard. "At least you tried."

She smiled. "That I did. And it'll be your turn soon."

Only when I did it, I wouldn't have fae healing and an army surrounding me. If I failed, there would be no one there to pick me up and get me out. I'd be stuck there. This time, it would be forever.

A biting power rippled toward me from Niamh's room, and I stuck my head out the door to see what was happening. My stomach dropped at the sight of the Mist King, clad in all-black leather armor with a long, gleaming sword strapped to his back. His eyes met mine, and I clutched the door tighter.

"You look more like yourself." The words settled into me in a strange, unexpected way that heated my cheeks. That was exactly what I'd thought when I looked into the mirror.

I frowned at him. "I've never dressed this way in my entire life. You think you know me, but you don't."

Irritation flickered in his eyes. "Hmm." He turned to Toryn and Alastair, who were lounging on the sofa watching our exchange with intrigue. "Have you made all the necessary arrangements?"

As if in answer, a knock sounded on the...window. Eyes wide, I watched as Toryn leapt up from the sofa and let a raven into the room. It held a tiny, rolled note in its curved beak. As Toryn read the note, the raven flew to the Mist King's shoulder and settled in, pressing the top of his head against the fae's neck.

I gaped at them.

"Teg got the message. He'll meet us at the base of the mountain with the horses." Toryn tossed the note into the fire. "We're all good to go."

"What is that?" I asked, pointing at the raven with a smile. "Do you have a pet bird?"

For some reason, it struck me as completely ridiculous. The Mist King. With a pet. The raven nestled against the fae's neck, clearly happy to be there. And then suddenly, Nellie's face popped into my mind. This raven could fly away, but my sister never could. The thought of her wiped away my smile.

"This is Boudica, my familiar." He tossed me a pair of heavy leather boots. "Now, put these on. It's time to go."

SEVENTEEN
TESSA

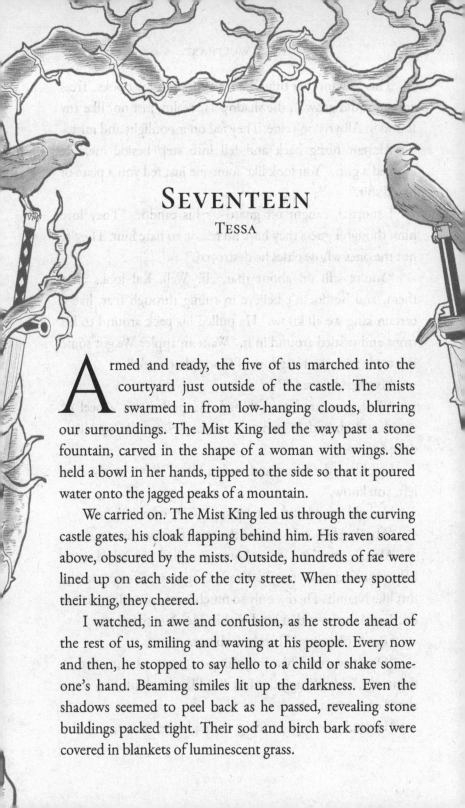

Armed and ready, the five of us marched into the courtyard just outside of the castle. The mists swarmed in from low-hanging clouds, blurring our surroundings. The Mist King led the way past a stone fountain, carved in the shape of a woman with wings. She held a bowl in her hands, tipped to the side so that it poured water onto the jagged peaks of a mountain.

We carried on. The Mist King led us through the curving castle gates, his cloak flapping behind him. His raven soared above, obscured by the mists. Outside, hundreds of fae were lined up on each side of the city street. When they spotted their king, they cheered.

I watched, in awe and confusion, as he strode ahead of the rest of us, smiling and waving at his people. Every now and then, he stopped to say hello to a child or shake someone's hand. Beaming smiles lit up the darkness. Even the shadows seemed to peel back as he passed, revealing stone buildings packed tight. Their sod and birch bark roofs were covered in blankets of luminescent grass.

This was another thing I'd read about in my books. Trees and grass did grow in the shadow fae realm, just not like any found in Albyria or Teine. They fed on moonlight and mist.

Alastair hung back and fell into step beside me. He cracked a grin. "You look like someone just fed you a plate of literal shit."

I snorted, caught off guard by his candor. "They love him, though I guess they have no reason to hate him. They're not the ones whose cities he destroyed."

"You're still on about that, eh? Well, Kal looks after them, and he doesn't believe in ruling through fear, like a certain king we all know." He pulled his pack around to his front and rustled around in it. "Want an apple? We got some in a trade with the Kingdom of Storms last week."

My chest burned. "No apples."

"Well, you need something." He pulled out a heel of bread and shoved it into my hands. "Here. Eat up, little dove."

I grabbed the bread and took a bite. "We've barely even left, you know."

He held out a hand and winked. "Give it back then."

"Absolutely not." I stuffed the rest of it into my mouth.

Alastair chuckled. "You know, I'm glad you asked us to help you find your family. I've been going stir-crazy lately, just like Niamh. There's only so much battle planning we can do. Toryn, he loves that kind of shit. Me? No, thank you."

"Battle planning?" I arched a brow.

"Don't worry. There's nothing to worry about on that front. Yet." He shrugged. "But Kal likes to think two steps ahead of everyone else."

"Hmm." We kept striding through the streets, and the

throng of people slowly started to ease. Dubnos was a larger city than I'd expected. Much larger than Albyria.

"You've got the wrong end of things, you know," Alastair said, fiddling with one of the rings in his ear. "Kal's not the bad guy here."

I scowled. "Not the bad guy to you. He didn't harm you or your people."

"This journey would go a lot easier if you gave him a chance."

"Have any more of that bread?"

His face brightened. "Absolutely."

After passing me the bread, he returned to his attempt at convincing me the Mist King wasn't so bad. I just chewed and chewed, a perfect excuse to refrain from a reply. I didn't even have to listen to all his words.

That worked until we reached the gates and I ran out of food.

When we pressed out into the wilderness, the mists surged in, thickening around us. Gone was any sign of grass and moss on the ground. All that remained was sand, dirt, and darkness. The shadow fae shuffled around, their bodies bent into the harsh wind. Alastair and Niamh took the front while Toryn rounded out the back. That left me stranded in the middle with the Mist King.

Of course he didn't take the lead.

"What's that look on your face?" he asked me as we started down the mountain on a rock-strewn path far steeper than I liked. My boots scuffed along the ground as we inched across the dirt.

"What look?"

"The one you got as soon as we left Dubnos."

I shrugged. "I just don't find it surprising that all your posturing inside your city was just for show. As soon as no one could see you, you put your soldiers in the front and back. You're protected in the middle. Just a typical king. You couldn't possibly be the one to face danger yourself."

From ahead, Alastair chuckled.

"Most kings don't lead a party because their death would bring instability to their kingdom, particularly if they don't have an heir. Like Oberon."

I snorted. "Oberon has *a lot* of heirs."

"None of them count to the light fae. They wouldn't want a half-mortal king. Those heirs are not *heirs*. They're soldiers and a way for him to wield power over the rest of his fae. *He* can have children. None of the rest of them can unless he gives them permission." Our boots crunched as we passed across a rocky stretch in the path. "If he dies, that city would tear itself to shreds, every fae there trying to grapple for power. And as there are so few of them left...that would be the end of Albyrian fae."

"I see your point. That doesn't explain you, though."

I glanced up at his face just as he smiled. "We take turns in the front and in the back. This formation isn't to protect me. It's to give each of us a break."

Alastair chuckled again, and I narrowed my eyes at his back.

"Go ahead," I said to him. "Laugh at my expense."

He grinned over his shoulder at me, though I could barely see his features through the mists. "You're cute when you're mad, little dove."

I narrowed my eyes.

"Don't worry," Niamh called out over her shoulder.

"Alastair is a shameless flirt, but he's harmless. It doesn't mean anything. He flirts with anyone who breathes."

"And fucks them, too." Toryn chuckled from behind us.

Alastair spread his hands before him. "You think I can help it if the ladies like the look of me? Who am I to disappoint them? There's enough of me to go around."

I took another step forward, and my boot sank into something soft and fleshy. Something sharp tore through my ankle. Hissing between my teeth, I glanced down to find a luminous black snake hanging off my leg. I screamed and tried to shake it off, fear thundering through me.

Steel arced through the air, and power thrummed across my skin. The Mist King slammed his blade down on the creature and sliced its head clean off. The fangs loosened from my leg, leaving behind a deep crimson stain that spread through the rolled cuffs of my trousers.

The pain. My knees buckled and I slid to the ground.

I couldn't see straight. A storm of black spots consumed my vision.

The Mist King knelt beside me and ripped open my trouser leg. I stared dumbfounded at the wound. Where the snake had bitten me, deep black lines were spreading across my skin. Pain rocked through me, and I hissed out another scream through my teeth.

"Hold still," the Mist King demanded, his face lined in terrifying concern.

Tears blurred my vision. I glanced up at the stony faces of the fae. Niamh gave me a nod and passed me a stick. Something to hold onto.

I took it in my hands and squeezed tight.

The Mist King lowered his head to my leg, pressed his lips against my roiling skin, and...sucked. A shudder went through me as his hands gently gripped my thighs, his mouth working, his lips caressing.

A spark of delirious pleasure went through me at the sight of him there.

And the fact it actually felt...good.

Another storm of pleasure coursed through my leg, despite the venom trying to tear my body apart. I tightened my grip on the stick and tried not to moan. This should not feel good. There were people watching. And this was *the Mist King*.

"It's working." Niamh loosed a breath and fisted her hand in victory. "You're going to be all right, Tessa."

The Mist King suddenly pulled back, his sapphire eyes glowing in the dark. He spat the venom on the ground, and hissing smoke swirled up to join the mists. As he stood, the glow of his eyes began to fade, and he held out a hand toward me.

Heart thumping, I stared at that hand. Large and calloused, strong. I took it and let him pull me to my feet. For a moment, no one said a word, and then Alastair clapped me on the back.

"Close call. That was a beithir, the deadliest snake in the known world. Its venom can kill you in ten minutes if you do nothing to stop it. You're lucky Kal here knows how to get it out."

I swallowed hard. "Ten minutes."

"Come on, let's get moving," Niamh said after giving me a gentle pat. "We have a long way to go before we reach somewhere we can camp."

They resumed their posts at the head of the party and started off down the path. The Mist King lowered a hand onto my shoulder when I moved to follow. He stared down at me with those softly glowing eyes, mist whorling across his face.

"There are dangerous things out here in the mists," he said in a low voice. His raven soared in to settle on his shoulder. "Be careful where you step."

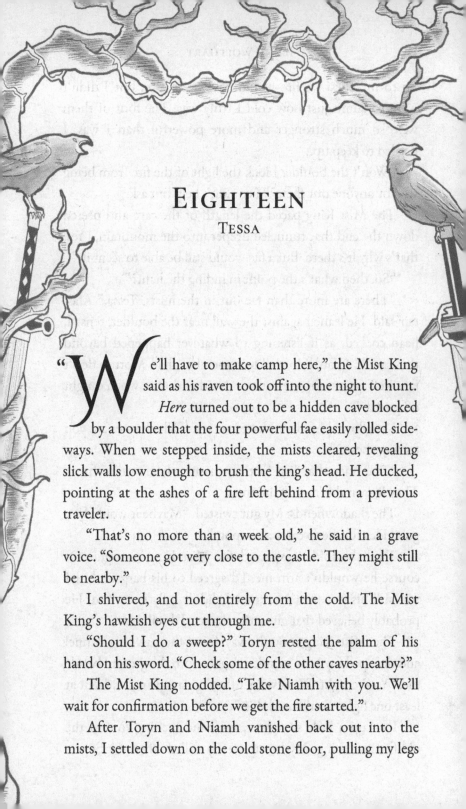

EIGHTEEN
TESSA

"We'll have to make camp here," the Mist King said as his raven took off into the night to hunt. *Here* turned out to be a hidden cave blocked by a boulder that the four powerful fae easily rolled sideways. When we stepped inside, the mists cleared, revealing slick walls low enough to brush the king's head. He ducked, pointing at the ashes of a fire left behind from a previous traveler.

"That's no more than a week old," he said in a grave voice. "Someone got very close to the castle. They might still be nearby."

I shivered, and not entirely from the cold. The Mist King's hawkish eyes cut through me.

"Should I do a sweep?" Toryn rested the palm of his hand on his sword. "Check some of the other caves nearby?"

The Mist King nodded. "Take Niamh with you. We'll wait for confirmation before we get the fire started."

After Toryn and Niamh vanished back out into the mists, I settled down on the cold stone floor, pulling my legs up to my chest. A fire would have been nice, but I didn't want to admit just how cold I truly was. The four of them were so much stronger and more powerful than I was. I needed to keep up.

"Won't the boulder block the light of the fire from being seen by anyone out there?" I couldn't help but ask.

The Mist King paced the length of the cave and peered down the end that tunneled deeper into the mountain. "Yes, that's why it's there. But a fae would still be able to scent it."

"So, then what's the point in hiding the light?"

"There are more than fae out in the mists, Tessa," Alastair said. He leaned against the wall near the boulder, tensed, head cocked, as if listening to whatever happened beyond these walls. "You'd do well to remember that. Mortals don't fare well against those creatures. Neither do fae, when caught off guard."

I swallowed hard and hated to ask. "Which ones are you talking about?"

"The ones that live in that chasm where you're from. They live on this mountain, too."

The shadowfiends. My gut twisted. "Maybe it would be a good idea for me to carry a weapon."

Truth be told, I expected the Mist King to argue. Of course he wouldn't arm me. I'd agreed to his bargain, but I was still his prisoner. He knew I didn't fully trust him. He probably believed that given the chance, I'd stab him.

The Mist King moved away from the yawning tunnel and dropped my little wooden dagger onto the ground beside me. "You're right. We never get through a journey without at least one fight. You'll need this."

I sat up a little straighter, my hand inching toward the old familiar thing. My breath nearly stilled when my fingers brushed the edge of it. King Oberon's blood still stained the pointed tip. "I assumed you'd destroyed this."

"It's yours. Just don't use it against me again, and you can carry it for as long as you'd like." He turned away again, boots echoing as he vanished down the dark tunnel. I could hear him long after I could no longer see him.

Standing, I flipped the thing in my hand, feeling out the familiar weight of it. A part of me wanted to toss it away and never see that horrible stain again. This was not the weapon that had killed my sister, but it had still caused her death. And Raven's. I could never forget that.

"I heard you stabbed him with that thing," Alastair said, his voice quiet. "Try not to do it again, eh?"

I glanced toward him, still flipping the dagger. "He should have included that in my vow if he's so worried about it."

He laughed. "You're going to end up driving him crazy."

"Good." With a little smile to myself, I settled back onto the ground, but regretted that decision within an instant. The cold seeped through the leather trousers, freezing my butt. Holding back a shudder, I stuffed the dagger into the front of my tunic and then shoved my hands up into the ends of my sleeves, curling the material over my fists.

"You're cold," Alastair noted.

"I'm fine."

"Don't lie."

The Mist King strode back into the cave's little room, cloak flaring behind him like a dark pair of wings. His face looked troubled. "I found some more evidence of travelers deeper in the cave."

Alastair inclined his head toward me. "Tessa's cold."

"I'm fine," I said through clenched teeth. Clamping

them together was the only way to stop my teeth from chattering. "So, what's the problem with more evidence of travelers?"

"It looks like they're trekking into the mountain itself instead of up and around it." The Mist King frowned when he spotted my cloth-covered hands. "Stop lying to us. We can scent it."

Suddenly, he whipped off his cloak and draped it across my shoulders. The intoxicating scent of mist and snow enveloped me. My mouth popped open to argue. I didn't want his cloak anywhere near me. For one, it had touched him. And two, well, it had *touched him*.

But for the love of light, it was warm. And it smelled so fucking good. Like him.

"I don't want this," I said with a scowl.

"Don't be so difficult," he shot back. "You're freezing."

"I'd rather freeze than wear a stupid cloak that belongs to the Mist King." I threw it off my shoulders.

Anger flashed through his eyes. He hovered over me, pure fury tensing every muscle in his jaw. I waited for it, what I knew came next. He tried to act like he was different than Oberon, but they were exactly the same. Eventually, he would snap and show the truth of his soul. He'd hit me. Or he'd make Alastair do it.

"*Do not call me that*," he said, every word punctuated by irritation.

"Why not?" I lifted my chin. "That's who you are, isn't it?"

"Only my enemies call me that."

"And isn't that what we are?" I whispered back. "Don't try to pretend we're allies just because we share a common interest—seeing King Oberon dead."

"I'd say that does make us allies," Alastair cut in.

"Stay out of it," the Mist King and I both shouted in unison.

Surprise flickered through the king's eyes, and a slight smile tickled his lips. He started to speak, but a sudden thunder stopped whatever he'd meant to say.

The boulder rolled away from the cave's opening. Niamh and Toryn darted toward us, eyes wild, faces drenched in sweat.

The mists swirled inside.

"We need backup!" Niamh shouted. "We've got eight pookas."

Pookas?

I sucked in a sharp breath and stood, instinctively reaching for my wooden dagger. I didn't know what pookas were, but by the flash of alarm on the Mist King's face, I knew I didn't want to find out.

"Get behind me," he barked, drawing the sword from the sheath at his back. Power rumbled in the cave. "Don't try anything stupid."

I scowled as he edged in front of me, blocking my body from anything that might shoot in from outside the cave. "What makes you so sure I'd try something stupid?"

"I've spent more than five minutes in your presence," he threw over his shoulder. "That was enough."

Heart pounding, I glared at his back, fully encased in the smooth leather of his armor. Still, I could see the strength of his muscles ripple as he raised his weapon, bracing for the impending attack.

Alastair made a move to shove the boulder back into place, but it was too late.

Several large forms hurtled into the cave. My chest

constricted. They were as large as horses but with great, sharp fangs bigger than my head. Dark matted fur shifted like whirling shadows, and their luminescent golden eyes were lit with impossible fire.

Where a horse had hooves, these creatures had claws. Their talons were so deadly sharp that it would only take one swipe to tear a man's body in half.

"Shadowfiends," I whispered.

And there were eight of them. My heart nearly faltered as I backed up against the slick wall of the cave, clutching my dagger to my chest. Eight of them and five of us. And I didn't really stand a chance against them on my own.

Niamh, Toryn, and Alastair lifted their swords in unison, roaring. They sprang into action, sweeping their blades at the creatures' dark heads. Only Niamh's sword hit its mark, the sharp edge sliding into the nearest beast's flesh.

Its head toppled to the ground, blood spraying her clothes.

Toryn and Alastair were flung back when two of the shadowfiends crept up behind them and swiped them aside. They flew through the air, shocked growls ripping from their throats. They soared back into the depths of the cave where the darkness swallowed them whole.

Another shadowfiend appeared at the mouth of the cave, grabbed Niamh by the waist, and tossed her out into the mists.

I swallowed hard, my heartbeat cantering wildly in my chest.

As if sensing my fear, the Mist King murmured, "Don't worry. They're fine. This is the pookas' strategy. Divide and conquer. Get the extra weight out of the way so they can more easily get what they want."

Blood rushed into my ears. "What is it they really want?"

His shoulders tensed as the shadowfiends began to fan out in the cave, stalking toward us. "You."

I wet my lips. "Me? Why? Because I'm weaker than a fae?"

For a moment, he stayed so focused on the approaching shadowfiends that I thought he hadn't heard my question. But then he spoke.

"You really don't know? No one ever told you?"

A tremor of unease tiptoed down my spine to join the blatant fear gathered there. It was starting to seem like King Oberon had kept us in the dark about a lot of things. This was clearly another one of them.

"Does it have something to do with me being the king's intended bride?" I asked.

"Pookas survive on human flesh," he growled as the beast sprang into action. "Stay here."

The Mist King stormed forward, sword slicing through the air in an elaborate twirl, powered by the intoxicating strength of him. Mist sprang from his skin, engulfing the entire cave in a strange, twisting darkness.

I watched, fear and dread churning in my gut. I could hardly see a thing. Every now and then, the mists would part and a splash of blood would arc through the air. The beasts roared, their screeches echoing through the cave.

Niamh reappeared at the entrance, looking none the worse for wear. She merely sheathed her sword, folded her arms, and leaned against the wall, waiting.

"You're not going to help?" My fingers twitched around my dagger.

"No need." She sighed. "He's almost done. A shame I only got to fight one."

Suddenly, the mists cleared. The king heaved in the center of the cave, his sweat-soaked muscles pulsing beneath his torn shirt. Blood dripped from his sword, and the shadowfiends were scattered around him. Their matted fur was the only thing that made them recognizable.

My stomach roiled and I twisted away. The sight of so much blood almost took me back to a time I couldn't stomach to relive yet again. *Nellie's face.*

"Those damn pookas," Alastair thundered as he and Toryn returned. "They threw us a mile away. We missed all the fun."

Fun was definitely not the word I would have used.

I felt the heat of their gazes on my back.

Toryn spoke. "Glad to see she's still with us."

"I wouldn't have let them touch her," the Mist King said.

My eyes were drawn to him, despite the sight I knew would meet me. He'd moved away from the bodies, toward the corner pile of packs. He tugged his torn shirt over his head and dropped it to the ground, his massive shoulders and V-shaped back gleaming, even in the dark.

His form was near-perfect, even with the blood splattered across his impressive pecs and chiseled abs. It almost hurt to look at him. My hand twitched, still locked around the dagger, and suddenly, I felt extremely self-conscious.

"You all right?" Niamh asked from beside me. I jumped and let out a little yelp.

Her eyes widened as an embarrassing amount of heat blazed my cheeks.

"Sorry," I said. "I guess I'm a little on edge after that. Those shadowfiends...you call them pookas?"

She nodded. "Yes. But you don't have to worry about

those things as long as you have Kal around. They don't stand a chance against him."

"Yes, I can see that," I said, my mouth a little dry. As impressive as it was, it was also a little terrifying. King Oberon had never demonstrated his power like that, though I supposed he'd never needed to.

The Mist King strode over, wiping the blood off his chest with a rag. The cloth dipped between each indented ab, and my eyes warred against me as they tracked his every move.

And then I realized what I was doing and decided I'd rather leap into the chasm to find more of those shadow-fiends. Biting the insides of my cheeks, I stared at the useless dagger in my hand.

"Find anything out there, other than those creatures?" the Mist King asked, turning to Niamh.

"No, Kal. No sign of any travelers out there."

He nodded. "So, they did go into the tunnels. We'll need to check that out before we move on."

"How long will that take?" I asked with a frown.

"However long it takes."

I folded my arms. "You vowed to help me find my family."

"And I will. We just have to check this out first." He took a step toward me, his muscles shifting with every movement. "Someone, most likely an enemy, is trying to reach the castle through these tunnels. We have to stop them."

"That's quite the leap," I countered. "There's a lot of pookas around here. Maybe the travelers were just trying to find somewhere safe."

He cocked his head, his eyes still narrowed. "You might be right, Tessa."

I started to loose my tensely held breath.

"But you also might be wrong. And I am not the kind of king willing to take a chance on the lives of my people. Don't force me to move on before this is taken care of."

Irritation bubbled up inside me. Damn him, I hated that he was right. What kind of king would he be if he didn't bother to check out a potential threat? Shivering, I wrapped my arms around my chest and scowled. "All right."

He glanced at my arms, noting my discomfort. "You're still cold." The danger in his voice did not match his words.

Truth was, with the excitement—and terror—of the battle, I'd momentarily forgotten how fucking cold this cave was. The fear had pumped blood through my veins, and adrenaline had chased away the chill.

But that was all gone now. In its place came a cold so deep I swore I could feel it in my bones.

Niamh edged in a little closer. "Look, her fingers are blue."

Roughly, the Mist King grabbed my hand and held it up before his eyes. A jolt of heat flashed through me. I swallowed hard.

He dropped my hand and scowled. "You should have taken my damn cloak."

"I don't want to wear your cloak," I parroted, though I kind of did.

"Hmm."

My teeth clicked together. I gripped my arms even closer, trying to hold back the shudders.

"She needs a fire, some food, and sleep," Toryn pointed out. "How about the three of us go search the caves? We'll meet you back here after we do a full sweep."

The Mist King frowned. "You really shouldn't go without me."

"We'll be fine," Alastair said, fiddling with one of his earrings. "Besides...I don't think it's a good idea for her to come. No offense meant, little dove."

"None taken," I muttered, though I did hate feeling useless.

"You're the best one to stay with her in case more pookas attack," Niamh pointed out. "Besides, we can forgo sleep for a night. Hopefully, we find the traveler by morning, and then we can be on our way to Itchen."

The Mist King agreed, though he didn't look too pleased by it. I wasn't thrilled either. It meant being alone with him for hours, although hopefully I'd be asleep for most of it. If I could actually sleep after everything that had happened.

After they hauled the bodies of the pookas out into the mists and rolled the boulder back into place, the trio vanished into the shadows of the caves. Wordlessly, the Mist King snatched his cloak from the floor and draped it across my shoulders, his body tense, as if he expected me to argue again.

I was too cold to make the effort. Scowling, I buried myself in the soft material and perched on a rock, teeth still chattering. Within moments, he had a fire blazing in the small clearing left behind by the previous traveler. Sighing, he grabbed a fresh tunic from his sack, tugged it over his head, and sat beside me.

For a long moment, neither one of us said a word. I stared into the orange flames, wondering exactly how I'd ended up here. In a foreign realm with an enemy king, surrounded by monsters that wanted to kill me.

But I had always been surrounded by monsters. They'd been hidden inside a pretty package, that was all. The fae who ruled over us didn't care about our lives. We were nothing but cattle to them.

Expendable objects to be beaten down and used.

Like my sister.

I closed my eyes as my gut twisted in pain.

"How many pookas are out there?" I finally asked, needing to talk about something—anything—to take my mind off Nellie.

"In the mountains?" A muscle in his jaw ticked. "It's hard to say. Fewer than there were a century ago but more than I'd like."

"I meant...out there. In the world. In the mists." Where Val and Mother were.

"Hundreds."

My chest burned, my thoughts turning back to those horrible, grotesque forms, their demented screams, the glowing eyes. I began to realize how much danger Val and Mother would face. Had probably already faced. And they didn't have powerful fae to fight beside them.

"Is there anywhere that's safe from them?"

"Caves can be, so long as they don't see you go inside."

"No, I don't mean here. I mean out there, beyond these mountains, back in the rolling fields that used to be part of the Kingdom of Light. It's where Mother and Val would be. Is there anywhere that's safe?" My voice came out strained and more high-pitched than I'd intended, but I couldn't stop thinking about my mother's face. She may have once thought about joining the rebels, but she was no fighter. How could she survive if even one of those things attacked her?

He shifted slightly toward me, his strong jaw illuminated by the glow of the fire. "There are still cities and villages out there. Itchen is one of those places. Endir, too. They'd be safe inside the buildings if they made it there. The pookas like being in the mists. They'll only go inside a place if they're lured there."

I grasped onto that tiny slice of hope and bottled it up to keep it safe. Everything I did now was for one thing. To find Mother and Val. If I didn't have hope they were alive, I didn't think I could keep moving.

"I won't lie to you, Tessa," he said quietly. "They're in a lot of danger, and there's more out there than pookas. I'm impressed by their bravery, though I am surprised they decided to risk it. Did they know you were going to escape Albyria?"

"They hoped I would," I said in a soft whisper. "But they left before I did."

"The bond of blood is powerful, even in humans. If I had the chance, I'd do whatever it took to save my mother."

I glanced toward him, curious. The tale of the Mist King's mother was ancient lore, passed down over hundreds of years. She had once ruled the Kingdom of Shadow, her raven hair and diamond eyes immortalized on a thousand paintings. Many believed her to be the most beautiful being to have ever lived. Songs were written about the gently falling snow that followed her, and the stars in the sky that had glowed brighter on the day of her birth.

Even King Oberon, who cared for little other than his own wealth, status, and power, had fallen in love with her. But that was where the tales diverged and myth and lore took over. There were a dozen different stories about what had happened after her fateful meeting with King Oberon.

But one thing was for certain.

She'd died not long after he'd proposed, after she had turned him down.

"Is that why you hate him?" I couldn't help but ask. "You think he killed her?"

His broad shoulders tensed as his eyes locked on the flames. When he spoke, his voice was a haunted, twisted thing. "Something like that."

A shiver went through me. His grudge against the king made even more sense than it had before. Hundreds of years, it had lingered. The bond of blood was strong indeed.

"He's been responsible for a lot of deaths," I said tightly.

"More than you know."

"But so have you."

He loosed a frustrated sigh, pushed up from the ground, and snatched the cloak from my shoulders.

My chin dropped. "Hey!"

"You're not cold anymore," he pointed out, his eyes flashing. "I'll be taking this back now."

He was right. The warmth of the fire had soothed me, melting away the ice. Even the tips of my fingers were nice and toasty. Despite the horrors of the night, I could easily curl up and fall asleep.

But still. "You're only doing this because you don't like what I said."

"You're right. I am." He threw his cloak around his shoulders and stalked over to the boulder where he found a flat rock to perch upon.

I frowned across the cave at him. "What are you doing?"

"Sitting here. Where I can get some peace." He pointedly turned away. "Go to sleep, Tessa. We have a long journey ahead of us."

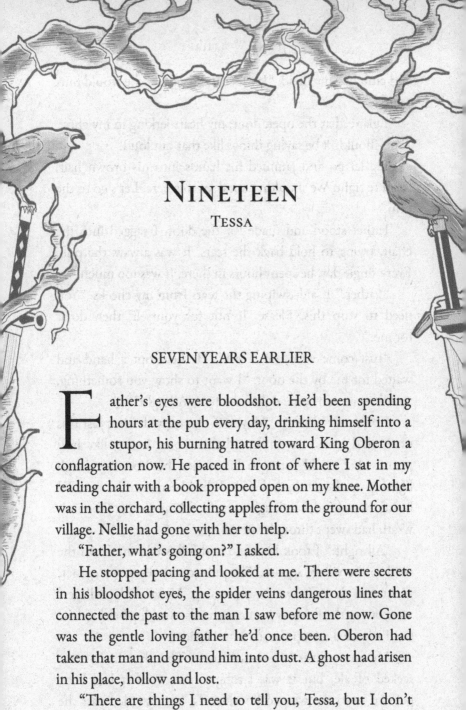

NINETEEN
TESSA

SEVEN YEARS EARLIER

Father's eyes were bloodshot. He'd been spending hours at the pub every day, drinking himself into a stupor, his burning hatred toward King Oberon a conflagration now. He paced in front of where I sat in my reading chair with a book propped open on my knee. Mother was in the orchard, collecting apples from the ground for our village. Nellie had gone with her to help.

"Father, what's going on?" I asked.

He stopped pacing and looked at me. There were secrets in his bloodshot eyes, the spider veins dangerous lines that connected the past to the man I saw before me now. Gone was the gentle loving father he'd once been. Oberon had taken that man and ground him into dust. A ghost had arisen in his place, hollow and lost.

"There are things I need to tell you, Tessa, but I don't know if I should. It's too dangerous." He knelt before me and clutched my hand. "If Oberon found out, he would hurt you."

I glanced at the open door, my heart jerking in my chest. "You shouldn't be saying things like that out loud."

He let go and jammed his hands into his brown hair. "You're right. We shouldn't speak of this here. Let's go to the pub."

Father stood and made for the door. I sagged into the chair, trying to hold back the tears. It was always the pub. Every single day, he spent hours in there. It was too much.

"Father," I said, swiping the tears from my cheeks. "You need to stop this. Please. If not for yourself, then do it for me."

"Just come with me, Tessa." He held out a hand and waited for me by the door. "I want to show you something, and then we can come right back here. All right?"

I blew out a breath. Maybe if I went with him, just this once, he'd have one drink and then come home, like he'd promised. I could listen to his stories, his booming laugh lighting up the dank, dark pub. It had been months since I'd heard that sound. His laughter had left him the day Oberon's wrath had swept through our village.

"All right." I took his hand and followed him down the road to the village square. The pub squatted on one corner, silent and dark. It was late morning. Most of the villagers were out in the fields or in the orchards, working hard for the fae. Father led me up the stairs and inside.

My eyes adjusted to the darkness. The place had always reeked of ale, but it was stronger now, as if it had been painted onto the warped floorboards. Dust swirled past the round wooden tables, mismatched chairs clustered around every one. An empty bar hugged the far wall, with kegs of ale stacked up beside it. A man named Ty poked up his head from behind the counter, caught sight of us, and frowned.

"What took you so long?" he asked, rubbing his hand along his thick beard. "We need to go now."

I twisted toward Father, confused. "Go where?"

Father didn't say a word as Ty hauled two bursting leather packs out from behind the counter and tossed them over the side. I stared down at them, taking a step back as if they were coiled snakes ready to strike. The truth clicked into place, why Father had been so insistent I come here with him, why he'd been acting so cagey, and why Ty had said they had to go.

"You can't," I whispered, my hands trembling. "Father, please."

Ty sighed. "You shouldn't have told her about this, Nash. She's not going to understand, and she'll tell people all about it."

I ignored him, turning to Father. "You can't go out into the mists. You'll die out there."

"Ah, Tessa." His hollow eyes stared into me as he cupped my cheek. "I'll die if I stay here. I have to go, for the good of everyone."

"But I need you." I clasped his hand, rough and strong. "Please don't leave me in this place. If you have to go, then take me with you."

He pulled out of my grip. "I can't. Not right now. But I'll come back for you, I promise."

"Why are you doing this?" My whole body trembled as I watched him cross the room and haul the pack onto his shoulder. "You said you had things you wanted to tell me, things you needed to show me, but all I've seen is that you're leaving me here with a monstrous king!"

Realizing I'd shouted those words, I clamped my hands over my mouth and stumbled away from the door. If anyone had heard that, if fae soldiers were on patrol...

Father took my arms and pulled me to his chest. The scent of leather and ale filled my head. My chest ached as though a part of me was being carved out and taken away, never to be seen again. I had meant every word I'd said to him. I needed him here. I couldn't stand the thought of living in this place without him.

My father's voice rumbled against me. "I'm doing this for you. You and Nellie. We're going out there to find a way to end King Oberon's reign."

"What?" I pulled back, certain I'd heard him wrong. No one ever spoke of such things. No one even dared. We were mortals. Even if we wanted to revolt, we'd lose, especially against an elite fae as powerful as Oberon. The magic of the sun ran through his veins.

"Nash is right," Ty said from behind us. "He can be killed. We're going out there to find out how."

I shook my head, not understanding. "But the only things out there other than mist are monsters that will rip you apart."

"And the Mist King," Ty said with a grunt.

My blood ran cold.

"I'll do anything to keep you safe, my love. I'll even take on a fae king." Father ruffled my hair.

"We need to go, Nash," Ty said. "The fae soldiers will be on patrol soon. We can't be here when they come."

Father clutched me against him one more time and then moved to the door without saying goodbye. He called over his shoulder, "I'll be back for you soon. Protect your sister. Keep her safe."

I fell to my knees when he left me in that pub, and I wept.

It was the last time I ever saw him alive.

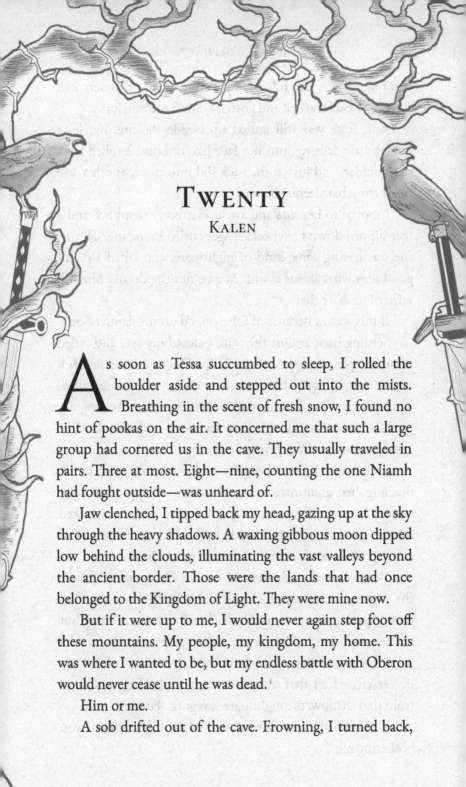

TWENTY

KALEN

A s soon as Tessa succumbed to sleep, I rolled the boulder aside and stepped out into the mists. Breathing in the scent of fresh snow, I found no hint of pookas on the air. It concerned me that such a large group had cornered us in the cave. They usually traveled in pairs. Three at most. Eight—nine, counting the one Niamh had fought outside—was unheard of.

Jaw clenched, I tipped back my head, gazing up at the sky through the heavy shadows. A waxing gibbous moon dipped low behind the clouds, illuminating the vast valleys beyond the ancient border. Those were the lands that had once belonged to the Kingdom of Light. They were mine now.

But if it were up to me, I would never again step foot off these mountains. My people, my kingdom, my home. This was where I wanted to be, but my endless battle with Oberon would never cease until he was dead.

Him or me.

A sob drifted out of the cave. Frowning, I turned back,

hand sliding to the hilt of my sword. If the travelers had somehow backtracked and gotten behind my warriors...

But Tessa was still curled up beside the fire, her long golden hair drifting into her face like ribbons. I rolled back the boulder, and just as the rock slid into place, another sob burst from her sleeping form.

I moved to her side and knelt. Her body trembled, and a tear slipped down her cheek. Anger curled inside me. Clearly, she was having some kind of nightmare, and I had a damn good idea what it was about. Maybe not the details. She still refused to share that.

If this wasn't because of Oberon, I'd eat my damn boot.

Settling back against the wall, I closed my eyes and called upon the power of the mists. Unlike Oberon, I still had full access to my magic, and few knew exactly all that entailed. Most of the time, I influenced dreams without showing my face. Communicating with Tessa had been a calculated risk to get my hands on those gemstones.

Focusing, I let my thoughts whisper into Tessa's mind, pushing her nightmare away. A dream sprang forth, one crafted from my few memories of Teine. That bird-soaked forest. The sun-drenched fields beyond it. And the feel of damp grass beneath my feet. Soft and grounding.

Tessa blinked as she turned from a flickering shadow— the nightmare. It vanished when she spotted me standing bare-footed in the grass, as if it were crafted from nothing but smoke and wind. Oberon couldn't harm her here. She wouldn't remember what she'd been dreaming before. My power chased all that away. As soon as she'd turned away from that shadow, the nightmare was gone. Forever.

She scowled. "I can't even sleep these days without you bothering me."

"I was bored," I said with a shrug.

She rolled her eyes. "You were the one who told me to get some rest."

"And now you're resting."

"Just go away. Please." Squaring her shoulders, she stomped right around me and started for the path away from the forest, leading into the village. I followed after her, curious.

"You know as soon as I leave, this dream will vanish?"

"And so will you," she called over her shoulder, her long hair whipping in the soft breeze. She continued down the path at a determined pace.

"Then, why are you heading into the village?"

She didn't answer. Instead, she marched to the edge of town, hung a left, and stood before a bright blue two-story cottage with flower boxes in every ground-floor window. A broom was propped up beside the front door, and the wooden steps gleamed like new.

"This was your home," I said, coming to stand beside her.

"*Is*," she whispered fiercely. "This is my home." Sighing, she shook her head and glanced up at me. "I don't want to make everyone leave this place. It's all they've ever known."

An uneasy flicker of guilt flared in my gut. "There's nothing I can do about that, Tessa. It won't be safe for them here."

"You can call back your mists." Her voice grew louder. "You can undo whatever it is that you did to cause all this!"

Slowly, I closed my eyes. "No, Tessa. I cannot. I have no way of stopping the mists from surging forward. I wish I did."

"Whose broom is that?" she demanded. "Where did it

come from? Because ours looks nothing like that. Green handle, brown bristles. That one is red."

My eyes flew open at the fury of her words. So much passion for something as small as a broom. "I do not know. Whoever lived here before, I suppose."

Her face scrunched up. "What do you mean?"

"This." I waved around at the dream. "It's all crafted from my own memories. Everything you see is what I have seen."

She pinched her brows together. "That's why everything looks so new. The paint on the house, the steps. This is from centuries ago. So, you're telling me I'm inside your head."

"No, *I* am inside *your* head."

"That's not any better," she muttered.

To my surprise, she didn't shout at me to get out. Instead, she drifted forward. Her feet hit the bottom step, and her hand found the railing's beam. Her fingers drifted along it as she whispered up the stairs.

I wasn't sure if I should follow her. The tension in her shoulders was so tight that her body looked like a statue. Something had happened here, with her family. More than whatever had happened up in that fucking crimson castle. I knew she was worried about her mother and her friend, Val, but this went beyond that. The way her body shook...her heart teetered on a knife's edge.

My teeth ground together. Whatever it was, King Oberon had caused it. What the fuck had he done to her?

Her fingers brushed the broom handle. A choking sound ripped from her throat. Then, she stiffened, turned, and ran past me, heading back the way we'd come.

I didn't follow. The last thing she needed was the Mist King haunting her every step when she needed time alone to process whatever she was feeling. Showing her the village, letting her see her childhood home, it had opened a wound that had barely begun to heal. I realized that now. This had been a mistake.

And so, I drifted out of her mind, draping my cloak back over her as the fire crackled. Her breathing had calmed. No more tears streaked down her cheeks. Not that I should care. She wanted me dead. To her, I was just as bad as Oberon.

Frowning, I strode back over to the boulder and sat hard. She'd done nothing but insult me since the day she'd opened her eyes in that dungeon cell. Every single time she got the chance, she threw that hateful title in my face. *The Mist King*. Over and over again, she taunted me with it.

Tessa blamed me for everything that had happened to her. The problem was, she was right. It *was* my fault. I'd lied to her. I was the reason Oberon had chosen her as his bride. I'd even drenched the lands in all that mist.

My eyes drifted back to her all the same. Those red-tinted lips. The dark golden hair falling across freckled cheeks. Fuller, the past few days. Stronger.

For fuck's sake, none of that mattered.

King Oberon needed to die. That was my top priority and the only reason I'd agreed to this bloody mission in the first place. Tessa was the key to getting to him. She was a mortal, one not trapped by ancient magic. She could come and go in Albyria without the gemstones' power stopping her.

And stab that blade into her king's heart.

I'd finally win this centuries-long war and let the mist flood those lands, and I didn't care if that meant she hated me.

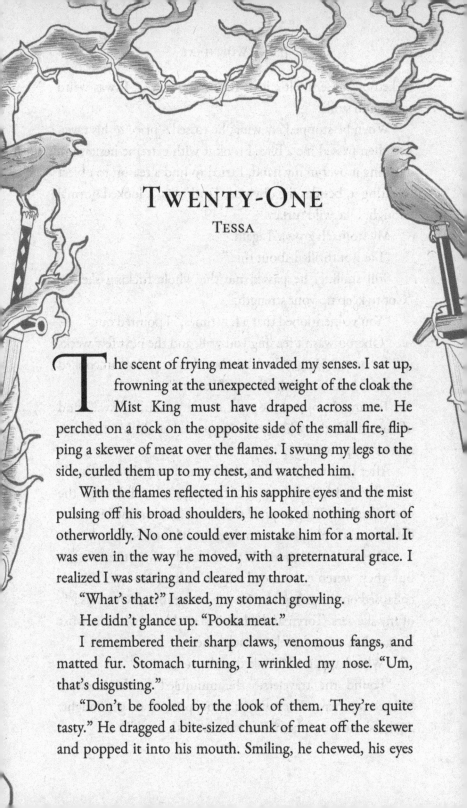

TWENTY-ONE
TESSA

The scent of frying meat invaded my senses. I sat up, frowning at the unexpected weight of the cloak the Mist King must have draped across me. He perched on a rock on the opposite side of the small fire, flipping a skewer of meat over the flames. I swung my legs to the side, curled them up to my chest, and watched him.

With the flames reflected in his sapphire eyes and the mist pulsing off his broad shoulders, he looked nothing short of otherworldly. No one could ever mistake him for a mortal. It was even in the way he moved, with a preternatural grace. I realized I was staring and cleared my throat.

"What's that?" I asked, my stomach growling.

He didn't glance up. "Pooka meat."

I remembered their sharp claws, venomous fangs, and matted fur. Stomach turning, I wrinkled my nose. "Um, that's disgusting."

"Don't be fooled by the look of them. They're quite tasty." He dragged a bite-sized chunk of meat off the skewer and popped it into his mouth. Smiling, he chewed, his eyes locked on mine. I felt a little funny about that. It was weird to see him smile.

When he stopped chewing, he tossed a piece to his raven and then passed me a bite. I took it with extreme hesitation. Turning it over in my hand, I tried to find a reason to object to eating it, besides the obvious. Truth was, it looked normal enough. Like wild turkey.

My stomach growled again.

"I'm not thrilled about this."

Still smiling, he passed me the whole fucking skewer. "Got to keep up your strength."

"You've mentioned that a few times," I pointed out.

"Oberon wasn't feeding you well, and the next few weeks will be hard." He grabbed another skewer full of uncooked meat and held it over the flames. "Eat up."

Tensing, I popped the meat into my mouth. It was kind of...bland. Nothing like what I expected at all. My stomach roared its approval.

After I'd eaten two entire skewers and my belly had finally started to feel full, the sound of footsteps echoed through the cave. The Mist King hopped to his feet and vanished into the darkness, returning a moment later with his trio of warriors.

They all looked tired. Dirt and blood stained their armor, but they weren't wounded as far as I could see. Niamh collapsed on the ground beside me and grabbed what was left of my skewers. Toryn and Alastair stayed back with the Mist King, whispering fiercely to each other.

"What happened?" I asked as she ate.

"Found the travelers," she mumbled as she chewed. "Three of them. They weren't too pleased to get caught. Archers, the lot of them. But we won in the end."

"Are you all right?" I asked, alarmed. For some reason, I'd expected them to find the traveler and escort him down the mountain where he could wander around somewhere else. I hadn't expected a fight, even though they'd been worried about a threat. Which meant...what exactly had they been trying to do? Did the Mist King have more enemies out there than King Oberon?

My gaze wandered to where he stood with the others. His face had gone hard, his eyes flashing with that rage he carried with him like a shield. They'd won, but he didn't look very happy about it.

"Course I'm okay," she finally answered. With a quick glance at me, she nodded. "Looks like you are, too. An uneventful night then?"

I wasn't sure if I could call it uneventful, what with the Mist King's irritating visit to my dreams again. What he was trying to accomplish with that, I didn't know. Was he hoping to make me more pliable by showing me glimpses of my home? By reminding me of what King Oberon had done to me and the threat that loomed over my people?

"There weren't any more pooka attacks," I answered.

She cocked her head at me. "Hmm."

The Mist King strode back over, with Toryn and Alastair in tow. He poured a bucket of ashes onto the fire and grabbed his pack. Niamh groaned.

"We need to go," he ordered. "We don't have time to waste."

He seemed agitated, although that wasn't far off from how he normally was. I started to ask Niamh what that was all about, but he tossed my pack to me. It thumped against my leg. Frowning, I grabbed it and stood.

"Why are you in such a hurry all of a sudden? What happened down there?"

"It's none of your concern. Now, if you want to find your mother, be quiet and come along."

"Be *quiet*?" My hands fisted as I stalked after him. Alastair and Toryn smartly backed away. "Stop ordering me around. I'm not your servant."

"Just do what I say, Tessa."

Everything within me went cold. "I know you're a powerful king, but I won't let you treat me like King Oberon did."

His feet slowed to a stop. Tensing, he cast a glance over his shoulder. "I'm sorry. This isn't an order. It's a request. We need to get going now. Please."

I blinked. He'd said please. That, I hadn't expected.

With a sigh, I nodded, reaching around to remove the cloak. He shook his head. "Keep it. You'll need it for a while."

My hands dropped to my sides. Niamh patted me on the shoulder as we watched the others push the boulder out of the way. As the mists rolled in, she leaned down to whisper, "I've never seen anyone get under his skin the way you do."

Frowning, I shifted on my feet. "Not even Oberon?"

"If Oberon spoke to him the way you do, he'd just stab him. In fact, Oberon wouldn't need to say a damn word. Get them in the same room, and you'd witness a fight of epic proportions."

"Who do you think would win?" I couldn't help but ask.

"Right now?" She inclined her head toward her king. "But that hasn't always been the case. Once, they were very evenly matched. The winner of the fight would be down to luck and..." She tapped her brain.

"Wait, how is the Mist King stronger now?"

"*Kal,*" she said, and then laughed. "Oh, you dear thing. Oberon's kept it all so close to the chest, hasn't he? He doesn't have access to his elite powers. The strength he currently possesses is a fraction of what he once had. He's just like any common fae now. We all have more strength and speed than mortals, fast healing, and an immortal lifespan, but that's it. Oberon has no extra magic, no light or fire power, no nothing. He doesn't have it. And despite his attempts, he can't get it back."

That made me take a step back. "What?"

"Conniving bastard, eh?" Niamh shook her head, patting me on the back. "Sounds like he's really had you all convinced he's as strong as he's ever been."

It wasn't something anyone had ever questioned. His power protected our little bubble of the world, and he'd never had any trouble keeping command of his throne. Of course, now that she'd pointed it out, I couldn't help but realize he'd never demonstrated his full fae magic. The fire and light at his fingertips. At least, not in my lifetime.

"When did he lose it?" I asked, already suspecting the answer.

She smiled. "Three hundred and seventy-five years ago. He poured all his magic into those gemstones, creating the barrier between our kingdoms. That's how he keeps the mists out. Unfortunately for him, that means he can't do anything else."

With another pat on my back, Niamh led me out into the swirling mists, trailing behind the others. I fell into deep thought as we took careful steps down the rocky path. Almost four hundred years ago, the Mist King had invaded the Kingdom of Light. The strength of his army had rushed across the sunlit cities and fields, destroying everything in sight. Behind him came the mists.

According to legend, Oberon took his last stand against the Mist King just outside of Albyria. He'd called upon the power of the sun, and he'd "thrown" it right at the enemy army. The Mist King had thrown his power right back, and the two magical forces had slammed into each other. Light and dark, mist and fire. The land shook from the clash of magic.

A chasm yawned wide in its wake.

Before the Mist King could find a way across the chasm, Oberon had created the protective circle around Albyria and Teine, keeping both the invading army and the dangerous mists out. But it must have come at a greater price than Oberon had ever admitted, least of all to the mortals he forced to obey him.

He'd lost his power.

"Wait a minute," I said when I caught up to Niamh. "If Oberon doesn't have access to his powers, how does he give immortality to his mortal brides? How does he protect the humans of Teine from wounds and disease?"

"That's a good question," she said, her armor clinking as we walked. "It's one we've tried to find the answer to ourselves. The truth is we don't know, but he shouldn't be able to do any of that, even *with* his powers. Elite light fae control fire and light. He's controlling life. Whatever power he's using, it isn't his."

Interesting.

Our party journeyed in near silence. We carried on down the mountain, the mists a cool caress against my cheeks. With every hour that passed, my eyes grew more adjusted to the strange and twisting darkness. I saw that it wasn't quite as dark as I'd first thought. I could spot vague shapes through the shadows. The mountain that rose up behind us was visible high above in sharp, jagged peaks, backlit by some vague light.

The Mist King fell into step beside me and saw me glancing up. "That's the moon."

I widened my eyes, taking in the soft round glow, fuzzing at the edges. "I've heard about the moon. In books, of course. But I didn't expect to be able to see it here. In Teine, there's no such thing as darkness. Not outside, at least. I didn't think you'd have any light at all."

"We're the Kingdom of Shadow," he murmured. "Not darkness. There's starlight, too. On nights the mists cleared, you'd be able to see them."

Surprised, I let my gaze wander to his face. Even in the murky darkness, his profile was striking. He was a tall, imposing figure beside me as we walked down the path barely wide enough for two, especially someone as broad-shouldered as him. The sword on his back swept between his shoulder blades, the curved blade illuminated by faintly glowing gems that matched the sapphire of his eyes.

The sight of him there in the mists was mesmerizing.

I swallowed hard and glanced away. "The mists clear?"

"In Dubnos? Not in centuries," he said in a voice that betrayed his pain. "The mists have always been here, of course, but they thickened after the war. They rarely leave now, no matter how hard I try to force them away."

"Right. I have to know. What in the name of light happened that day?"

Pebbles crunched beneath our boots as we continued forward, Alastair leading the way in the front of the group.

The Mist King sighed. "Oberon and I fought. All of this is a result of that."

"More specifically..." There was more to it than that. I was certain of that now. And if I was going to be the one to kill King Oberon for him, then I wanted to know everything I could. Something told me it all went back to the Mist King's mother and whatever Oberon had done to her. Kalen had attacked to avenge her death. And Oberon would never back down against a threat.

"Oberon was playing around with the power of the gods, power he never should have touched," he said, causing a jolt of shock in my gut.

I lifted my brows. "What power? What gods?"

"The five immortal riders who wanted to rule this world." With a shake of his head, he let out a bitter chuckle. "Do you know, it almost sounds like Oberon likes living in his little bubble. With so few mortals and fae under his reign, and with so little land, he can control every single aspect of it. He must have burned every book that mentioned any of this and made the fae swear never to speak of it to you."

Unease slithered through me. "So, you're telling me those gods are *real*?"

"Oh yes," the Mist King said with a harsh laugh. "And they are far more dangerous than any fae you've ever met. Long ago, fae and mortals banded together to banish them from this world. Those things you accuse me of doing— burning living souls and then eating their charred flesh? They did that, long ago. Now, King Oberon not only wants to bring them back. He wants to become one of them himself."

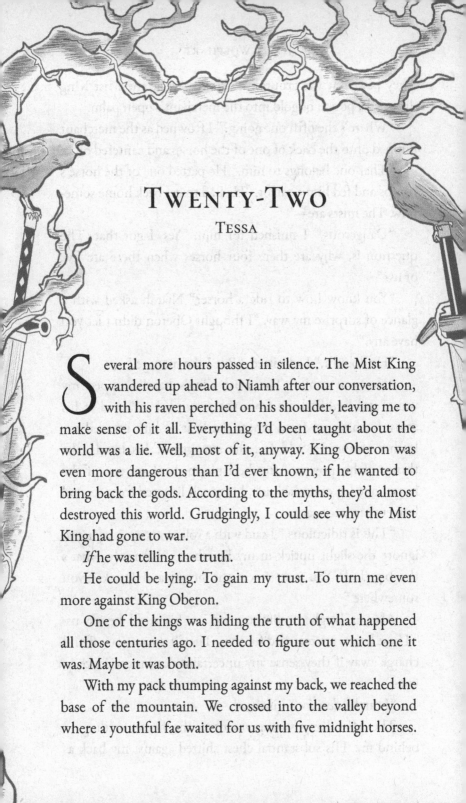

TWENTY-TWO

TESSA

Several more hours passed in silence. The Mist King wandered up ahead to Niamh after our conversation, with his raven perched on his shoulder, leaving me to make sense of it all. Everything I'd been taught about the world was a lie. Well, most of it, anyway. King Oberon was even more dangerous than I'd ever known, if he wanted to bring back the gods. According to the myths, they'd almost destroyed this world. Grudgingly, I could see why the Mist King had gone to war.

If he was telling the truth.

He could be lying. To gain my trust. To turn me even more against King Oberon.

One of the kings was hiding the truth of what happened all those centuries ago. I needed to figure out which one it was. Maybe it was both.

With my pack thumping against my back, we reached the base of the mountain. We crossed into the valley beyond where a youthful fae waited for us with five midnight horses.

They pawed at the ground, nickering, while the Mist King dropped a pouch of gold into the merchant's open palm.

"Where's the fifth one going?" I frowned as the merchant hopped onto the back of one of the horses and cantered off.

"That one belongs to him." He patted one of the horse's rumps and fed him a carrot. "He had to get back home somehow. The mists are—"

"Dangerous," I finished for him. "Yes, I got that. The question is, why are there four horses when there are five of us?"

"You know how to ride a horse?" Niamh asked with a glance of surprise my way. "I thought Oberon didn't let you have any."

"He doesn't," I admitted. "But I can manage."

"No, you can't." The Mist King's hands cupped my waist, and he lifted me from the ground. I smacked at his arms, burning up from where the heat of him invaded my leather armor. I could feel the strength of his hands, the thrum of his power. After he'd plopped me on top of the horse, one leg on either side, his touch lingered for a second longer than necessary.

"This is ridiculous," I said with a roll of my eyes, trying to ignore the slight uptick in my heartbeat. "Honestly, what's the big deal? You just sit on the horse, and it takes you somewhere."

Alastair laughed, climbing up on his steed beside us. "These beasts are too wild for that. They'll throw you off and charge away if they sense any uncertainty or inexperience in you."

"I can be *decisive*," I insisted.

The Mist King swung up onto the horse, settling in behind me. His substantial chest shifted against my back as he reached an arm on either side of me to grab the reins. I scowled as his hands settled onto my thighs, just above my knees. The heat and power of him pressed into me.

Something within me clenched.

"This is not necessary," I said hotly as the group flicked their reins, and the horses took off into an alarmingly fast canter. The ground jolted beneath me as we tore through the mists, the cool wind snatching at my hair.

I clung to the horse's coarse mane. We were moving so fast, the mist clouded my eyes, causing a steady stream of tears. As we galloped ahead, the Mist King kept my thighs firmly trapped beneath his steady hands. I shifted slightly to the side when we hit an unexpected ditch, and my hands slipped off the mane.

But his hands kept me steady.

I wanted to hate every moment of this. He was rude and monstrous and cruel and murderous and hateful and...also very muscular and strong. The wind blew his wintry scent into my nose, and the steady thrum of his body against my back chased away the anxious nerves. But only because I didn't want to die, of course.

I really needed to learn how to ride these horses so I would never have to do this again.

He leaned forward and pressed his mouth so close to my ear that a tremor went down my neck. "Relax. I'm not going to let you fall off."

"No, because then I wouldn't be alive to do your bidding," I snapped back.

There. That was better. Gone were the thoughts about how comforting and strong he was. He was those things, but that didn't erase everything else.

"That's right," he said with a dark laugh that shot his

breath against my neck. I pressed my lips together. "If you die, neither one of us gets what we want. So you will stay safely tucked here against my chest where I can stop Midnight from launching you into the mists where you'd have to fend for yourself. Or is that what you'd prefer, Tessa?"

Damn him, he was obnoxious. "I'm stronger than you think I am."

"You might be right, but there are some things you need to learn." His hands tensed against me once more when we hit another bump. "We need to train you to use that dagger."

"I know how to fight," I said with a scowl. "I hit Oberon square in the chest when I tried to kill him before. If I'd had the Mortal Blade, he'd be dead."

"Confident." I could hear the smile in his voice. "Regardless of how well you fared before, I want to train you. You won't be able to catch him off guard the same way you did before. In fact, if he sees you coming, he'll likely expect an attack. You ran from him. He won't trust you when you go back."

I snorted. "All I have to do is apologize and massage his ego. I'll tell him I went out into the mists, realized how stupid it was to run, and then I'll offer myself back up to him. I'm his betrothed. He won't kill me."

"He won't kill you, but he might..." His chest stiffened against my back. "There are other things he could do to you."

My hands fisted tighter around the horse's mane. When I spoke, my voice was barely a whisper. "Yes, I know."

"We need to train you," he said again, his voice more insistent. "I won't let you step one foot on that bridge until we can be certain you know how to defend yourself. He *cannot* harm you again."

A strange sensation fluttered in my belly. The Mist King only spoke that way because I'd be no use to him if I got caught. Tortured and ridiculed. Broken down. The first thing the light fae would do was take that dagger away from me. And then *no one* would be able to kill King Oberon, especially not me.

The passion in his words had nothing to do with my actual well-being. I was just the Mist King's tool, like I'd been for King Oberon.

A forest rose up before us, its trees' gnarled fingers stretching toward the sky, vacant and whistling in the wind. Their slate-gray bark blended in with the shadows. As the horses thundered into the rotting brush, dread curled through me. There was a strange presence to this place, like watchful eyes tracked our every movement in the woods.

I found myself leaning just a little farther back to feel the Mist King there.

He might not truly care about my well-being, but that didn't matter when I knew he'd do whatever it took to keep me safe in this place.

The woods swallowed the noise of hooves on dirt. When we'd gone several yards into the forest, the fae pulled to a stop and hopped to the ground. The Mist King swung off behind me first and held out a hand. Ignoring him, I dismounted with the gracefulness of a toddler.

"What are we doing?" I asked in a hush. This forest set my teeth on edge, and there was no telling what kind of monsters lurked nearby. More pookas, most likely. And whatever else lived in the mists.

"There are some hostile fae who have invaded a village just ahead," the Mist King said, a dark look in his sapphire eyes. "We need to take care of it."

I blew out a breath. "You think my mother and Val are there?"

"They're unlikely to have made it this far away from Albyria." He reached into the pack he'd strapped to the horse and dug out a pale gray gemstone. Its light glowed in the swirling mists as he tucked it into his pocket. "If they've taken shelter in one of the cities, my guess is it'll be Itchen or Endir."

I took a small step toward him and tapped the center of his chest, frowning. "Then, let's keep moving. You can't go against our vow unless I say it's all right."

"We have innocent people who live in Vere. Civilians," Niamh explained as she plucked an arrow from her quiver and flipped it in her hands. "They need our help. Are you really going to insist we keep moving, Tessa?"

Something my chest stirred. *Damn them.* Of course I wouldn't insist, not if innocents were in danger.

"All right. Do what you must," I said, turning back to the Mist King. "This is why you were in such a hurry to leave the cave, isn't it?"

He nodded and took my shoulders in his firm hands. A moment later, I stood in the center of the four horses, their inky bodies boxing me in. That was when I realized the fae were going to leave me here.

"Absolutely not." I folded my arms. "You can't leave me here alone."

"We can, and we will." He arched a brow. "Are you going to try to run? Because you know the vow won't let you."

I narrowed my eyes and shoved through the horses, taking off through the forest. Almost instantaneously, a force wound an invisible rope around my waist and hauled me back. My body hit the ground as the force dragged me toward the horses, dirt and sand spraying into my face.

I skidded to a stop, right where I'd just been, trapped in the middle of the horses.

Alastair guffawed.

I glared at them all. "You can't leave me here like this. What if some pookas attack?"

The thought terrified me more than I wanted to admit. Those things were monstrous. They could throw full-grown fae a mile. And while the Mist King had taken down eight of them at once, he'd seemed drained and tired when he was done. Not to mention the only weapon I had was my little wooden dagger. One blow from that would do nothing more than annoy a pooka.

"These beasts will protect you just fine, and Boudica is in the sky keeping watch," the Mist King said. "We're walking into a fight. These fae are archers. You need to stay here."

"What fae?" I asked, climbing to my feet. "Is something going on with your kingdom? You have rebels or something? Is that why your castle is so empty?"

"That is none of your concern."

"Might as well tell her, Kal," Alastair said with a shrug as he tightened his ponytail. "She's involved in this shit now, whether you like it or not."

I nodded. "*Thank you.*"

The Mist King's lips flattened. "Fine. The fae are invaders from the Kingdom of Storms. They've taken the people of Vere as prisoners and are using the village as an outpost while they plan an attack against my castle. The fae we found traveling in the mountains were scouts. Now, there's your answer. We need to go now."

Toryn shot me an apologetic smile but turned to go as

the others did. My heart thundered in my chest as the Mist King's words echoed in my ears. I hadn't thought much about the Kingdom of Storms in years. According to our history books, there wasn't much to them anymore. Was that just another lie? Why did they want to take the Mist King's throne?

I clearly wouldn't get those answers right now. The fae had left me alone in these woods with nothing but a few horses to keep me company. Breath hissing between my teeth, I pulled the dagger from my tunic and pointed it toward the vanishing forest path, waiting.

Every now and again, one of the horses would flick his ears or stomp his hooves, as if hearing something from the distance. Sounds that I couldn't hear myself. What was happening out there? Were they winning? With the Mist King's powers, how could they not?

As the moments stretched on, the silence and stillness of the forest became unbearable. A small twig cracked in the distance, and I jerked so hard that the horse behind me shoved his long snout into my back. The force knocked me to my knees where tiny purple flowers glowed in the night.

Scowling, I didn't bother to stand back up. Instead, I crossed my legs and settled in for a wait. The horses snorted, as if speaking their approval.

"This is annoying," I said to them. "Don't you want to go help them?"

No answer, but what did I expect? They were horses.

With a sigh, I wound my arms around my legs and tugged them to my chest. I was going to have to take the Mist King up on his offer to train me. Weakness could be conquered. Being left behind, so that I would be out of the way, was an aching reminder of just how little use I was out here. And if I wanted to kill Oberon, once and for all, I needed to be at my best.

A scorpion the size of my fist scuttled through the horses' legs, crawled up my side, and perched on top of my hand. I squealed and shook my arm, knocking the scorpion to the ground. It thunked into the dirt only an inch away.

Sucking in a breath, I stared at the creature, my heart trembling like a leaf.

"What in the name of light is that?" I hissed.

The creature rolled onto its back, its stick-like legs curled inward, and its body went still. For a moment, nothing happened. I glanced around, hoping there weren't any others creeping toward me. But the forest was silent and empty, save for the stomping of the horses' hooves.

Was it dead? Had I knocked it off too hard? I leaned forward and poked its frozen body.

The creature sprang up with a shriek and then raced off into the darkness.

I leapt to my feet. "All right. That's it. I really hate this forest."

A long low wail echoed through the silence. Chills stormed across my arms. The horses snapped to attention, their heads whipping toward the direction the fae had gone. Heart thundering, I slowly turned.

Something was out there, and I didn't think it was a scorpion.

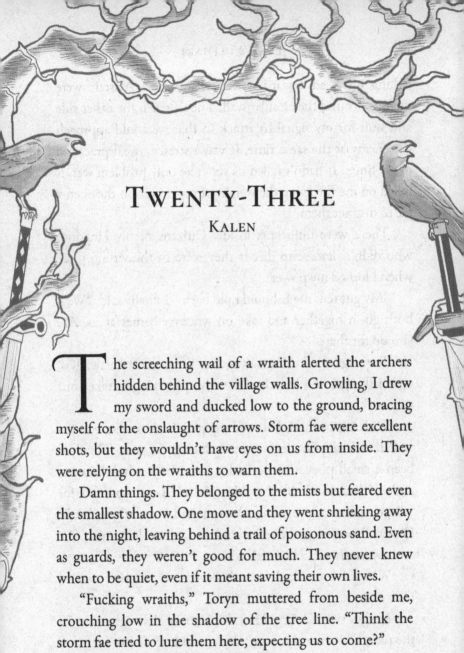

TWENTY-THREE

KALEN

The screeching wail of a wraith alerted the archers hidden behind the village walls. Growling, I drew my sword and ducked low to the ground, bracing myself for the onslaught of arrows. Storm fae were excellent shots, but they wouldn't have eyes on us from inside. They were relying on the wraiths to warn them.

Damn things. They belonged to the mists but feared even the smallest shadow. One move and they went shrieking away into the night, leaving behind a trail of poisonous sand. Even as guards, they weren't good for much. They never knew when to be quiet, even if it meant saving their own lives.

"Fucking wraiths," Toryn muttered from beside me, crouching low in the shadow of the tree line. "Think the storm fae tried to lure them here, expecting us to come?"

My lips flattened. "Let's hope not."

Wraiths loved blood and could scent it from miles away. If the storm fae had lured the wraiths here, they'd killed to do it.

"So, how do you want to do this?" Toryn whispered,

jerking his head toward where Niamh and Alastair were inching around the circular wall. They'd reach the other side and wait for my signal to attack so that we could approach the enemy at the same time. It was a strategy we'd practiced many times. It hadn't failed us yet. The only problem was, it relied on me throwing the weight of my power on the enemy fae to distract them.

There were innocents inside. Citizens of my kingdom who didn't deserve to die. If they were in the wrong place when I loosed my power...

"My gut tells me I should hold back," I finally said. "We'll both go in together and take on whoever comes at us. Are you up for that?"

Toryn grinned. "I'm always up for a good battle, Kal, especially against a bunch of fae who are trying to take your throne."

With a grim nod, I turned my gaze back to the wooden wall that had only been erected during the war. This had been a small pocket of normalcy once, back when humans and fae had lived side by side. There'd been no need for village walls. Before King Oberon had ruled these lands, Queen Bronwen had been a kind and benevolent ruler. She and my mother had been friends.

Why Oberon had ever believed my mother would marry him...

My gut twisted. I couldn't think about that right now. In the past, I'd let my rage control me, and I needed to focus on this fight.

"You and I have faced many battles together, Toryn." I held out a hand. He placed his palm against mine, and then we tapped the back of our knuckles together, before bringing our thumbs to our lips. We let out a low whistle that only the two of us could hear.

For so many years, we'd faced danger together. So many times, we'd sprayed blood on the ground. It did not thrill me to do it, like it did some fae. Niamh reveled in it. But it was what must be done. And I would never turn my back on my duty to my realm.

The village ahead was home to light and shadow fae alike. It was one of the only places in the world where our kind did not hate each other, where we lived together in peace. After the war, some of the people in Dubnos had wanted to explore the lands I'd taken from the Kingdom of Light. They'd ended up settling here, where there were empty homes left behind by the fae who had died fighting in the Battle of the Great Rift.

At first, I'd been surprised. Surely the light fae would hate us.

But it turned out they hated Oberon far more, and they were happy to be free of him, even if it meant they now had to live in permanent darkness.

Arrows rained down on the ground just ahead of where we hid, dashing aside my thoughts of the past. Toryn and I waited for the last arrow to punch the ground, and then we leapt to our feet, rushing forward before they could loose their next storm. We made it over halfway before they came again.

I dodged to the side, my heart raging in my chest. One arrow hit its mark, slamming into my shoulder. Pain flared through me, but I batted it away. I yanked the arrow out of my arm and tossed it onto the ground.

We made it to the wall, breath heaving between us. Sweat coated Toryn's brow, but he looked none the worse for wear.

The storm fae were good shots, but we'd surprised them. And we'd gotten lucky.

I nodded toward the barred door. "We knock it down together. I'll use some of my power, but not the full force of it. How is yours faring?"

Toryn grinned and held up his hands, wreathed in lightning. "All charged up."

The son of storm fae. I would never forget what he'd given up to join my side.

"Good." In the distance, something like an eagle let out a long, high-pitched whistle. "That was Niamh. They're ready on the other side."

I lifted my fingers to my lips and whistled back.

Pulling the mists into my body, I placed a palm against the door, the warped wood scratching against my palm. And then I *shoved*, just as Toryn blasted his lightning at the gate. The door splintered, shattering inward. I held up my hands to protect my face from the wind tunnel of wood and stone. Power stormed through the opening, rattling my bones.

When the dust finally cleared, both of us peered inside. An empty courtyard stared back at us. Frowning, I strode through the rubble, stepping over a pile of fallen stone. There wasn't a fae anywhere to be seen. No civilians. No soldiers. No assassins lurking in wait. Just pure silence, until a pair of footsteps echoed in the silence. A moment later, Niamh and Alastair joined us in the courtyard.

Al grunted. "Where the fuck is everyone?"

"Long gone." Niamh let out a low whistle as she pointed a finger at the empty battlements at the top of the wall. "They couldn't have fled that quickly."

Toryn frowned. "They shot arrows at us only moments ago. The storm fae have power over the elements, but they can't *vanish* into thin air. Trust me. If they could, I would know."

"It was a trick." I spun in a slow circle, eyeing up the old village. Some of the doors had been knocked down, and windows were smashed. Old, dried blood painted some of the wooden walls. "An illusion. That's why most of those arrows missed. No one was manning the bows."

"That doesn't make a lick of sense," Niamh argued. "They can't shoot arrows from afar."

"They set it up," I said, rubbing my chin. "They had the arrows ready to go, and then used a blast of wind to release them. They knew the arrows were unlikely to hit their mark, but it gave the impression soldiers were in here."

"Why the hell would they want to do something like that?" Alastair asked.

Alarm flashed through me as my thoughts went straight to Tessa. Those horses would protect her, even against a small army of storm fae. There was more to them than met the eye. But I could not stop the jolt to my heart, the instinct to rush to her side and make sure she was alright.

"It was a trap," Toryn said grimly.

Something in his voice snapped me out of my thoughts. I followed his gaze to where a group of storm fae on horseback charged into the village, grinning wickedly. Swords raised, they raced forward, bearing down on our group. I looked at each and every face. There were at least thirty of them and only four of us. A blast of wind shot into our faces, blinding me momentarily.

They were elites. Some of them were, at least.

"Run!" I shouted, grabbing Niamh's arm and tugging her toward the buildings. I would stand against the storm fae alone, but I had to get the others to safety first. Toryn's powers needed recharging before he could use the lightning again. Niamh and Alastair were common fae and had nothing other than their brute strength.

That would not hold up against a charging army of thirty, with elites in their ranks.

Fear flashed across Niamh's face as another blast of wind hit us hard. It knocked us off our feet, throwing us onto the ground. Alastair crawled to his feet, his face paling. He lifted a shaking finger.

I looked over my shoulder and my stomach dropped. The storm fae had surrounded Toryn. He curled his hands into fists and shot his magic, but it did nothing but fizzle on his fingers. One of the storm fae leaned down and grabbed Toryn's arm.

And then they took off into the mists, dragging him behind them.

I dropped back my head and roared just as the wind hammered into me and threw me at the wall.

TWENTY-FOUR
TESSA

"What's happening?" I jumped to my feet as Niamh raced down the path, her violet, braided hair flapping behind her like the loose rope on a ship. Her eyes were wild, brows pinched. Whatever had screamed out there must have attacked them. My mouth went dry. Was it pookas? Were they coming here? And where in the name of light was the Mist King?

I held up my dagger as my heart thundered against my ribs.

"It's Toryn," Niamh grabbed the horn of the nearest saddle and leapt up onto the horse in a single fluid movement. "The storm fae took him. I need to ride hard if I want to catch up to them."

"*Took* him?" I gaped up at her, picturing the strong fae and his gentle smile. "How? Why?"

"I don't have time to explain." She pointed at the horse called Midnight. "Get on. We'll meet the others by the village. Kal is beside himself, and trust me, you do not want to make him wait. When it comes to the ones he loves, he can be vicious."

I swallowed hard. "Understood."

Of course, that meant riding one of these things, and I'd been distinctly told that was a terrible idea. Niamh didn't make any other suggestion, though, so I shoved my foot into the stirrup and hauled myself onto Midnight's saddle. There was a silver streak in his mane. Other than that, it was impossible to tell the horses apart.

The hooves thundered against the ground as we charged toward the village. I clung on, my eyes half-closed as the branches whipped at my face. A sharp thorn made contact with my cheek, slicing a deep gash into my skin. I gritted my teeth against the pain, but I didn't slow down.

When we exploded out into a clearing just before a tall wooden wall, I spotted the Mist King storming in a circle and shouting into the wind. Alastair stood with his fingers jammed into his hair, jaw muscles ticking. His eyes looked haunted, as if he'd just stared death in the face.

Maybe he had.

"Alastair!" Niamh shouted from atop her horse. "Come on! We still might have a chance of catching up to them."

The Mist King whirled on his feet, his lip curled back in a menacing snarl. My stomach did a little flip. "They have a head start. You'll never reach them in time, and they could kill both of you if you do. And you know I can't go with you."

The vow, I thought.

"Stop being so pessimistic," I called out before Niamh could come up with a reply herself. "As long as there's a chance, we have to try."

The Mist King whipped his head toward me. I braced

myself for that ever-present anger, but instead, I found surprise. "*You* want to go after him? They've headed back toward the Kingdom of Storms. Away from Itchen and Endir, where your family might be."

A snake wrapped its way around my heart. Val and Mother were out there somewhere, and the last thing I wanted to do was go the wrong way. I needed to find them. I needed to make sure they were okay. They'd already been in the mists far too long. I worried that we didn't have any time to waste.

But how could I let Toryn get carried away for slaughter or worse? That would make me no better than King Oberon.

"We can't abandon him out there," I said.

It wasn't right.

The Mist King's body shuddered as he let out an audible sigh. He and Alastair joined us on the horses, though the Mist King chose to sit behind me once again. I didn't complain or try to shove him back. Right now was not the time for that. He looked distraught.

As we charged through the mists, turning back toward the looming mountain, I cast a glance over my shoulder, drinking in his face. His jaw was hard, his eyes flickering with a dark intensity. He looked like he was ready to rip the entire world apart. The Mist King cared *deeply* for his people. I'd never seen King Oberon worry about anything other than gaining power.

The Mist King had the look of a man who loved. A man who had already lost so much. A man whose soul had been shattered.

His eyes flicked down, and he caught me staring. Tensing, I shifted away, nibbling on my bottom lip as I gazed out at the vague shape of the mountain growing larger in the distance. I didn't like him very much, but I did understand him. And I couldn't help but wonder, what would I have done in his place, if I'd been pitted against Oberon all those years before?

I scowled. Well, for one, I wouldn't have destroyed entire cities.

Some of it, I could understand. The fight against Oberon. The clash of powers. The determination to see the king dead. But I could never justify the rest.

Ash filled my mouth.

"I know what you're thinking," he said in a low voice as the rough canter of the horse jolted my skull.

I shook my head. "Unlikely."

"How does the monstrous, terrible, wicked Mist King have an actual heart?" he asked bitterly. "Surely he can't care about anyone but himself."

"Close. It's hard to picture you as anything else when I can list off all the horrible things you've done to the world. Maybe you didn't eat human flesh, but you did destroy cities in the war."

"Then maybe this is the world paying me back for all my crimes."

His voice broke, and for a moment, I felt a stab of grief for what I'd said. No matter what the Mist King had done centuries ago, Toryn did not deserve to die like this. He was only following the orders of his king, and I'd seen the goodness in him.

"He'll be okay," I said, although I scarcely believed it. "We'll catch up to them."

"I can smell the lies on your breath."

My lips slammed together, and I turned back to face the mists. He was angry and scared and in no mood to talk. It was hard for me to blame him. For this, at least. I knew what it was like to be scared for a loved one's life. I'd suffered that fear far too many times, and I knew the twisted, biting pain when that fear became realized.

"I'll do anything to keep you safe, my love. I'll even take on a fae king." Father ruffled my hair.

I squeezed my eyes tight as a tear slipped down my cheek.

Up ahead, a form solidified in the mists. A broken body, abandoned on the ground. A gasp ripped from my throat as a familiar pair of vacant green eyes stared unseeing at the sky. His fighting leathers had been torn open, exposing his mangled chest. The wounds sizzled. Smoke curled off his body and drifted up to join the mists. These storm fae had hit him with powerful magic.

Nausea bubbled up in my throat as the Mist King roared. He launched from the moving horse and raced toward Toryn, sand storming up in his wake.

"Oh my moon," Niamh cried out, slowing her horse a few feet away from Toryn. A sob shook her body.

"Stay back!" the Mist King shouted as he stared ahead at the army of storm fae inching out of the darkness. A heavy gust of wind blasted into our faces, bringing with it the scent of thunder and steel. "Stay behind me!"

"The fucking bastards," Alastair growled, thumping his chest as he screwed up his face in anger. "I will fucking kill them all."

Mist swirled around the king's powerful form, his arms outstretched on either side of him. The storm fae rushed forward, oblivious to the threat. The two in front blasted more wind and rain in our direction, but the Mist King batted it away as if it were nothing.

"Kal, stop," Niamh called out, her voice shaking.

"They're trying to goad you into fighting them, and there's too many for you to take at once. I know you're angry, but—"

"I said stay back," he thundered, his voice raw and full of an otherworldly power that skittered across my skin. "Get Tessa away from me."

"What?" I whispered. "Why?"

Alastair grabbed the reins of my horse and pulled me away from the Mist King and the approaching storm fae. Niamh followed, her eyes cast to the ground until we were so far away that all I could see were vague shapes in the mists. Alastair dropped the reins and folded his arms, while Niamh paced back and forth with her hands rubbing against her thighs.

"What's going on?" I hissed at them. "What's he doing?"

"He's going to kill them," Niamh said bitterly, her eyes haunted. "And I'm not going to try to stop him this time."

Fear throbbed through my veins as I turned back to the Mist King and his growing whirlwind of mist. The enemy fae were blasting all kinds of elements at him now. Rain and snow. Icy pellets. It all slammed into some kind of invisible shield around the king and Toryn's body, and then shattered into mist.

He lifted his eyes from the ground and stared them down. Hands clenched, he threw his arms at the storm fae. A sudden thump of power radiated toward me, wave upon wave of pure, unyielding darkness. I braced myself against the force of it. And then it crackled and exploded outward, straight at the gathered storm fae.

Invisible and silent, his power sucked everything inside of it, even the mist. For a moment, starlight danced in the inky sky, and then his awesome power hit them hard.

The entire army collapsed, dead within seconds.

My jaw dropped, and for a moment, I could do nothing but stare at the fallen bodies. So many, and all it had taken was one burst of power from the Mist King. I slid my eyes his way. He'd fallen to his knees beside Toryn's body, his fists pounding the sand. Boudica flew in from the shadowy sky and settled on the Mist King's knee, curving toward him.

"I'm sorry you had to see that, little dove," Alastair said as he shoved his sword back into its sheath. "But you don't need to be scared. He would never use that power against you."

It took me a moment to get my jaw working again. I dropped my voice into a whisper. "It's like nothing I've ever seen. Why didn't he...?"

"Use it against the pookas? Or back in the village when the storm fae first came at us?"

I nodded.

"Kal's power is dangerous. He hasn't used the full strength of it like that in over three hundred years. The last time he did, well. You know what happened."

"The Great Rift," I murmured, understanding at once. His power was beyond anything I could have dreamed. Enough to crush entire armies.

"It's difficult for him to control, and the mists have gotten worse since that day he fought Oberon. He's worried something like the Great Rift will happen again. Or worse," Alastair continued. "Even when he holds back, he won't let us be anywhere near it." His lips flattened. "Normally, that is."

"He's alive!" The Mist King's shout tore through the mists.

I whirled toward his booming voice. He curled over his

friend, clasping his raised hand. With a gasp, I rushed toward them, Niamh and Alastair by my side. When we reached them, I noted Toryn's pained eyes, his grimace, the hiss between his clenched teeth. Smoke still curled off his body.

"Toryn." Niamh fell to the ground beside him and began to weep while Alastair jammed his fist into his mouth, pacing beside the group. The Mist King's body shuddered. He leaned down and whispered words to Toryn, words I couldn't hear.

I pressed my lips together, emotion blasting me like a sudden gust of wind. He was badly hurt. His wounds still gushed blood, and his skin looked like pieces had been burned away. But he was alive.

The fae clustered together, a circle of love and unbreakable bonds. I almost felt as if I should leave them alone to process all this. So, I drifted back over to the horses and rubbed Midnight's snout. He nickered in answer.

After a moment, Niamh drifted over to me, wiping the tears from her face. Alastair followed. He had a dark look in his eye, one I understood all too well. The storm fae had launched an attack on their kingdom. They'd almost killed their dearest friend. The perpetrators were dead, but that wouldn't be enough. The storm fae queen had likely sent them here. The Kingdom of Shadow would want to retaliate.

"We need to take Toryn back home," she said as she motioned for me to join them where Toryn had slumped back onto the ground. "He's going to be all right, but he has a long road ahead of him. Those are magical wounds. It's going to take time. There is no way he can continue on like this, and he certainly can't travel home by himself. We need to go with him."

My heart ached. "Of course."

"What about the...you know?" Alastair inclined his head toward me. The mission. The vow. Finding my family so that I could kill Oberon. To them, that likely mattered very little now. They had far greater things to worry about. Their friend was half-dead, and a war was brewing. It would not be long before the storm fae tried something else.

"Tessa and I will continue on to Itchen," the Mist King suddenly announced, his voice raw and hollow and *wrong*. "You two will return to the castle with Toryn, and I'll keep in touch with the communication stones. Alastair, you take charge while I'm gone. I trust you more than anyone else."

My breath stilled. I could hardly believe his words. "Are you sure that's what you want to do?"

"Don't argue with me, Tessa. I made a vow." He remained hunched over Toryn, clutching his sleeping friend's hand.

Alastair and Niamh exchanged a dark look before helping the Mist King lift Toryn onto the back of one of the horses. He cracked his eyes open for a moment, took the reins, and then slumped forward, wincing in pain. The Mist King murmured to his friend, his whispered words snatched away by the wind.

Then, he turned to his raven. "Go with them. Make sure they stay safe."

The bird cawed.

Niamh walked back over to me. I hugged my arms to my chest, unsure what to do now. I didn't want them to leave me with him, but I couldn't say that out loud. Not when they had to return their wounded friend home. It would be wrong of me to do anything but stand aside and let them go.

She gave me a strained smiled. "You be careful now, Tessa. And keep an eye on him."

"I'm pretty sure he's the one who's supposed to keep an eye on me."

She nodded, but then dropped her voice to a whisper. "Do me a favor, eh? For the next few days, could you just drop the Mist King thing? Use Kalen. All right?"

I heaved a sigh. There'd been something so satisfying about the clench of his jaw every time I'd called him by that name. He hated it with a ferocity that made me smile. But I saw where Niamh was coming from. He'd almost lost someone important to him. Maybe, just for a few days, I could soften my jabs.

I nodded.

Alastair handed me another chunk of bread and gave my cheek a pinch. "We'll see you soon, little dove. Be on the lookout for snakes, eh?"

"I'll do my best."

And then they were gone, riding off into the mists, Boudica following close behind. Their king watched them go, rage and pain burning in his eyes. My heart pounded out a frantic beat. This was exactly what I'd worried would happen. It was just me and him now, alone in the darkness.

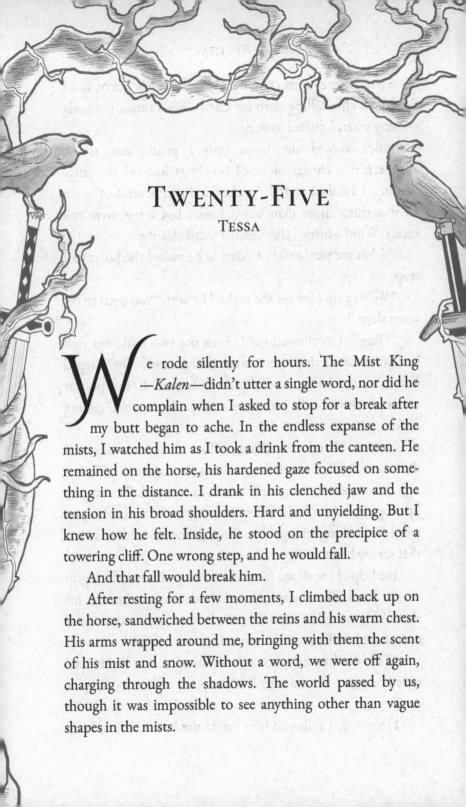

TWENTY-FIVE
TESSA

We rode silently for hours. The Mist King —*Kalen*—didn't utter a single word, nor did he complain when I asked to stop for a break after my butt began to ache. In the endless expanse of the mists, I watched him as I took a drink from the canteen. He remained on the horse, his hardened gaze focused on something in the distance. I drank in his clenched jaw and the tension in his broad shoulders. Hard and unyielding. But I knew how he felt. Inside, he stood on the precipice of a towering cliff. One wrong step, and he would fall.

And that fall would break him.

After resting for a few moments, I climbed back up on the horse, sandwiched between the reins and his warm chest. His arms wrapped around me, bringing with them the scent of his mist and snow. Without a word, we were off again, charging through the shadows. The world passed by us, though it was impossible to see anything other than vague shapes in the mists.

Several more hours crept by. My eyelids grew heavy, and I found my chin lolling onto my chest several times, my body starting when I drifted to sleep.

Kalen slowed the horse into a gentle gait as we approached a cluster of small buildings just off the path. Blearily, I blinked at the ramshackle huts. Several of them were nothing more than burnt husks, but a few were still intact. Wind whistled through the small clearing.

"What are we doing?" I asked as he pulled the horse to a stop.

"We'll camp here for the night," he said. "You need to get some sleep."

"Here?" I swallowed hard. Even the two buildings that had survived all these years were falling apart. The warped boards were rotting, and the roofs sagged. If the pookas attacked, those walls would not stop them from getting inside.

"It's an abandoned village, which means no one will disturb us." His voice held no room for argument. With a sigh, he dismounted and held out a gloved hand. Pressing my lips together, I took the offer. My fingers slid into his open palm. Something strange shot through me, an odd sensation that set my heart racing.

He helped me down from the horse and released his grip on my hand, like it was a sword about to slice through his skin. After tying his horse to a nearby post, he strode toward one of the buildings and motioned for me to follow.

"This used to be a home, and there's a bed inside," he called out over his shoulder. "It's as good a place to camp as any."

Frowning, I followed him inside the house. It had been

completely ransacked. The front room had once been a kitchen and living space. To the right, a round wooden table had been tipped to its side, one of the legs snapped in two. I couldn't see where the missing piece was, and I had a feeling I didn't want to know.

Soot stained the floorboards in the living space. Chairs were upturned, stuffing pulled out. Someone had carved words into one of the walls, but it was written in a script I didn't understand. Something about it seemed to reach out toward me, long fingers of darkness that scraped down my spine. Stomach twisting, I turned to the Mist King, wondering why in the name of light he wanted to spend a night here.

"I don't think this is a good idea," I said as he leaned over one of the chairs and flipped it back onto its legs. "This seems like the kind of place where dangerous criminals like to stay."

"Don't worry," he said in a low voice. "I won't let them touch you."

A chill swept down my spine. Kalen sat on the chair, placed his sword across his lap, and stared at the door. His jaw ticked.

"You're just going to sit there all night?" I asked. "I thought you said we needed to stop for some sleep."

"*You* need some sleep." He jerked his thumb over his shoulder at the half-open door leading into darkness. "There's only one bed in there. You take it. I'll keep watch."

"Um." My cheeks filled with heat as I turned on my heels and poked my head into the dark room. As he'd said, it held a small single cot. A pile of blankets were bunched up in one corner, and only a thin mattress covered the sagging frame. A window sat just above the bed, giving me a view of the unyielding darkness outside. I did not want to sleep in this place.

"Tessa."

I jumped, my heart jerking up into my throat. Kalen had suddenly appeared behind me. I hadn't even heard his footsteps. Sucking in a deep breath, I tried to settle my nerves.

His brows arched. "Are you all right?"

"This place creeps me out," I admitted.

With lips set into a grim line, he pulled a small blanket from his pack. "I thought you might want to place this on top of the mattress. And then you can use my cloak as a blanket to keep you warm."

Something in my heart clenched. That was strangely sweet. I might've been touched if it had come from anyone other than him. With a slight smile, I took the blanket and gave him a nod. "Thanks. Why are you being so nice to me?"

"Why wouldn't I be?"

I didn't know how to answer that without rubbing some salt in his wound, so I chose silence as the best option for now. "You're right. Thank you for this."

He leaned closer and brushed his thumb across my cheek, making my heart jolt. "You have blood on your face."

Frowning, I reached up and felt my cheek. Dried blood caked on my skin around a tender spot—where the branch had scratched me. It felt so strange. I'd been wounded before, of course, but I'd always healed fast, thanks to Oberon's protection. Most of the time, we didn't get scars. No marks were left behind unless Oberon wanted them to be.

I still didn't understand how he had the power to do any of that without his magic.

"I got cut in the forest," I said. "I'm fine."

He nodded. "Good. Now, get some sleep. I'll be in the other room if you need anything."

Kalen trailed out the door but didn't close it behind him. From within the cocoon of darkness, I watched him retake his seat facing away from me so that his eyes were on the front door. His back stiff, he curled his hand around the sword resting in his lap and waited. For what, I didn't want to ask. I'd already seen enough to know that we were in danger no matter where we went, and this little shack was far less safe than the cave had been. I would never forget what had happened there.

With my heart pounding in my chest, I spread Kalen's blanket across the mattress and climbed on top, pulling his cloak across my body. And then I stared at the far wall with wide-open eyes. My whole body felt tense. The truth was, I didn't want to be inside this room without him. I didn't feel safe. The window just over my head seemed like the perfect place for a pooka to smash through, so that it could drag its claws through my skin...

Tears in my eyes, I shuddered. I hated this. Being useless and fearful and no closer to finding Mother and Val. I needed to know how to fight. I'd always yearned for that skill, but I'd never realized how important it was until now. In this world, skill with a blade was far more useful than anything else. King Oberon had known that. And he'd ensured mortals would never have the tools and training needed for revolt.

"Tessa," Kalen murmured from the open door.

Heart jerking, I twisted onto my side to see his shadowy profile filling the entire frame. His sapphire eyes gleamed in the dark. My mouth went dry as he slowly stalked toward me.

"Is something wrong?" I asked.

"You tell me." He knelt beside the bed until his face was

right in my eyeline. Furrowed brows enhanced the tension in his face, but there was a softness in his eyes that shook me. "You're tossing and turning."

"I can't sleep in here," I admitted to him. "I'm too on edge. It feels like a pooka will crash through that window and kill me."

For a moment, I wanted to take the words back. I hated admitting any kind of weakness to this king who had once reveled in the misfortune of his enemies. The king who only cared about my life because I could do the one thing he could not. But then he glanced at the window and nodded.

"Understandable. What would make you feel safer?"

My heart pounded. I was *not* going to tell him that. It was embarrassing and also completely ridiculous. Even though I didn't trust him, the only way I'd feel safer was if he sat in this room instead of the one out there. Right beside me. Close enough, just in case the worst happened.

But he was the Mist King.

He'd sent his mists and monsters across all of Aesir.

He'd trapped Teine beneath Oberon's horrible rule. Everything was his fault. He'd destroyed cities! I should fear him.

Instead, he made me feel safe.

And I could never tell him that.

My breath caught. He gazed at me as if he were looking inside my mind to read my every thought. He reached out a hand, his fingers dragging along the edge of my shirt. Everything within me tightened. My heart roared in my ears. What was he doing? Why was he—?

Oh. His fingers whispered across the edge of my dagger, and then he pulled the weapon from where I'd hidden it in my shirt. He placed it in my hands.

"Hold onto this tonight. I'll start training you tomorrow." He pushed up from the bed and started to go.

"Wait," I breathed, but then I stopped myself.

With a frown, he paused and gazed down at me. "What is it, Tessa?"

My name curled off his tongue, almost making me shudder.

"Nothing. Never mind," I said tightly.

Without another word, he retreated to the other room. I gripped the dagger, holding it against my chest. It had been a nice idea, but it wasn't enough. Deep down, I knew that this little wooden thing would do nothing against a real threat. It was a safety blanket and nothing more.

Footsteps thumped on the hardwood floor. Kalen appeared by my side once more, dropping his chair right beside the bed. He settled into it without a word. Inwardly, I let out a strangled breath. He was right here now. If a pooka came through that window...well, it wouldn't stand a chance.

Still, I found it difficult to sleep. I was all too aware of his presence by my side. It was like he took up the entire room. Even when I turned my back to him, I could feel him.

Eventually, I finally found myself drifting away, only to be woken by the cold not long after. My teeth chattered. The temperature had dropped. Sniffling, I reached up to feel my nose, and my hands were like blocks of ice. Shivering, I clutched the cloak tighter around me, but it did little good. Without a fire, I would not get warm.

Kalen reached out and placed the back of his hand against my cheek. The bastard's hands were as warm as the sun in Teine. Another annoyingly unfair advantage the fae had over us. Turned out they didn't feel the cold quite the same.

"You're freezing," he said, his voice sounding worried. "Is the cloak not helping?"

"Doesn't seem so."

"Hmm." Without another word, he pushed up from the chair and climbed into the bed. Alarm jolted through me, making me forget about the cold for a moment.

"What are you doing?" I tried to squirm away from him, but he curved a strong arm over my body and pulled me against his chest. My heart nearly stopped. The warmth of him seeped into my bones, chasing the cold away.

"I'm making sure you're warm," he said gruffly.

Face to face, it was impossible not to look into his eyes. Up close, their sapphire color was even more breathtaking. Black lined the edges of them, making them pop. But there was pain in those eyes, too. A pain so deep that it looked as though something had broken his soul in two.

Without thinking, I caught myself asking, "Are you all right, Kalen?"

His lips parted. "You called me Kalen."

"Just for now," I whispered back. "Don't get used to it."

With a shake of his head, his eyes swept across mine. "Are *you* all right?"

"No."

He nodded. "Well, all right then. Neither am I. Toryn will heal, but he's in a lot of pain. He almost didn't make it. I...don't know what I would do without him in my life."

"I realize I haven't known him for very long, but...Toryn seems like a good soul."

"You have no idea," he ground out, closing his eyes. "Toryn stayed beside me when most of the world turned me into a monster. Someone to be hated and feared. Someone to be scorned. Even in my own kingdom, not everyone believed I was worthy of trust for a long time. But it's more than that. Toryn is good to everyone. He goes out of his way to help those who need it. Those bastards just committed an act of war."

My heart pounded. It was the most emotion he'd ever shown me. About anything. And his words had set fire to a question in my mind, one that had been a little spark for the past few days but was growing almost impossible to ignore now.

What exactly had happened all those years ago? If King Oberon had lied to us about so much, what else had he said that was untrue?

But most importantly, had the Mist King *really* burned down those human cities?

"You really didn't do it, did you?" I whispered to him. "You didn't kill thousands of innocent mortals in the human kingdoms beyond the sea."

For a moment, I thought he might pull away. Instead, his arm around me tightened. "Tell me, Tessa. Whose power stems from light and flames? And whose power stems from mist?"

I sucked in a sharp breath. Even though I'd begun to suspect it, hearing those words come out of his mouth shook my very soul. All my life, I'd been taught that the Mist King was the enemy to be feared. Never cross that bridge. Never step foot in the mists. Because he'd sneak up behind you and gobble you up. You'd never be seen again.

Stay on the right side of the chasm, do what you're told, and you'll be safe. The Mist King can never get to you while you're under Oberon's protection.

It had all been a lie.

"Those are Oberon's powers," I whispered to him, heart pounding so hard I nearly shook from the force of it.

"*Were*," Kalen said firmly. "They *were* his powers."

"Was he the one who did it?" My voice faltered. "He destroyed those human kingdoms?"

"No." Kalen shook his head. "Those were just lies, likely woven together to make you scared of me. All those human kingdoms still exist. My army did destroy villages in the Kingdom of Light when we invaded, though. Like this one. I wished they hadn't, but the war was...brutal."

"Why didn't you explain that before?" I asked him, my hands fisting around the blanket.

"I tried. You wouldn't listen to me, Tessa," he said with a sigh. "In fact, I'm surprised you believe me now. Until today, you've insisted on calling me by that name he gave me. There was a part of me that thought you might decide not to kill him after all. That you'd want to undo our vow."

"Oh, I would never decide that." My whole body started shaking, and before I realized what I was saying, I whispered, "You don't understand. He killed my sister. And then he dropped her head right at my feet."

My voice broke off, my heart thundering against my ribs. I'd never said it out loud. I'd never even whispered it to anyone. But as I'd listened to Kalen's story, the words had built up on my tongue, begging to be spilled, like chaotic paint across a canvas.

There was no taking it back now. Even if I found a broom and brushed all the paint back inside, the color had already seeped into the canvas. It would leave behind a stain, a memory I could no longer turn away from. And now Kalen could see it, too.

Even if he wasn't a monster, I still couldn't trust him. I couldn't trust anyone.

Kalen drew in a long, slow breath. After a moment, he lifted his arm from my body and cupped my cheek. Every single cell in my body zeroed in on where his skin touched mine. An impossible heat spread through me.

"I am so sorry, Tessa." Anger flashed through his eyes. "You deserve none of what he's done to you."

I shook my head. "You're wrong. I tried to kill him, and he retaliated. Nellie's death is all my fault."

"No, it isn't," he said, his voice rough and full of emotion. "It's all *him*, and I would kill him for what he's done to you if I could. I would rip his head off his body. And then I would feed the rest of him to the mists. He would be nothing but ash when I got done with him."

I sucked in a rattling breath.

His hand slid along my neck before he wound his arm around me once more. He tugged me a little closer. Heart hammering, I tried to focus on anything other than the heated look in his eye, the strength of his chest against mine, the closeness of his lips.

He was just trying to keep me warm. That was all. And I definitely didn't want it to be more. Yes, I'd discovered he wasn't *exactly* the monster I'd always believed him to be, but that changed very little. He'd still captured me. He'd still lied to me.

"Tell me about her," he murmured.

"My sister?"

"Yes. What was she like?"

Surprised he'd ask, I waited a moment before answering. But it didn't take long for the floodgates to open. I told him about the time Nellie had grabbed my hand and jumped into the mud, back when she'd been only five and hadn't discovered dresses and boys. I recounted the time she'd learned a dance for that damn King Oberon song and wanted to teach me every move. Memories of her beautiful life filled me up, and I told story after story until my words grew hushed and a warm relaxation finally settled over me.

I drifted to sleep with her name on my tongue and Kalen's steady strength by my side.

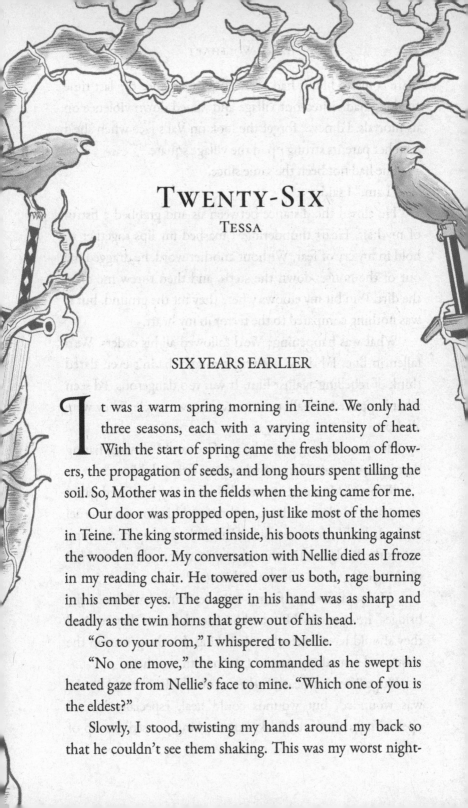

TWENTY-SIX
TESSA

SIX YEARS EARLIER

I t was a warm spring morning in Teine. We only had
three seasons, each with a varying intensity of heat.
With the start of spring came the fresh bloom of flowers, the propagation of seeds, and long hours spent tilling the
soil. So, Mother was in the fields when the king came for me.

Our door was propped open, just like most of the homes
in Teine. The king stormed inside, his boots thunking against
the wooden floor. My conversation with Nellie died as I froze
in my reading chair. He towered over us both, rage burning
in his ember eyes. The dagger in his hand was as sharp and
deadly as the twin horns that grew out of his head.

"Go to your room," I whispered to Nellie.

"No one move," the king commanded as he swept his
heated gaze from Nellie's face to mine. "Which one of you is
the eldest?"

Slowly, I stood, twisting my hands around my back so
that he couldn't see them shaking. This was my worst night-

mare come to life. It had been over a year since the last time the king had visited our village and rained down violence on us mortals. I'd never forget the look on Val's face when she'd seen her parents strung up in the village square.

She had not been the same since.

"I am," I said.

He closed the distance between us and grabbed a fistful of my hair. Heart thundering, I mashed my lips together to hold in my cry of fear. Without another word, he dragged me out of the house, down the steps, and then threw me onto the dirt. Pain bit my elbows where they hit the ground, but it was nothing compared to the terror in my heart.

What was happening? We'd followed all his orders. We'd fallen in line. I'd done nothing wrong. I hadn't even dared think of rebelling against him. It was too dangerous. I'd seen what happened to Val's parents, to my own uncle. They were all dead.

He spat on the ground by my face, and I winced, hating that I was so weak. "I know what your father did."

"What?" My mind stuttered. I lifted my head and gazed up at him. He leaned down and twisted his lips into a cruel smile. It had been a year since Father had escaped, running across the Bridge to Death and vanishing into the mists. Had the king only found out about this now?

"My soldiers just found him, coming back over the bridge," he sneered. "Him and his friend. Seems they realized they should have listened to their king. It's dangerous in the mists, and something attacked them both out there."

Hope lifted my heart. Father was back? It sounded like he was wounded, but wounds could heal, especially here. I opened my mouth to speak, but the king pressed the tip of his dagger against my lips. "No speaking. Your father defied me. Do you know what I do to traitors?"

I shuddered. Unwanted memories flew through my mind like circling vultures that searched for a way to swallow me whole. So much blood. So many vacant eyes. If the king had decided my father was a traitor, he was dead. I slumped, shoulders bent like a sagging roof, a tear burning down my cheek.

"That's right." He roughly grabbed my arms and flipped me onto my stomach. My breath rushed out of me as the weight of him pressed against the back of my legs. The dirt scraped against my face and the cloying taste of bile clogged my throat. He'd killed my father, but it hadn't been enough. He was going to kill me, too.

King Oberon grabbed my tunic and ripped it open, exposing my back. The sharp tip of his dagger dug into my skin, right at the base of my spine. I sucked in a rattling breath, too terrified to do anything but lie there like an insect trapped beneath the boot of a giant.

He leaned down and hissed into my ear, his breath saturated with the scent of lavender. "What was your father doing out there? Tell me what you know."

I squeezed my eyes tight. "Getting far away from you."

"How dare you!"

Brutal pain lanced through me. Oberon scraped his blade through my skin, dragging the steel in a line down my lower back. I screamed, thrashing against the ground, but that only made it worse. Black dots stormed my vision. Darkness called for me, welcoming me into its sweet embrace.

Two small bare feet appeared just before my eyes. I blinked and twisted my head to see Nellie standing beside me, her entire body trembling. She clutched the green handle of our broom and waved it at the fae king.

"Stop it!" Tears ran down her face. "Let go of her!"

My heart nearly stopped. The blade on my back vanished, and the king's weight shifted.

"No." I tried to flip over, but he still had me pinned to the ground. "She's just a child. She doesn't know what she's doing. Nellie, go back inside the house and stay there no matter what happens."

"Just a child?" the king asked in a deadly calm. "How old?"

"Seventeen," I said. "But only just."

"Hmm. Not truly a child." Tension pounded my skull as the king dragged the moment out for far too long. And then he relented. "But I'll spare her if you take on her punishment as well."

"Yes, of course," I said without even missing a beat.

"No, don't," Nellie said, her chest heaving from her sobs. "Leave her alone. Please."

"Nellie." With my cheek still pressed against the dirt, I looked up and met her eyes. She looked so scared. Terror made her lips wobble and her hands shake, and her entire body looked as though it might crack into pieces, like shattered glass. "Go back inside. This will be over soon."

"Listen to her, love," one of the villagers called out from down the street. Several others whispered their agreement. We had an audience now. And none of them would do anything. They couldn't.

Nellie choked out one last sob, whirled on her feet, and raced up the steps. She stopped just inside the open door, still holding tight to that broom. The brown bristles shook like branches in the wind.

The king turned back toward me with a wicked grin. He shoved one hand against the back of my neck, holding me down. His knife dug into me once more. "That first one was for your father. This one is for your sister."

The blade sliced through me, carving me up like a slab of meat. I screamed as the pain tore through me, as hatred boiled in my veins like acid, burning every part of me. My sister's eyes never left my face. I kept my own locked on hers, finding a strength there I did not know I had. I would get through this. As long as he didn't kill me, I'd soon heal. And then this pain would be nothing more than a distant memory.

But I would never let go of this hatred.

Oberon drew the blade away from my throbbing back and dropped it onto the ground. A river of blood wound through the dirt beside me. His clothes rustled, and the sound of a snapping string followed.

Sweat dripped into my eyes. "What are you doing?"

"Be quiet," he demanded.

Another rustle sounded, and then liquid fire flowed across my wounds. The flames consumed me, lashing my entire body. The pain was so great that I could barely think around it. The fire licked at the wounds, blazed past them, and then spread deeper, burning up everything inside of me, including my heart.

I flailed against the dirt, gasping for breath. Darkness flooded my vision. Death called for me, and I no longer had the strength to turn away from it. My hands stilled as my body went limp.

The last thing I heard was the king's smug voice saying, "Just as I thought."

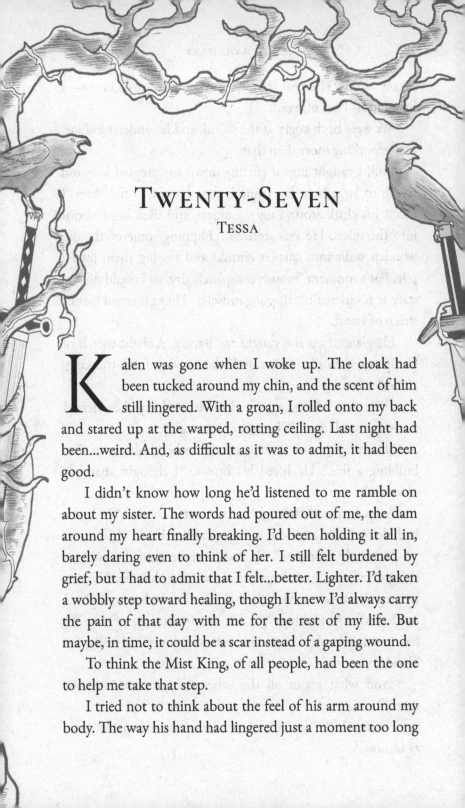

TWENTY-SEVEN
TESSA

Kalen was gone when I woke up. The cloak had been tucked around my chin, and the scent of him still lingered. With a groan, I rolled onto my back and stared up at the warped, rotting ceiling. Last night had been...weird. And, as difficult as it was to admit, it had been good.

I didn't know how long he'd listened to me ramble on about my sister. The words had poured out of me, the dam around my heart finally breaking. I'd been holding it all in, barely daring even to think of her. I still felt burdened by grief, but I had to admit that I felt...better. Lighter. I'd taken a wobbly step toward healing, though I knew I'd always carry the pain of that day with me for the rest of my life. But maybe, in time, it could be a scar instead of a gaping wound.

To think the Mist King, of all people, had been the one to help me take that step.

I tried not to think about the feel of his arm around my body. The way his hand had lingered just a moment too long on my cheek. The heat in his eyes when he'd gazed at me—a heat I must have misread.

We were both angry at the world, and he understood me. It was nothing more than that.

Still, I caught myself patting down my tangled hair and trying to straighten my tunic before I went to find him. I threw his cloak around my shoulders, and then stepped out into the mists. He was shirtless, chopping some of the old wooden walls into smaller chunks and tossing them into a pile. For a moment, mouth completely dry, all I could do was stare at his incredible rippling muscles. They glistened from a sheen of sweat.

He glanced up and caught me staring. A slight twitch of his lip was the only indication he knew what I was thinking. "Good morning."

"Morning." Holding the cloak around my shoulders, I moved toward him. "What are you doing?"

"Found this axe in one of the other houses, so I'm building a fire." He lifted his brows. "I thought that was obvious."

A flush spread through my neck and cheeks. "Isn't it a bad idea to build a fire out in the open like this?"

"It's early morning." He shoved the end of the axe into the ground and leaned against the wooden handle. My eyes tiptoed down to his bare chest again. For the love of light, I needed to stop looking. "Pookas sleep this time of day. We have a solid window now where they're not out hunting for blood."

"And what about all the other dangerous things out there?"

He smirked. "I'm the most dangerous thing out here right now."

Another burst of heat filled my cheeks. *Come on, Tessa.* What was wrong with me? One night in the same bed with him, and I'd completely lost sight of reality. I just hoped he couldn't tell.

He continued, thankfully, saving me from having to respond. "We'll break our fast and then we'll have a training session."

"A training session?" I liked the sound of that.

"And then we'll be on to Itchen. We should reach it by the end of the day."

I took a step closer, my heart in my throat. "Itchen? That's where you think Mother and Val might be."

A strange expression flashed across his face. "I don't want you to get your hopes up, Tessa."

Again, the way he spoke my name curled through me.

"They might be there—it's a good city for humans. But there's no guarantee." He heaved up the axe and got back to work. The crack of splitting wood rang through the silence, filling up my head with distant memories of a time, seven years ago, when the king had allowed the mortals of Teine to build a few new homes. He'd even given us a single axe to use under strict supervision. Father had helped.

But thinking of him hurt almost as much as thinking about Nellie, especially because that day had not ended well. A few of the humans had taken a break in the pub, resting their weary feet and tipping ale down their parched throats. The fae soldiers had thought the humans had sneaked away to plot against them. So, the soldiers had slaughtered them all, and then they'd hung the traitors' bodies up in the village square. One of those humans had been my uncle, my father's brother. Both of Val's parents were killed, too. My father had vanished into the mists not long after that. He was gone for a full year.

And when he'd finally returned to the Kingdom of Light, Oberon had taken his head.

After Kalen built the fire, and we had a small breakfast of pooka meat and a heel of bread, he pulled a pale gray gemstone from his pocket. He extracted metal tongs from his pack and used it to hold the gemstone over the flames.

"What are you doing?" I asked, pulling the cloak around my shoulders to ward off the cold.

"Checking on Toryn." The gemstone turned black. "Niamh."

A moment later, Niamh's face appeared on the gemstone. I gasped, leaning closer. She was as clear as day, and I could even see the walls of the castle behind her. I'd never seen anything like it before.

"How is Toryn? Is he all right?" Kalen demanded.

"He's fine. We reached Dubnos without any issue, and he's healing in his quarters."

Kalen visibly relaxed, the tension in his body unwinding like a spool of thread. "And the city itself?"

"No sign of any storm fae," Niamh replied. "Alastair sent some scouts down to the border. They should be back this afternoon."

Kalen nodded. "We'll reach Itchen today. Keep me informed."

The gemstone cracked just as Niamh's face vanished from the surface. Kalen dropped the instruments into his pack, his gaze distant, his lips a thin line.

"That's good news, isn't it?" I asked.

"It is. I just hate not knowing what the storm fae are

planning. They didn't attack us for no reason. But don't you worry about that. It's time for you to train."

Kalen stood, drew a circle in the sand, and told me to stand in the middle of it. I did as he said, my wooden blade clutched in my right hand. He sized me up and then shook his head.

"You're very tense and rigid."

I rolled my eyes. "Thanks."

"You need to relax more." He crossed the circular line and held out his hand for my dagger. Hesitatingly, I passed it to him. Closing his eyes, he rolled back his shoulders, and then sank into a crouch. There was something so graceful and natural about his movements. He didn't clutch the dagger with fisted hands. He was poised to strike, but he wasn't tense. Kalen screamed strength and power, his muscular form impossible and deadly and—

His eyes flipped open, that dark gaze meeting mine. A little tremor went through my gut. "Understand?"

I loosed a breath. "Yes."

He passed the dagger back to me. As I took it, our fingers brushed. Our gazes suddenly locked. Something flashed in his eyes that called to me. Instinctively, I leaned toward him, even as my mind screamed at me to stop.

There was just something so...mesmerizing about the way he moved.

What are you doing? a little voice shouted in the back of my head.

I shuddered as he pulled his hand away. With a slight smile, he murmured, "Your turn, Tessa."

Knees shaking, I tried to mimic what he'd shown me. Fingers relaxed, shoulders loose but firm. But I still felt the tension rattling inside me. My entire body was coiled so tightly, it might snap at any moment.

Strong hands wrapped around my shoulders, kneading them. My eyes flipped open, and his face was right there. Only two inches from mine. Our breaths mingled in the mists. Heat tore through me, chasing away the last shred of logical thought.

"What are you doing?" I whispered.

"You're too tense. Staying calm and collected in battle is one of the biggest advantages you can ever get." His gaze dipped to my lips, and then snapped back up to my eyes. "Oberon is passionate. He's full of rage and often does things without a second thought. You need to be better than that."

"And you don't feel passion?" I couldn't help but ask, eyes still locked on his as he continued to rub my shoulders.

His chest rumbled. "I feel too much passion. It's what twisted everything into what it is now. If I'd stayed in control of my emotions better, I never would have thrown the full strength of my power at Albyria. I was trying to stop your king from destroying my army, but I did too much, and it caused all of this. I did what you've always accused me of—trapped your people with Oberon."

"At least you stopped him from winning and bringing back the gods."

His hands stilled as his eyes searched mine, scouring for answers I didn't know if I had. "I thought you hated me for what I did. I thought you wished it had never happened."

I blew out a breath. "I did. But I think maybe I was wrong."

Kalen pulled himself up tall and dropped his hands to his sides. "Explain."

"I wasn't told the truth about you. Everything you've

said to me paints a very different portrait than the one I was given. You're not the enemy of the world, Kalen. I see that now."

He ground his teeth and glanced away. "You've gotten the wrong idea about me. Again. I caused *all of this*, Tessa. I need you to know that. My armies did attack villages and cities on our way to take down Oberon. And I want you to see that I would do it all again if given the chance. I'd drench the world in mist and shadow and all the danger that lurks within it. Anything to trap Oberon and stop him from bringing back the gods. That makes me a villain."

The pain in his voice ripped through me. With a shaky breath, I stepped closer to him and took his hand. He jerked his head toward me in shock. I could tell that he thought I'd be angry at him for what he'd said, but it was the opposite. He'd make himself the villain if that meant saving the world from the gods. I could not hate him for that.

"I understand what you tried to do, even if I don't like the result of it."

He swallowed and glanced away. "Tessa, I..."

"I'm not sure I trust you, but I don't hate you." I frowned at his profile. "Can you at least look at me?"

Jaw clenching, he dragged his eyes toward mine. Shadows churned in the depths of the blue, the softness I'd seen before driven away by whatever was going on inside his head.

Kalen pulled my hands up toward his heart. I could feel it beating against my skin, the steady *thump, thump, thump* that had kept me company all night. The scent of him curled around me as he tugged me a step closer. My heart racing, I tipped back my head, scared to find out what he would say or do next.

His palm swept across my shoulder before cupping my

cheek. I shuddered as his thumb brushed across my chin. He searched my eyes, looking surprised at what he found in them.

"Tessa, you are—"

A bloodthirsty shriek shattered the silence. Heart jolting, I stumbled away from Kalen and whirled toward the thickening shadows that surrounded the abandoned village. Through the haze of the mists, I couldn't see a damn thing, not even the vague outline of whatever had made that noise.

I glanced up at Kalen. His hand had gone to his sword.

"Please tell me that was a fluffy rabbit."

Kalen took my shoulders and shoved me behind him. "Afraid not. That was a pooka call. One has picked up our scent and told others where we are."

I choked on my fear. "I thought they slept this time of day."

"They usually do," he said grimly. "It seems things are changing in the mists. Stay behind me. No matter what happens."

Heart rattling in my chest, I clutched my wooden dagger and gazed across the silent expanse of nebulous mist. Nothing made a sound, not even Kalen. He held his sword before him, shifting to the left and then the right, but his footsteps were silent. Kalen was like the darkness itself.

Another wail crashed down on the village like shards of ice.

Bracing myself, I cast a glance over my shoulder at the little shack. The front door hung open, swaying in the wind. A shadow moved behind the window.

I shifted closer to Kalen, my shoulder brushing his back. He tensed against me.

"It's in the house," I whispered.

Whatever was inside must have heard me, because it threw itself against the glass window. Shards exploded toward us. I held up my arm to block my face and sharp spikes dug into my skin, slicing through the tunic.

Kalen shoved me behind him and whirled toward the wolf-like monster stalking toward us, its matted fur thick with sprinkles of glass. It didn't even seem to notice the wound on its snout, its eyes locked on my face, churning with a hatred that shook my soul.

Its claws punched the sandy ground. One step after another, saliva dripping off elongated teeth.

"Kalen," I whispered as he angled his sword at the monster. "It looks like it wants to eat me."

"Don't worry," he said in a low growl. "It would have to kill me before I would let it take you from me."

A shudder went through me at his words. I knew he was only talking about saving my life so that I might do what I'd promised. He didn't truly care for me. But still...those words wormed their way into my heart and heated my chest.

The beast roared and leapt toward us. I stumbled back as Kalen took a swing, his brutal sword arcing through the mists. The steel sang when the blade made contact. It sank into the pooka's fur, cutting down to marrow and bone. Blood splashed onto the sand like droplets of vibrant paint.

A claw sliced through my back, pain blinding me. I stumbled forward with a horrified scream as another beast leapt before me, its jaw gaping so wide that I could see rows of sharp teeth. The pain took me to my knees, and my teeth knocked together from the force of my fall.

I stared up into the dark eyes of the beast as the poison of its claw spread through me, numbing my mind, dulling my eyes, dragging me away to a world where I no longer existed.

I'd fought so hard for so long. Every horrible thing the world had thrown at me, I'd somehow survived, but the flickering flame inside me started to dull. Ashes consumed me, snuffing out that spark.

This was the end for me.

I'd never find Mother and Val. I'd never again look up into a bright sky filled with puffy white clouds. I'd never see my home again.

A horrifying growl cut through my dark thoughts. Kalen appeared just behind the beast and swung his sword. He sliced the pooka in half. The beast thudded to the ground beside me, a broken thing. Kalen hurried toward me with a look of pure fear on his usually stoic face.

I reached up as he roared. Then the shadows finally claimed me.

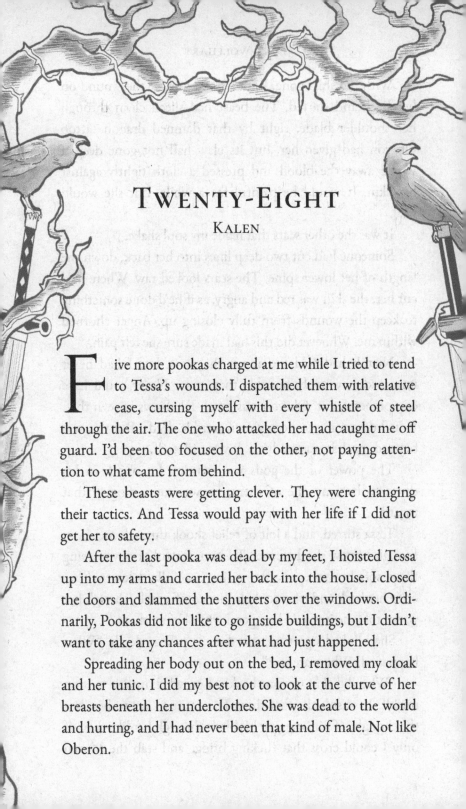

TWENTY-EIGHT

KALEN

Five more pookas charged at me while I tried to tend to Tessa's wounds. I dispatched them with relative ease, cursing myself with every whistle of steel through the air. The one who attacked her had caught me off guard. I'd been too focused on the other, not paying attention to what came from behind.

These beasts were getting clever. They were changing their tactics. And Tessa would pay with her life if I did not get her to safety.

After the last pooka was dead by my feet, I hoisted Tessa up into my arms and carried her back into the house. I closed the doors and slammed the shutters over the windows. Ordinarily, Pookas did not like to go inside buildings, but I didn't want to take any chances after what had just happened.

Spreading her body out on the bed, I removed my cloak and her tunic. I did my best not to look at the curve of her breasts beneath her underclothes. She was dead to the world and hurting, and I had never been that kind of male. Not like Oberon.

With her shirt gone, I got a good look at the wound on her back and started. The beast had sliced clean through her shoulder blade, right by that damned dragon tattoo Oberon had given her, but its claw had not gone deep. I wiped away the blood and pressed a cloth tightly against her skin. It would be painful for a while, but she would heal.

It was the other scars that made my soul shake.

Someone had cut two deep lines into her back, down the length of her lower spine. The scars looked raw. Where he'd cut her, the skin was red and angry, as if he'd done something to keep the wounds from fully closing up. Anger churned within me. Whoever did this had made sure she felt pain.

Niamh had told me about the scars, but I had never imagined how truly horrible they were. Never could have comprehended it. Oberon was cruel. I'd always known that. It had driven me to do my own terrible deeds. But this was beyond cruel. It was madness. It was evil itself.

The power of the gods was twisting his mind. In his quest to become one of them, he was succeeding in that regard.

Tessa stirred, and a jolt of relief shook through me. Even though I knew she'd recover, I'd been fearful of never seeing those soft brown eyes open again. Carefully, I lowered her onto her back and tried to make her comfortable, though her wince told me it would be a good while before that.

She blinked up at me, her face as pale as death. "What happened? Where are we?"

"Who did that to your back?" I growled, unable to stop myself. It wasn't the first thing I'd meant to say to her, but the thought of him digging his blade through her like that...if only I could cross that fucking bridge and stab the Mortal

Blade into his heart myself. Instead, I would have to be satisfied with Tessa doing the deed.

She swallowed hard, and pain flickered through her eyes, as if the memory itself was too much for her to think about.

"Never mind," I said quickly. "You don't need to tell me. We're—"

"You know who it was," she said in a scratchy voice. "Oberon did this."

My heart hardened at her words.

"It happened six years ago." She winced and shifted slightly on the mattress in a struggle to get comfortable. "My father defied him. Oberon took his head, but that wasn't enough for him. He punished me, too. And now, he's forced me to become his bride. He killed my maidservant and my sister, and then he spent an entire month breaking me apart so that I would not have the will to fight him anymore. He destroyed me, Kal. If you and Morgan had not gotten me out of there...if you hadn't done what you did, I would be wed to that monster, so broken that I never would have recovered."

My chest expanded as emotions churned within me. I hated seeing her like this—her voice trembling, her eyes full of pain.

"What happened out there after I passed out?" she asked again. So, I told her. Her face paled as I recounted the events, and when I mentioned the new wound, she stiffened. It would be another scar to add to the others.

"It felt like poison," she said when I was finished explaining. "Like the pooka's venom had gotten into my blood."

I nodded. "They have venom in their teeth and claws that can stun you. It's how they're able to attack so successfully."

Her body shook as she loosed a breath. "So the venom can't kill me?"

"No," I said quietly. "You're going to be fine, Tessa. No thanks to me."

"You couldn't have known that one would sneak up behind us."

"No, but I could have guessed it. I should have put you someplace safe." My hands fisted at the thought of what might have happened if things had gone differently. She could be dead right now.

She reached out a hand and brushed my knee. Everything within me stiffened at her touch. I flicked my gaze down at where her fingers curled against the side of my leg, and for a moment, the only thing in the world that existed was this. It shouldn't have unnerved me so. It was just a hand—only the slightest touch. But it caused something to stir deep within me.

She swallowed hard and then snatched her hand back as if she'd shocked herself. I shouldn't have been surprised. I was the bloody Mist King. Why would anyone want to touch a monster like me?

Her cheeks brightened as she twisted her face away. "I'm safest by your side, Kalen. If you'd put me somewhere else— like this house—they would have killed me. And you would have been too far away to do anything about it."

"Regardless of all that, we can't stay here much longer. I know you're in pain, but we need to move on before other pookas smell the blood of their brethren on the winds."

She winced. "I want to keep going, but I have to admit, I don't feel wonderful."

"If I could share my healing powers with you, I would not hesitate for even a second to save you from this pain, Tessa."

Her eyes shone as she gazed up at me, a slight smile

tugging at her lips. It was so different from how she'd looked at me only a week before that it made my gut twist. She said she understood why I'd loosed the full strength of my power on Albyria, but I couldn't even forgive my damn self. I'd ruined this entire kingdom, and I would do it all over again. How could she, having been trapped behind the chasm with Oberon all this time, look past that?

And now I was sending her right back in there to finish something I should've been taking care of myself.

I knew what she was walking into, even if she didn't realize it herself. Even with the Mortal Blade, trying to kill King Oberon was a dangerous mission. He didn't have full access to his powers, but he was still strong and difficult to kill. He surrounded himself with soldiers who worshipped at his feet.

Tessa was just as likely to die as she was to sink that blade into his heart.

It was a fact I'd been wrestling with for days. How could I send her in there, knowing she might not make it out alive?

"Kalen?" she asked, whispering up at me. "What's wrong?"

I ground my teeth together. Right now, none of that mattered. She wouldn't be sneaking back into Albyria until we'd found her family, and that could take weeks or even months, especially if we needed to return to Dubnos soon. I still had time to train her. Or find another way.

"Nothing." I shook my head. "I'm just sorry we'll have to travel with you injured and bleeding, but as soon as we reach Itchen, you'll be safer. There will be plenty of comfortable beds where you can rest, too. I daresay there will even be some clean sheets."

"Sounds luxurious after this. The pookas don't go there?"

Rubbing my chin, I glanced at the shutters that blocked my view of the churning mists beyond the village. "They never have before, but things are changing. Don't let down your guard. They might very well follow us there."

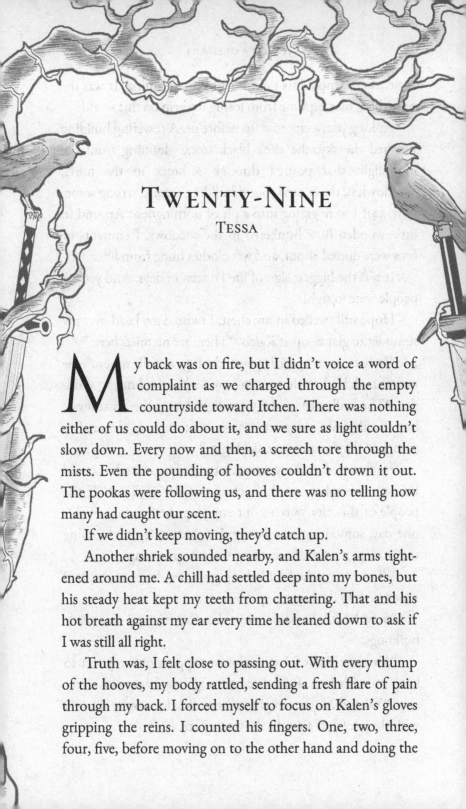

TWENTY-NINE
TESSA

My back was on fire, but I didn't voice a word of complaint as we charged through the empty countryside toward Itchen. There was nothing either of us could do about it, and we sure as light couldn't slow down. Every now and then, a screech tore through the mists. Even the pounding of hooves couldn't drown it out. The pookas were following us, and there was no telling how many had caught our scent.

If we didn't keep moving, they'd catch up.

Another shriek sounded nearby, and Kalen's arms tightened around me. A chill had settled deep into my bones, but his steady heat kept my teeth from chattering. That and his hot breath against my ear every time he leaned down to ask if I was still all right.

Truth was, I felt close to passing out. With every thump of the hooves, my body rattled, sending a fresh flare of pain through my back. I forced myself to focus on Kalen's gloves gripping the reins. I counted his fingers. One, two, three, four, five, before moving on to the other hand and doing the same. As the moments ticked by, I kept counting. It was the only thing that kept me from losing my grip on this world.

At long last, a city rose up before us. A towering building brushed the sky, the sleek black stone gleaming from the moonlight that poured through a break in the mists. Windowless, the central round building seemed wrong somehow, as if I were gazing into a pit of nothingness. Around it, little wooden huts hunkered in the shadows. Remnants of fires were dotted about, and wet clothes hung from lines.

It was the biggest sign of life I'd seen in days. And yet, no people were in sight.

Hope still swelled in my chest. I twisted my head over my shoulder to glance up at Kalen. "There are no mists here."

"Itchen is a special place during a full moon," he murmured, his breath caressing my neck. I tried not to shudder. "The brilliance of the moonlight burns the mists away, but it only lasts a day and comes twice a year, if that. I'm surprised they're not out enjoying it."

He frowned, and my stomach twisted in on itself. I could hear his unspoken words as clear as a day in Teine. If the people of this city weren't out enjoying the freedom of this one day, something was wrong. I closed my eyes, clutching the cloak in my fists. Something was *always* wrong.

When we reached a hitching post, we dismounted, and Kalen tied up the horse.

"Stay here," he said before heading toward the silent buildings.

"Absolutely not," I said, almost tripping over my feet to keep up with him. Pain sliced through my back with every step. "Val and Mother might be here. Besides, you're the one with the sword. If a pooka shows up here, I—"

"Pookas can't leave the mists," he threw over his shoulder, carrying on without even a moment of hesitation.

I scowled. "Yeah, and they don't like going into buildings, and don't tend to sneak up on you, either, right? They're doing things now that they didn't do before."

He came to a sudden stop, whirled toward me, and placed his hands firmly on my shoulders. My lips parted, heat creeping through my chest. I was so focused on the strength in his fingers, the heat of his touch, I almost didn't hear his words.

"This is not like that, Tessa," he said, a roughness creeping into his voice. "If they step out of the mists, the moonlight will burn them to death. So, even if they threw all caution to the wind and tried to attack this place, they'd die before they reached you. You can relax. They can't get to you here."

But I couldn't relax. Not with his hands on me.

"I'd still rather go with you than wait here."

His eyes softened, and my heart did something strange in response. I wasn't sure I'd ever seen him make that expression before. Almost as though he...cared. My eyes betrayed me as they drifted down to his full lips. For a moment, neither one of us said a word. I wasn't sure I even breathed.

"All right," he finally said. "Stay with me, but brace yourself. There's a hint of blood on the air, and you might not like what we find."

Fear for Val and my mother rushed through me.

Had they come here, hoping to find shelter from the mists? Had anyone been inside these homes? Or had they been a part of whatever had happened here? My heart beat painfully beneath my ribs. What if they'd somehow made their way here, but then the worst had happened? The pookas had attacked them just like they'd targeted us.

"Stay close," Kalen murmured as we slowly stalked toward the nearest building. Its front door was wide open, hinges creaking as it swung in the steady breeze. I shivered beneath the cloak and tried to find the strength inside myself to carry on, knowing that my worst nightmare might lie just beyond that doorframe.

Mother and Val dead, ripped apart by vicious claws.

Nausea churned in my gut. If we found them in there, I didn't know how I'd have the strength to carry on.

We went up the small set of creaking steps. Kalen hovered in the doorway just in front of me, wincing when a gruesome stench wafted toward us. I threw my hand over my mouth and stumbled back down the steps, curving forward as I vomited on the ground. Tears streamed from my eyes, a horrible knowledge twisting me apart.

I knew what death smelled like. King Oberon had made certain of that.

Steps creaked as Kalen came to my side. He lifted my hair from my shoulders and pulled it back, waiting silently while I composed myself. Gripping my knees, still curved forward, I sucked deep breaths in through my nose and blew them out through my mouth. Slowly, the nausea passed, even as my heart raged like a bonfire.

"Thanks," I whispered, finally daring to stand straight. Kalen met my eyes as he loosened his grip on my hair. "You didn't have to do that."

"You should braid it," he said gruffly. "Better for fighting."

I ground my teeth and glanced away. "I don't know how. Nellie used to do it for me."

Kalen was silent for a moment before he said, "I can go inside without you. There's no reason why you should have to see this."

"Yes, there is," I said, nearly choking on my words. "You don't know what Val or my mother look like. How will you know if it's them in there or not?"

"You are brave," he murmured before striding back up the steps and waiting for me just outside the door. I appreciated that he didn't try to talk me out of it or insist I stay down here. I could tell by the look on his face that he understood, that he'd do the same damn thing if he were in my shoes.

Gulping air into my lungs, I nodded to myself and followed him inside the building. Shadows crammed the small space, making it difficult to see much. I waited for a moment to let my eyes adjust while Kalen began a slow stalk around the room.

As I settled into the darkness, I had to put a hand to my mouth to hold back the scream. Blood painted the walls and the floorboards. Bodies littered the ground, arms and legs ripped from their torsos. Some of them looked half-eaten.

There were at least a dozen of them. Men and women, old and young. They were all dead.

Squeezing my hands into fists, I whispered through the room, not daring to touch a thing. Revulsion twisted through me as I peered down at each tormented face, searching for two familiar sets of eyes. Faces I had longed to see for so long, but now prayed to the sun that I wouldn't find—not here.

After I'd gone through the entire room, I went outside and sat on a stump far enough away that I could no longer smell the stench. Val and Mother were not here. Not in this building, at least. But that did not make the horror any less real. These people had suffered. Their lives had been cut short.

All because of those monsters. The same monsters who were determined to do the very same thing to me. The moonlight must have chased them away before they'd finish their meal, but it had been too late.

I heard footsteps behind me. Kalen sat down on my left side and stared across the empty city.

"Are you all right?" he asked quietly.

"I haven't been all right in a very long time."

"I take it your family isn't in there."

"Not in that home, no." Swallowing hard, I scanned the rest of the buildings. "But they could be in one of those. Just give me a moment. I need to catch my breath."

"There's no one inside those buildings, Tessa. I can scent them from here. Nothing dead or living inside. They must have fled when the pookas attacked. Hopefully most of them got away."

Slowly, I stood, all my hope dashed in a single sentence. "You think they fled into the mists? What if the pookas followed them? They wouldn't have gotten very far before the beasts caught up."

His eyes were heavy when he spoke. "The pookas might have been distracted by..." He didn't finish the sentence. Didn't need to. "It might have been enough."

"But we don't know that," I argued, sweeping my hand toward the hidden horizon. "We need to go see if we can find them. See if they're...see if they made it away from here."

It wasn't over yet. If we didn't search the mists surrounding the city, I'd never know if Mother and Val had been here and tried to escape. Maybe Kalen was right. Maybe they did get a head start. We needed to see if we could find something out there.

"All right." Kalen pushed up from the ground. "We can do a loop around the city, see what we can find. It's a vast land out there, but if they're anywhere nearby, I should be able to scent them."

Because the smell of blood and flesh was strong. And fae were able to sense things mortals could not.

I jogged down the steps and headed toward the horse. When he spotted me, he stamped at the ground, kicking up dust. Rearing back, he let out a horrible noise, nothing like any neigh I'd ever heard before. This was something else entirely. A shriek of pain and fear, the kind of sound that could cut through bone. With wild eyes, it stared right into my soul, screaming and stomping and jerking its head at the rope attached to the reins.

Stumbling backward, I slammed into Kalen. Pain flared bright and hot in my wounded back. He gripped my arms and pushed me behind him.

"What's happening?" I whispered.

Kalen's palm rested on the hilt of his sword. He gazed around. "He's sensed something. We need to get inside."

"Sensed *what*?" I asked, my voice rising.

He took in a long breath through his nose, scenting the air. A moment later, he unwound the rope and shoved the reins into my hands. "Take him into the castle. A storm is on the way. You *cannot* be outside when it hits."

"A storm? What do you mean, a storm?"

Storms were nothing I'd ever experienced before. The Kingdom of Light didn't have them. Rain showers, yes. Cloudy days, occasionally. They came just often enough to keep the hardy plants happy and the dirt from drying out too much. But I'd never been through anything like the storms I'd read about in books. Lightning and thunder, blackened clouds that lurked in the sky like shadows of death.

"A storm," he repeated. "One that is far worse than anything you could dream."

Tension pounded in my skull. "I didn't know your mists brought storms."

"They don't. This is no natural storm, Tessa."

I read between the lines. If this wasn't a natural storm, then it came from somewhere else. Somewhere with power over the elements. My heart dropped to the sandy ground by my feet. How could that even be possible?

"The Kingdom of Storms is attacking us?" I took a step away from him, shaking my head. "I thought you killed all those fae."

"They've clearly sent more." He curled his hands and faced the mists, calling to me over his shoulder. "You need to get inside. I'll fight it off."

My mouth went dry. "You're going to fight *a storm* on your own?"

"It isn't safe for you," he replied, pointing at the black castle in the distance. "Go in there. The storm will knock down the wooden buildings, but you should be safe within the stone. Now, *go*, Tessa. Get inside before these fae claim your life."

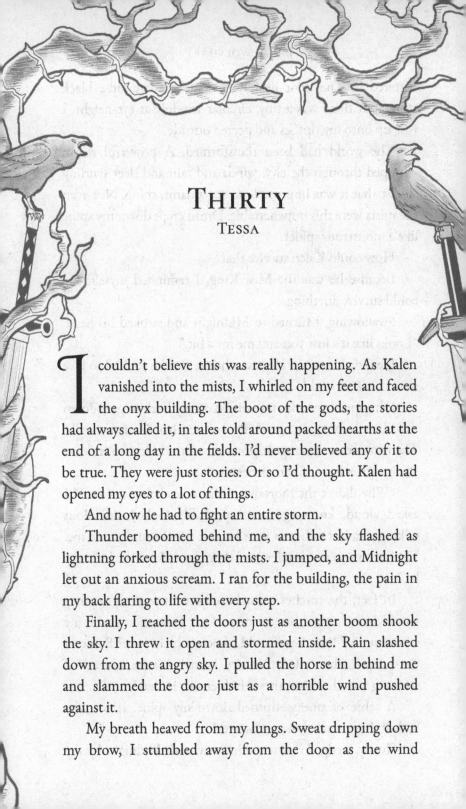

THIRTY
TESSA

I couldn't believe this was really happening. As Kalen vanished into the mists, I whirled on my feet and faced the onyx building. The boot of the gods, the stories had always called it, in tales told around packed hearths at the end of a long day in the fields. I'd never believed any of it to be true. They were just stories. Or so I'd thought. Kalen had opened my eyes to a lot of things.

And now he had to fight an entire storm.

Thunder boomed behind me, and the sky flashed as lightning forked through the mists. I jumped, and Midnight let out an anxious scream. I ran for the building, the pain in my back flaring to life with every step.

Finally, I reached the doors just as another boom shook the sky. I threw it open and stormed inside. Rain slashed down from the angry sky. I pulled the horse in behind me and slammed the door just as a horrible wind pushed against it.

My breath heaved from my lungs. Sweat dripping down my brow, I stumbled away from the door as the wind battered it. The door itself was made of that same black stone, but there was a tiny, circular window at eye-height. I rose up onto my tiptoes and peered outside.

The world had been transformed. A powerful storm whipped through the city, winds and rain and sleet swirling so fast that it was impossible to see a damn thing. Not even the mists were this impenetrable. Dread crept down my spine like a monstrous spider.

How could Kalen survive that?

Because he was the Mist King, I reminded myself. He could survive anything.

Swallowing, I turned to Midnight and stroked his head. "Looks like it's just you and me for a bit."

He didn't answer. He was a horse. But he seemed to give me a thankful nod.

I dropped his reins and twisted on my heels to gaze down the silent hallway. It was chilly, but torches lined the walls. The flames cast dancing shadows across the black stone floor. My breath echoed in the silence.

"Why didn't the mortals and fae take shelter in here?" I asked aloud, knowing that I probably looked ridiculous talking to a horse, but at least no one was around to see me. "This seems so much safer, and they clearly kept the hallways lit."

In fact, the torches must have been lit recently or they would have burned out by now. That realization made my stomach do a little flip. Could someone be in here? Some of the people who called this city home? Maybe instead of running into the mists, they'd hidden out in here?

A sense of unease tiptoed down my spine. If so, why hadn't they revealed themselves yet?

Slowly, I edged down the hallway with Midnight by my

side. He seemed to sense my hesitation, his hooves clacking along the stone. I pulled my dagger from my tunic and aimed it straight ahead, even knowing it would do little to keep me safe.

A part of me wanted to call out to the darkness, to ask if anyone was there. But I couldn't bring myself to voice the words. Something felt off about this place. The certainty of it settled into my bones.

And then the door behind me flung wide. Rain and wind rushed inside, blinding me momentarily. The door thundered shut, and my heart pounded as I tried to make sense of the looming figure standing before me.

I held up my dagger, ready to fight.

And then I saw the tortured face. My hand dropped to my side. "Kalen?"

He let out a monstrous growl that sent skitters of terror across my arms. "I can't fight it."

"What?" I asked, blood draining from my face.

"I can't fight it!" He shouted the words, and then shoved away from the door, his entire body trembling with anger. "I tried to go out into the storm, but it pushed me back. Again and again and again, until I had no more strength to fight it." He sagged forward, gripping the wall. "The storm fae could be attacking Dubnos, too. My people need me."

"But how?" I whispered. "Your powers..."

He should have been strong enough to weather the storm. All he had to do was throw his mists around him and shove against the wind and rain raging outside. I'd seen what he'd done to those storm fae. This should not be any different.

"It's not working." He shook his head. "I do not know why."

I took a step toward him and touched his arm. "Are you using the full force of your power? You're the Mist King. Surely there must be something you can—"

"Do not call me that, Tessa," he growled, shoving away from me. He shot me one last look of rage before storming down the corridor, away from where I stood with the horse, gazing after him.

"Hmm." Narrowing my eyes, I followed, his cloak fluttering behind me. The horse stayed right where he was. *Smart*, I thought. Kalen was in a mood, and he looked ready to tear the entire building apart. Not that I could blame him. I knew exactly how he felt. Those he loved might be in danger, and there was nothing he could do.

"Kalen, stop," I called after him as he took the first turn to the left. The next hallway was the same as the one before. Long, empty, quiet. "I'm sorry I said that, but I didn't mean it the way it came out. You're one of the most powerful beings in the entire world. That's all I meant."

He came to a sudden stop and whirled toward me. His eyes still churned with anger and pain. "What good does all that power do if it's impossible for me to *use it*?"

His booming voice echoed down the stone halls. *Use it, use it, use it.*

"We'll figure something out," I said. "Don't forget I'm trapped here, too, while Val and Mother are out there." I shivered at the thought of them caught out in that storm. Would they have had any warning like we had? Likely not. "How long does a storm like this last?"

"This isn't a normal storm." He twisted away. "It will last as long as they fucking want it to, unless I can somehow gain control of enough power to push it back."

I nodded. "All right. So, then let's find somewhere to sit

down and think this through. Are there any rooms with windows in this place? It would be good if we could keep an eye on the storm while we think."

With a muscle ticking in his jaw, he relented. "Up on the fifth floor. There are some viewing circles high enough to see any approaching threat."

"Viewing circles?"

"Like the one on the door. The creator of this building was paranoid. She did not want any weakness in the design of it. To her, windows are weakness. Glass is easily shattered."

"The myths say this building is the boot of a god. She lost it when she fell to earth, though it remained upright for whatever reason." I arched a brow. "But that's not true, is it?"

"Myths and legends are often rooted in the truth, but no, that's not the full story." He motioned toward the end of the hallway where a set of stone stairs curved upward to the next floor. "Come. We can talk about this more another time."

"I want to understand all this," I said, falling into step beside him. "I need to know what happened in the past. The real history. Not the stories whispered before bedtime. Not the tales sung around hearths. I want the reality of everything. Who were the gods? When did they come? What in light's name is this building?"

"This building," he said, "is cursed."

A shiver went down my spine as we began our trek up the stairs. "Cursed how?"

"Death lives in this place." He continued to climb.

"Are you going to elaborate on that?"

Heaving out a sigh, he pushed open the door to the fifth floor. "When most of the gods were banished from this realm, one of them got trapped. The God of Death. She's here, in this building. Her soul lives on, though she's unable to do anything but watch and listen. It is a cursed place."

My heart thumped. "You're telling me that we're trapped inside a god's house. And she's *here*."

"Yes."

My mouth dropped open, and then I snapped it shut. I didn't even know where to begin with that information. It was bad enough that we were stuck inside because of a storm that Kalen couldn't fight, but to add this on top of it...

"We need to figure out how to leave," I whispered.

"Trust me," he ground out. "I know."

We fell into tense silence as Kalen led the way through the dimly lit hallways. There were no torches to light the way here, and the tall, angry fae king beside me was the only reason I didn't get lost. When we reached a set of looming oak doors, Kalen shoved inside.

The expansive room stretched out before us, filled with oak dining tables hidden under a thick layer of dust. Empty chandeliers hung from a ceiling held up by wooden beams. Red-and-gold tapestries hung from the wall—Oberon's banners. But it had been a very long time since the king had stepped foot in this place.

"This was one of Oberon's cities, before you conquered this part of the world," I murmured, trailing over to pick up a helmet emblazoned with the king's sigil. Kalen put a hand on my arm before my fingers touched steel.

"Best not do that," he warned. "This place is cursed. Don't touch anything."

I snatched back my hand. "You think picking that up will do something to me?"

"I don't know. But let's not test it." Kalen moved away from my side and approached a wall where five little windows lined up, side by side. Bracing his hands on either side of one, he leaned close to peer out into the storm. The muscles in his back clenched beneath his tunic.

I went over to him and looked through one of the other windows. It was impossible to see a damn thing.

Kalen pulled one of his communication stones from his pocket and held it up in the dim light. It shattered in an instant, and the shards rained down on Kalen's boots.

He scowled. "Whatever is affecting my powers is destroying my stones. I can't contact Dubnos without them until this storm is over."

"I guess it might be a little while before it dies down."

He grunted. "If I were them, I wouldn't let up for weeks. What better way to destroy your enemy kingdom than by battering them with a brutal storm they're unable to fight? Shattered remains, the only thing left behind. No one left to fight. It's the perfect form of attack, particularly when they've discovered a way to neutralize my powers."

I shivered. "You make it sound so hopeless."

"Because it is."

Kalen grabbed a chair, dragged it over to the windows, and sat. His entire body coiled tight, he stared at the storm with so much concentration that it felt like he was trying to stop it with his mind. Maybe he was. After a while, I grabbed my own chair and set up camp beside him. If he was going to do this, so was I. Silence stretched between us for a good long while.

And then something occurred to me. "You said this place holds the power of a god. Could we use it somehow for our own benefit? Maybe it could stop the storm."

He whipped his head toward me and looked at me with so much dread, I almost wondered if a pooka had materialized behind me. What I'd said wasn't *that* shocking. "Absolutely not. That's far too dangerous."

"But you're the...well, you're you."

"I would do *anything* to protect my people," he said roughly. "*Anything*. Except one thing. And that's use the power of a god, especially this one. That's how dangerous it is. That's how much horror it would bring."

I frowned but decided not to argue. He was pretty damn convinced about the whole thing.

"So, what are we going to do?" I asked. "If we can't use this power, we have to do something else. We can't just let them trap us here for weeks."

In that amount of time, the storms could do so much damage, the entire kingdom would be left in ruins. More ruins than it already was. Any human and fae left alive in this part of the world...would be gone. A shudder went through me.

"I don't understand how they're doing all this. Your powers are beyond anything I've ever seen. You're the *Mist King*, for light's sake, and—"

"My entire kingdom is likely under attack right now. The people I love are in danger, and I am forced to sit here and listen to you call me the bloody Mist King. Maybe the gods really are punishing me. Because I can't think of a single worse thing than that."

Tears sprang into my eyes from the harshness of his words. Growling, I shoved up from the chair, my body trembling. "You know what? That's fine. I don't want to be stuck here with you, either. Just sit here and mope all day and night for all care. It's been a long fucking day. My ass hurts and so does my back. I'm going to find a room where I can get some sleep. *Away from you.*"

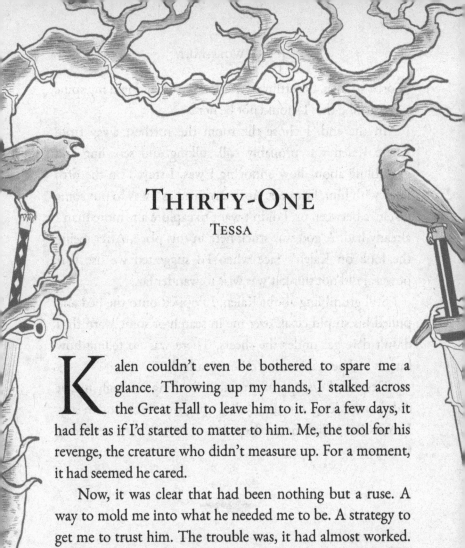

THIRTY-ONE
TESSA

Kalen couldn't even be bothered to spare me a glance. Throwing up my hands, I stalked across the Great Hall to leave him to it. For a few days, it had felt as if I'd started to matter to him. Me, the tool for his revenge, the creature who didn't measure up. For a moment, it had seemed he cared.

Now, it was clear that had been nothing but a ruse. A way to mold me into what he needed me to be. A strategy to get me to trust him. The trouble was, it had almost worked. I'd stopped seeing him as the bloody Mist King. He'd become Kalen to me. I never should have let down my guard around him.

I couldn't trust anyone.

Brushing away angry tears, I wandered the halls in search of a room. I passed several, but I didn't like any of the ones I found. They were all grand rooms, of course. Four-poster beds. Soft, lush carpets. All dark and cozy, hidden from the onslaught of the storm and Kalen's harsh words. But they were all cold and lifeless, too. Every time I stepped through a door, a strange, unsettling sensation skittered down my spine —a warning that I should not be here.

In the end, I chose the room the furthest away from where Kalen was probably still sulking and scowling and grumbling about how annoying I was. I stayed on the fifth floor with him, however. As determined as I was to put some distance between us, I didn't want to explore any more than I already had. A god was stuck here in this place. After seeing the look on Kalen's face when I'd suggested we use that power, I did not think it was wise to wander far.

Still grumbling about Kalen, I flopped onto the bed and pulled his stupid cloak over me in search of some warmth. I didn't dare get under the sheets. There was no telling how long it had been since they'd been washed.

Despite the surge of emotions rushing through me, it didn't take long for my eyelids to grow thick and heavy. Exhaustion lulled me to sleep. It had been a very, very long few days.

I awoke to the scent of fire on the wind. A star-studded sky filled my vision, a million little lights that twinkled against an inky tapestry overhead. For a moment, all I could do was stare up at them. It was a sight I'd always dreamt of, one I never thought I would have the chance to see. Beneath the vastness of the majestic sky, I felt so small. Such a tiny spark in an endless universe, but somehow, it filled me with hope. If something as breathtaking as the stars could exist, surely this world could be a better place.

"It's beautiful, isn't it?" Kalen asked from beside me.

Irritation flared in my gut. He was ruining the moment. "This is one of your stupid dreams, isn't it?"

"How could it be anything else?" he asked, his voice just as laced with irritation as mine. "We're trapped in a storm."

"Go away."

"I would if I could. I'm afraid this wasn't my choice."

I scowled. "And now you're just lying. You're the one who controls the dreams. Now, go away and leave me alone. Sleep is the only time I can escape you. Most of the time."

"My powers are behaving strangely in this place. I don't have any control over this."

"Are you actually serious?" I frowned and glanced over to him. He didn't look like someone who was joking. In fact, he just looked...tired. Weariness hung around his eyes in the form of purple shadows. A moment ago, he hadn't looked like this. Fae never suffered like that. Their faces never showed their age or exhaustion. Their powers wiped all that away. Was this how he really felt inside? What he hid from the world? Or was it just the magic playing tricks on us both?

His jaw ticked. "I don't want to be here any more than you do."

"Wonderful," I said flatly. "Time for me to wake myself up then."

Anything to get away from him. I'd sleep some other time.

I tried to wake myself up. Obviously, nothing happened. There was one person who could control dreams, and it wasn't me. He didn't say a word as I growled and threw up my hands.

"Tell me how to wake up."

"You can't control it."

"Can *you* wake yourself up?"

"I'm not asleep. I got pulled into your dream when you started sleeping, and I can't seem to get out of it. So, it looks like we're both stuck here until you wake up."

I fisted my hands. "Wonderful." Frowning, I glanced around us. We stood on some sort of battlement, gazing out at a field of sapphire flowers. They glowed beneath the light of a full moon. The scent of fire drifted toward us again, along with the distant sound of cheers.

"Where are we? What is this?"

"A memory of mine from a very long time ago," he said quietly. "The eve of battle. The last time the Kingdom of Storms took up arms against us."

"Oh." Now that I knew what this was, the signs were all there. Along the battlements, I spotted archers at the ready. That fire I smelled was from the enemy camp far across the field. Every now and then, orange flames flicked up into the sky, burning higher from the wind. Kalen was even dressed the part. Having donned black leather armor with steel capping his shoulders and elbows, he looked like a soldier of the night itself.

I thought back to the history books I'd read growing up. There were many tales of war and battles, but I'd grown bored of most of them. They'd always been such dry stories with lists of names and titles and whether they'd lived or died. And with Oberon controlling the narrative, I had no way of knowing if anything I'd ever read was true.

"I'd ask you when this was and what happened, but you made it clear how you feel about the annoying mortal asking you questions."

His gaze hardened. "This happened a very long time ago. The details hardly matter."

"It must matter, or we wouldn't be here right now."

"All it means is that my power is out of control. Nothing more."

"I bet it means a lot more than that. It's kind of a strange coincidence, don't you think? We get stuck inside one of your dreams that has to do with a Kingdom of Storms attack against you. When the Kingdom of Storms is now attacking again. Tell me what it means, Kalen."

"I don't owe you an explanation for any of this." He shoved away from the wall and strode down the length of the battlement, the fortress stones cast in the silver glow of the moon. I grabbed his arm.

He stopped. "Let go of me, Tessa."

"No," I said, tightening my grip around his bicep. "You can't just shut me out every time something uncomfortable happens. That's not fair to me, when you were the one who *dragged* me into your world."

"This has nothing to do with you." He turned back toward me, but I kept hold of his arm. If I let go, I had a feeling he'd just keep on walking away from me. "This war began long before you were born, and I daresay it will continue a long time after you're gone from this world. Focus on your own problems and on Oberon. I'll take care of the rest."

When he didn't immediately start walking away again, I took another step closer. My fingers twitched against his impressive muscle. "Unfortunately, I don't think it's that simple. Everything you do affects everyone else. Including me."

"Well, it shouldn't," he said roughly. "Your life is far worse with me in it."

I curled my lip at him. "You say that like you're not the one who *took* me from my *homeland*."

"Oh, don't act like you're still mad about that," he said with a hollow laugh. "You're free from Oberon. You've had a chance to see the world and learn the truth about what happened hundreds of years ago. You can act like you're angry with me, but I know deep down inside, you're happy I stole you."

"So smug," I hissed up at him. "To believe you know anything about me."

He shrugged out of my grip and started walking. I followed behind, mostly because I didn't have anywhere better to go. It wasn't like I could leave.

"I know more about you than you want to believe," he said, taking deep strides down the battlements. "You're brave and reckless and full of heart. You're also—" He stopped and turned.

"What?" I demanded, propping fisted hands on my hips.

"You're more like me than you want to admit."

I glared up at him. "I'm not like you. For one, I don't invade other people's dreams. Or steal girls from their homeland after lying to them for months."

With a growl, he leaned toward me, lowering his head so that his eyes were even with mine. "You keep saying that, but you must be confused about what that word means. I didn't *steal* you, Tessa. You were given the choice to run from Oberon. And you took it."

My heart fluttered beneath my ribs at the heated look in his eye. "Yes, I did run. But I did not choose *to go with you*. If I had, you wouldn't have felt the need to poison me."

He let out a hollow laugh. "You said you didn't hate me anymore."

"Yes, well, I said that before you started acting like an asshole again!"

His eyes flashed, his body curving over mine. "Why are you so *vexing*?"

"Maybe it's you," I whispered back as my eyes caught on how the mists seemed to curl off his skin. "Have you ever stopped to think it's your fault?"

"Is it my fault you called to me from your dream?" he asked, his lips tilting upward at my surprise. I called to him? That couldn't be true. Could it?

A flush crept up my neck. "Oh, *please*. Don't even try to pretend that's what happened. You said it yourself. Your power is acting strangely here. *Your* power. This has nothing to do with me."

He let out a chuckle and tucked a finger beneath my chin. The heat of his touch stormed through me, curling my toes. The feeling only made me hate him more. "You're right about part of that. My power is acting strangely here, and it's out of my control. But you also called for me. You've done it before, back when you were in Teine. You just didn't realize it. How do you think I always knew when you had mined some gemstones? Why do you think I chose you in the first place? It's because you called out for me, whether you realized it or not. Your soul was pleading for someone to *do something*. And so I did."

My mouth dropped open, and I tried to take a step back, but my feet were rooted in the stone. Dropping my voice to a harsh whisper, I said, "You're lying."

"I am not lying, Tessa."

The heat in my neck raced up to my cheeks, burning me up from the inside. "If that's true, you should have told me."

"And where would be the fun in that?"

He gave me a little smirk and then removed his finger from where he'd pressed it against my chin. But he didn't move. Irritation flaring in my gut, I put my hands against his chest and *shoved*. I hated the idea that I'd been calling out to him in my sleep. He would take it the wrong way. He'd decide that it meant something it definitely did not.

Kalen would believe I actually *wanted* to be near him. That I wanted his help.

That was so far from the truth, it was laughable.

Like an enormous boulder, he didn't budge an inch. Growling, he wound his fingers around my wrists and trapped them there, right where I could feel the thunderous beat of his heart. Not a steady thump. It was racing.

My mouth went dry as his gaze tripped down to my lips. A spark lit in his eyes that matched the flames burning up my heart, chasing away the ever-present cold of the Kingdom of Shadow. He ran his rough palm over the side of my neck, then tangled his fingers in my wild hair.

"I told you to braid that mess," he said in a low murmur. "When it's like this, it'll just get in the way when you fight."

"Fight you?" I whispered with an arch of my brow.

He wrapped a hand around my waist, and my heart nearly shook out of my chest. Not in fear, but in something else that scared me far more than he ever had. A want curled through me. A *need*. Heart racing, I gazed at his strong, angular face. Those eyes, so full of darkness and passion, icy blue here in the dream.

Suddenly, he pulled me closer. His mouth found mine, and a shudder went through me. Heat engulfed every part of me as his lips whispered against me, and he gripped my waist tighter.

I grabbed his leather armor, held on for dear life, and found myself kissing him back. His lips were agonizingly soft.

His powerful body brimmed with a passionate need that made my bones turn liquid.

For a moment, all that mattered was this and him and all that remained unsaid between us.

And then something jolted me awake.

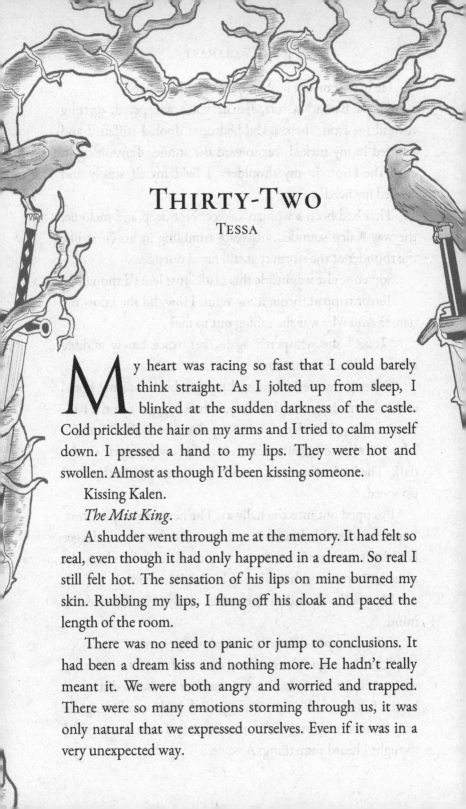

THIRTY-TWO

TESSA

My heart was racing so fast that I could barely think straight. As I jolted up from sleep, I blinked at the sudden darkness of the castle. Cold prickled the hair on my arms and I tried to calm myself down. I pressed a hand to my lips. They were hot and swollen. Almost as though I'd been kissing someone.

Kissing Kalen.

The Mist King.

A shudder went through me at the memory. It had felt so real, even though it had only happened in a dream. So real I still felt hot. The sensation of his lips on mine burned my skin. Rubbing my lips, I flung off his cloak and paced the length of the room.

There was no need to panic or jump to conclusions. It had been a dream kiss and nothing more. He hadn't really meant it. We were both angry and worried and trapped. There were so many emotions storming through us, it was only natural that we expressed ourselves. Even if it was in a very unexpected way.

He hadn't meant it. And neither had I. All it—

"Tessa Baran," a soft, female voice whispered, drifting toward me from the cracked bedroom door. I stiffened and whirled in my socked feet toward the sound. Tension tightened the knots in my shoulders. I held myself steady and cocked my head.

That had been a woman's voice. Not deep and melodic, the way Kalen sounded, his voice rumbling in his chest like the thunder of the storm that still raged outside.

Someone else was inside this castle. Just like I'd thought.

Terror tripped through my veins. How did she know my name? And why was she calling out to me?

"Tessa," she whispered again, her voice barely audible over the whistle of the wind.

Gritting my teeth, I shoved my feet back into my boots and held my dagger at the ready. When I crept into the hallway, nothing but dense, whirling shadows waited for me. The voice hissed again, somewhere far away, down in the dark. The back of my neck prickled, and my heartbeat picked up speed.

I stepped out into the hallway. The heavy thump of footsteps thundered behind me. I spun around with my dagger held high and my heart in my throat. Kalen's hand caught mine just two seconds before my blade hit his chest.

My cheeks flamed as memories of the kiss flooded my mind.

"What are you doing?" he asked with a frown.

"Um." Tongue thick in my mouth, I tried to come up with an explanation that made sense, but I was too distracted by the fullness of his lips. The lips that had been kissing me only moments before. But none of that had even been real. "I thought I heard something. A voice."

A deep frown carved his face. "I thought I heard you calling for me. I came to make sure you were all right."

Heat spread through my entire body. "I wasn't calling for you. It was that voice."

His jaw clenched as he dropped my hand and turned to gaze down the corridor that stretched out beyond where we stood. "Hmm. It seems the god who is trapped here is trying to get our attention. Best to ignore it."

"All right." Swallowing hard, I tucked the dagger back into my tunic. His eyes tracked the movement, lingering a moment too long on where the top of my shirt dipped low. "Why would she be doing that?"

"For nothing good, I'm sure. Ignore her, Tessa. She's dangerous."

A long moment of silence passed between us. Tension pounded the air like a hammer of war. My feet seemed frozen in place. For a good long while, I barely even breathed.

And then there he was. Within two quick steps, he'd palmed my cheek with his rough hand and looked into my eyes with an intensity that made my soul shake.

"I'm sorry, Tessa."

His hand dropped away. Cool air whispered in to replace the heat of him. With a shake of his head, he stepped back, turned away, and vanished down the corridor. I stood there, staring after him with a racing heart. I had no idea what had just happened. My mind felt full of a million twisted thoughts.

What had he apologized for? Being rude to me earlier, when he was upset about the storm? Or for kissing me? If it was the latter, did that mean he regretted it? I shook my head at myself. Why would it matter if he did? It wasn't like I'd wanted him to kiss me. Or that I had enjoyed it. Or that I ever wanted it to happen again.

Still, a part of me wanted to march after him and demand he explain.

Instead, I returned to my room, slammed the door, and slumped against it, my heart still careening wildly in my chest.

I didn't think I would sleep any more tonight.

"D o you ever sleep?" I found Kalen still sitting before the row of "windows" the next morning. Or maybe it was only several hours later. It was impossible to tell without the sun to guide me. He perched on the edge of the chair, hunched forward with his elbows resting on his knees. He didn't even glance my way as I approached him.

Truth be told, I hadn't gotten much sleep myself. After our little...incident, I'd tossed and turned until I got fed up with trying. Now, I was back here again. It wasn't like I had anywhere else to go.

"I only need sleep every few days," he said, his eyes still locked on the windows. "And then only for a few hours. The mists rejuvenate me more easily than rest."

Interesting. I wondered if the same could be said for Oberon and the sun, although I supposed not. He didn't have his powers right now.

I wandered through the room, coming to stop beside his pack. It was partially opened, and inside, the Mortal Blade gleamed, the gemstone sparkling with the heat of a thousand suns.

"You brought it with us."

He glanced over his shoulder, saw what I was looking at, and frowned. "Considering using it against me, are you?"

"I..." My heart faltered. Strangely enough, the thought hadn't even occurred to me. "Actually, no."

His eyes flickered as he sensed my words were the truth. "Hmm."

He pushed up from the chair, his powerful muscles rippling. At some point, he'd tugged off his leather armor and unbuttoned the tunic beneath it. The soft material whispered open, revealing the hard planes of his stomach. It was all I could do not to drop my chin and stare.

"Might as well take the opportunity to train," he said, thankfully not noticing the direction of my thoughts.

I snapped my eyes back up to his face. "With the Mortal Blade?"

He raised his brows as he strode toward me. "And let you stab me with it?"

"I said I hadn't considered doing that. You know I'm not lying."

"That doesn't mean you wouldn't accidentally nick me with it. Or change your mind." He pointed at my breasts. The hilt of my dagger stuck out. "We'll start with that. Once you're competent with it, we'll move on to something more deadly."

"You're worried about me trying to stab you, but you're happy enough to call me incompetent."

He folded his arms. "You're plenty competent. Just not with the blade."

"I bet it's fun having someone around who can't sniff out your lies."

"What am I lying about?" he murmured, watching me as I pulled the wooden stake out of my tunic.

"You see me the same way every fae does." My grip tightened on the dagger. "You think I'm weak. Useless. Mortal."

"Well, you're partially right," he said with a slight smile, motioning me forward. "You're as mortal as they come, but nothing about you is weak and useless. Tell me, Tessa. How is it you mined all those gemstones from the chasm?"

"I..." I shifted on my feet, not expecting the direction of this conversation. "I got a rope and I scaled down the chasm wall. And I used some tools my father had hidden away in our cellar. Why?"

He smiled. "You are strong, Tessa. And brave. Now, use that fire and try to wound me with that dagger of yours."

For a moment, I hesitated. "You told me to relax before."

"That didn't work. Now, I want to see what you can do when you really fight."

I didn't need any more encouragement than that. Staring into the sapphire depths of his eyes, I focused on all the pain and rage I'd felt most of my life. The fear of the fae who ruled over us. The hatred when I looked up at their city of crimson. The pain from Oberon's cruelty. He'd ripped out a part of my soul and left behind a gaping hole. I was a shell of the person I used to be.

With a roar, I charged at Kalen, picturing Oberon's face. I raised the dagger and swung it hard, pointing the sharp, stained end at Kalen's bare chest. His lightning quick reflexes cut in, and his hand swung up to block my blow. He shoved me back and folded his arms while I tried to catch my footing.

"Again," he demanded.

I growled and shot forward again. He caught me and easily swatted me aside like a pesky bug.

"Again," he said, his voice growing louder.

Sweat beaded my brow as I took another shot at him. Again and again, I ran at Kalen. Each time, I wasn't quick enough. Finally, I'd had enough. Heaving, I dropped the dagger to the floor and held my side, trying to catch my breath.

Kalen strode over, picked up the dagger, and pushed it back into my hands.

"Good," he said, as I took it without complaint. "Now that you've burned off all that rage, I want you to do what I suggested before. Relax and think about what you're doing. Don't just run at me blindly with all that beautiful passionate anger."

I flushed and watched as he took five big steps away from me. "So, all that? It was just to get me to calm down?"

He cocked his head. "It worked, didn't it?"

"Yes," I admitted. All that running, and tumbling, and shouting had done something to me. Adrenaline still charged through my veins, but I felt...still. Focused. Calm. The hatred still lurked deep within me, but it no longer made me feel like my skin was trying to jump off my bones and run. For once, my mind was clear, and I felt like I could actually focus on what he'd asked me to do. It was the best I'd felt in a really long time.

"Good." He beckoned me forward. "Now, let's see what you've got."

Slowly, I began to circle Kalen. He turned with me, hands relaxed by his sides, eyes locked on my every movement. Realistically, I knew that no matter what I did, he'd see me coming. But that didn't mean I wouldn't try.

Maybe I could distract him.

I flicked my eyes to the wall behind him, pretending I'd spotted something. He smiled.

"Nice try," he said. "That won't work on me."

"The storm has stopped," I tried.

He laughed and shook his head. "I can smell your lies."

I huffed out a breath, frowning. "If I rush at you like this, you'll just knock me away again."

"Correct." Brows arched, he cocked his head. "So, what will your move be, Tessa? Say you get inside the castle without being spotted. You find Oberon in his throne room, and none of his advisors or guards are around. It's just you and him, but he sees you coming. How will you attack?"

I mulled over his words. The truth was, that was the worst possible outcome, other than being caught. If King Oberon saw me coming, it wouldn't work. Sighing, I dropped the dagger to my side.

"At that point, I've already lost," I admitted.

"And that outcome is a real possibility." He advanced a step toward me, his eyes churning with something I didn't understand. "You need to be prepared for the possibility he'll see you coming and that you'll be forced to fight him head-on. If you don't, and you admit defeat, he'll capture you. So, what will it be, Tessa? Give it your best shot."

My heart raced as Kalen stared me down, challenging me to this fight. What did he expect me to do? Every time I'd run straight in for the killing blow, he'd blocked me without a second thought. Which meant...I couldn't race toward him. I sucked in a breath. That was why he kept asking me what I'd do. Because the obvious move was not the answer.

Heart thundering, I dropped the dagger to my side and slowly walked toward him. He stood his ground, cocking his head in curiosity. I smiled as I stopped just an inch way from him, our bodies separated by a small gap of air.

"Hello," I said to him, tipping back my head to gaze up at him with a timid smile.

"What are you doing, Tessa?" he murmured.

"Just saying hello." I lifted a finger to his chest and tiptoed it across his bare skin. He stiffened against me, shooting a thrill down the length of my body. "You looked lonely over here by yourself."

A slow smile spread across his face. "This is an interesting approach."

"Are you going to stop me?" I whispered back.

"Depends on what you plan to do with that dagger in your hand."

My breath caught in my throat as he leaned toward me. Before I could talk myself out of it, I flipped the dagger and jammed it into his side.

Only the fucking thing didn't hit its mark. He grabbed my hand just before the blade hit. My feet twisted beneath me. Stumbling, I fell, and he came with me. My back hit the floor. Kalen caught himself just in time, bracing his forearms on either side of my head. A deep chuckle rumbled from his chest, and my entire body burned from the warmth of him.

"Hello," he murmured, grabbing my arms and raising them above my head. He put his weight behind him, trapping me there.

His hard, muscular body pressed against me. My heart pounded so hard I could barely think. The scent of him enveloped me, drowning all my thoughts under an avalanche of mist and snow. That strange need roared back to life again, clenching my core. His eyes locked on mine, and for a moment, the world stopped. I swore it was as if he stared right into the very depths of me. He saw all my anger. All my rage. And he didn't flinch away.

I arched my back, lifting my hips to brush against where he straddled me. Surprise sparked through me at the hardness I found there. Kalen nearly purred, and his hands tightened around my wrists.

"What are you doing?" he murmured.

I tried to ignore the fire in his eyes and the tension pounding between us. Sucking in a breath, I wriggled against him one more time.

A low growl rumbled from his throat, and his eyes went dark.

His grip on me loosened just enough for me to free my hands. Still wriggling, I wrapped my arms around his massive chest and then threw all my weight to the right. Our bodies flipped over. I grabbed his wrists and pinned him down.

Delight whipped through me when he laughed.

"Impressive. You're even stronger than you look." He shifted beneath me, the length of him still hard between my thighs. "But you will *not* be using this move against Oberon."

"Oh, is that so?" I whispered, my heart racing. "Why not?"

His eyes darkened even more. "Because I can't stand the thought of his hands on you."

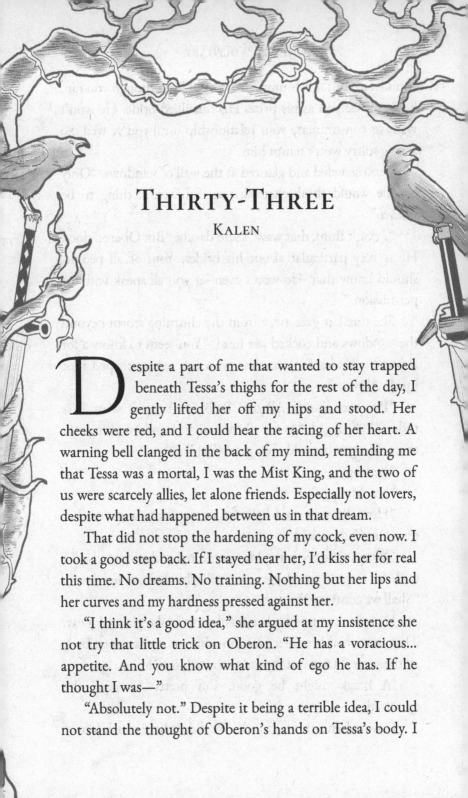

THIRTY-THREE

KALEN

Despite a part of me that wanted to stay trapped beneath Tessa's thighs for the rest of the day, I gently lifted her off my hips and stood. Her cheeks were red, and I could hear the racing of her heart. A warning bell clanged in the back of my mind, reminding me that Tessa was a mortal, I was the Mist King, and the two of us were scarcely allies, let alone friends. Especially not lovers, despite what had happened between us in that dream.

That did not stop the hardening of my cock, even now. I took a good step back. If I stayed near her, I'd kiss her for real this time. No dreams. No training. Nothing but her lips and her curves and my hardness pressed against her.

"I think it's a good idea," she argued at my insistence she not try that little trick on Oberon. "He has a voracious... appetite. And you know what kind of ego he has. If he thought I was—"

"Absolutely not." Despite it being a terrible idea, I could not stand the thought of Oberon's hands on Tessa's body. I shuddered. But it was more than that. "Even though you ran, he'll still see you as his prize. His unsullied bride. He won't want to consummate your relationship until you've wed. So acting sultry won't tempt him."

Tessa scowled and glanced at the wall of windows. "Only a male would think that way, as if I were a thing to be *sullied*."

"*I* don't think that way," I said darkly. "But Oberon does. He is very particular about his brides. You, of all people, should know that. He won't even let you all speak without permission."

She tore her gaze away from the churning storm beyond the windows and cocked her head. "You seem to know a lot about his brides for someone who has never stepped foot inside Albyria."

"I've been inside Albyria. Before it became what it is today." I shrugged. "As for all the insight into how things are there, Morgan has told me a great deal."

"Your spy."

"Yes. My spy."

"How did you get a light fae to spy for you against her own king?" she asked.

"Morgan's story is for Morgan to tell and no one else." I nodded toward the dagger she still clutched in her hand. "Shall we continue?"

Her cheeks turned a beautiful pink as she glanced away. That move had been her idea, but she was embarrassed by it all the same. I tried not to read too much into it.

"A break might be good. I'm pretty hungry," she admitted.

I swore beneath my breath. We didn't have much left of

the pooka meat reserves, and I had no way of going into the storm to hunt for some more. Anything that had once been left behind in the castle stores was likely long gone by now. Or rotten. Three hundred and seventy-five years is a very long time.

Just another reason why we needed to get out of this moonforsaken place as soon as we could.

I glanced over at the dust-blanketed hearth. "I'll get a fire going and cook up some meat for you. I'm afraid that's all we have."

"And how much, exactly, is that?"

Smart girl. "A few days' worth. Maybe a week if we can stretch it."

She paled. "That's it? What if we're stuck here for longer than that?"

"We won't be." My arms itched to wrap around her, but I kept them right where they were. "I'll get us out of here. One way or another."

Tessa nodded, but she did not look convinced.

We fell into a rhythm over the next few days. First thing in the morning, Tessa and I trained. I taught her how to dodge a blow. I showed her how to sneak silently up behind someone. Her footsteps would never be as silent as a fae's, but it might be good enough.

Might.

The word haunted me as we sat beside the hearth after another torturously long day. She held her hands close to the blaze of the flaming chair—furniture was all we had to burn now. I found myself drinking in her striking profile. The long slope of her nose. Her slender neck. The wild tangle of deep golden hair the color of sunflowers.

An image popped into my mind, of Oberon grabbing that hair and jerking it to the side while he pressed a blade against her throat. I fisted my hands and turned back to the fire. Tessa was strong and brave and determined as hell. But if Oberon got his hands on her...

Maybe this was a terrible idea. She could get killed.

"Come here," I told her.

She started and slid her gaze my way. "What?"

"Come here." I patted the floor just in front of me. "It's time we took care of that hair of yours."

Her face flushed. "You can't be serious."

"If you're not going to braid it, I will."

I'd never braided anyone's hair before, but I'd watched Niamh do it time and time again. I might not get it perfect, but it'd be better than the messy strands that fell into her eyes. In a fight, those would blind her. In training, they often did.

She shifted on her backside and didn't make a move to come near me.

I flashed her my teeth. "I won't bite."

Her neck bobbed as she swallowed. I couldn't help but stare.

"You do kind of look like someone who would bite, Kalen." Her voice was hushed.

The way she said my name shot a thrill down my spine. It

had been days since she'd called me by that fucking name Oberon had given me, but I still could not get used to how *Kalen* rolled off her tongue. I could listen to her say it all damn day.

"You're right. I do bite sometimes. But I wouldn't do it to you. Unless you asked."

She sucked in a sharp breath, and then she finally shifted closer to me. Turning her back to me, she pulled her knees up to her chest and gazed ahead at the fire. I could see her pulse thrumming in her neck, as quick as a rabbit. Something within me yearned to reach out and touch it.

Instead, I focused on her hair. Pulling a deep breath into my lungs, I swept the tangled strands behind her shoulders. Her arms tensed.

"Is this all right?" I murmured.

A breath spilled from her parted lips. "It's fine."

Gently, I slid my fingers into her hair and eased them through the strands, careful not to pull too hard when I hit a tangle. The moments ticked by, the warmth of the fire drenching us as I tried to comb her hair with my hands. There was only so much I could do without a brush.

After a quarter of an hour, she leaned a little closer. Her shoulders even relaxed, though the frantic beat of her heart remained.

"There," I said, in more of a growl than I'd intended. "That should be good enough to braid it for now."

She patted the back of her head. "It's still a mess."

"That's why we're braiding it." I separated her hair into three thick chunks the way I'd watched Niamh do. Slowly, I wound them together. With every sweep of her hair, I saw more and more of that delicious neck, to the point I almost forgot what I was doing. Clenching my jaw, I finished it off with a bit of rope tied at the ends. I sat back, wondering what in moon's name had gotten into me.

She reached behind her and ran her fingers along the braid. It was messy, I'd admit, but it'd keep the hair out of her eyes, and that was all that mattered.

"Thanks." She twisted toward me. "How does it look?"

Without all that hair in her face, I was struck by how big and beautiful her eyes were. They seemed to leap toward me to grab hold of my shirt and force me to stare into the depths of them... and get lost there forever.

"Not bad," I said, clearing my throat. "Niamh would have done a better job, but it'll do for now."

Her eyes softened. "I know you're worried about her. Maybe tomorrow will be the day we get out of here."

My chest tightened. Every damn day, I'd tried to force the storm back. And every day, I'd failed. We would not leave this place until the storm died. And that could be a very, very long time.

"Perhaps," I said.

Sighing, she turned back to the fire and leaned against my legs. Shock jolted me, though I stayed put. Tessa hadn't tried to flip me onto my back since that once, and I hadn't entered her dreams again. This was the first time we'd touched in days, other than blocking blows during training.

"How much more food do we have?" she asked so softly that I almost didn't hear her over the roar of the fire.

No sense in lying to her, although I didn't want her to worry more than she should. "Two more days." Because I wasn't eating anything myself. "I'll try to set a trap out in the storm tomorrow. It's possible a pooka could wander close enough."

She twisted toward me and frowned. "You really think they'd be out there in this?"

No. But it was the only shot we had of getting enough food to survive another week in this place. I'd already raided the kitchen stores. There was nothing left. Not even some grains. Mortals did not like coming into this god-cursed place, but hunger could make even the wisest man do foolish things.

"It's worth a shot," I told her. "They'll get hungry, too. There's only so long they can wait out the storm."

If they weren't all already dead.

She searched my eyes, and then sighed. "You're lying."

I couldn't help but smile at that. "I'm not lying, love. But you're clever to pick up on the fact that I'm also not telling the full truth. We would be very lucky if one walked into our trap."

A shudder went through her. And that was when I realized I'd called her *love*. A name I reserved for only those closest to me. It had just popped out.

"I didn't mean..."

"No, obviously not." She flushed. "It's just one of those sayings. Many of the men back in my village call all the women that. It's a very normal thing to say. In fact, I don't know why I'm even talking about it right now." Her flush deepened, spreading through that delicious neck that just begged for the skim of my teeth against it.

I glanced away. "Are you tired?"

"What?"

"Are you tired?" I turned back toward her and saw surprise in her eyes. "It's been a long day. You probably need to get some sleep."

She laughed. "You're embarrassed that you called me *love*."

"You're the one who blushed."

Her mouth dropped open. "Oh, you can't be serious."

"Your face is the same color as a tomato." I folded my arms and gave her a smug smile. "Should we find a mirror so I can prove it to you?"

"As if the King of Shadow has any idea what a tomato is."

The King of Shadow, I noted. *Not* the Mist King.

"I love tomatoes," I said. "In fact, I miss them dearly. It's been far too long since I had one."

"Over three hundred years, in fact," she said dryly.

"A little longer. Oberon stopped trading with us a couple of years before the Battle of the Great Rift."

"What's it like?" She cocked her head. "To live so long?"

I blew out a breath. "Where do I even begin? For one, it's very...freeing. There is always tomorrow and many days and years after that. If there's something I want to do, I know I have the time to do it. But it can also feel very empty and lonely at times. That same freedom means that sometimes it doesn't feel like anything matters. No matter what happens, I will just carry on..."

"Lonely?" she whispered.

I nodded, my heart twisting.

"Why have you never..." She cleared her throat, blushing again. "You know, mated with someone. You have no wife."

No heirs, I thought.

"You sound like Niamh."

She arched a brow. "Niamh is beautiful. And she clearly adores you."

I chuckled. "I'm not her type. Besides, I could never see her that way. She is like a sister to me."

"All right then. So, why not someone else? Surely there are many beautiful fae in Dubnos who would be thrilled to be your wife. You're the king. And you're...not bad to look at."

My eyes caught on her parted lips, the hollow of her throat. Something within me warmed. "I have never met someone who I felt matched my soul."

She smiled. "That's a pretty intense requirement, Kalen."

"It is not," I said. "Mates are a forever thing. It is a bond that cannot be broken. It transcends even death. I do not want anything less than the deepest connection I could ever find. Anything less than that is not worth the trouble. I want —no, I *need*—someone whose soul matches mine."

She gazed up at me. "How can someone ever match your soul? You're...*you*, Kalen."

Something in her eyes drew me toward her, and her body seemed to curve my way in response. So badly, I wanted to kiss her again. I had for days. The dream might not have been real, but it had felt real to me. And it had been killing me to pretend that it had never happened. Neither of us had mentioned it. Not a word.

But I knew I could not do this. It wasn't fair to Tessa. Hell, it wasn't fair to me, either. So, I sucked in a breath and turned my gaze toward the wall of windows. Black clouds churned outside, whipping bands of rain against the glass.

She let out a little sigh. "All right. I suppose I should get some sleep."

"That's a good idea," I said tightly. "Rest now in case we can get back on the road tomorrow."

As soon as her eyes closed, she called to me. With my powers out of my control, there was nothing I could do to stop myself from going straight into her dreams. She stood in the center of the fields near her village, her hair free and flowing in the wind.

"Where's the braid?" I asked with an arched brow, trying my best to appear nonchalant about this whole thing. But it was hard to look at her like this after our conversation beside the fire. All I could see was the strength in her body, the fire in her eyes. She was breathtaking.

"Where are your sapphire eyes?" she countered.

I frowned. "What color are they?"

"The color of ice."

I pressed my lips together as pain rocked through me. "That's the color of my mother's eyes."

"Oh, I'm sorry, Kalen. I didn't realize."

"You don't need to be sorry, Tessa. There's no way you could have known. *I* didn't even know I brought them into the dream like this." And I couldn't bear to dwell on it much longer. It had been centuries, but the pain was as fresh as it had been then.

She blew out a breath and glanced around. A shadow crossed her face when her eyes snagged on her village, on the home she'd left behind. "I guess you're stuck here with me again. What should we do?"

"I'm guessing you don't have any desire to take a stroll through Teine. Or even Albyria."

"Teine feels like a tomb. There's no one there, and things are wrong. Like that broom."

Her and that bloody broom. "Teine was empty when I

visited, but Albyria wasn't. In fact, I could show you something interesting there. It'd be good for you to see it."

She cocked her head. "That sounds deliciously intriguing."

"I thought you might say that."

Together, we took the winding path up the side of the hill to the city of Albyria. I gazed up at the walls that glittered beneath the sun. It had been a long time since I'd been here, even in my own dreams. It held nothing but terrible memories for me. Coming here was like taking a step into a past I wished I could erase. If only I could go back to the days before my mother had met Oberon. I might have been able to stop everything that had happened.

We reached the top of the hill and stepped through the guarded gates, though none of the soldiers paid us any mind. To them, we didn't exist. Tessa let out a pent-up breath and glanced around. Her face was ashen.

"It looks different like this," she whispered. "You know, when I'm not being paraded around as Oberon's silent mortal bride. It almost looks like a normal city." She sounded sad about that.

I followed her gaze to a child laughing, running after his mother's long skirts. His pink cheeks glowed.

"Ah." I winced. "You're forgetting, this is all crafted from my memories. Nothing like that exists in Albyria now. Light fae can no longer bear children."

"And King Oberon won't allow anyone else to touch a mortal." She swallowed and cast her eyes to the ground. "Most of the time, that is."

"No children. No heirs," I said with a nod. "It's his way of controlling them all. And so, I would imagine there is a lot less laughing. It is not a world in which I would want to live."

"Shadow fae," she said, turning toward me. "Do they have the same...difficulties?"

"No," I said, my thoughts growing dark. "But that does not mean we have fared well, either. We lost so many during the war. Many others abandoned our kingdom for a life beyond the sea. When they discovered what I'd done, they left."

Her eyes widened. "Oh. I had no idea."

"It doesn't matter," I said gruffly before taking off down the street. "Come. I want to show you something."

She followed me through the maze of streets. Back then, Albyria had been a bustling, cheerful town. Bolstered by trade, the light fae were wealthy beyond measure. We needed their crops, their fresh fruits and vegetables, the leather from their cows. And they needed our gold and crimson gemstones. How else could Oberon design such a flashy, glitzy, sparkling castle without our mines?

Humans and fae alike wandered the streets, the former free to do whatever they liked. Trade in shops, drink ale in pubs, or spend their days soaking up the sun in a hammock by the river. They all bustled about. This memory was from one of the very last days before their world—and mine—had changed irrevocably.

We came to a stop just outside a pub. I held up a hand for Tessa to wait. "You won't be able to change anything. Just watch."

She swallowed and nodded, and then I pushed inside. Dimly lit by a handful of candles, the pub was cloaked in shadows and scented with ale. Boisterous, cheerful fae boomed out laughter as they shared drinks and tales. In the corner, several fae and humans sat around a table playing cards. I motioned for Tessa to move nearer to them.

There were six of them, every eye glassed over. They were a dozen pints in, I guessed. A mangy-haired human suddenly shoved to his feet and shouted at the fae across from him, "You're cheating, you filthy fucking fae."

The fae's glowing emerald eyes narrowed, and he stood. "What did you say to me, you mortal piece of shit?"

The rest of the humans leapt to their feet. One pulled out a dagger. A very familiar dagger with a plain hilt and a glowing gemstone in the center. Tessa gasped.

The first mortal laughed and pointed at his friend, who had pressed the blade against the cheating fae's neck. "This is what ya get for messing with us. You don't think you're so high and mighty now, do ya?"

Laughing, the fae rolled his eyes. "Your pitiful blades can do nothing to us, mortal."

With a smile, the man dragged his blade across the fae's throat. Tessa's hand flew to her mouth as blood arced through the air. But that was not where it stopped. The fae's body bucked, his eyes rolling back into his head. He fell, crashing against the table. Cards and drinks clattered onto the floor.

The fae crumpled to the ground beside the man's boots, his blood pooling around his neck. Another tremor shook his body. His face turned to ash first, melting away his features. The curse of pure iron whispered down his chest, and then his arms and legs, transforming every part of him into nothing more than black ash. Soon, that was all that was left of him. Even his clothes had burned away.

It was as if he'd never existed at all.

Tessa whipped toward me. "What in light's name was that?"

"That," I said grimly, "is what happens when you stab a

fae with the Mortal Blade. And it's exactly what Oberon will become. He'll soon be nothing but ash."

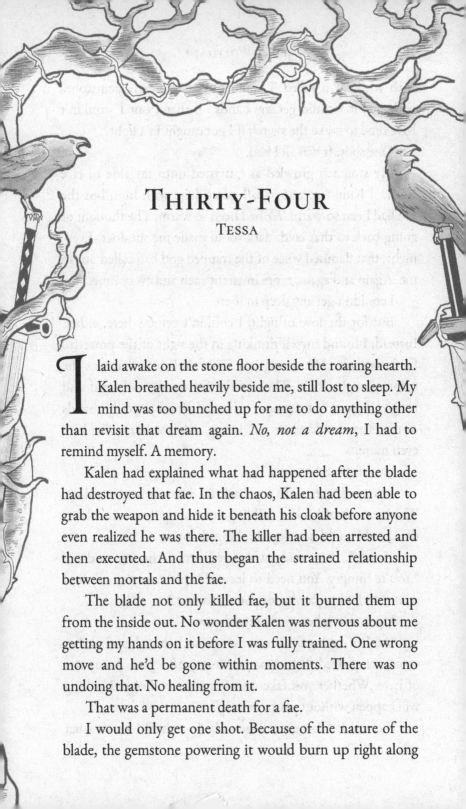

THIRTY-FOUR

TESSA

I laid awake on the stone floor beside the roaring hearth. Kalen breathed heavily beside me, still lost to sleep. My mind was too bunched up for me to do anything other than revisit that dream again. *No, not a dream*, I had to remind myself. A memory.

Kalen had explained what had happened after the blade had destroyed that fae. In the chaos, Kalen had been able to grab the weapon and hide it beneath his cloak before anyone even realized he was there. The killer had been arrested and then executed. And thus began the strained relationship between mortals and the fae.

The blade not only killed fae, but it burned them up from the inside out. No wonder Kalen was nervous about me getting my hands on it before I was fully trained. One wrong move and he'd be gone within moments. There was no undoing that. No healing from it.

That was a permanent death for a fae.

I would only get one shot. Because of the nature of the blade, the gemstone powering it would burn up right along with whoever it killed. I could carry some extra gemstones with me, if I could get my hands on them, but I wouldn't have time to make the switch if I got caught in a fight.

One shot. It was all I had.

My stomach growled as I twisted onto my side to face Kalen. I hadn't meant to fall asleep here with him, but the fire had been so warm. *He* had been so warm. The thought of going back to that cold, dark room made me shudder. Every night, that damned voice of the trapped god had called out to me. Again and again, more insistent each and every time.

I couldn't get any sleep in there.

But for the love of light, I couldn't get any here, either. Instead, I found myself drinking in the sight of the powerful fae beside me. His strong jaw. That dark hair that was the color of night itself. Those powerful hands, calloused and rough. He was not someone who was afraid to get his hands dirty. That should scare me, but it only made me like him even more.

He infuriated me, yes, but...

I flopped over onto my back to stare up at the ceiling. The memory of his kiss still lingered on my lips. It had been days, and I could not stop thinking about it.

"Tessa," that voice whispered from the open door. "You're hungry. You need to leave this place so you can find some food. I have a way for you to do that."

My stomach betrayed me and growled.

"All I'm asking for is a conversation," she whispered, her voice full of need. "I have something to offer you. A way out of here. Whether you take my offer is your choice. Nothing will happen without your consent."

I scowled. "You expect me to believe that? I know what you are."

She sighed. "All right then. I will you offer you something else. Your sister."

My heart lurched into my throat as I sat straight up. Hand flying to the dagger beside me, I scanned the silent Great Hall, half-expecting to find a monstrous wraith watching me, knowing exactly what to say to rile me up.

I hissed out between my teeth as I slowly stood.

"That's right," the voice said. "I will return your sister to you if you do what I ask."

I cast Kalen a glance before following the voice out into the hall. I knew what he'd say if I told him about this. He'd been more than clear many times—the god trapped here wanted out, and she was dangerous. I knew this, but I could not stop my feet from moving. Not with the image of my sister in my head.

Could a god bring a girl back to life?

My heart thundered at the thought of it. At seeing my sister smile again. At erasing the horror of what Oberon had done to her. What I'd done to her by not falling in line.

If I could save her now, after failing her so greatly, what kind of sister would I be?

The god's voice led me down the stairs, back to the ground floor where the horse pawed at the ground. It glanced up as I passed by, its dark eyes full of knowing. I swallowed hard when I came to another set of stairs that descended into the depths of the earth and pure, unyielding darkness.

I hesitated on the top step.

"I cannot hurt you even if I wanted to," the voice said. "I am trapped. My powers are muted. All I can do is speak to you."

"If you could hurt me, it isn't as though you would outright tell me," I mumbled.

"No." The voice sounded amused. "I suppose not. Still, all I can do is swear to you that I mean you no harm."

I blew out a breath. The god could still be lying, of course. But I needed to hear what it had to say about my sister.

And so I went down. Down into the dark where the shadows lurked like wraiths. At the bottom of the steps, I walked into a cavernous room where water trickled down the stone walls. A dim light shone ahead, casting a pool of gold upon a deep onyx stone embedded into the rock face.

It glittered as I approached.

The voice sighed, the sound coming directly from the gemstone. "Thank you for coming down here. It's so much harder to speak with you when you're above ground."

I shifted on my feet and frowned. "So, you're trapped inside that gemstone."

"My power is. My body is somewhere else."

"And you can't get out? Or do anything as long as you're trapped in there?"

"For the most part. Most importantly, I cannot do anything that directly harms you."

"All right then. Tell me about my sister."

"I have an offer for you, Tessa Baran. Your sister was taken from you. Release me from my captivity, and I will return her to you. She will be restored to everything she was before."

The world paused around me. I stared at the stone, her words echoing in my ears. For a moment, I couldn't do anything but wonder if I'd heard her right. But then the full weight of her words slammed into me. My knees wobbled. I clutched the wall, blinking back the burning tears, hating myself for the horrid hope twisting through me.

I could get Nellie back.

"Nellie," I whispered, her name like acid on my tongue. *Nellie, Nellie, Nellie.* Her bloodied face flashed in my mind. The image of her head rolling toward me and—

My hand slammed against my mouth as nausea shook my stomach. A sob choked me. Buzzing filled my head.

I couldn't be here. I couldn't hear this.

But I couldn't turn away from it, either.

I had the chance to bring her back.

Desperation clawed at my gut. Everything within me wanted to say yes. The god had known there was only one thing I could say when presented with this choice. I had to take it. I had to let her out.

And loose a god back on the world once more.

My stomach twisted. I could barely breathe.

"What is your decision, Tessa Baran?" the god asked in a voice that betrayed her emotion. She desperately wanted me to say yes, and she thought she had me. Who could turn something like that down? Who would say no to saving her beloved sister, the sweetest creature who had ever walked this earth? Her life had been stolen far too soon by a monster who wanted to bring back the gods—who wanted to become one himself.

I hissed between clenched teeth. "What will you do if I let you loose? Where will you go?"

The gemstone flickered. "That is none of your concern."

My heart twisted over on itself. "Yes, it is. If I let you out of there, I'm responsible for whatever happens next. What will you do?"

The stone rumbled, shaking the ground. "I will find a way to reunite with the rest of my soul."

"And where is that?" I asked sharply.

A sigh. "King Oberon of Albyria has the rest of me. You, of all people, should understand why I would want this."

Alarm flashed through me. "*Oberon* has part of a god's soul?"

"Trapped in a stone," the god said quietly. "But you don't need to concern yourself with any of that. You can reunite with your sister and leave these lands for the human kingdoms beyond the sea. Start a life somewhere new, far from war and mists and wicked kings."

I leaned against the wall. Nellie's face flashed in my mind. I could hear her laughter echoing through my ears. My heart shattering into a million pieces, I brushed my tears aside and tried to imagine a future where we took off on a grand adventure, Mother and Val by our sides. Maybe we could find an island somewhere and feel the hot sand between our toes. No one would follow us. Oberon and his cruelty could be long forgotten far away from here.

And destruction would rain down on everyone else.

I blew a breath through parted lips, pain ripping through me. "No."

My voice echoed through the cavern.

Stunned silence was my only answer. And then a scream. So loud and so harsh, it scraped against my bones. The ground began to rumble, knocking me sideways.

I slammed my hands over my ears as I whirled away from the god, only to come face to face with a tall, muscular figure sheathed in mist. Kalen stared at me from the entrance to the cavern, his gaze hard, his eyes full of harsh fire.

Swallowing hard, I fisted my hands and braced myself for his shouted words. He'd told me, time and time again, to ignore the call of the god. Instead of listening, here I was. And I'd come so close to releasing her.

He would never look at me the same again.

"Come here," he murmured, surprising me.

I squared my shoulders. "You can't just order me around."

"Just come here, love." He held out a hand as the lurching ground shook my bones.

My heart flared with heat at the look in his eyes, a look I had not expected. Without another word, I crossed the room and took his hand. He pulled me up the stairs behind him, and the screams died in the god's throat. When we reached the top of the steps, Kalen slammed the door and whirled to me. I tensed, bracing myself for the anger. It would come now that we were out of there.

Kalen stepped forward. He tucked a finger beneath my chin and searched my eyes. "You turned her down."

I swallowed hard. "Just barely."

"She offered to bring your sister back to life, and you turned her down," he repeated, his voice building in intensity.

My body almost crumpled, but he snaked his hands around my waist to keep me steady. Tears blurred my vision. "What else could I have done, Kalen? She's one of the gods. I could not sacrifice my people and these kingdoms to undo my broken heart. As much as I wanted to, I couldn't. I just couldn't."

I started crying. Real sobs, this time. My entire body shook from the awful, twisted truth of it all. I could have had my sister back. It had been within my grasp. All it would have taken from me was one simple word.

"Tessa, love." Kalen pressed his lips to my forehead and then gathered me into his arms. I didn't fight against him as he cradled me against his chest and carried me back up the stairs to the fifth floor. He kicked open the door of the Great Hall and strode straight over to the hearth where the fire still flickered, its embers glowing bright.

He lowered my feet to the floor, but he did not let me go.

My cheeks burned as my sobs subsided. His chest was damp with my tears from where he'd carried me in his arms. The scent of snow still lingered in my nose. Rubbing at my face, I glanced away. "This is embarrassing."

He caught my hand, curling his fingers around mine. "You have no reason to be embarrassed."

"I broke down in front of the King of Shadow. This is not my finest moment."

He smiled. "I love it when you call me that."

Heat blazed around my heart. "I thought you'd be angry."

"Why in the name of the moon would I be angry, Tessa?" He gestured at the open door. "Do you not realize what you just did? You stood strong in front of *a god*. You turned down what most never could, for the good of the living. I could never be angry at you for that. No, Tessa. I'm awed."

He gazed at me with a ferocity that curled my toes. Swallowing hard, I gazed right back. Something within him called to me. Shuddering, I felt my body lean forward. His eyes sparked.

"Fuck it," he growled.

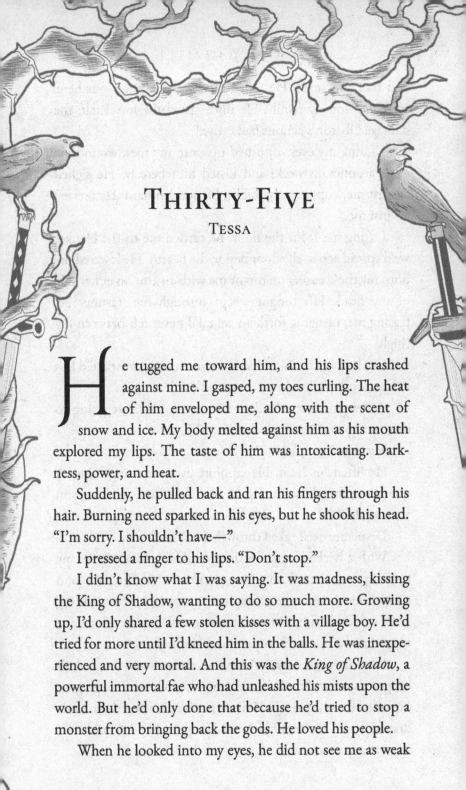

THIRTY-FIVE

TESSA

He tugged me toward him, and his lips crashed against mine. I gasped, my toes curling. The heat of him enveloped me, along with the scent of snow and ice. My body melted against him as his mouth explored my lips. The taste of him was intoxicating. Darkness, power, and heat.

Suddenly, he pulled back and ran his fingers through his hair. Burning need sparked in his eyes, but he shook his head. "I'm sorry. I shouldn't have—"

I pressed a finger to his lips. "Don't stop."

I didn't know what I was saying. It was madness, kissing the King of Shadow, wanting to do so much more. Growing up, I'd only shared a few stolen kisses with a village boy. He'd tried for more until I'd kneed him in the balls. He was inexperienced and very mortal. And this was the *King of Shadow*, a powerful immortal fae who had unleashed his mists upon the world. But he'd only done that because he'd tried to stop a monster from bringing back the gods. He loved his people.

When he looked into my eyes, he did not see me as weak

and frail and small. He called me strong. He was out here, searching for my family. He understood the loss I felt, the damage Oberon's actions had caused.

Closing my eyes, I pushed up onto my toes, wound my arms around his neck, and kissed him fiercely. He sighed against me, cupping my thighs, his sudden hardness pressed against me.

Lifting me from the floor, he carried me to the blanket we'd spread across the floor beside the hearth. He lowered me onto my back, easing on top of me with an arm on either side of my head. His tongue swept through me, tasting me, teasing me, bringing forth an ache I'd never felt between my thighs.

I arched against him, a soft moan escaping my parted lips as his mouth trailed down to my neck.

A low growl rumbled in his throat. "You are going to drive me to madness with that sound."

My breath caught.

He lifted his head, his sapphire eyes searching mine. A question echoed in the depths of them. "Are you sure you want to do this?"

Desperate need raked through me. "Yes."

With a wicked smile, he dragged the bottom edge of my tunic up my stomach, exposing my breasts. A guttural sound escaped his throat as he gazed down at them, his eyes lighting with a furious fire. He swept his thumb across my aching nipple, and a storm of shivers shook through me.

"You like that, do you?" He leaned down and dragged his tongue across it. Need clenched my thighs, and a rough gasp exploded from my throat. I fisted my hands around the tunic draped across his shoulders and clung on like I would float away at any moment.

He massaged my nipple with his tongue, softly rubbing the other with his thumb, driving me so wild that I bucked against him. Moaning, I angled my hips so that I could rub against him, anything to release the building tension between my thighs.

Eyes flashing, he shifted back to meet my gaze. I shuddered at the raw power reflected there. A lazy grin played across his lips. "Tell me, love. What else makes you squirm like this? I need to know exactly what you like."

Heat rushed into my cheeks. Nibbling on my bottom lip, I glanced away. "I, um, I'm not sure."

He shifted on top of me, took my chin gently between his thumb and forefinger, and turned my face back toward him. "You've never lain with another?"

I swallowed hard, embarrassed. "No. We were forbidden. Unmarried girls must remain pure for the king. Any of us caught even kissing someone would have been beheaded. It happened once, just before the third Festival of Light. The story has been passed down over the years. A warning of what Oberon would do."

His gaze darkened. "Of course. I should have known."

Something in my gut twisted and I suddenly felt cold. Now that we were talking about Oberon, that clenching between my thighs was gone. The moment was ruined. I never should have spoken his name aloud because all I could picture now was his orange-red eyes, those terrifying horns, and the smug look on his face when he'd killed my sister.

Swallowing hard, I glanced away.

"That bastard." With a clench of his jaw, Kalen pushed off me and stalked over to the bay of windows. I tugged my shirt back over my breasts. "Did he do something else to you?" His voice was low and dangerous, mist curling off his skin.

"Not like that, no," I whispered.

His fists clenched as he whirled toward me. "I can't let you kill him."

I pulled my knees to my chest and gaped up at him. "*What?*"

In two strides, he'd crossed the room and knelt by my side. He took my hand in his, staring at me fiercely. "It's too dangerous. If you walk back into that city, your life is forfeit. He will kill you, Tessa. Or worse." His voice cracked. "Even with the Mortal Blade...it's too much of a risk."

Defiance rose up inside me like an iron fist. I pulled my hand out of his and stood. "I'm not that fragile, Kalen."

He rose with me. "You're as strong as the moon, Tessa. But you are still a mortal. He could easily kill you."

"I thought you said he wouldn't," I replied hotly. "That I'm too valuable to him. He branded me as his bride."

"You *were* valuable to him," he said in low voice. "But he may very well have replaced you with someone else. If that's the case, you're dead. And even if not, if you fail, if he catches you...he will bind you to his will until you're dust."

I shivered beneath the intensity of his gaze, but I did not back down. I lifted my chin. "We always knew this would be dangerous. I want to do this, Kalen. You said it yourself. He needs to be stopped."

"We'll find another way."

"There is *no other way*. No one else can reach him. It has to be me." My heart pounded as I spoke the words, making me realize just how badly I wanted to see Oberon dead. Not just for revenge but for the safety of this world. Now that I'd met one of the gods and heard the venom in her voice, I knew the people who called this realm their home would never be safe as long as Oberon tried to bring the gods back.

"Tessa, love," he said softly. My heart squeezed as he took my hand and placed it against his thumping heart. Skin against skin. The heat of him overwhelmed me. "I can't let you do this. I won't sacrifice your life this way. It would make me just as bad as he is."

I ground my teeth, the heavy thump of his heart rocking through me. "It's my life. It should be my decision."

He pressed his lips together. I thought he would fight me more on this, but then he nodded. "You're right. It *is* your choice, and I won't steal that from you. But you need more training before you go after him. You're not ready. Surely you can see that."

Frustration churned like a storm-swept sea. I narrowed my eyes but didn't argue, because I knew he was right. I'd been improving during our daily training sessions. I was far more comfortable with combat stances and sneak attacks than I had been a week ago...but it was just that. A week.

King Oberon was five hundred years old—ancient, especially compared to a twenty-five-year-old mortal like me. Even without his elite fae power, he was strong and fast and deadly. There was only so much I could learn in a week. If I wanted to beat him, I knew I needed to be better than I was.

"I thought you were in a hurry to stop him," I said. "Training me properly could take months." Or even a year.

"Oh, I am," he said with a slight smile. "But my definition of hurrying might be different than yours."

Right. A year to him likely meant nothing.

I sighed. "So, where does that leave us? My people are still stuck beneath Oberon's rule. Val and my mother are still lost in the mists."

He tucked a finger beneath my chin. "You're right. I will continue to help you find your family, and you can make your choice on what to do after that. I release you from our deal."

A rush of magic coursed along my arms.

Frowning, I glanced at them. "What was that?"

"I release you from our deal," he repeated, his voice low and dark. "Repeat the words, and you'll be free to make your own choices once reunited with your family. You may leave this continent behind or you can stay and train with me. It will be your choice, and I will not make it for you."

Heart pounding, I gazed up at him. "You're really doing this."

He nodded.

"But..." I hated that I even dared ask this. "If I say the words back to you, how can I be sure you'll still help me find Mother and Val?"

A flicker of pain went through his eyes. "I suppose you'll have to decide if you can trust me, Tessa."

I gazed up at him, my lips parted, tension wracking my body. Could I trust him? He'd lied to me, about who he was, about why he wanted the gemstones. But that had been before I knew him. How could I not believe him now, at least about this? He was offering me freedom to go anywhere I wanted. I could do whatever I liked. It was a freedom I'd never had. One that meant I fully decided my fate, even if it was one that did not involve him or his plot against Oberon.

He was letting me go, if I wanted to run.

"All right," I whispered. "I release you from our deal, too."

Another wave of magic skittered along my arms. The tension in my shoulders loosened its grip on me, and the tight noose of the vow burned away to ash. I was free. It was done. Our deal was over. Kalen sighed and stepped back. My hand dropped away from his chest.

He gazed down at me, though his eyes churned with worry. "This is for the best."

"I'm still going to kill him."

"After you've trained more," he countered, following me back to the blanket beside the hearth.

I settled down and folded my legs beneath me. "Maybe. It's my choice, after all."

"Tessa," he warned as he joined me.

I shot him a winning smile. "What?"

"I thought you agreed you need more time."

"I do." I knocked his shoulder with mine. "Maybe you'll even train me with the actual Mortal Blade instead of my dinky wooden thing."

He glanced my way, his expression unreadable. "Hmm." And then he changed the subject. "I'm curious. You rebelled against the king's orders in other ways. Substantial ones at that. Why not with sex?"

I nearly choked. I hadn't expected him to suddenly ask about *that*.

Face heating, I focused on the fire. "Maybe if I'd met someone who made me want to rebel in that way, I would have. But I grew up with all the boys in the village. I didn't see them that way. I tried kissing one of them a few times. Aidan was his name. But I just didn't feel anything. And all the older men...they reminded me of my father." I swallowed hard. "There was no one else."

"I see," he said quietly, his eyes gleaming.

I wet my lips. "I'm guessing it's difficult for you to relate to. You've been around a long time. You're...not unattractive."

He chuckled at that. "High praise."

"And you're a powerful king," I added. "You must have..."

"Fucked a lot of people?" he asked.

"Yes, have you?" I asked boldly.

"Not as many as you'd think." He gazed into the fire. "Only one ever meant anything, and that didn't last."

I drank in the hard edges of his face, the tension around his eyes. "What happened?"

"She said she didn't trust me," he said flatly. "Could not stand the idea of being with *the Mist King*. After she left, I discovered she'd been sneaking messages to Oberon, trying to work with him on a way to take me down. She was a spy. In the end, she was too cowardly to go through with it."

"A lucky escape for you. She sounds like a terrible person."

Kalen shifted toward me, his gaze dark. "You thought the same of me."

"That was before I knew you."

His gaze dropped to my lips. "I want you safe, Tessa. But for the love of the moon, there's a part of me that hopes you don't run."

"Only a part of you?"

"You should go to the human kingdoms," he said. "Away from Oberon's cruelty. Away from these horrible fae lands."

"Away from you?" I couldn't help but whisper.

He wound a hand around the back of my neck, gripping tight. "You should go. Once we find your family, you should go."

I leaned into his touch, dipping back my head to expose my lips and neck to him. "I don't want to run from you."

His lips were on me a second later, hungry, fierce, full of need. I gasped as his grip on me tightened, as the ache in my core flared to life. His teeth skimmed my neck. A low guttural sound rumbled in his throat.

I leaned into him and basked in the heat of his touch and—

The entire building shook with the force of a thousand angry fae.

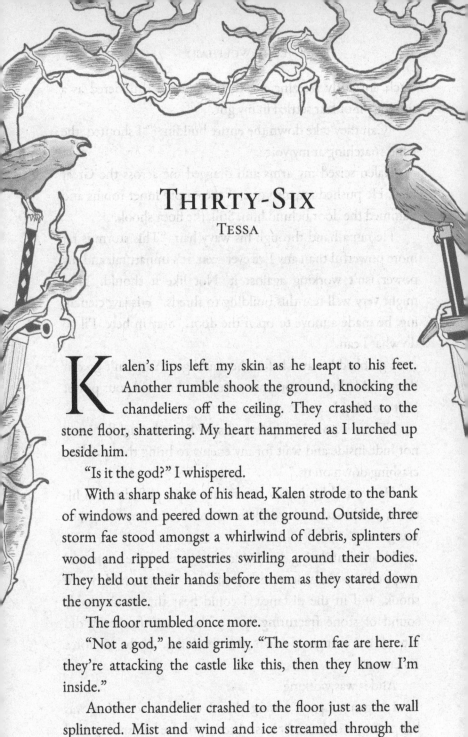

THIRTY-SIX

TESSA

Kalen's lips left my skin as he leapt to his feet. Another rumble shook the ground, knocking the chandeliers off the ceiling. They crashed to the stone floor, shattering. My heart hammered as I lurched up beside him.

"Is it the god?" I whispered.

With a sharp shake of his head, Kalen strode to the bank of windows and peered down at the ground. Outside, three storm fae stood amongst a whirlwind of debris, splinters of wood and ripped tapestries swirling around their bodies. They held out their hands before them as they stared down the onyx castle.

The floor rumbled once more.

"Not a god," he said grimly. "The storm fae are here. If they're attacking the castle like this, then they know I'm inside."

Another chandelier crashed to the floor just as the wall splintered. Mist and wind and ice streamed through the crack, instantly freezing me to the bone. I shuddered as a sinking pit of fear settled in my gut.

"Can they take down the entire building?" I shouted, the wind snatching at my voice.

Kalen seized my arms and dragged me across the Great Hall. He pushed me into one of the empty inner rooms and slammed the door behind him. Still, the floor shook.

He ran a hand through his wavy hair. "This storm is far more powerful than any I've ever seen. It's unnatural, and my power isn't working against it. Not like it should. They might very well tear this building to shreds." His jaw clenching, he made a move to open the door. "Stay in here. I'll go do what I can."

I grabbed his arm before he could go. "You can't go out there and fight them on your own. You just said your power isn't working."

"There is no other option, Tessa," he said roughly. "I will not hide inside and wait for my enemy to bring this building crashing down on us."

He wound his hands around my hips, pulled me to his chest, and kissed me hard. Before I could catch my breath, he was gone.

Heart thundering, I stood in the center of the room and wrapped my arms around myself. The floor rumbled and shook, and in the distance, I could hear the unmistakable sound of stone fracturing apart. The storm fae really did intend on bringing down this building, likely to force Kalen out.

And it was working.

I began to pace, hating that I couldn't see what was happening out there. At least three storm fae had surrounded this place. Maybe even more. And they'd found a way to mute Kalen's powers. In his current condition, he did not stand a chance against them.

But what could I do? I had no magic of my own, no brutal powers that could stop them. All I had was a little wooden dagger.

And the Mortal Blade.

A weapon that could kill a fae.

I threw open the door and hurried back into the Great Hall, where rain and wind poured through half a dozen new cracks. Another tremor shook the building, and I slid sideways. My legs buckled, and I almost banged my head on the stone, but I caught myself just in time. Heartbeat racing, I crouched on the bucking floor, my eyes caught on the world beyond the windows.

Kalen stood outside, roaring at the storm fae. In his hands, he held a swirling ball of mist. My breath caught as he hurled it at the storm fae.

It died, as if it were nothing more than smoke on the wind. His powers were still useless against them.

A blast of wind hit him square in the chest. He hurtled backward, his body hitting stone.

Hands shaking, I rushed to his pack and searched for the Mortal Blade. I found a small ration of pooka meat, a canteen, and a pair of metal tongs. Fear rushed through me. The blade was gone.

Where the fuck had he put it?

"Tessa," the goddess whispered, her voice filling the Great Hall despite the lashing rain and wind. Ice twisted through my veins. I fisted my hand around Kalen's pack. "Tessa."

"Stop talking to me," I said around my tight throat. "I told you I'm not letting you out."

"Do you know what it is that stops your lover from being able to draw upon his powers?" she whispered.

I stiffened and stood, ignoring the word she'd used to describe Kalen. "No, but let me guess. You do."

"It's me. *I've* been muting them since you arrived." She laughed. "Or toying with them in the shape of your dreams."

"I don't believe you," I whispered, even though it made so much sense.

"You're smart to distrust a god, but how do you think it is you got trapped in this castle with me?" she asked. "Why do you think the enemy's powers are greater than his right now? Kalen Denare is one of the strongest beings in the world. Their powers pose no threat to him. While I numbed his, I amplified theirs. He stands no chance against them unless I release my hold on it all. Your choice, Tessa Baran."

Tears burned my eyes as I bolted out of the Great Hall and took the steps two at a time. I raced into the ground hallway, stopping when I met Midnight just by the door to the dungeon. He blinked at me, nodded, and then shifted aside.

I didn't stop to ponder what that meant as I hurried down the stairs, not pausing until I stood before the glowing onyx gemstone. Even down here, the walls shook. "Tell me why you're doing this."

"Why do you think? I need you to release me. Do that, and I'll return the Mist King's power to its full capacity, and I'll stop amplifying theirs."

I ground my teeth, my hands shaking by my sides. "You know I can't do that."

"Can't?" she asked with a tsk. "Or won't?"

"Does it matter? I'm not doing it."

"And your lover will die. Because of *you*," she said with a snap.

My breath hitched. "What is that supposed to mean?"

"Oh, you pitiful little thing. Don't you understand why the storm fae are here, attacking you?"

"They're trying to take control of Kalen's kingdom."

"Yes and no. They want *you*, Tessa Baran. You are their path to an alliance with King Oberon of Albyria. He wants you returned to him. You're branded as his bride, after all. And once the storm fae and light fae have joined together, they can banish the mists and return the gods to this world."

For a moment, all I could do was stare at the glowing onyx gemstone, hating every word the god had said. "If that's true, then why are you offering to help Kalen? Aren't you on Oberon's side? Don't you want the gods returned? You're one of them."

She let out a laugh as another boom shook the building. A chunk of rock slammed into the ground only a few inches from my feet. "I'm on no one's side. I want to be released, and nothing else matters to me. Now, let me out."

My belly knotted as I stared at the flickering gemstone, wincing as the world shook once more. "Maybe. If you promise to go far away from here."

"Happily."

"Vow it to me." Narrowing my eyes, I waited for her response.

She tsked. "Fine. I vow it."

No magic skittered along my arms in response. I didn't feel a hint of power at all. It did not surprise me that the gods were not bound to the same rules of magic that mortals and fae were. She had not truly vowed a damn thing.

But she had no idea that I realized that.

Mouth dry, I nodded. "All right. How do I release you?"

The gemstone seemed to expand, the glow intensifying.

"I knew you would make the right choice, Tessa Baran. We are so alike, you and me. Now, come closer."

Frowning, I did as she asked, though her words scraped through me. I was nothing like the God of Death.

"Place your hand against the heart of me and pull me into your chest."

I stepped back. "I beg your pardon?"

Her voice turned sharp. "Do what I said. You're running out of time. Your beloved Mist King is on his knees. He has wounds all across his back from where the rocks have slammed into him. He will bleed to death if you do not release me. I won't let him heal until then."

My breath hitched, horror snaking through me with venomous fangs. "You're stopping him from accessing his healing powers, too?"

"Oh yes. Now, let me out."

"You're a monster," I whispered.

"I am a god." Her voice boomed in the cavern.

Sucking the biting cold into my lungs, I lifted a trembling hand and placed it in the center of the glowing stone. It hummed beneath my fingers, the light flaring in anticipation. Power curled through me, beckoning me closer. Closing my eyes, I tried not to think about what this could mean. I'd gone up against a powerful being once before and had failed. Oberon was no god, but he was the closest thing the humans of Teine had to one. Could I risk doing anything other than what the god had asked? Would this kill me?

What other choice did I have?

Kalen would die if I didn't do something. The building would crumble down on top of me. Nothing would stand in Oberon's way anymore. The gods would return.

I leaned into the rock, a silent prayer on my lips. Not to

any god or fae or mortal alive. But to the person I'd always wanted to be. Someone who could make a difference.

The girl who had always dreamed of a better world.

With a roar, I whipped the wooden dagger from my tunic and slammed the blunt end into the glowing stone. Power shook, throwing me back. My teeth slammed together when I hit the ground hard, and ringing filled my ears.

The god's brutal power ripped through the rumbling cavern, filling up my head with its guttural, inhuman sound. I clapped my hands over my ears and pushed up onto my feet, eyes wide at the sight before me.

My blade had cracked the gemstone, shattering it in the middle. A dark power rushed out of it like liquid smoke. As soon as it hit the air, it misted, swirled, and then vanished like it had never been there.

I stood in the center of the cavern, my heart thundering, until the last remnants of the power disappeared. Hugging my arms to my chest, I inched closer to the stone. It was silent and dark and dead. The cracked gem held no more power now. But was it really gone? Had I destroyed the god? Could it really have been that easy?

Either way, Kalen should have his powers back. He could fight now.

Hope flaring to life in my chest, I raced up the stairs. Midnight stood waiting for me, his body blocking the door that led into the storm.

"Move, Midnight," I said, tugging at his reins. "I have to go out there and help Kalen."

Help Kalen. As if there was anything I could do against a group of storm fae. But I couldn't leave him out there to fight them alone, especially if he was wounded. I needed to draw the enemy away from him. Just for a few moments. Long enough for him to heal.

"Come on," I pleaded with the horse, who didn't so much as blink in my direction. And then I had an idea. "He needs *our* help."

Midnight looked at me.

"That's right." I nodded. "We ride out there into that fucking storm and distract those assholes long enough for Kalen to heal. And then they're dead."

He whinnied, stomping his massive hooves, and then he shifted to the side, as if inviting me to climb onto his back. I hauled myself up, grateful that some of my strength had returned to me. I was going to have to ride like light through that storm and hold on with everything I had in me.

"I'm trusting you," I muttered to the horse before leaning forward to shove at the door. "I know you like the buck people off and—"

Midnight charged into the raging storm, knocking the door off its hinges. I yelped and gripped his mane to keep from tumbling off onto the rain-battered ground. Wind and ice still churned through the city, but the strength of it was nowhere near what it had been at the start.

Bending forward against the storm, I risked a glance around. Three storm fae were converging on Kalen, who knelt on the ground. Blood dripped down his back and his shoulders curved forward as his head lolled to his chest.

Something in me cracked at seeing him like that, and furious tears filled my eyes.

"Oi!" I shouted at the trio. "Leave him alone!"

The three storm fae jerked up their heads, and their gazes fell upon me. I shuddered. Midnight jerked sideways, galloping away from the center of the town toward the thickening mists. But the quick glimpse I'd caught of the storm fae had rattled my bones.

Their eyes were hollow and as bright as ice. They had silver hair that cascaded around their broad shoulders. A symbol was branded on each of their necks—a symbol that made my soul ache. I didn't know what it meant, but I could feel the darkness of it reaching toward me. There was something wrong with those storm fae, more than just the god's boost of power that had been helping them trap us here.

And I needed them to hunt me.

The shouted cries from behind told me they'd taken the bait. If they'd come here for me, so that they might ally themselves with Oberon, they couldn't risk letting me get away. Holding on tight, I leaned into Midnight as we charged through the mists. A blast of wind hit me in the back.

"Come on, Midnight," I whispered into his ear. "Run like you've never run before."

His hooves thundered against the ground, spraying sand and dirt onto my legs. Mist burned my eyes, and the world transformed into a field of shadows and darkness. I could hear the hooves of the enemy echoing close behind, but as I twisted to glance over my shoulder, I couldn't spot them through the dense fog.

Good. That meant they might not be able to see me, either.

An arrow whistled through the air and punched Midnight's rear leg. I screamed as he stumbled to the side. His cries of pain ripped through the night. I flew off his back, skidded across the ground, and rolled out of the way. My palms scraped against the coarse sand as Midnight crashed toward me.

As he came to a heavy stop on his side, he blinked at me

through the fog. A pitiful sound escaped his throat. My chest ached, but as I began to reach toward him, footsteps sounded nearby. I sucked in a breath and stood on shaky legs, whirling toward the approaching attackers.

A storm fae on a silver steed rose from the mist. I angled my body in front of Midnight, my heart hammering so hard, I thought I might be sick.

The storm fae smiled, slowing to a stop only a few feet from where I stood. "King Oberon's bride."

His voice crackled like ice, and a powerful wind whipped toward me, tugging at my long braid.

I narrowed my eyes. "I'm no one's bride, especially not his."

"He believes differently. And what Oberon wants, Oberon gets. You're coming with us." The storm fae dismounted, his heavy leather boots thudding against the sand. A spray of dark mist washed over me as I stumbled backward.

I whipped out my dagger and pointed it at his chest. The storm fae merely smiled and pressed himself against the bloodied tip. Eyes flashing, he leaned closer to me, so close I could smell the rain on his breath.

"You truly think a mortal like you could harm me? That you could run from your fae king and never get caught? There is nowhere you can go in this world that he could not find you. You are *his*."

With an angry growl, I shoved my pitiful blade into his chest, but it barely did a damn thing, his leather armor protecting him. Not that it would have mattered. Even if the wood slid into skin, he would have healed, just like Oberon had.

The storm fae laughed, wrapped a hand around my neck,

and lifted me from the ground. My feet dangled beneath me as he shook me hard. I sucked at the air, desperate to get in a breath, but he squeezed so tightly that all I could do was choke on it.

Fear tumbled through me. He clearly wouldn't kill me, not when he needed to deliver me alive to Oberon. But he would make me suffer. He'd steal all the breath from my lungs, just enough to knock me out. And then I would have no way to fight back.

The world went dark in the corners of my eyes.

And then a tall, mist-enshrouded figure rose up behind the storm fae like a wraith from my worst nightmares. A pair of sapphire eyes gleamed in the shadows.

Strong hands grabbed the storm fae's head. Surprise flickered in the silver eyes. The Mist King twisted hard, snapping the enemy's neck.

I sucked in a desperate breath of air as the storm fae collapsed. Pain still ripped through my neck, and dark spots flickered in my vision. But I could breathe, and Kalen was here. Relief and hope tangled in my gut. He was here.

He caught me before I fell. With a shuddering breath, he yanked me to his chest, and the scent of snow consumed me.

I awoke with my head on his lap and his fingers caressing the strands of hair that had sprang free from my braid. His hand tensed when he spied me staring up at him, at the mist swirling across his jaw.

"Thank the moon. You're awake." His voice sounded rough, and the look in his eye was the whisper of a ribbon curling around my heart. For a moment, I forgot to breathe, too caught up in the heat of him, the feel of his hand against my hair, and everything still unspoken between us.

Swallowing, I sat up and felt my neck. It was tender on one side, and my back hissed with pain. The wounds must have reopened during the fight.

"What happened?" I asked as I pressed trembling fingers to my forehead. Every single part of me felt wrung out, like a dirty rag left too long in the sunshine.

Kalen's eyes flashed. "The bastard tried to choke you. So I snapped his fucking neck."

My memories flashed back to the moment Kalen had risen from the shadows like some kind of avenging god. I shuddered, though not from fear. He'd looked so...powerful and deadly. And while I knew he'd killed the storm fae because of the threat they posed, I also knew that part of the reason was me.

"You saved my life," I whispered. "Again."

His eyes sparked. "You saved me first. Although, I should be angry at you for rushing out into the fight, risking your life like that after I told you to stay inside."

"I do what I want, Kalen."

A tantalizing smile curled his lips. "Yes, I'm well aware of that. Now, explain to me what happened. One minute, I couldn't use my powers. The next..."

I filled him in on everything, how I'd confronted the god, smashed the gemstone to release her grip on his power, searched for the Mortal Blade and come up empty, then ridden Midnight out into the storm.

My gut twisted at the thought of the horse.

"Is he all right?" I asked. "The fae hit him with an arrow..." Sorrow pulsed through me. I couldn't bear the thought of him dead because he'd helped me. I couldn't stand the thought of him dead at all.

"Midnight is no normal horse. He's almost fully healed." Kalen brushed soft fingers against my neck, staying clear of the tender spot. "The storm is over. As long as you're all right to travel, we can leave this cursed castle now."

I sagged in relief. "And the god? Did I destroy her?"

His lips flattened, and his eyes grew haunted. "I'm not sure, love. We can only hope. It seems unlikely a wooden stake could do something as powerful as that, but you didn't do what she asked, so I don't think you released her, either."

"Where *was* the Mortal Blade, Kalen?" I asked. "Why wasn't it in your bag?"

"I took it out into the storm."

I frowned. "I thought you couldn't use it."

"I can't." A grin spread across his face. "I thought you might go after it and try to use it against them. I didn't want you risking your life, though it appears you found a way to do that anyway."

"Seriously, Kalen? I want to be annoyed at you for this, but..."

His voice dropped. "But what?"

I stared at the blanket, my heart pounding. "I'm just happy you aren't dead."

"Is that so?" he murmured.

"And I know you're not happy about what I did, but—"

"Quite the contrary, love." His hand skimmed up my neck to palm my cheek. "You are exquisitely brave."

Our gazes locked, four eyes caught in a sudden cloud of darkness. I sucked in a gasp and glanced around. The mists seeped from Kalen's skin, and it fogged around us, transforming the red-and-orange Great Hall into a thickening gray. The mists reached for me. They caressed my cheek and trailed down the side of my face like tender fingers. My lungs no longer seemed to work, though my heart had yet to fail. It beat doubly hard, like a roll of thunder had been trapped inside my chest.

All the while, Kalen's gaze stayed locked on my face, the intensity in his expression taking my breath and holding it right in my throat. As if a moth to a flame, I leaned toward him. His mists parted and swirled until another tongue of that delicious power curled around my body, licking at my neck.

Pain shot through me, and I winced.

Suddenly, the mists vanished, blinking away like they'd never even been there at all.

"What's wrong?" Kalen asked, his voice laced with anguished concern. "Did I hurt you?"

"You're not the one who hurt me." Hissing between clenched teeth, I touched my neck. Another blast of pain thundered through me. "It's from where that storm fae tried to strangle me. And my back is hurting again, too. Stupid mortal body."

"There is nothing stupid about your body." He took my chin between his thumb and forefinger before turning my head to the side. His eyes swept across my neck and then his expression darkened. "You're bruised. You may need to rest before we travel."

"I'll be fine," I said. We'd been trapped here for days. Val and Mother were still out there. Kalen's kingdom needed him home. I couldn't be the thing that held us back.

"Hmm." He released his grip on my chin and looked as though he intended to argue, but his back snapped straight.

"I've just felt Boudica arrive. I need to go see what she's brought me."

"Word from Dubnos?"

He nodded. "Let's hope so."

Kalen pushed up from the blanket and vanished out the door. As soon as he was gone, I pressed a hand to my racing heart. What had *that* been? And why did it feel as if I were teetering on the edge of a very tall cliff? I was flirting with danger, tempted by sapphire eyes, strong arms, and a gentle touch.

Yes, Kalen was not who I'd thought he was. I'd been so wrong about everything, but...was I getting too carried away? Could I truly trust him? I hoped I could.

A moment later, he returned with two letters, his raven, and a smile I'd rarely seen. It was a smile of hope. "I've had news from Dubnos."

I stood. "Is everyone all right?"

"The city was attacked, but they were able to push the storm fae back. For now. The enemy army has gathered in the fields beyond the wall, and it looks as though they plan to renew their attacks soon. But the city and castle have survived." He took a slow step toward me. "There's more, Tessa. A second letter from Niamh. I don't quite understand it, but your mother and friend are in Dubnos. They arrived a few days ago. They're alive, love. And they're safe."

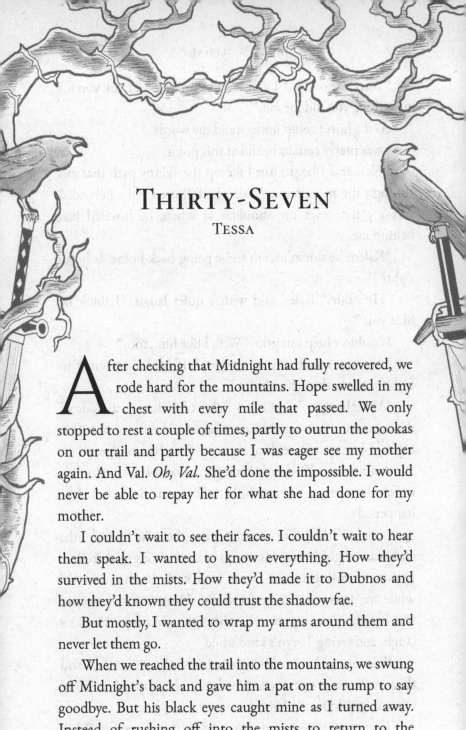

THIRTY-SEVEN
TESSA

After checking that Midnight had fully recovered, we rode hard for the mountains. Hope swelled in my chest with every mile that passed. We only stopped to rest a couple of times, partly to outrun the pookas on our trail and partly because I was eager see my mother again. And Val. *Oh, Val.* She'd done the impossible. I would never be able to repay her for what she had done for my mother.

I couldn't wait to see their faces. I couldn't wait to hear them speak. I wanted to know everything. How they'd survived in the mists. How they'd made it to Dubnos and how they'd known they could trust the shadow fae.

But mostly, I wanted to wrap my arms around them and never let them go.

When we reached the trail into the mountains, we swung off Midnight's back and gave him a pat on the rump to say goodbye. But his black eyes caught mine as I turned away. Instead of rushing off into the mists to return to the merchant, he pawed at the ground, watching me.

"You can go now," I said to him, smiling. "Thank you for everything you did for me."

As if a horse could understand my words...

I was pretty certain he did at this point.

Kalen and I began our hike up the skinny path that cut through the mountains. Midnight followed right behind. I cast a glance over my shoulder at where he hovered just behind me.

"Kalen, he doesn't seem to be going back home. Is he all right?"

"He's fine," Kalen said with a quiet laugh. "I think he likes you."

I couldn't help but grin. "Well, I like him, too."

"Teg, the merchant, won't mind. If Midnight wants to come with us, that's his choice."

"All right then." Smiling, I followed Kalen up the side of the mountain, passing the cave where we'd camped that first night. Now, it felt so long ago, as if it had happened in another lifetime. We'd only been gone a couple of weeks, but it felt like years. So much had changed. So much had happened.

I couldn't help but wonder what the next few months and years might bring. Mornings spent training with Kalen. Evenings feasting in the Great Hall with Mother and Val while we dreamed of a better world. Hours packed around the hearth, listening to Niamh's tales, hearing Alastair's laugh, and seeing Toryn's kind smile.

Kalen would win this fight against the storm fae, and then we'd turn our focus south, to the day when King Oberon would finally fall.

There was a piece of it that I didn't dare hope for. What had happened between me and Kalen in Itchen had been...

intoxicating. I couldn't lie to myself and pretend I didn't want that with him, and so much more. There was something about Kalen that drew me in. He saw me for who I was, and he understood me in the same way I understood him. When I looked into his eyes, I felt as though I saw the core truth of who he was.

But I didn't know if it would ever be more than what it had been—a moment of passion in the middle of a storm of danger. We hadn't spoken a word about it since, and we'd been traveling at such a furious pace that I'd barely had time to eat and catch my breath, let alone anything else.

After another long night spent trekking up the mountain, Kalen and I strode through the looming city gates on tired, aching feet. My eyes were puffy, and my throat felt a little raw from all the mist I'd sucked into my lungs, trying desperately to keep up. I needed to sit down, and then sleep for days.

But first, I needed to see my mother and Val. The thought of them spurred me on.

Niamh sprinted out of the castle and threw her arms around Kalen's neck, Alastair just behind her. Tears were in her eyes when she pulled back and scanned her king's face. "You're here."

He grasped her hands in his, pressing his forehead against hers. When he spoke, his voice was rough with emotion. "And you're all right. How's Toryn?"

"So much better. He's waiting for you in his room," she said.

Alastair thumped Kalen on the back, and then turned to me with a smile. "Glad to see you're alive and well, too, little dove."

"Where are they?" I blurted, knowing how rude that

came across, but I couldn't wait even a second longer to see them. I had hoped they'd come out to meet us with Niamh and Alastair.

Niamh cocked her head as she pulled away from Kalen. "Where's who?"

"My mother. And my friend, Val."

Niamh's brows furrowed as she glanced at Alastair and then at Kalen. "I'm sorry, Tessa. They're not here. Should they be?"

My heart pounded my ribs as Kalen frowned. "We got a letter from you. Boudica brought it to me with your first letter about the storm fae attack. It said they're here."

I tried to calm my panic as Kalen pulled the two letters from his pack and showed them to Niamh. Surely, there was some kind of confusion, and they'd clear it up right here and now, and then they'd take me to see my family.

Val and Mother were here. We'd received a letter saying they were. There had to be some sort of explanation for this.

Niamh scowled as she read the page. "I didn't write *that* letter. Someone else did." She lifted her eyes to my face and winced. "I hate to say this, but someone has tried to trick you. Probably the storm fae. I'm so sorry, Tessa. I know how upset you must—"

"This can't be right." My chin began to tremble. "They have to be here somewhere."

Alastair heaved out a breath, compassion in his eyes. "The storm fae must have intercepted our letter about the attack and then forged this other one."

"But why would they do that?" I asked in a hoarse voice. "What would be the point? It makes no sense. Where are Mother and Val?"

I couldn't accept that they weren't here. The truth stared

me right in the face, but I refused to look at it. If they weren't here, then that meant they were still out in the mists, alone. Or dead. That was impossible. I had to believe they were inside that castle, *alive*.

My knees nearly buckled.

Kalen's voice was soft when he spoke. "They're trying to capture you and take you back to Oberon. Perhaps they think it will be easier to get to you if you're here. I am so sorry, Tessa. I had no idea."

The truth hit me square in the gut. Val and Mother had not made it to Dubnos, and I would not see their faces tonight. Tears burned my eyes.

"I need to go back," I whispered, glancing to each of the shadow fae. "I have to go find them. They're still out there in the mists and—"

Alastair clapped his hand on my shoulder and nodded. "You look like you're about to pass out, little dove. Why don't you get some rest, and then we can come up with a plan tomorrow? Plus, we could really use Kalen for at least a few hours. A fight is looming. His power is greater than ours and—"

"Kalen doesn't have to go with me," I said in a hollow voice, studying his tense face. "We released each other from our vow."

Niamh shot Kalen a scowl. "The vow about killing Oberon? Why the fuck did you go and do that?"

"We can discuss the details later," Kalen said, turning to me. "Alastair is right, Tessa. You need to get some rest. We only briefly stopped on our way back here. You can barely stay upright."

Midnight nudged me from behind and nickered his agreement. The traitor.

"But Val and Mother," I whispered, my heart flaring with pain.

"You can't help them if you run yourself into the ground," Kalen said firmly. "Get some sleep, and I promise we will come up with a plan to find them tomorrow."

Even though I felt too numb to argue, my mind was screaming. My body trembled from all the exhaustion and fear and pain, building on top of me until I felt I might crumple beneath the weight of it. A part of me had started to heal these past few weeks, but the wound threatened to rip wide open once more.

Midnight nudged my arm, rubbing his snout against me. I leaned on him and closed my eyes. This couldn't be happening.

Val and Mother were supposed to be here. I was no closer to finding them than I had been before. And I had no way of knowing if they were even alive.

Kalen went to see Toryn before heading to the war room with Niamh and Alastair, while I was left to fend for myself and the horrible revelations that had slammed into me. It was hard to blame him for that. His city was being threatened by an enemy determined to destroy them all—the same enemy that had tried to kill him in the mists. The very same enemy that had sent that letter tricking me. They'd made me believe my family was here.

I felt adrift in a world that was not my own. I had no one to talk to. There was nothing to do but wander through the fire-lit corridors of deep gray stone. Nothing to do but go over everything that had happened again and again until I could make sense of it all.

Nothing to do but worry.

If the storm fae knew about Mother and Val leaving the Kingdom of Light, did that mean Oberon did, too? Had he gone looking for them in Teine to punish them for my escape? He hadn't found them, of course. They were already gone. But what had happened to the other villagers?

Had he punished anyone else?

Running a hand along my braided hair, I paced the halls until my feet felt like two bruised peaches. I needed to at least sit down, even if I couldn't sleep. Kalen and the others had been right about one thing. My body was broken after our journey through the mists. My back still ached from the pooka's wound. The bruise around my neck had barely begun to fade.

So, I would eat and sleep, if I could. And then I'd head back out into the mists, regardless of whether Kalen joined me.

I would never stop trying to find my family.

I trudged through the castle until I found the room they'd prepared for me. My quarters for the night. Inside, I found a large bed draped in the finest cottons. The fresh scent of washed linens hung in the air. A fire had been lit in the hearth and was crackling and warm. Crossing the room, I gazed out the single window at the mountainside. Through the mist, the moon shone bright.

Sighing, I closed my eyes and leaned against the wall. My heart ached for Mother and Val. Despite the looming battle, this castle was the safest place in both kingdoms. But maybe they'd made it to Endir. Maybe the fae and mortals who lived there had taken them under their wing, protecting them from the wraiths and the pookas and all the other dangers of the mists.

I had to hope they still stood a chance out there. And I had to believe I could find them before it was too late.

Something glittered in the corner of my eye. Tensing, I whirled toward the bed. A folded piece of parchment sat squarely on the duvet, and a length of golden chain stuck out. I'd been so wrapped up in my thoughts when I'd entered the room that I hadn't noticed anything was on the bed until now.

I snatched up the paper, and Val's golden necklace tumbled onto the bed, along with a pale gray gemstone. Gasping, I unfolded the note and read the words.

Tessa,

    I've found your mother. She and your friend are trapped in the dungeons beneath Albyria. The captain has known all along.

    Use the communication stone to contact your mother. Hold it above fire and speak her name. I've given her a stone, too, but the guards will see the fire. You won't have much time to speak with her.

    Make it count.

    Yours,

    Morgan

Hands shaking, I dropped the note like it was a viper. Val's mischievous grin flashed in the back of my mind. My mother's sweet smile. Nothing made sense. It was too much for my exhausted mind to comprehend, and my heart felt on the brink of destruction. All this time, they'd been trapped in Oberon's dungeons...or had they?

I paced the room, twisting my braid in my hands. There were so many letters, so many lies, so many fae with agendas. I had trusted Morgan to get me out of the Kingdom of Light. She'd followed through, but she'd also hidden the truth from me. She'd never told me who the captain was.

Kalen had lied to me, about a lot of things, but things had changed these past few weeks. He'd helped me. He'd cared for me...hadn't he? A scream built up in my throat, but I held it back. I swallowed down my rage and tried to *focus*. Something wasn't right about this.

My heart hurt from the twisting thorns that wrapped around it. They dug in deep, the sharp points like knives. I brushed away tears as I plucked the communication stone from my bed and held it up in the dim light. Letters were nothing but words, and they easily held lies. If Morgan was telling the truth, I wanted to see it with my own eyes.

If Kalen had betrayed me, I needed to be sure of it.

I went over to the door and locked it before kneeling in front of the hearth. Metal tongs were propped up beside it, and I used them to hold the stone over the flames. Dark lines curled across the pale surface of the gemstone, twisting like snakes. The shadows consumed the entire jewel until it was black.

"Ula Baran," I whispered, my hand trembling and shaking the tongs.

A moment passed with nothing but the crackle of the fire. And then the surface of the stone wavered. My mother's face blurred into view, and behind her I could see the bars of a cell. I sucked in a breath and almost dropped the stone, my heart leaping at the sight of her. Even with the matted hair and the dark shadows beneath her eyes, she'd never looked more beautiful.

A sob choked out of me. She was there. She was alive.

"Mother?" I gasped.

"Oh, Tessa, my love," she said, leaning forward. "I have never been happier to see your face in my life. Are you all right?"

I opened my mouth to tell her everything, but Morgan's warning rang in my ears. We wouldn't have much time to talk before the guards spotted the flame that powered the communication stone.

"I'm fine. Don't worry about me." I mashed my lips together. "Is it true you're in Albyria's dungeon?"

She glanced over her shoulder at the bars. "I'm afraid so. Listen, your Mist King knows about it, too. You need to get away from him, Tessa. Don't listen to his promises about finding me and Val. We've been here this whole time, and he *wanted* us in here. He's been lying to you, and we can't be sure why, but it's—"

The stone cracked in two, and Mother's face vanished. A vicious monster rose up inside of me, causing my entire body to shake with anger. With a silent roar, I hauled back my hand and threw the stone into the fire. It shattered, just like my heart.

All this time, Kalen—the Mist King—had known where my family was. He'd taken me on a wild chase through the mists, tempting me with the idea that they were out there, that all we had to do was find them.

All to trick me into trusting him. I never should have listened to a word he'd said.

It had all been a lie.

THIRTY-EIGHT

TESSA

Chest tight, I perched on the edge of the bed and focused on the words that blurred before me. I couldn't stop reading the letter from Morgan. A tear dripped from my cheek and splattered on the ink, smudging it until it was unrecognizable. Kalen had lied to me. He had never wanted to help me find my family.

That was why he'd released me from our vow. So that he would no longer be bound to his promise. But then what about his plot against Oberon? I shook my head, crumpling the note in my fist. Clearly, the Mist King had done all this to get me to trust him. Then, I'd no longer need the motivation of our vow to do what I'd promised him.

He was free to stop looking for my family. Now, he could go back to what mattered most to him: winning a war against the other kingdoms.

He'd known I'd still want to kill Oberon. This way, he got what he wanted without giving me anything in return.

My heart thumped as I strode to the window and gazed outside. Through the mists, I could spot the flicker of torches from the battlefield. What was the real reason for this battle? Why did the storm fae want to fight him now? For me or for something else entirely? I had no way of knowing. The lies were so thick that I could not swim in them. Soon, I would drown.

My stomach twisted in on itself. Sucking a sharp breath, I sat hard on the bed. How much of what he'd told me had been true? What had been false?

Which king was the liar?

I knew the answer to that, at least. They both were.

For the first time in my life, I did not barrel head-first into action without thinking things through. The Mist King had taught me that. What was better than using his own advice and training against him? He had no idea that I knew about his betrayal, and right now, he was distracted by battle plans.

I had some time to plot.

I lay flat on my back, legs crossed at the ankle, staring up at the ceiling. A mural in deep violets and blues spread across it, a night sky lit up by thousands of stars. Mist sprayed in at every corner. Beautiful but deadly. Like him.

First things first, I needed to get out of here. But if he'd gone to so much trouble to keep me in Dubnos, spinning elaborate lies, I doubted he'd let me walk out of the castle gates. All that talk about giving me freedom, he hadn't meant it. He'd just wanted me to trust him.

So, I needed to get out of this castle. I needed to make it through the mists alive—thankfully, Midnight might help me with that. And then I needed to sneak back into Albyria so that I could free Mother and Val.

Anger rushed through me at the thought of Oberon and everything he'd done to my people. I still wanted him dead, especially now. Deep down, I knew that some of what the Mist King had told me was true. Oberon was a monster who needed to be stopped, and he stood in the way of my family's safety.

If he caught me, I'd never be free. He'd probably murder my mother and Val to break me once again.

I needed to get the Mortal Blade and kill him.

But if I killed him, his protective circle around Albyria would vanish. The mists would swarm Teine. Death and danger would follow. I could no longer trust the Mist King to provide safe passage to somewhere beyond the sea. The mortals would die.

My heart hammered as my mind spun through a thousand different answers. But there was only one way. One brutal way for me to save my family and everyone else in Teine.

I not only had to kill Oberon. I had to kill the Mist King, too. If he was dead, I did not think the mists would vanish entirely—they existed beyond him. But it would stop him from spreading them further across the lands. It would stop him from invading Teine.

Unfortunately, the gemstone that powered the Mortal Blade would only work once. I'd need to replace it to use the blade a second time.

But I had an idea.

When the clock chimed midnight, I cracked open my bedroom door and peered out into the silent corridor. My body tensed in anticipation of being seen by a soldier or member of the court, but the crackle of the torches was my only answer. With a deep breath, I slipped out into the hall.

My boots tapped against the stone as I crept forward, my eyes aimed on the path to the Mist King's quarters, which were situated just beside the war room. I doubted he'd be sleeping now. Instead, he'd be at his table with Niamh and Alastair, plotting their moves well into the night. He wouldn't see me slither into his room to snatch the Mortal Blade.

As soon as I got my hands on it, I would topple one of the stone statues that lined the hall, the bust of a former king from centuries past. Niamh and Alastair would rush into the hallway to investigate, and I would slip inside the war room to confront the Mist King alone.

And then I would stab him.

Hands sweaty, I pressed my fingers against his door and carefully pushed it open. My heart pounded in my ears, muted by the roar of my blood. With every other step, the memory of his lips against mine flashed through my mind. Eyes burning, I shoved that image away over and over, hoping it would vanish for good. I couldn't think of him like that. Not anymore. He wasn't the fae I'd grown close to in Itchen. That had been Kalen, a person who didn't exist.

This was the Mist King.

I closed the door behind me and pressed my back against the wall, barely daring to breathe as I stared at the empty bed. Relief shook through me. He wasn't here. If he'd been asleep, that might have made things easier, but I wanted to look into his eyes when he realized I knew exactly how much he'd betrayed me.

I would never again let a fae king rip my heart to shreds.

Quickly, I crossed the floor, spotting the abandoned pack in an instant. He'd left it hanging open on the floor beside his bed, as if he'd hastily dumped it before rushing off to his battle meeting. I knelt beside it and rustled through the contents.

Canteen. Blanket. And...my hand brushed iron.

The world slowed around me.

Breath catching, I pulled the Mortal Blade from the Mist King's bag and held it up before me. The gemstone gleamed in the center of the weapon, flickering with eternal fire. It was the color of the eversun, whose power rushed through it.

Enough power for a mortal to kill a fae king.

I was so transfixed by it that I did not hear the door open.

"Tessa?" the Mist King asked from behind me. His voice held none of the softness he'd shown me in the final few days of our journey. Now, his words were laced with suspicion, as if he understood at once exactly why I was here, kneeling on the floor beside his open pack.

Slowly, I stood and turned to face him, careful to hide the blade behind my back. My heartbeat thrummed in my neck at the look in his eye. Pure, unyielding darkness.

"What are you doing in here?" he asked in a lethal quiet.

"I..." Swallowing hard, I glanced around. My fingers trembled around the blade. "I thought I might sleep better in here."

His eyes narrowed. "You're lying."

"No, I'm not. I truly couldn't sleep."

"Why have you taken the Mortal Blade from my bag?"

My muscles tensed. "What makes you think I did that?"

"Do not take me for a fool," he growled, pushing away from the door to close the distance between us. I sucked in a breath and stumbled a few steps back, knocking my backside against the edge of his bed. Fumbling, I whipped the dagger around to my front. And just as he reached me, I pointed it at his heart.

He froze. Pain flickered in his eyes. Rage and hurt tangled together like thorny vines around my heart. *No.* I couldn't be weak now when it mattered the most. He was the one who'd caused this. All of this was his fault. If I did not do what had to be done, my people would not survive.

He'd lied to me.

"What are you doing, Tessa?" he asked in a low, dangerous voice. "You want to train? Is that it? Because you want to go find your family? That's fine. Just remember that if you even so much as graze my skin with that, I die."

"I know exactly what it does," I whispered fiercely, tears building in my eyes. "That's why I'm here, Mist King. To do what I should have done the first time I saw it in your bag."

His sapphire eyes widened with a flash of pain, but then his expression went flat. "So, you've come here to kill me. I don't suppose you want to explain why."

"Why do you think?" My hand shook, the dagger point whispering against his unbuttoned tunic. Just one little push up, that was all it would take. The knife would graze his skin, and he'd be gone. "Morgan sent me a letter. She told me Oberon has had my family all this time. I used a communication stone to see my mother, so don't even pretend like it's not true. They've been trapped in his dungeons while you've led me around in the mists like an idiot, tricking me into... They're *my family*." My voice cut off as an unwanted sob shook me. "All this time, they've been trapped there. All this time, you knew. Oberon could have easily killed them, and I wouldn't have been able to do a damn thing to save them because I was stuck wandering the mists because of your lies. You're exactly what I thought you were. You're the Mist King." I lifted my eyes so that he could see the true depths of my hatred for him. "And you betrayed me."

Understanding lifted his brows, but the rest of his face remained blank. As if he'd checked out, as if this conversation was beneath him. "I see."

"*You see?*" Tears blurred my vision. Heart roaring with pain, I angled the blade so that all it would take was one tiny shove to hit his heart. "After everything that's happened between us, that's all you have to say to me? *You see?*"

His hand wound around my wrist as anger blazed in his eyes. Tears streaming down my cheeks, I pulled against him.

"You did the one thing I could never forgive, Kalen. *The one thing.* The women in my life mean more to me than anything else in the world, and that includes men who whisper sweet words with their poisoned tongues. And if they fall, *I fall.*"

"Let go of the blade," he said, reaching out his other hand to try to snatch the weapon from me.

He was stronger than me. So much stronger. If he grabbed my other hand, he'd have the dagger, and there would be nothing I could do to save my family. He'd keep me here.

It would all be over. Desperation raked through me.

And so I shoved.

The blade inched into his chest, slicing right into his left abs. Something within me shattered, the pain so great I gasped. Gritting my teeth, I let go, horror twisting my gut.

The Mist King's eyes widened in shock. Shadows fled. The gemstone cracked, light spilling out. As a storm of mist blasted me in the face, his entire body shuddered.

The most powerful fae alive thundered to the ground.

My hands flew to my mouth. Shaking, I knelt and pulled the blade from his chest before wiping the blood against the bed. I couldn't look at him as I grabbed his pack and stuffed the knife back in. I couldn't watch the life leave his eyes. Despite how horribly he'd betrayed me, despite knowing he'd wanted to use me for his own gain, pain tore my heart into a million tattered ribbons.

I had cared for him. Kalen, the shadow fae who was willing to do anything to save the world, who had looked at me and saw the truth of my heart. But that wasn't the real him. Kalen had been nothing but a lie.

Brushing away the tears, I threw open the door and ran.

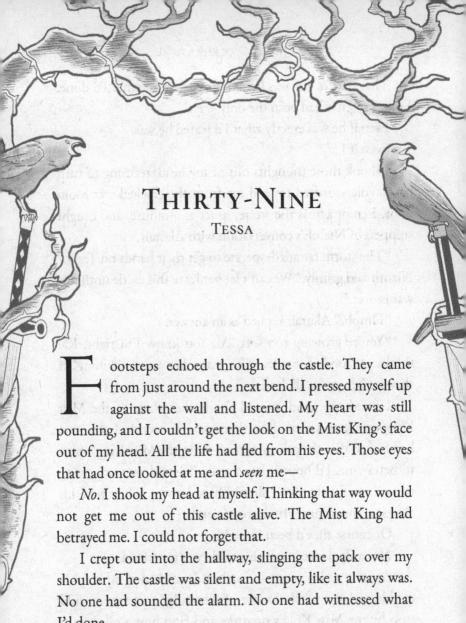

THIRTY-NINE

TESSA

Footsteps echoed through the castle. They came from just around the next bend. I pressed myself up against the wall and listened. My heart was still pounding, and I couldn't get the look on the Mist King's face out of my head. All the life had fled from his eyes. Those eyes that had once looked at me and *seen* me—

No. I shook my head at myself. Thinking that way would not get me out of this castle alive. The Mist King had betrayed me. I could not forget that.

I crept out into the hallway, slinging the pack over my shoulder. The castle was silent and empty, like it always was. No one had sounded the alarm. No one had witnessed what I'd done.

Thank the light for that.

For a moment, I paused, halfway between the Mist King's door and the entrance to the war room. My gut twisted, a vision of his vacant eyes haunting me. A part of me wanted to turn back, to try to revive him, to try and stop the power of the blade.

That part of me was breaking apart from what I'd done. Even though it had been the only way...

Even if he was exactly what I'd feared he was.

Even if I...

I shook those thoughts out of my head, refusing to turn back. Voices drifted toward me from the cracked war room door. I crept across the stone, quiet as a mouse, and caught snippets of Niamh's conversation with Alastair.

"The storm fae are desperate to get their hands on Tessa," Niamh said grimly. "We can't let her leave this castle until this war is over."

"Hmph," Alastair replied as an answer.

"You're growing too soft, Al. You know I'm right. Kal thinks so, too." A rustle. "She is the key to us winning. If they get her, we're all dead."

I fisted my hand around the leather strap of the Mist King's pack and carried on. For some nonsensical reason, I had hoped that the others weren't in on the Mist King's plan to betray me. I'd hoped they'd truly believed we were trying to save my family. But I should have known. They were his closest companions. His dearest friends.

Of course they'd been in on it.

Not a single fae inside this castle was my friend.

As soon as I was out of earshot, I quickened my steps. I couldn't dally much longer. Eventually, someone would stop by the Mist King's quarters and find him a pile of ash inside. They'd quickly realize I was on the run and come after me.

I needed to be out of this castle before that happened.

No guards blocked my way as I rushed into the shadowy courtyard. Midnight was in the stables, munching on hay.

"Hello, Midnight. I'm back already." I grabbed a saddle

and prepared him to run, tying the pack on as well. "We need to go. Fast."

He gave me a strange look but didn't object as I led him out of the castle gates and down the hill. We didn't stop, as painful as my feet felt. Exhaustion was ripping my eyes and body to shreds, but I knew I had to keep moving. Every moment wasted took me one step closer to the shadow fae catching up to me.

At the base of the mountain, I swung up onto Midnight's back and urged him forward. He took off through the mists. Hours passed. My vision grew blurry, and a few times, I started to slide off his back. Once, the jar of his gallop nearly knocked me off into the blowing sand.

I desperately needed to rest. I wasn't going to make it unless I did.

Midnight slowed outside the abandoned village where Kalen—no, the Mist King—and I had stayed. Heart in my throat, I dismounted and scanned the empty courtyard. My eyes caught on the home with its broken window and rotted, swinging door.

Sorrow filled my heart.

Here, he'd saved me from a pooka. Here, he'd broken down my walls.

And I thought I'd broken down his. At least partially.

Sagging against the horse, I closed my eyes. Why did all that have to be a lie?

"It's no use wishing for things that never were and never will be," I whispered to Midnight before opening my eyes. He stared at me and stomped his hooves. I couldn't tell if he agreed or if he was angry at me. After all, he'd tried to help the Mist King, too.

"Come on, let's go inside."

The bed was just as we'd left it. No one else had stayed here from what I could tell. Sighing, I settled onto the empty mattress and pulled the cloak up to my chin. I'd brought it with me. It still smelled like him.

"Goodnight, Midnight," I whispered.

Some might've found it odd to bring a horse inside a house, but I wouldn't leave him out there in the mists to fend for himself. Pookas could decide to enter this building, but he'd fare better in here than out there. Wooden walls were better than mist.

Besides, I felt safer with him by my side.

Despite my raw emotions and churning thoughts, it did not take long for sleep to claim me. With the Mist King's heavy cloak warm against my body and the soothing sound of Midnight's breaths, I drifted away into a familiar dream.

I blinked around me at the forest rising up at the edge of a verdant field. In the distance, the familiar rooftops of Teine reflected the eversun's morning light. My breath caught as I gazed at the old tree and its bent trunk where the Mist King once sat.

Once. Pain tore at my heart. He wasn't there now, of course. Because he was dead.

Still, my presence here unnerved me. I'd never dreamt about this forest unless led here by him. But he was gone. I'd stabbed him with the Mortal Blade and had watched the life drain from his eyes. My subconscious was playing tricks on me. Awake, I could not stop thinking about what I'd done, regardless of knowing that it had been my only choice.

My face felt wet. I lifted my fingers to my cheek and found tears. Even in a dream, I was crying over him. *Stupid girl.*

The dappled forest called to me. I wove through the flowing grass and perched on a branch in the Mist King's tree. As I leaned back, settling into the bark, I could understand why he'd liked it here. Birdsong filled the sweet air thick with the scent of wildflowers. A tree limb dipped low overhead, its brilliant leaves swaying in the breeze.

It was peaceful here. And quiet.

And it made my bones feel as if they were home.

I tried not to think about the times we'd come here. Before, when I'd thought of him as Captain, that mask had hidden his face from view. For a long time, I'd only known him by those brilliant ice-blue eyes. In memory of his mother.

My chest ached. With a sigh, I swung my legs over the side of the trunk and decided to pay my village another visit. Since this dream was so much like the ones I'd shared with the Mist King, the broom would probably be wrong, but at least—

A familiar roar shook through the dream, knocking me off the branch and into the brush beneath the tree.

I glanced up, heart pounding. That had sounded just like...but it was impossible.

Another roar echoed through my mind.

Jolting awake, I sucked in gasps of frantic air. Midnight stomped his feet, shoving his wet nose into my face. He looked distraught. And outside, a wail whipped through the night.

"Oh fuck." I blinked the sleep out of my eyes and jumped to my feet, throwing the cloak over my shoulders. I grabbed Midnight's reins and made for the door. "We have to get out of here fast. I don't know if it's a pooka or a wraith or something else, but we have to go now."

Midnight flicked his ear once.

"Pooka?" I asked him.

I swore the horse nodded.

"All right. We need to move fast." We ran to the door together. Out in the cold night, the mist flowed like rivers of fog, blinding me to anything that hid in the darkness. I leapt onto Midnight's back just as a monstrous beast thundered into the courtyard, fangs bared.

Its claws were drenched with blood, leaving behind a wicked trail as it thundered toward us. I took in its matted gray fur, the violence in its beady eyes. The pookas had found me.

"Go!" I shouted.

Midnight lurched forward. I swallowed down a panicked cry as I clung to his mane, gritting my teeth against the rough, jarring speed of his gallop. The monster screamed behind us and took off in our direction with a terrible swiftness. I glanced over my shoulder, watching the beast give chase. He was only a few steps behind us.

I turned forward once more, trusting the horse to take us in the right direction. "Come on, Midnight. Don't let up. We're both dead if it catches us."

Midnight's skin grew slick with sweat as we hurried onward, tunneling into the darkness.

Another pooka launched out of the shadows, thundering down beside the first. Midnight did not even flinch. He kept charging through the shadows and mists, his eyes locked on the ground ahead. I had no idea what we were going to do once we reached the chasm. We couldn't stop. If we did, the pookas would rip us to shreds.

My mind raced as we kept moving forward. Would someone spot me if I stormed out of the darkness on a horse that reeked of the mists? Did Oberon have guards stationed on the other side, waiting to capture me if I ever dared to return?

I glanced down at the leather bag that held the Mortal Blade. It was strong enough to kill a king. It would be strong enough to kill a foot soldier. But I had no gemstones to power it. Yet.

Another pooka joined the two hot on our trail. I shot a quick glance over my shoulder, mist stinging my eyes. They were not slowing down. If Midnight faltered for even a moment, they'd be on top of us.

I'd have to risk the bridge. We had no other choice. I could stop on this side of the chasm and get ripped to shreds...or cross into the sun-drenched lands and hope no one had an eye on the bridge.

Clutching the horse's mane, I leaned forward. "Can you make it to the bridge?"

He let out a soft whimper but nodded. Poor thing. His skin was so slick with sweat that it beaded as he charged. I knew how he felt. My entire body ached, but especially my back, my butt, and my feet. I'd barely slept an hour back in the abandoned village before the attack.

But there was nothing else we could do. If we gave in to our exhaustion, if we did not keep moving forward, those gaping jaws behind us would swallow us whole.

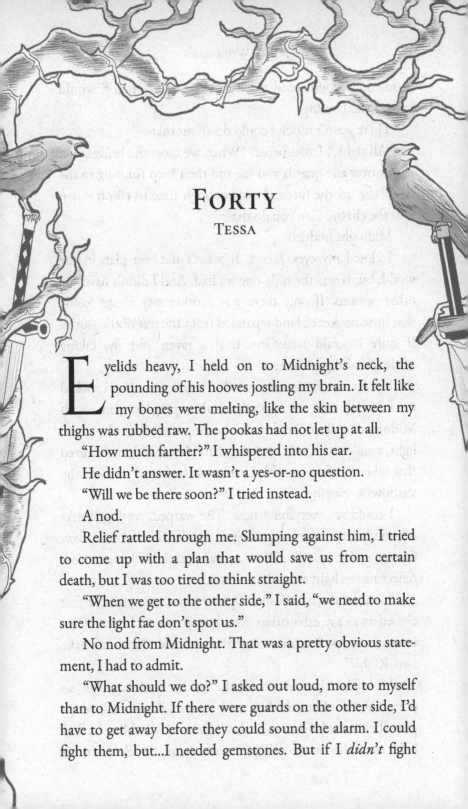

FORTY
TESSA

Eyelids heavy, I held on to Midnight's neck, the pounding of his hooves jostling my brain. It felt like my bones were melting, like the skin between my thighs was rubbed raw. The pookas had not let up at all.

"How much farther?" I whispered into his ear.

He didn't answer. It wasn't a yes-or-no question.

"Will we be there soon?" I tried instead.

A nod.

Relief rattled through me. Slumping against him, I tried to come up with a plan that would save us from certain death, but I was too tired to think straight.

"When we get to the other side," I said, "we need to make sure the light fae don't spot us."

No nod from Midnight. That was a pretty obvious statement, I had to admit.

"What should we do?" I asked out loud, more to myself than to Midnight. If there were guards on the other side, I'd have to get away before they could sound the alarm. I could fight them, but...I needed gemstones. But if I *didn't* fight them, they would send word to the castle. Oberon would know I was coming.

There wasn't much I could do about that.

"All right," I whispered. "When we cross the bridge, just knock over any guards you see and then keep running to the right, toward the forest. I need enough time to climb down into the chasm. Can you do that?"

Midnight nodded.

I closed my eyes. Good. It wasn't the best plan in the world, but it was the only one we had. And I didn't have any other options. If only there was another way to get inside that little pocket of land separated from the rest of the world. If only I could transform into a raven and fly, taking Midnight along with me.

Up ahead, a hazy sun seemed to pierce the mists. I sucked in a breath and sat up, heart thumping in time with Midnight's gallop. We must be nearing the bridge. It was so light, even on this side of the chasm. How had I not realized that when I'd first stumbled across? It had been so dark, the shadows so cloying.

I could see everything now. The warped, rotting planks of wood where the bridge began. At the far end, two hazy figures stood watch. Their massive steel blades gleamed, reflecting the light from the eversun.

"Two of them, Midnight," I said as a new rush of fear chased away my exhaustion. My skin seemed to jump off my bones, anticipation throttling through me. "You can take two. Right?"

Midnight charged across the bridge with a neigh so powerful it could rattle the world. The soldiers jerked, whipping their swords from their shoulders and stumbling back. I held on tight as we galloped past them. Shocked shouts exploded from their throats, and then they sprang into action.

Suddenly, Midnight bucked. My hands slipped on his sweat-soaked mane, failing me. I tumbled off, soaring through the air. When I hit the ground, sand sprayed into my face.

I swiped the sand aside and rolled over onto my back, trying to recover from the new waves of pain wracking my body. What had happened? Why had Midnight thrown me?

That was when I spotted him in the distance, the fae soldiers circling him. And something strange was happening. The horse shuddered as he transformed. His skin rippled, the sleek coat melting away to reveal rough bark. His snout elongated; his teeth grew sharp. The entire creature grew, punching up from the ground so that it towered over the terrified guards.

The beast hauled back his clawed hand and swiped the fae aside, blood spraying the grass.

I swallowed down a ball of nausea. I recognized this creature. It was a joint eater. Tall, with skin the color and texture of a tree, the joint eater's fangs were powerful enough to rip through armor. Spine curved, it lurked there, with blood staining his elongated claws, skinny and sharp like the whittled wooden dagger by my side. As he rose up to his full, terrifying height, his bones creaked like ancient trees swaying in the wind. And then his skin began to burn.

The Mist King's words echoed in my ears. Pookas were allergic to moonlight. I bet they were allergic to sunlight, too. Maybe all the monsters of the mists were, which meant... Oberon's protective circle had never prevented them from crossing the bridge, not like it did to fae. They just did not want to burn to death from the eversun.

I swallowed hard. "Midnight?"

"Run," he hissed in a voice that was a slip of parchment rattling in the wind. "Get your gemstones. I'll hold off anyone who tries to come for you. I can keep watch from the mists."

I slowly stood, awe lifting my chest. "Thank you."

Whirling on my feet, I did not stop to think about what I'd just witnessed. The truth about what Midnight was, hidden beneath the gentle exterior he'd shown until now. I sprinted along the edge of the chasm, my feet still aching with every step. Just ahead, the old familiar forest rose up, tall limbs scratching a clear blue sky. Beyond it sat my village. My heart ached to go there, to see familiar faces, to walk back into my faded blue home and sit in my favorite chair. Pick up a book. Read.

But if the castle fae had somehow spotted me cross the bridge, I couldn't risk leading them to Teine. They'd slaughter everyone who so much as looked at me, let alone helped me.

Branches slapped my arms as I tore through the forest, aiming my sights on the edge of the chasm just through the clearing on my right. Here, no one would be able to spot me. The trees were my shields.

I slowed to a stop at the edge of the chasm. I hadn't scaled down this section of the rock face before, so plenty of gemstones should be waiting near the top. Without a rope to ensure my safety, I couldn't risk climbing too far down.

As I stared into the shadowy depths of the chasm, nerves tangled around my gut. This was a very bad idea. I could die trying to get my hands on more gems. But I also wouldn't be able to protect myself if I turned back now. I'd done this before, I reminded myself. Well over thirty times. I *knew* how to do this. My body was weary, but I was still strong.

After shoving up my sleeves, I gripped the edge of the cliff and eased my legs around the side. They skidded against the rock as I searched for purchase. Heart hammering, I jammed the toe of my boot into a crevice. Thank the light. Carefully, I glanced around at the surface beneath me.

There, another place my feet could grip. I followed the motions, my instincts taking over. Muscles groaning from weeks of no climbing, I inched down the side of the cliff so slowly that an hour must have passed by before I found my first stone.

Sticking my tongue between my teeth, I clung on with one hand while I fumbled for the wooden dagger strapped to my waist. My fingers screamed, my body shaking.

"Light, I wish I had a rope," I hissed between my teeth, sweat beading on my forehead.

My hand closed around the dagger. Arms shaking, I pressed against the chasm wall. I had to grip the rock face with the edges of my fingers, since the dagger was in the way. It was barely enough to hold me in place.

This was going to be even harder than I'd thought.

"Come on, Tessa. You can do this." Now, I was talking to myself. The fear was making me a little delirious.

Forcing myself to remain calm, I got to work on the gemstone. It was slow work, prying the thing out with what I had. My old tools were back home, and I couldn't risk going back for them. But soon, the gemstone popped free and dropped into my hand. I pocketed it and moved on to the next.

I was three gemstones in when an inhuman shriek echoed through the whistling cavern.

I craned my head to glance over my shoulder, my body tense. There, on the opposite side of the chasm, the three pookas who had chased us here were prowling through the mists.

They'd found me.

"Fuck," I whispered, pocketing the third gemstone and starting to climb. I tipped my head back to gaze up at the top of the chasm. It would take a few minutes to reach it, and the pookas wouldn't follow me there, but as long as I was in the chasm—

A pooka screamed as it launched off the opposite side and hurled its body through the air. With a rasping breath, I scrabbled up the rock face as fast as I could. It was coming right for me.

The pooka slammed against the rock face a yard farther down. Sweat dripped into my eyes as I stared down at him. His claws punched the rock, stopping him from tumbling into the abyss. And then, slowly, he lifted his head toward me and snarled.

My heart jolted and I scrambled up the cliff. Hand over hand, foot over foot, I moved as fast as my mortal body would allow.

I didn't know what I would do if it reached me. I wouldn't be able to fight it off.

Another pooka threw itself off the cliff.

I kept climbing.

This one didn't fare as well. It missed its mark and fell into the darkness.

The third continued to pace on the opposite side of the cliff while the first chased me up the rock. It was gaining fast. I climbed, closer and closer to the top.

A shadow darkened the sky above as a figure leaned over

the side of the chasm's edge. Midnight, still in his joint eater form, glared down at me with venomous eyes. Smoke curled from where his bark-like skin burned.

"Hurry," he scraped out in that strange, terrifying voice. Kneeling, he held out a blood-drenched claw. The pooka grabbed my ankle, shrieking, while the third soared from the opposite side, claws outstretched.

It hit the rock, scrabbling up behind us.

I grabbed Midnight's rough hand and clung on tight while he tried to pull me out of the pooka's grip.

"Hold on," he wheezed, planting his feet firmly in the soil. With a roar, he yanked hard.

I reached the edge, body scraping against rock. My elbows dug into the grass as I tried to kick off the pooka. A bone snapped in my ankle, blinding me with pain. I screamed, the sound echoing through the cavern.

"Let go of my hand," Midnight said. "Let go of my hand!"

Blinking the stars out of my eyes, I did as he said, planting my palms on the grass. The weight of the pooka started to drag me back over the edge, but it was gone a second later.

I climbed the rest of the way to safety and then turned to stare down into the chasm, my heart in my throat. Midnight had thrown himself over the side, slammed his flaming body into the pookas, and now they were all tumbling down, flipping over and over and over...

They vanished into the darkness. The light of the fire blinked out.

A moment later, silence chilled my veins.

"Midnight?" I whispered, fisting the grass in my shaking hands. "Midnight, are you there?"

No answer.

My forehead met the soft, damp ground as a sob shook me. There was no way he could have survived that. It was a very, very long way to fall. Even if he lived through the impact, the chasm was swarming with pookas. He wouldn't stand a chance, especially if he was wounded from those burns.

He must have known that when he threw himself at those creatures.

For a moment, I knelt there on the ground, mourning the joint eater, one of the bravest souls I'd ever met. With a sigh, I brushed my fingers against the gemstones in my pocket. Three of them. He'd sacrificed himself so that I could get away—so that I had three chances of stabbing Oberon. I could not let him down.

I stood. It was time to kill the king.

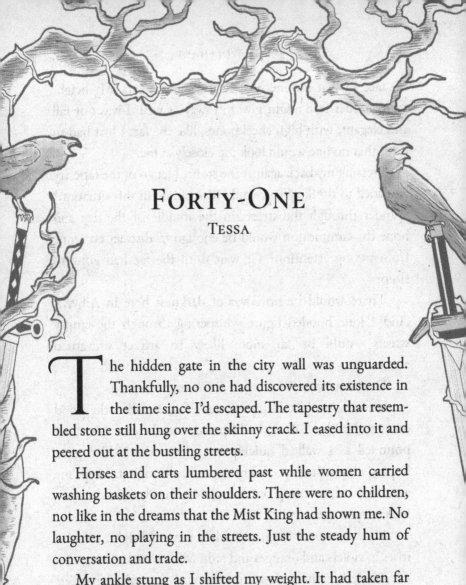

FORTY-ONE
TESSA

The hidden gate in the city wall was unguarded. Thankfully, no one had discovered its existence in the time since I'd escaped. The tapestry that resembled stone still hung over the skinny crack. I eased into it and peered out at the bustling streets.

Horses and carts lumbered past while women carried washing baskets on their shoulders. There were no children, not like in the dreams that the Mist King had shown me. No laughter, no playing in the streets. Just the steady hum of conversation and trade.

My ankle stung as I shifted my weight. It had taken far more effort for me to climb the hill than I'd hoped. I shouldn't have survived what had happened at the chasm. Somehow, I had, and the only remnant I carried with me was a throbbing ankle. And as painful as it was, it was already healing, thanks to being back inside Oberon's circle of protection. The wound would slow me down, though.

That was not ideal, when I needed to blend in. As a human, I would have to keep the cloak's hood tight around my face so that no one spotted my smooth ears. My height and rounder face might give me away as well. I was not tall and elegant, with high cheekbones, like the fae. I just had to hope that no one would look too closely at me.

Pressing my back against the stone, I let go of the tapestry and tried to think. What would Morgan do in this situation? Wander through the streets in the middle of the day and hope the commotion would be enough to distract everyone from paying attention? Or wait until the fae had gone to sleep?

There would be no cover of darkness here in Albyria. And a lone hooded figure whispering through the empty streets would be far more likely to attract unwanted attention.

Decision made.

Before I could talk myself out of it, I pulled the hood over my braided hair and whispered into the city. My heart pounded as I walked quickly away from the hidden gate, hoping no one had spotted me squeeze through it. I kept my gaze forward, focusing on the sandy ground, careful not to look anyone in the eye.

My eyes were wrong, too. Most fae had bright, colorful irises in violets and oranges and reds. Mine were brown.

Barely breathing, I wound my way through the streets and strode into the market where the fae of the city hawked their wares. There were colorful silken gowns and brushed leather armor, knives and swords and arrows tipped with golden points, loaves of fresh bread, and fruits from the fields around Teine.

My mouth watered, but I didn't dare stop.

None of this was for me, and it never had been. Most of these merchants' stalls were packed full of things the humans had made, not the fae themselves. The weapons were theirs, but everything else? Built and grown by the mortals down below who rarely got a chance to enjoy any of it themselves.

It didn't have to be this way, I thought, as I hurried toward the end of the market. We could have a better world, a city where humans and fae worked together. We could build a place without golden walls keeping us apart or whips to keep us down. A place without so much hate and brutal violence. A place where we understood one another and did not burn with so much rage.

A kingdom without Oberon.

I turned off the main street and into an alley, the bottom of the cloak floating behind me. A heavy hand gripped my shoulder just before I made another turn. A fae stopped me short, whirling me around to face him.

His sharp yellow eyes glowed with curiosity. He leaned in, the stench of stale beer a cloud on his breath. Sharp ears cut through a wild mess of black hair. He gave a little sniff. "What's a mortal doing here?"

I'd thought about this. With my best nonchalant smile, I said, "I work in the castle. King Oberon sent me to the market to buy some things."

A wicked smile curved his lips. "Is that so?"

And that was when I remembered. Fae could scent lies. My stomach flipped as he backed me up against the wall, leaned in, and shoved his lips against my ear. His breath was hot on my skin.

"I love my missus and all, but I might just claim you for myself. Can't have a lost little mortal wandering around the Sunlit Market, now, can we? Someone needs to look after you. And you're just so...useful. If you know what I mean."

Muscles tensing, I reached a hand around my back and

thumbed the iron hilt of the Mortal Blade. Unfortunately, I knew exactly what he meant. Another fae, desperate for an heir. It would make him one of the most powerful fae in this city, probably giving him access to Oberon himself.

I shuddered and slid the blade from its holster, wincing at the slight *zing* it made. "Get off me. I really am going to the castle, and if you try to steal me, then the king will be extremely angry."

His brows pinched. He could tell that was the truth.

"Who the fuck are you?" Roughly, he snatched my wrist and shoved back my hood. His eyes swept across my face, widening. I didn't know how he recognized me. Maybe he'd attended one of the many balls I'd endured that month before the wedding. But I knew that look. Recognition, followed by greed.

A guttural laugh escaped his throat. "My, my. What do we have here? The long-lost mortal bride. I cannot wait to see the look on the king's face when I take you straight to him." His eyes went distant. "The reward will be far greater than anything I could have gotten with your spawn."

He yanked me toward him. Trembling, I pulled the dagger from behind my back and slid it right into his gut. The fae gasped, loosing the grip on my arm and stumbling away from me. Fingers of blood stretched out from the gaping wound in his stomach, where the blade had sliced through his tunic. I swallowed hard, hating all this death, even as a part of me, deep down inside, rejoiced.

"What?" he asked, blood bubbling out of his mouth and trailing down his chin. His eyes rolled into the back of his head, and then he fell.

"Dammit." I grabbed the blade and hurried down the length of the alley to put as much distance between us as I could. I'd already burned one of my gemstones. Now, I only had two left. Two chances to kill Oberon.

And I still had to get inside the castle.

I wound through another set of alleys until I reached the courtyard just beyond the front doors of Oberon's castle. The shadows of its towering spires splashed onto the stone ground. Several soldiers wandered through the courtyard. Two stood firm with spears beside the closed oak doors. There was no way to walk inside without being spotted.

Morgan had mentioned a secret tunnel from one of the nearby inns. Before one of the soldiers could spot me lurking about, I ducked back into the alley and came out on a different street. Several inns sat silent and empty, cobwebs clinging to shuttered windows. Albyria had not needed inns for centuries now. Mother once told me that the fae had kept them open for years, hoping that one day a traveler would cross that bridge and grace their steps.

But over time, they'd accepted the truth. No one was ever crossing that bridge.

Until now.

Casting a furtive glance over my shoulder, I pushed into the nearest inn. Dust rose around me with every step, reminding me of the mists. My heart dropped as I took a quick look through the vacant building. All I found were spiders, old sheets draped over furniture, and glass bottles that had been emptied long ago.

A dead end. But it gave me a chance to pop out the fried gemstone and replace it with a new one.

I tried the next inn and then the next, until I finally found the creaking wooden stairs leading to a basement, with a tunnel just off it. The cloak flapped behind me as I hurried down the hidden corridor, leaving a storm of dust in my wake.

At the end of the tunnel, I came to another set of stairs leading back up. With a quiver in my stomach, I climbed them, pulling out the Mortal Blade. The gemstone flickered with the trapped fire within, illuminating the way. When I reached the door, I pressed my ear against the wood and listened. No sound came from the other side.

The hinges creaked as I pushed the door open and slipped into the castle. I glanced one way and then the next, thankful that no fae were in this corridor. I couldn't afford another fight.

Tugging the hood back over my head, I moved through the silent corridor, trying to get my bearings. King Oberon had not allowed me any freedom during my month spent here. Most of the time I'd been trapped in my room, in the Great Hall for balls, and in the current queen's quarters where she had poked and prodded at me.

Queen Hannah.

I wondered what she was doing now. Had she retired from her duties as expected? Or had my disappearance forced her to remain by Oberon's side until he found a replacement? If the fae from the alley was any indication, it did not sound like he'd chosen another. That, plus the storm fae's actions, suggested that the king still meant to make me his wife.

But why? If a new mortal bride every seventy-five years was so essential to his reign, why hadn't he chosen another?

And what did he really do to them? To *us*? I knew it was far more than what we'd been told. It didn't fully add up, and I wanted to know why.

Maybe I could force Oberon to explain before I shoved

my blade into his heart, and then I could ensure no fae ever tried to do what he had done again.

I reached another set of winding stairs and ascended with quiet steps. The light from a bay of windows splashed onto stone archways etched in thorny vines. This was the Great Hall. I bypassed it completely. Up and up and up I went until I reached the highest floor where I knew Oberon slept.

No guards stood outside, which meant Oberon wasn't there. He was likely plotting in his own war room or listening to his advisors drone on about whatever it was kings talked about with their council.

With one last glance over my shoulder, I slipped inside the door and waited for his return.

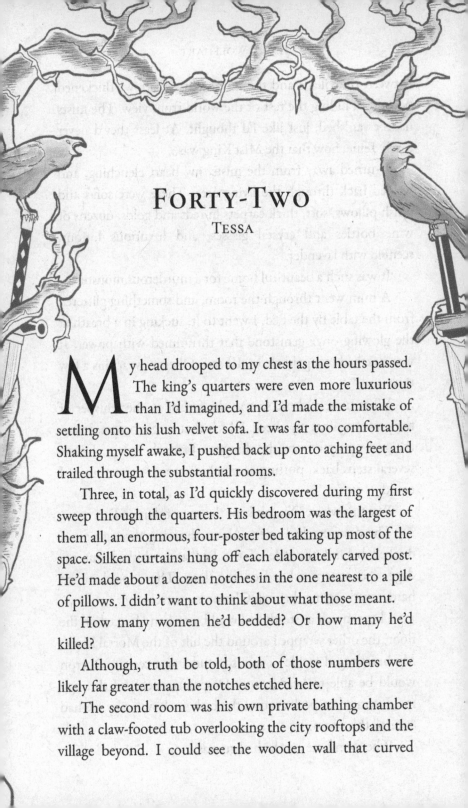

FORTY-TWO

TESSA

M y head drooped to my chest as the hours passed. The king's quarters were even more luxurious than I'd imagined, and I'd made the mistake of settling onto his lush velvet sofa. It was far too comfortable. Shaking myself awake, I pushed back up onto aching feet and trailed through the substantial rooms.

Three, in total, as I'd quickly discovered during my first sweep through the quarters. His bedroom was the largest of them all, an enormous, four-poster bed taking up most of the space. Silken curtains hung off each elaborately carved post. He'd made about a dozen notches in the one nearest to a pile of pillows. I didn't want to think about what those meant.

How many women he'd bedded? Or how many he'd killed?

Although, truth be told, both of those numbers were likely far greater than the notches etched here.

The second room was his own private bathing chamber with a claw-footed tub overlooking the city rooftops and the village beyond. I could see the wooden wall that curved between the village and the mountains. Shadows thickened beyond it, hiding the rest of the world from view. The mists hadn't vanished, just like I'd thought. At least they'd never reach Teine, now that the Mist King was...

I turned away from the mists, my heart clenching, and walked back through the living area. There were sofas and plush pillows, soft, thick carpets in reds and golds, dozens of wine bottles and crystal glasses, and luxurious lotions, scented with lavender.

It was such a beautiful home for a murderous monster.

A hum went through the room, and something glittered from the table by the bed. I went to it, sucking in a breath at the glowing onyx gemstone that thrummed with power. It was attached to a gold chain. I'd seen Oberon wear this a few times.

What unnerved me so was the feel of it, the whisper of the power against my cheek. I'd felt that magic before. It was the god's power from the dungeon beneath Itchen. I took several steps back, putting as much distance between us as I could.

Was this where Oberon kept the rest of that god?

The door cracked open. Alarm shooting through me, I ducked behind the side of the bed and whisked out my dagger. Footsteps echoed on the floor. The door slammed hard, reverberating through Oberon's quarters.

I kept myself as steady as I could, one hand braced on the floor, the other wrapped around the hilt of the Mortal Blade. My heart raged inside of me, so loud I was certain Oberon would be able to hear it, too. Desperation clawed through me. I wanted to peek around the bed, see how many fae had entered this room.

If he found me and he had guards...

"I know you're in here, Tessa," Oberon announced. "There are dead guards by the Bridge to Death. Not to mention all the reports I've had in the past few hours from people who have spotted a human scurrying around like a frightened mouse, heading into inns and poking around. Did you think I'd be too stupid to realize you'd come here?"

So much for sneaking up on him from behind. Quietly, I hid the blade behind my back and stood.

Oberon lounged on the bed, arms folded, lips quirked with a wicked smile. Those horrible horns gleamed from the light of the sun streaming in from the window behind him. He gave me a quick once-over before shaking his head. "You look worse than you did when I found you stealing from me, which is quite the accomplishment. Did the shadow fae not treat you well?"

"They have nothing to do with this," I hissed between my teeth, though that wasn't entirely truthful. They had been the ones to start this. But I would be the one to end it. On my own fucking terms.

"I'll admit, I'm surprised to see you here," he drawled, sprawled across the bed as if this conversation had no effect on him at all. As if he were bored of it already. "I assumed I'd have to kill the Mist King and pry you out of his cold, dead hands. He gave you up far more easily than I expected, which was fairly stupid of him. I wouldn't have done the same in his place. He's let me win."

"The Mist King is dead," I said flatly.

His brows arched. "Dead?"

"I killed him." My entire body stiffened as Oberon leapt off the bed and edged closer. "The same way I'm going to kill you."

He stopped and laughed, an eerie sound that sliced

against my eardrums. I couldn't help but shudder. "You think that *you*, a mortal girl, could kill a five-hundred-year-old fae king? I may hate the Mist King with every fiber of my soul, but I am not willfully blind to the fact he's one of the most powerful beings alive. You could never kill him, Tessa. You could not even harm him. You wouldn't know how."

It was my turn to smile now. "I'm really going to relish the look on your face when you realize just how wrong you truly are."

I pulled the blade out from behind my back and angled it so that he could spot the gemstone gleaming in the center of it. "Ever see this before?"

His eyes slightly widened. "Impossible."

"*Not* impossible," I said, my smile growing wicked. "The Mist King has had it all these years, just waiting for a chance to find a mortal who could use it against you. I stole it from him and brought it here."

Oberon launched toward me, his hand outstretched. His body slammed into mine. The world tipped sideways as I tumbled to the floor, as his fingers began to close around my wrist. Heart pounding, I twisted away from him, rolling across the floor to escape his grip. I barely slid out of the way just in time, but the dagger clattered across the stone, away from me.

Seething, he climbed to his feet and gazed down at me. My back was against the wall, Oberon blocking the only route out of this room. The fire in his eyes burned with venomous hate. I was trapped. And as he laughed, I realized I would not get out of this alive.

I'd *never* had a chance of surviving this. Deep down, I'd known it, too. And still, I'd come anyway. Because the Mist King had betrayed me.

One boot hit the floor hard, and then the other, as Oberon came closer. "You have made a very terrible mistake, little human. You do not have the strength to kill a king, and you never will. And I will make sure that you remember this moment for the rest of your pitiful life. I have your family in my dungeons. I cannot kill you for what you are to me, but there's *nothing* stopping me from killing them. They will pay for your crimes against this crown."

All the blood drained from my face. I saw the truth in the depths of his ember eyes. Oberon meant every word he said. He would not only force me to do everything he demanded, he'd punish those I loved. He would cut off their heads and parade them through the streets, just as he'd done to Nellie.

He still wouldn't kill me, despite everything I'd done, which meant he'd take it out on someone else.

"You're a monster," I whispered up at him. "I know everything you're trying to do. The Mist King told me all about your quest to return the gods to this world."

He smirked. "Oh, the Mist King told you, did he? And you believed everything he said?"

My heart thundered. "No. But I believe him about that."

"The Mist King is no better than I am." Oberon knelt, wrapped his hand around my aching ankle, and smiled. Pain lanced through my body. "But you already know that, or you wouldn't have tried to kill him. I'm just surprised he let you get away with it. Attempted murder of a king?" He shook his head. "You're just as bad as us. Just as bad as *me*."

I blinked at the harshness of his words, but deep down I knew he was right. What I'd done was unthinkable. What I planned to do to Oberon was just as bad. Killing in cold blood. *Murder*. I had blood on my hands, same as them.

"The difference is I did it to save my people," I hissed through my teeth.

Oberon's hand tightened on my leg. I winced in furious pain. "Why do you think *I* do what I do?"

"Don't act like you're some kind of hero, Oberon. I know you're not."

He leaned forward and growled into my face. Fear tripped down my spine at the look in his eyes. "You have no *idea* what my people have been through over the past four hundred years. We're cut off from the world. We cannot breed. Beyond the bridge, the Mist King lurks, plotting our demise. I am trying to keep my people safe. I want the light fae to survive. And everything *you* have done has threatened that."

My heart thrashed in my ears, his words echoing in my head. It was the most I'd ever heard him say. The most truth he'd ever spoken, at least in front of me. He was scared. His power—his reign—teetered on the precipice. One wrong move and it would all crumble down on top of him.

I saw it now. All his boasting, all his puffing out his chest. It was because his place as the ruler of this land was far more tenuous than he wanted everyone to believe.

"You need me, far more than you want me to know." I sat up a little straighter, back still pressed against the wall. "There's something about this mortal bride thing that gives you power."

His brows slammed down. "We need mortals to breed. Do not begin to think of yourself as someone important."

"Except that I am," I countered, flicking my eyes to the bedroom behind him. Perhaps if I could distract him, I could launch myself over the bed and run for the living area. There, I might stand a better chance of fighting him. "This tattoo on my upper back. It must have done something magical. It's why you haven't tried to replace me with another mortal bride, even though that would have been far easier than convincing the storm fae to track me down."

A low growl rumbled from his throat, and he curled back his lips.

"What is it, Oberon?" I asked, slowly easing up onto my feet, despite the hand he still clamped around my ankle. "What is the *Oidhe* really about?"

"It is *King* Oberon to you," he thundered, yanking on my leg. My backside slammed into the hard floor, and my teeth knocked together. Stars filled my blurring vision as he hauled me across the room, my braided hair dragging behind me.

I thrashed, kicking at his face. My ankle screamed in pain as he jerked me out of the bedroom and into the living space. Shaking, I snatched at the first thing I saw. The leg of a table. I grabbed on tight as he tried to haul me to the door.

"Let go!" He squeezed my ankle.

Pain filled my entire body, shattering my soul. I screamed, and my fingers slipped against the wood. Dark spots crept into the corners of my vision. My body begged for relief. I'd demanded so much from it these past few weeks, and it could barely take any more.

Laughing, he leaned down, sneering into my face. "I need you alive, but it doesn't matter if you're a broken, battered thing. You're in the Kingdom of Light. You'll heal."

He twisted my ankle harder. The pain was so great, I almost blacked out. Maybe I did. Because one moment, he held tight to my throbbing ankle, the next he'd hauled me to my feet.

He shoved me toward the door. "I'm taking you to the

dungeons. You can spend some time in a cramped, dark cell with your family. They won't be in there for long, I'm afraid. Well, they will. They just won't be alive."

Horror twisted through me, nearly taking me to my knees. He would kill them, and then he'd force me to sit only feet away from their bodies, from their blood.

"*I will break you,*" he whispered into my ear. His breath smelled of lavender and blood.

Tears blurring my vision, I jerked away from him. I raced back into the bedroom, hobbling on my screaming ankle. The dagger had slid just beneath the bed, the sharp end sticking out from the shadows. I leapt toward it, fingers closing around the hilt and—

Oberon hauled me from the floor, roaring. He tossed me across the room, but I clung to the dagger. My body slammed into the wall. My back screamed from the contact. I slid into a lump, trying to catch my breath.

The king stalked toward me. "You will not defy me ever again!"

He reached for me, and I knew if he got his hands on me this time, he'd never let go. It was now or never.

I screamed, shoving the Mortal Blade's tip straight down through his boot. The blade pierced his foot. Oberon roared. Yanking out the dagger, he threw it across the room as the gemstone blinked out. Seething, he wrapped his hand around my throat and yanked me into the air.

My lungs squeezed as he growled at me. "You failed. Your fucking dagger is useless in mortal hands. Only fae can kill fae. You're not strong enough, you pitiful little *insect.*"

Oberon suddenly choked, and his grip on me loosened. Eyes rolling back into his head, he stumbled sideways, and then he hit the floor.

I gasped, pulling breath into my lungs, palming the wooden boards as pain wracked my entire body. But I could take it. I could take it all. After all my years spent in anguish from the violence he'd wrought, it was finally over.

King Oberon was dead.

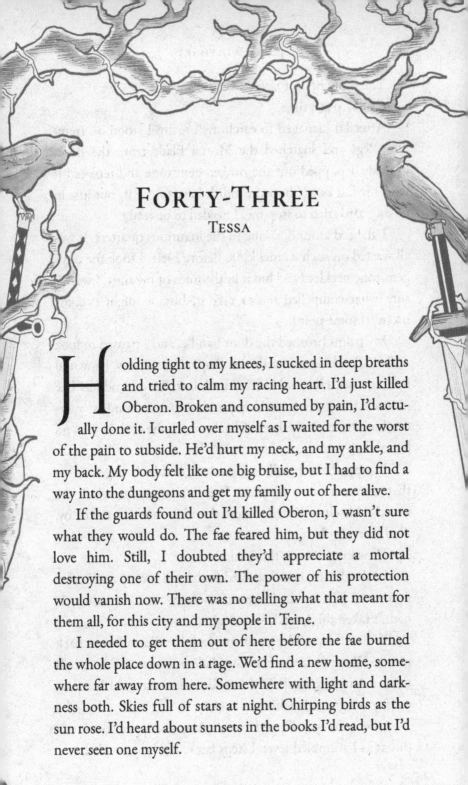

FORTY-THREE

TESSA

Holding tight to my knees, I sucked in deep breaths and tried to calm my racing heart. I'd just killed Oberon. Broken and consumed by pain, I'd actually done it. I curled over myself as I waited for the worst of the pain to subside. He'd hurt my neck, and my ankle, and my back. My body felt like one big bruise, but I had to find a way into the dungeons and get my family out of here alive.

If the guards found out I'd killed Oberon, I wasn't sure what they would do. The fae feared him, but they did not love him. Still, I doubted they'd appreciate a mortal destroying one of their own. The power of his protection would vanish now. There was no telling what that meant for them all, for this city and my people in Teine.

I needed to get them out of here before the fae burned the whole place down in a rage. We'd find a new home, somewhere far away from here. Somewhere with light and darkness both. Skies full of stars at night. Chirping birds as the sun rose. I'd heard about sunsets in the books I'd read, but I'd never seen one myself.

The thought of it tasted like hope.

One step at a time.

After I'd managed to catch my breath, I stood on trembling legs and snatched the Mortal Blade from the floor. Quickly, I popped out the broken gemstone and replaced it with my last one. I hoped I didn't have to use it, but just in case a guard tried to stop me, I needed to be ready.

I glanced around, taking in the luxurious quarters. It was all wasted on such a cruel king. Before I left, I took the onyx gemstone necklace and hid it in the folds of my shirt. I wasn't sure what compelled me to take it, but...it might become useful at some point.

My palms brushed the door handle, and I paused to look at the fallen king one last time. Any moment now, he would turn to dust. He would be fed back into the ground just like mortals, those beings he'd spent almost four hundred years crushing beneath the heel of his boot. In the end, he was no better than any of us.

I gripped the handle and waited, suddenly eager to see that moment come to pass. The final moment when the world rid itself of King Oberon. Another moment ticked by. And then another.

How long did this thing take?

In the dream, it had seemed as though it only took a few moments. The fae had almost instantly turned to dust. It hadn't taken this long. I was certain of it.

With a frown, I let go of the door handle and went back over to Oberon's body. Had the blade not gone in far enough to turn him into dust? Did I need to do it again? I hated to use my last gemstone, but...

Oberon's eyes flipped open. A gasp ripped from my throat as I stumbled several steps back. My heart rattled, fear twisting through my gut like a thousand angry snakes. What was happening? How was he alive?

I'd stabbed him. The blade hadn't gone in deep, but it didn't have to—this was the Mortal Blade. I'd watched his eyes go vacant. His skin had grayed. His body had collapsed.

I didn't understand what was happening.

He looked like he wanted to rip my heart from my chest.

Brushing his tunic, he rose to his feet. I trembled and raised the dagger before me. I had no choice but to try again. One more gemstone. One more chance.

Oberon smiled. "That won't work, Tessa. The blade is not the one you think it is."

My stomach dropped.

He chuckled at the look on my face. "That's right. The Mortal Blade would have destroyed my body, turning me to ash. All that one did was poison me for a moment. Useful for a mortal trying to flee a fae. It gives you enough time to run. Pity you didn't think to do that."

"You're lying." My voice was rough, scraping through my tight throat. It couldn't be true. Something must have gone wrong. I didn't stab him hard enough. But...it should only need a scrape.

Oberon grabbed my arms, his nails digging into me. I trembled at the rage in his eyes. "I am not lying. The blade has a twin. Did he not tell you that?"

Shock slammed into me. My lips parted, and my knees almost buckled as a strange sense of relief filled my heart. "But that would mean..."

"The Mist King didn't die." Oberon laughed. "You truly thought you'd killed him. And that an ant like you could kill me, too. You're pathetic."

He reared back his hand. I didn't have time to think, time

to breathe, as he brought it down hard against my head. The last thing I knew was pain and a darkness as deep as death.

Chains rattled as the guards yanked me down the gloomy dungeon corridor. I winced with every step, the bonds too tight around my wrists. Exhaustion weighed heavy on my shoulders, tugging on my eyelids, but I forced myself to stay alert.

I glanced into every cell we passed, but the dungeons were mostly empty. Oberon didn't need to take captives, not when we all so readily fell in line. And those who disobeyed didn't end up behind bars. They ended up with their heads on spikes in the village square.

"Tessa!" a familiar voice exclaimed from a cell just ahead. *Val!* Hope surged in my chest, propelling me forward. I'd fought so hard to find her. My feet had kept moving when the rest of me could not, all so I could save her and my mother from a cruel fate. Failure was a lead weight strapped to my heart, but at least they were here and not lost to the mists. At least I would see their faces again. And I would take my last breath if it meant they could escape. The chains jangled as I tried to get a better view, but the guard yanked me back.

As we passed the cell, Val and Mother pressed up against the bars. Tears were streaming down both their faces. They looked tired, their clothes wrinkled and dirty, but their beaming smiles was the thing I noticed most.

I slowed, my entire body shaking. The world stilled around me, and for a moment, it all felt worth it. Every excruciating wound. Every hour of sleep I'd lost. Every choice I'd made had led me right back here. They were trapped in a dungeon beneath a castle full of cruel fae, but they were alive. My fingers brushed the bars, but the guard tugged on my chains until my boots skidded across the stone away from them.

"Tessa." My mother shoved her hand through the bars and reached toward me, but the guard dragged me farther down the passageway. The strings of my heart unraveled at my feet, and I tried to pull it back, but the guard didn't give me a chance. He hauled me away from their cell, away from the pieces of me that had always been with Mother and Val.

"Aren't you putting me in there with them?" I asked, craning my head over my shoulder to keep my eyes locked on their faces. This couldn't be happening. I'd only just seen them. We hadn't even had a chance to say a word to each other.

"No," the guard said gruffly. "You're going in with the other one."

"The other one?" I asked as we reached a door and pushed through. Had another human rebelled against the fae? I tried to think of who it could be. Most of the mortals in Teine would never even blink in the wrong direction. So, who else had Oberon captured? And why?

Surely not Morgan...

The guards didn't answer. Instead, they yanked open the nearest cell, shoved me in, and slammed the door behind me. I looked around, and then everything stopped. A girl with chestnut hair stood before me, her brown eyes glassy with tears. Her smile was one I'd recognize anywhere. An impossible smile. A smile that froze the blood in my veins.

"Is this some kind of trick?" My back hit the bars as I

stumbled away. "Are you making me a hallucinate? You killed my sister. She's not alive!"

My rough voice echoed down the stone corridor. This was almost worse than anything they'd done to me so far. To make me see my baby sister, to make those brown eyes gaze at me with soft worry. I almost fell to my knees.

"It's me, Tessa," she whispered.

For a moment, there was nothing I could do but stare. This was impossible. Oberon's guard had thrown her head at my feet. She was dead. Nellie had been taken from me. It had been the worst moment of my entire life, and the wound from that day still festered, poisoning my heart against the world.

She spread her hands in the shape of wings. "You did it. You flew away like the ravens."

Those words. Our secret language born from our tears and our pain. No one else knew them. No one understood the bond we shared. A bud of hope stirred inside me like a seedling stretching through the dirt to reach for the sun. Could this be real?

I shuddered from the fear of hope.

"Please don't just stand there." She swiped at her cheeks, the tears smearing across her skin. "You're looking at me like I'm a stranger. I need you, Tessa."

Something in me cracked. I almost fell to my knees from the wave of grief that rolled over me, dragging me down into the bottomless depths of the sea. But right in its wake, just before I drowned beneath the weight of it, something else followed, pushing that grief away. It was an emotion I had not felt in so long that it was a stranger in the shadows, a ghost of who I'd once been.

I took two steps toward her, trembling. "Nellie?"

She rushed at me and launched into my arms. Our bodies collided, my breath knocked from my lungs. I clutched her against me, fisting her dress, breathing in the scent of her hair. She still smelled like apples after all this time. Sagging against her, I wept.

I had no idea how, but my sister was here.

Nellie was *alive*.

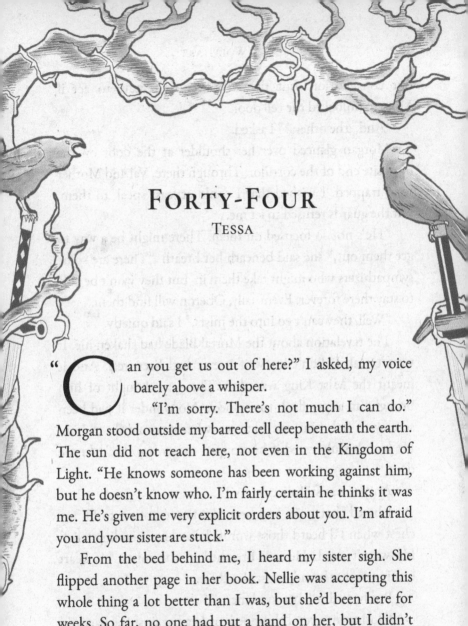

FORTY-FOUR
TESSA

"Can you get us out of here?" I asked, my voice barely above a whisper.

"I'm sorry. There's not much I can do." Morgan stood outside my barred cell deep beneath the earth. The sun did not reach here, not even in the Kingdom of Light. "He knows someone has been working against him, but he doesn't know who. I'm fairly certain he thinks it was me. He's given me very explicit orders about you. I'm afraid you and your sister are stuck."

From the bed behind me, I heard my sister sigh. She flipped another page in her book. Nellie was accepting this whole thing a lot better than I was, but she'd been here for weeks. So far, no one had put a hand on her, but I didn't trust that Oberon would hold back much longer, especially now that he had his bride back.

I lifted my tired eyes. The pity in Morgan's gaze made my soul ache. She nodded toward the end of the corridor where five soldiers stood watch. They weren't close enough to hear our conversation, but they would not hesitate to act if Morgan unlocked the cell door.

"And...the others?" I asked.

Morgan glanced over her shoulder at the door on the opposite end of the corridor. Through there, Val and Mother were trapped. I wished that I could at least speak to them, but the guards refused to let me.

"He's not so focused on them. There might be a way to get them out," she said beneath her breath. "There are some sympathizers who might take them in, but they won't be able to stay there forever. Eventually, Oberon will find them."

"Well, they can't go into the mists," I said quietly.

The revelation about the Mortal Blade had shaken me. It wasn't real. I didn't know if it ever had been real. And it meant the Mist King was alive. The very thought of him brought an angry flush to my neck. No wonder it had been so easy to stab him. He'd known what it would do to him. He hadn't truly cared if he stopped me or not. He'd *let* me do it.

And he was still alive.

I hated that relief had been the first emotion to fill my chest when I'd heard those words. Pure, knee-bending relief. He wasn't dead. He still breathed in the mists, his heart beating in that broad, muscular chest.

But he had still betrayed me.

Closing my eyes, I thumped my head against the bars and tried to shove thoughts of him out of my mind. What was he thinking now? What was he doing? Had he heard I'd failed and been caught?

Did he even care? He hadn't told me the weapon was the Mortal Blade's twin or that it even had a twin at all. Maybe he'd wanted me to come here and fail.

It didn't make any sense, but none of it did.

"They'll be all right," Morgan whispered. "We'll figure it out."

"It's hard to have that kind of hope. Oberon threatened to kill them, and the wedding has been rescheduled."

"I heard."

"Two weeks from now." I waved at my dirt-caked body. "Apparently, he wanted to do it sooner, but he doesn't like the state of me."

"You've had a hard time of it, love."

Love.

My heart squeezed. I swallowed down a lump of nausea, trying to force my lips to form the words. "Have you heard from him?"

Had Kalen visited Morgan in her dreams?

"No," she said tensely. "I doubt he wants to speak with me, knowing I told you the truth about him. Besides, if I got caught communicating with him, Oberon would realize I've been the one helping you. And then he'd try to force me to talk. I'm strong, Tessa, I am, but…I've experienced his torture before. I did not fare well."

"You have?"

She nodded grimly. "A very long time ago."

Morgan didn't elaborate, and I didn't want to push her to share things that were that painful. Even now, after being reunited with Nellie and finding out she'd been alive all this time, my heart still felt like a shattered mess I'd never piece back together. Anger was a formless monster inside of me, its teeth snapping at Oberon, at the Mist King, at everyone except Val, my mother, and my sister. And it wanted blood.

"Did you find out how all this happened?" I tipped my head toward Nellie. My sister didn't have the answers herself.

King Oberon had taken her the very same day he'd taken me, only hours later. She had no idea why.

Morgan nodded. "It turned out he used a decoy, a girl from your village with the same hair. That's why she was so bloodied and bruised. He wanted you to think she was Nellie."

"Oh." I sagged against the bars. "That would have been Sanya."

For a moment, I'd had to wonder—was this the doing of the god? But as relieved as I was that I hadn't unintentionally released her onto the world, the truth was no better. It meant an innocent girl had died.

"I'm afraid so. Were you close?"

"We grew up together." Frowning, I searched Morgan's face for more answers. "I don't understand. Why would Oberon have done that? Why not just...?"

I wouldn't say it out loud, but Morgan heard my question. If Oberon had wanted to break me, why had he only pretended it was my sister he'd killed? He didn't care about her life, and he'd made it more than clear that mortals were meaningless to him. Instead, he'd put on an elaborate ruse and kept her trapped in a dungeon.

"Honestly, Tessa, I have no idea," Morgan answered.

I opened my mouth to ask for more, but she took a step back, glancing down the corridor. A fae soldier was striding toward us, his face hidden behind a metal helmet painted crimson.

"Morgan," he barked, his hand on hilt. "King Oberon has ordered us to get the mortal to sleep. You know how he is about these things. The girl has to recover, despite what she did."

"I understand." Morgan gave me a silent nod and

vanished down the hallway, leaving me and Nellie to deal with the soldier alone. Another guard trailed behind him, his arms full of pillows and blankets and what I assumed was valerian-spiked wine.

"You'll drink this," the first one barked. "And then you'll sleep. Any questions?"

Stomach in knots, I shook my head. "There's not much to ask. I'm to obey the rules so that I can become the king's silent broodmare."

"Say another word and we'll inform the king," the pillow-carrier said in warning.

"I don't really care," I hissed back. "There's not much more he can do to me."

"He'll kill your family." The soldier unlocked the door and motioned the other to dump the blankets just inside. "Your sister in there can be first."

I snapped my mouth shut.

"Good girl," he said, and then slammed the bars in my face. "Now, go to sleep."

They resumed their watch beside the dungeon doors and left me to sort out the bed myself. Nellie joined in to help, draping a blanket across my mattress. The soldiers had been surprisingly generous with the pillows, and the resulting nest swallowed my aching body like a cocoon of clouds. I still wore the Mist King's cloak. Despite the scent of mist and snow that followed me around, I couldn't bring myself to take it off.

Nellie climbed back into her bed and curled up on her side. She hadn't been given any wine, and she stared at mine with a frown. "Are you going to drink that? It'll knock you out."

"Absolutely not."

"Good." She smiled, and the sight of it tore at my heart. Even now, hours later, I could scarcely believe she was alive. "I'm glad you're with me. I'm just sorry it has to be *here*."

"It's not your fault."

She sighed into her pillow. "What are we going to do?"

"I don't know." I fisted the blanket, picturing Oberon's wicked face. "But I'll figure something out. I won't let him do this."

Her throat bobbed as she swallowed hard. Nellie didn't look convinced, but could I blame her? She'd been stuck down here for well over a month by now. Mother and Val had been here for weeks. I'd have lost hope, too.

I reached a hand toward my sister. Her fingers wound around mine, clutching tight. "I love you."

"I love you, too, Tessa." Closing her eyes, she relaxed against her pillow. I watched her for a good long while, holding tight to her hand, until sleep dragged her into peace and her breathing deepened. Something dark stirred in my heart as I stared at her dark lashes flared across her cheeks. By trapping my family, Oberon thought he'd won. What he didn't know was that he'd made me more determined than ever.

I grabbed the chalice and mimed taking a sip before brushing the back of my hand across my lips. Heaving out a sigh, I flipped over so that my back faced the soldiers. And then I poured the wine onto the floor, letting it trail down the wall beside the bed. After a few moments, I flipped back over, my heart hammering, and placed the empty chalice on the table.

Soon, sleep claimed me. I was too exhausted to fight against it anymore.

The dream began with the cool brush of twilight. Night

encased the forest, splashing moonlight onto the drooping branches. I rose from the long swaying grass and stared ahead at the dense evergreen trees so unlike the oaks and the black-thorns back in Teine.

A cool wind whipped at my braided hair, and a cloud of mist rushed toward me from the forest.

My body tensed, and a part of me wanted to run. I'd been waiting for this moment ever since I'd learned the truth. I'd been counting down the moments until I could dream again.

But now that I was here, fear snaked around my heart.

"Hello, love." The Mist King strode out of the shadows. "Surprised to see me?"

ACKNOWLEDGMENTS

This book was a beast to write, and I absolutely could not have done it alone. First and always, to my husband, for listening to me ramble on about plot points, making sure I eat, and throwing ideas at me when I get stuck.

To Christine, Anya, Alison, Jen, Marina, and Tammi, for the daily chats. Writing can be an isolating job, but your friendship means I'm never alone.

To the incredible Sylvia, for designing the most gorgeous book cover. I fell in love with it the second I saw it.

To Maggie, for your editorial insights and suggestions. And to Lindsay, for your keen eye when polishing this book. The story is so much better because of you both.

To Dian and Beth, for illustrating the most gorgeous artwork of Kalen, Tessa, and Nellie. You brought these characters in my head to life.

And to all the readers who took a chance on a new series and began this journey with me. Thank you so much for reading. There is so much more to come.

ABOUT THE AUTHOR

Jenna Wolfhart spends her days tucked away in her writing studio in the countryside. When she's not writing, she loves to deadlift, rewatch Game of Thrones, and drink copious amounts of coffee.

Born and raised in America, Jenna now lives in England with her husband and her two dogs, Nero and Vesta.

www.jennawolfhart.com
jenna@jennawolfhart.com
tiktok.com/@jennawolfhart

9 781915 537096